PEDRO the Enigma

Robin Matchett

Piercemore

First published 2005

10 9 8 7 6 5 4 3 2 1
Copyright © Robin Matchett, 2004
James Piercemore Books ®
www.piercemore.ca

All rights reserved. Without limiting the rights under copyright reserved above, no part of this publication may be reproduced, stored in or introduced into a retrieval system, or transmitted in any form or by any means (electronic, mechanical, photocopying, recording or otherwise), without the prior written permission of both the copyright owner and the above publisher of this book.

*Publisher's note: This book is a work of fiction. Names, characters, places and incidents either are the product of the author's imagination or are used fictitiously, and any resemblance to actual persons living or dead, events, or locales is entirely coincidental.

Printed and bound in Canada

National Library of Canada Cataloguing in Publication
Matchett, Robin
    Pedro the enigma / by Robin Matchett.

ISBN 0-9730798-4-3

I. Title.

PS8576.A7996W48 2003   C813'.54   C2003-900145-8
PR9199.3.M3935W48 2003

Is it not the wonder of the world that cannot be discovered?
—Gwion (Celtic Bard)

Chapter One

Furthermore, we have not even to risk the adventure alone, for the heroes of all time have gone before us. The labyrinth is thoroughly known — we have only to follow the thread of the hero's path, and where we had thought to find an abomination, we shall find a god. And where we had thought to slay another, we shall slay ourselves. Where we had thought to travel outward, we will come to the center of our own existence. And where we had thought to be alone, we will be with all the world.

—Joseph Campbell

The car flew into the black night like a banshee and its time, it appeared, was a foregone conclusion when it missed the turn and ploughed through stone markers in a blaze of light. As it plunged, with the motor's whining revolutions, the car arced in a half twist, the wind sounding strangely remote and silent softly buffeting the windows. Headlights caught rocks awash in the ocean, which for a precious moment illuminated the moonless dark in an incandescent ghostly yellow. There seems to be a blind numbing, nothingness. It is a density impossible to comprehend, but a faint sensing of light chances to hover very near, just above, out of sight — the feeling of turning, turning, turning within an orbit of confinement, striving for that light, intensely, irresistibly, born of consciousness . . .

A sickly sensation extended from his lower body to his head as he strained to reach the warmth. But he shivered until, in his pain, he gulped the air, jarring him from the netherworld to the real one, blue and magnificent. On his tongue he could taste gritty earth, his eyes caked in blood.

How the sun burned! And he was immobilised, yet the earth was warm and comfortable. Blades of grass tickled his nose as he noticed heavy breathing nearby. An intense pain then cut him to the core of his being. He knew where he was. He managed to lift his head enough to see the hulking form of his enemy, Vron the Barbarian, ramming with a moronic intensity and bulk of his weight in the violation of his young wife. He noticed the glint of his own impressive sword on the ground in the waving grass. All efforts to reach it were in vain. He was helpless as he looked upon her terrible ordeal, her gentle face tear-stained and the breeze caressing strands of blonde hair, flailing silently to the angels of death.

Gwydion groaned and felt his dagger sheathed at his side. The Saxon monster jerked and collapsed in a satisfied grunt. Around them in heaps, Gwydion could hear the death throes of others; in the distance, screams and shouts could be heard in the final vestiges of battle. Vron and his brutal horde had surprised the Caerymwy fortification with an overwhelming force, killing and mutilating everyone except those who had escaped with Bran. Gwydion's strength ebbed from loss of blood, and he knew he was done for by the gaping gash in his side, among numerous other slashes. He had fought them all with Olwen, his warrior bride, at his side. She had stubbornly refused to go with Bran. Their sacrifice had been carried out to save the others so that they would be free to remember and avenge that day.

"Olwen!" Gwydion cried in anguish. The mad Saxon turned and looked at Gwydion in a wild leer before he stood up slowly to survey the field of death and pillaged fortifications now in flames. Vron smiled down at the lifeless girl-woman rudely prostrated before him and then saw Gwydion's extended arm reaching for his sword. He bent down and picked it up. The ornate design far surpassed his own rough piece. He swung it, cutting the air in clean incisive swings and glared down with his ugly boar face at Gwydion who struggled resolutely to hold Vron's eye, indomitable even in death.

"Evil monster!" Gwydion heard himself utter. "When you die, I will be watching." And with a superhuman effort he sprang from his place and stabbed Vron in the groin.

The blow was not effective as it glanced off a hard leather guard, cutting his thigh instead.

"Aaagh!" bellowed Vron, but he recovered. "You are weak! I am strong! My line will rule forevermore." Incensed, he spat on his victim, and lifted the Celtic sword high above his head, the blade floating weightlessly against the blue sky, shining in the setting sun. Gwydion heard Vron growl as the sword sliced down through the air. "Gorgon will never die!"

Pedro George jolted awake in a sweat. Sitting up in the dark, he mumbled incoherently, struggling to focus his eyes, and then touched himself reassuringly. Bands of light raced across his ceiling in rapid strokes as the familiar rolling steel of a passing streetcar mollified his anxiety. He pulled back his unzipped sleeping bag, laid out like a quilt, and walked to the open window to kneel with his elbows on the sill and look out onto the street. It was deserted now. Above, low clouds of the city's night sky were a resinous yellow-purple like a grotesque bruise. The globular surfaces of the clouds made him think of his brain pulsing to the electrical hum of the metropolitan matrix. He felt like a component, one of millions, wired into some kind of techno-germ, yet he was different — a kind of ancient strain adapted to resist the dilemma: sacrifice yourself or be sacrificed. One must conform, however: wear a smile, drive a car, be material, be normal, hyper-normal. His time was imminent:as an innocent, a fool, a poet — all fancy prerequisites for a notable death. Blessed was the dreamer.

Pedro sighed. The ancient myth was the modern reality. And they had long turned to stone: Gorgon, the specter of death, staring down upon civilisation on a collision course with apocalypse. What they didn't know today, it had known yesterday; and tomorrow it would remake what it had known the day before, incarnating time and transformation. Call it God. Call it beauty. Call it ugly. Call it Gorgon. Call it hell. Pedro called it Nature.

Yet there was still time before such a fate stampeded into action. In bed he curled up and felt the massive earth rotate in silence.

The early morning sounds below on St. Clair West brought Pedro to his senses. From his bed, he could hear the mezzo-soprano voice of his landlord, Giovanni, calling out as he received a delivery for his café-bakery-delicatessen. The aroma of freshly baked bread from the ovens below permeated the apartment. Pedro thought of Donna del Rio, Giovanni's niece, now stacking the shelves with hot crusty loaves. Soon she would knock on his door and patiently wait for him to answer. He would answer, sometimes with a towel about his waist, dripping wet from a shower. Increasingly, Donna would invite herself in, handing over a bag of buns or a loaf as if an exchange for right of entry. She would then pull out a scrap of paper to read her poem. This persistence was actually an aberration for her in that she felt too strongly about him as if he had a mysterious authority over her. Often, she added cautiously that he was the only one to whom she would ever pay this homage.

Donna was not quite twenty, a voluptuous young woman of Bohemian-Italian stock, and a no-nonsense history honours student. Her powder-blue eyes, thick auburn hair, pout-sensual mouth, and robust disposition were universal to the generic male libido and also somewhat exasperating as Donna's charm embraced the simple notion that all creatures are equal. Pedro, however, defied categorization, coming across as someone so remote, perhaps belonging to an unknown species. Donna had just recently moved into the adjacent apartment, and Pedro found their proximity a pleasant surprise as she was the only friend he had at present. She reminded him of someone or something he couldn't place, and thus rejuvenated his old spirits.

Today was different. Pedro paced the room, dressed in jeans and a navy T-shirt. He was anxious because it was time to level with Donna: their relationship had been cordial as a friendship only, but now Donna was imposing her femininity with increasing ardour; the last thing in the world he wanted was to hurt her feelings, indeed anybody's for that matter. Romance of any kind couldn't have been further from his mind at that particular juncture of his life. He kept seeing himself hurtling through the darkness over a cliff and believed that perhaps it really was time to die. What had become such a wayward life had turned from sublime to ridiculous; it made him laugh at this tacky melodrama which had reached the low point as when an audience empties the theater before the punch line because nobody cares. There he was: the recluse, the pained, the artist: that damned aura of his imploding toward some new threshold opening onto the same monotony day after day. How careful he had been to avoid being great, how cowardly to deny his latent passions, perhaps to otherwise stand up like a maniacal street speaker and preach utopia. Thus, he ruminated: he must either hold his course or self-destruct; he felt too close to the source of nature, and the sun was beginning to blind. He knew what bearing he must take: onward, into the unknown; that seemed never in question, preordained. He hadn't any choice now. He could feel it actually already happening, continuing to unfold from something that had begun a long time ago.

The quiet knock came. Pedro heard it but didn't answer, preferring to relish its perfect Donna-tone. "It's open," he said after a few moments, feeling weightless in his faded crimson antique-sofa chair by the window. "Pedro?" came the voice clear as a mountain rivulet. He faced her as she entered, smiling with that cool benevolence that was so captivating about her. She stood there holding a loaf of crusty bread, her hair a little tousled about her Renaissance face.

"I was hoping you would come to your senses today," lamented Pedro behind his gloomy brown eyes. He then turned to the window, breaking eye-contact. She saw his intangible profile, skinny yet soft, fair skinned, a man-boy luminescent in the sunlight with his wild light-brown hair unkempt about his head. Yet there was a sadness, a burden that wore on him like an invisible shroud. "And leave this urban hermit to his demons."

"Oh shut up. I was hoping to get you out of the shower again," she declared, attempting to cheer him up. "I'm a little disappointed."

"So am I. You know, you should really find a nice man, one who works for a living," he remarked, facing her again, adding, "No poem today?"

"That's a revelation," she said, ignoring the inquiry, as she gently closed the door behind her. "And what is eating you?" She put the crusty bread on the table and provocatively edged her way toward him, yet moving haltingly as if their meeting was more propitious than usual.

Pedro turned to the window again, appearing pensive for a moment, then turned back to her as she saw on the fat arm of the chair.

"You know," he said, "if you weren't so intelligent and beautiful, I'd ask you to leave with me."

"What! Don't trifle with me, you jerk! Where are you going?" She put her arm around his head and squeezed it in a lock. "You think you're so damned cool. Punishable, by no poem."

"I used to be cool," he said laughing, then slipped out of her grip. He stood up and went to the window with his arms folded like Mister Clean. Donna made herself comfortable by slipping into his seat, with one leg remaining over the armrest.

"So ya wanna elope? With a virgin?" she proposed, half-teasingly.

Pedro turned to look at her. Her blue eyes intensified as if to underline her sincerity. She was so vulnerable: her lips parted seductively. It was a sign too obvious to brush over.

"I think you should stay that way for awhile," he replied delicately.

Then turning her face away, with a note of trepidation in her voice, she quietly responded, "What's wrong with you today?"

Pedro sighed and, dropping his arms, he looked out the window seeming to stare at a point in the street that the traffic passed through. He could feel her exuding emotions. He turned and watched the room transpose its colour to a granite hue.

"I don't know, Donna. I'm not the person you think I am," he explained, resisting the impulse to put his hand on her head and gently caress her hair. "Without trying to sound cryptic, I feel I'm living in a dream like a dead man in a dead land. I don't know what to say. Maybe we could . . . but I'm too self-serving . . . at present . . . and differ from most people who seem to crave involvement in normal relations. I'm really strangely average and anti-social to boot; you might even call me a loser because I opt out, in the extreme."

He began to pace.

She frowned. "You're in a rut, that's all. It's lonely."

"I'm a freak of nature, Donna. I told you I was into past-life regression, and I could find your twenty-fifth great-grandmother and tell you what she dreamed at night. So what." He stopped pacing then started again. "But I like it this way, feeling free," he continued. "My faculties are raw and impoverished and alive."

He stopped again, revealing an energy or desperation, that Donna had never seen before. He appeared to be hiding something.

Donna stood up haughtily; it was her turn at the window. "So where are you going? Why are you going? And why tease me about going with you? Do you want to torture me?" She turned to face him on the last syllable. "Christ! And we haven't even kissed! Pedro what's going on?" she blurted out.

"Why don't we go downstairs and get some coffee," he suggested. "I'm sorry. I don't want to torture anybody; I've hurt too many as it is."

"Like who?" she pried impudently.

"Like my friends . . . my parents."

"Well, what did you do?"

"Let's go; I'll try to explain."

"I'm dying to hear it," she uttered almost sarcastically, but lowering her eyes.

The winch strained as the wreck it was retrieving snagged on a jutting rock. The wreck, however, broke free from the rock, and soon the truck had hauled in its catch and laid it by the side of the road. Inspector David Thomas walked slowly around the thoroughly charred, almost unrecognizable red Rover. He already knew no body would be found; the divers were still looking with great difficulty along the violent shoreline. Thomas wasn't about to make any judgements, but had the occupant or occupants not been wearing seat-belts, the sea undoubtedly would have swept them away and would not have given them up. The problem of course was: who was it? Thomas peered inside the wreck and poked about, finding nothing except an umbrella under the front seat. He opened the map compartment and found the soggy, scorched ownership document. All he managed to make out was the name of a leasing company in London.

A few motorists had stopped along that stretch of road to watch the dismal proceedings. Inspector Thomas, a portly, graying individual in tweeds, with piercing eyes, complacently fancied himself the city detective-turned-country-gentleman, a sort of Holmes-Watson fantasy. He didn't mind an audience because usually someone came up with a lead.

"Good morning," he said to a motley group of men now standing to the side, speaking amongst themselves in low voices. "And prayers to the departed," he added as an afterthought.

The response was a mumble. Thomas hesitated, expecting the collective inquiry. His prominent square jaw and ruddy clean-shaven complexion commanded a reaction. He had a disarming twinkle in the blue of his eyes.

"Bloody 'ell, not the best place for some bloke to nod off at the wheel," spoke up a fat little fellow with a falsetto voice and moustache.

"Looks that way, doesn't it," said Thomas, priming for more.

"Either that or 'e thought 'e 'ad wings! Not a tire mark!"

"Maybe his lights failed," said a man in overalls.

"Not a chance," said an old farmer. "I live up there," he said pointing up the hill. "By a stroke of fate, I saw him go over, lights a-leading his way. Llewelyn's the name. I reported it last night."

"Would you mind showing me from where you saw it, sir?" asked Thomas. "A bit later." he added.

"Always humbled 'ere the law, sir."

"Right you are, much obliged."

Later, Inspector Thomas drove his Range Rover following Llewelyn's truck. The lane rose steadily around the hill and came to a sheltered vale. They got out and Llewelyn led the way past the old stone house and yard to a low shed nestled beneath the top of the hill. Before they reached the shed where ewes and lambs were foraging in an outside manger, Llewelyn stopped and faced the ocean. From this height, they had a good view of the coastal road. The ocean beyond looked shiny blue-gray and very inhospitable, its long white-capped swells crashing against the coastal rocks in massive white explosions.

"This is where I saw it, Inspector," said Llewelyn. He pointed with his weather-beaten finger. "See the corner? Well, at night you could only see the lights."

Inspector Thomas scrutinized the visible stretch of road. "Describe to me again what you saw, Mr. Llewelyn."

"As I said, I saw the lights, like I see 'em any night the fog's not in. By God, not like this time though; them lights never turned. They just dipped and vanished, then I sees a bright flash, but the night swallowed it too. It happened in seconds; not a chance he had, not a chance." Llewelyn shook his head.

"Did you see another car before or after?"

"Not a one, sir," answered the farmer.

"Strange," was all Thomas could say.

"The poor sod met his Maker, I warrant," said Llewelyn.

The district station was in the old coastal port town of Aberystwyth, from which, at one time, emigrants had departed for the new world. An old Norman castle graced the promontory and the medieval vestiges of an earlier period remained about the town. The station building itself could have been mistaken for an oversized tavern. Inspector Thomas sat at his desk, studying the partially charred ownership papers. He had just gotten off the phone with a woman at Fitzooth & Fitzooth, a London based investment firm, who said the car had been leased by them on loan to Pedro George. The woman, Marsha Dickson, to whom his call had been forwarded, seemed quite upset when Thomas wouldn't respond to her heated inquiries. He did find out, however, that George was a Canadian doing some research in archaeology as an assistant to Dr. Augustus Woods, who lived near Caerymwy, a local village not far inland. Further delving revealed that Pedro George's residence was with the Willobies, who actually owned the property where he had been working. The inspector would have to apprise the Willobies of the accident to find out whether Pedro was driving the car and certainly before he would convey news of the accident to the man's family. David Thomas opened and closed his ballpoint pen methodically with his thumb. He called the Willobies and spoke to Mrs. Willobie about the crash. He asked if Mr. George had been driving his car that day. She replied tearfully that he hadn't been seen by them in months but was expected any day to resume work with Dr. Woods. Thomas then asked her if she could refrain from telling Mr. George's family until conclusive information was available so as not to cause undue anguish. He added that, in the event of Mr. George's death, the news should be relayed through the proper authorities in person.

Later that day, the sea-divers reported that no body could be found, nor would likely be found off that particular stretch of rocky coastline. They did, however, find a leather jacket with a wallet containing two five pound notes, the driver's license and other items belonging to Peter W. George. Llewelyn was right, thought Thomas. This Peter had indeed met his Maker. Resigned to that seemingly ineluctable conclusion, he chalked the case up as yet another, albeit quaintly tragic, episode in his long career. He reflected on his decision made a few years before to leave London and a proffered desk job after pressure-treated years as a homicide detective. His interests had evolved into farming and history, which accorded well with his present fortuitous post and harmonious pastoral existence. In London he had earned his spurs by displaying an uncanny sense for turning up the right stones and a certain empathy for the human condition. At this stage of his career, he thought he had seen it all in virtually every strata of society, sometimes even among those thought to be above reproach. However, his fascination with serious crime, which initially spurred his interest in police work, made him dismiss this fatal auto accident as nothing more than a simple tragedy. Yet down in his soul he minded the adage: cursed be he who leaves the stone unturned.

He rubbed his eyebrows, then drew his fingers slowly over his lips and chin. Abby, a secretary, came in with a fax which she handed to Thomas. It said that Peter Willobie George entered Britain at Gatwick on Canadian Airlines from Toronto over a year ago, and that he had spent almost the last six of seven years in Britain. Inspector Thomas then lifted the telephone receiver.

The warm spring sun cast a celestial glow over the beautifully manicured Rosedale garden. The leaves were out in full, some blossoms were still in bloom, the expansive lawns were lush and glistening with dew; myriad coloured flowers lit up the various paths and spaces. The back of the property sloped toward a ravine in front of which was a stone patio with ornate, black steel garden furniture. John George was reading the newspaper; his physique, tall, erect and resolute, firm mouth set in concentration, smooth face with light complexion, bright blue eyes, and a thick full head of grey hair gave one the impression of profound intelligence — a very bastion of upper-class Rosedale. By profession he was a lawyer and by trade, a business entrepreneur, which had made him a rich man. His friends were few, as he was self-absorbed and possessed a cynical intellect; yet he was known to like a drink and throw a good party.

Connie George came out of the huge, greystone house and placed a tray with coffee, toast, and honey on the table. She was still in her bathrobe, wearing her dark-brown hair loosely to her shoulders; she had smooth tanned skin, brown eyes, and high cheek bones. Although known at times to be somewhat irreverent, she was a sociable and engaging woman, whose charisma and grace could only allay such rumours.

"I have a tennis game this morning, dear," said Connie, as she poured coffee.

"Mm," was all he could muster.

"I'm playing Sadie McPherson," she went on.

John put down his paper for a moment. "Sadie?" he uttered trying to sound nonchalant; he had always had a soft spot for Sadie, who, besides being a distant relation, had been the girlfriend of their only child Peter during and slightly beyond adolescence.

"How's our friend Sadie?" he asked, shaking the paper, as he appeared to be reading something with renewed interest.

"Oh, she's fine. You know she's in journalism — actually she's presently working on a book," said Connie stirring cream and honey into her coffee.

"Any idea what it's about?" said John.

"She said it had something to do with New Age and mysticism; you know, psychic phenomena."

"Mmph. She was always one to take on the strangest things, our son included. That's your side of the family, I might add."

"You can be so dry, John; at least we're interesting. You must admit we do have a flair for living."

The telephone began ringing inside.

"That's probably Sadie now," said Connie.

"I think Sadie's a wonderful girl and wish to hell she could've influenced that boy of ours."

But Connie had disappeared into the house. In a minute she quietly returned and sat down pensively. John, anticipating more about Sadie, looked up over his paper. "Well?" he said.

Connie didn't respond at first, which compelled John to put down the paper and reiterate, "What is it? Can't she make it?"

"John," she said in a sad, euphonic voice, "that was a Detective Dumont on the phone; he's coming over to see us."

"What?" he said, as the pit of his stomach constricted.

"There's a policeman coming here; it's about Peter."

"Peter? What's wrong?"

"He wouldn't say."

"I have some bad news," said the officer finally, after they had settled in the living-room. "It appears that your son, Peter, has been killed."

John and Connie were frozen in time as the moments lapsed, with only expressions of shock on their faces. The room seemed dark, sunk in a funereal shadow, the police officer fading before their eyes. Connie began trembling, and John helped her to the sofa. He then walked to the window and opened the curtains, as Detective Dumont watched.

"I am sorry. It's a terrible thing," said Dumont, trailing off, his fleshy face reddening. He now glanced at the floor, shaking his head. "We received the call this morning from Wales."

"I don't know what to say; we haven't heard from him or spoken to him in months. He was impossible to reach; he never called us. I can't believe this. How can this have happened?" said John tremulously, as he shot a piercing, pained look at the officer.

"It was a car accident, Mr. George. He apparently drove over a cliff on a coastal road. Did you know that he was in Wales?" asked the officer.

"He lives in London during the winter, but he used to drive to Wales often and spent his summers there. He was doing research. Dear God!" said John as he began to pace. Connie sat immobilized in shock.

"Unfortunately, they never recovered the body; it must have . . . washed out to sea."

"Christ Almighty!"

Connie began to sob. John went over to her. "Our boy," he said, "washed out. Such a wasted life."

"He was coming back. He was doing so well," said Connie tearfully.

"What am I to say? I guess I have a strange life," said Pedro. He was sitting with Donna in the shade of the tree on the terrace of Tina's cafe just down the street from their apartments. "I am what I am. Life is wonderful; at least it should be. I avow sensibility, if people are to get along. It's a feeling I get that follows a path leading to some distant mountains veiled in mist; it began thousands of years ago."

Donna del Rio loved his fair skin and perfect lips and his concerned eyes. She had her elbows planted on the table and was sipping her tea. She raised one hand to place wayward strands of hair behind her ear. She liked what he had to say.

"So what were you doing thousands of years ago?" asked Donna, smiling and looking again into the unfathomable wells that were his eyes.

"I'll give you the manuscripts," said Pedro. "You may keep them." He turned, shying away from her infatuation but knowing that, once he began to tell her, she would either blow the whistle on him or stay by his side until the end. "My circumstances at present are the result not only of events in this life of mine as Pedro George but of the reaction to my life in the past."

"How do you know this for sure?" said Donna sceptically. "I mean, I want to believe you, but I can't imagine you saying something like that without some very strong evidence."

"I was sued once," he began. "A couple of years ago I did a family history — my first client, the family of a friend of mine—."

"Sued? I don't understand. For what?"

"Let me begin by saying I grew up an only child in Rosedale . . . a bit stifling; at any rate, I was considered an anomaly in my family, whose interests were mainly financial — old Toronto trusts, and so on. Well, you know, as a child I was into literature: I read most of the classics — Dickens, James, Hugo, Dostoyevsky, Joyce, et cetera — before I was ten. At any rate, my interests evolved to the human condition and that great archetypical myth-minded social creature that he/she is, and our so-called God and Its great permutation. I became obsessed in a way; I thought I could find the truth, the secret, the ultimate knowledge, which was all just waiting for me to discover. I was predestined — a thousand voices confirmed this for me, voices from nature, the trees, waters, flowers, all things, even rocks and animals, the least of which was humanity. I guess you could say I have been on a quest. After I finished university, I became a genealogist, which provided a respected front to both earn a living and give me autonomy to pursue my real interests such as regressive karma, dreams, and resonances of life where few dare to tread; it's a bit like being an astronaut in the mind. The point is, we are not necessarily what we think we are. But without going further into such semantics, which can take on the guise of a psychological blowtorch, I was sued, sued for shedding light on a family's sordid origins which I had researched at their own request. We settled out of court, but the damage was done. Word was leaked to the press, I was blacklisted from the Genealogy Society for being unprofessional, and called both a "charlatan and a notorious fraud."

"What on earth did you find out about these people?" asked Donna.

"Well, basically that they had hacked a swath through history, murdering, raping, torturing, doing anything to achieve power and wealth; mind you, their methods have mellowed a bit these days; but what's past is prologue, as the saying goes. Anyway, they didn't like the mirror, so-to-speak, held up to their background and nature. My father, by the way, works with them."

"Who are they?"

"Morgan of Morgan-Willobie Inc. My mother is a Willobie; so you see, the whole thing was close to home."

"Name sounds familiar."

"I thought I was doing them a service; I did what they asked of me, didn't get paid, got shafted, and ended up having to pay their legal fees! They did waive that, thanks to Ronald, the son, but I bolted the country and moved to Britain."

"But how does this relate to your 'evidence' concerning this thousand-year thing?" Donna reminded him, as she put her hand on his.

"I have an aunt and uncle — my mother's younger brother — living in Wales, whom I was free to visit; they were very liberal and understanding of my situation. Well, through them I met a neighbour of theirs, an old man, Dr. August Woods, a retired archaeologist. So, I began to work with him from time to time and eventually made some fascinating discoveries on a little dig we started right on my relatives' property."

"Wow. What did you find?"

"A burial chamber, some runes, but, paramountly, presence. I knew in advance where everything was, all that was there, and the story behind everything because that's where I had lived before; for a number of years, I had had recurring dreams, or so I had thought them, until my arrival in

Wales. I made two very close friends, Hero and Niko, both of whom I had met separately over there; at the same time Ron Morgan, the young scion of the Morgan family, was visiting and spent time with us. He was making personal reparations after his parents sued me, and I was willing to forgive him as an old friend. Ron had been my friend since youth and I had always treated him much like a pet or something akin, not that I disliked the guy, just that he was kind of oppressive, which was his character. You see, by nature he was rather bellicose, fitting the family mold. As a kid, he was a holy terror, and probably in a relative way still is now. He causes general pain and discord for all who know him. I think I was the only person he couldn't consume or overpower in his way. I suppose he respected that but was incapable of tuning into my particular wavelengths. I think he envied me somehow."

"So did your being sued change your relationship?"

"Funnily enough, not really; and he was the one who had pushed for the family trace. When I told him I had discovered a link during the Saxon invasions of post-Roman Britain, he was exhilarated, even at the news that his ancestor had cut a swath of suffering difficult to take lightly. He boasted in fact, "I am descended from Vron the Barbarian." Then he proceeded to chant and beat his chest, completely lost in a brainless reverie. I thought it amusing and even laughed at the time, but he was quite serious."

"So, it was obviously his parents."

"Oh, he was in on it too, nothing personal; they were ruthless; I was inconsequential. They were truly without feelings, at least for anyone but themselves."

"No wonder you're living the way you are," said Donna, as she put her arm around him. "You've simply discarded normal human relations; it's your protection against insensitive assholes who've ruined your career. Listen, why don't we go back to your place . . . forget about all your troubles and get on with our lives. Together. You should pursue this psychic thing and archaeology; everything will be fine. Come on Pedro, you'll see!" Donna stood up. "Come on. I know I'm right."

Pedro wouldn't move. "Donna," he said into his empty teacup, "you don't know the half of it. All of that doesn't matter; that's just life. You wouldn't understand what's happening now . . . I can't explain, but I don't think I'm long for this planet."

"What? Whaddaya mean 'not long for this planet'? Are you going to another one? Come on, let's go; I don't have all day."

"There is something ominous, disquieting in the air." Pedro stood up and put some money on the table. He just couldn't get out what he wanted to say.

"What? What is it?" said Donna apprehensively.

Pedro sighed and walked out. She followed, keeping right behind as they joined the busy pedestrian traffic on the sidewalk. She had to half-step around a few people who blocked the way then half-jog to catch up to him.

"I'm a dreamer," he said, "and you don't want to know me; I'll bring wrack and ruin. Believe me, Donna . . . my circumstances impose a harsh lesson. Some brush me off as mistaken; some demand a piece of my flesh; and the remainder look to me for guidance. The truth, I believe, is more radical. I can exert power that may bring about change in a spiritual sense. August said I was a guardian of the secret of life, according to an ancient Celtic myth."

"But what's this about 'not long for this planet'?" said Donna, sidestepping people, persisting in her question, not really listening to what he was saying.

"That was something that could've gone without saying," he said.

"Do you believe you're not long for this world?"

Pedro didn't respond; it seemed that words only impeded the gravity of such an apocryphal pronouncement.

"There is so much to say, isn't there, Pedro," said Donna. For a moment she felt like giving up on him.

They arrived at Giovanni's.

"In time" was all he could come up with.

"So what's this secret of life then?" she asked, as he opened the door up to the apartments.

Pedro turned and smiled, put his hand on her shoulder, then leaned over and pecked her cheek with a little kiss. "The secret of life?" he whispered. "Food for thought." He turned to walk up the stairs. Donna stood there and hesitated, wondering whether or not to follow him, but watched him go instead. Then she closed the door and went back into the groceria.

Back in his apartment, Pedro went to his bedside table and pulled out the newspaper. He sat down and stared at the obituary which he had read a hundred times:

> George, Peter Willobie — Tragically on Thursday, June 14, 1992, in Wales. Beloved son of John and Constance George. Will be sorely missed by all who knew him. Service in Grace Church-on-the-Hill at 1:00 p.m. Saturday, June 30. Donations may be made to Sunnybrook Hospital Research Fund 2075 Bayview Avenue, Toronto, M4N 3M5.

His mind reeled. A sudden gush of blood coursed through his body, and he threw himself back on the bed. His unconscionable support through inaction of his fraudulent death sickened him. He thought of his parents and how they must be suffering on account of him, not to mention his friends. The tingling in his body was symptomatic of his terrible guilt. Yet he knew he must purge himself of this guilt, extricate himself without compromise from the web of the Wicca. His abjurement of them three months before had been a moral obligation not only to himself but even to the Wicca. Now the stakes were pushed to their limit: his personal apocalypse, it appeared, would lead to the resolution of his fragmented life, during which he had been relentlessly pursued by the specter of his nemesis, Gorgon. Yet he couldn't decide whether it was just his imagination. He could hardly fathom what on earth could have led someone to fake his death. But, conversely, he found the new anonymity strangely appealing: it was an unexpected twist to his self-imposed exile from untenable circumstances. It even seemed to be a necessary sequel to his disappearance. Knowing his desire to be alone, they obviously felt, in Wales, that he would welcome their morbid gesture as a kind of compliment — a fait accompli — but the witches didn't work that way: they must have seen his disappearance as a retreat, a weakness, and symbolically they were simply washing their hands of him for good. Pedro, though, could not really believe that. Maybe they thought more highly of him and were doing him a favour. Maybe it was to lure him back. It certainly got his attention and morbid gratification; at least they were thinking of him. Although it had occurred to him to give himself up, nothing could distract him from his present course and his need for absolute solitude. Furthermore, he knew that he must protect others from being swept up into the vortex of a leprous spell.

Chapter Two

Only a fool thinks life was made his way.
—Alun Lewis (Welsh poet)

Two weeks had passed since news of the accident. He was declared deceased. It was all so tragic for those who knew him. And the rain that day seemed to be nature's own response. Low dark clouds spewed forth wave upon wave of alternating drizzle and downpour that still would not deter about thirty resolute people huddled under their umbrellas around a newly erected gravestone in a lonely besodden expanse of Mount Pleasant Cemetery. Tears mixed with rain cascaded around the mourners, forming puddles of hopelessness and a sense of futility. John and Connie George stood together with Charles Willobie and Sadie McPherson; other friends and relatives were there, including Ronald Morgan and his parents who, notwithstanding their past acrimony with Pedro, were there in support of the Georges. Ronald couldn't take his eyes from Sadie and the Georges, seeming almost to marvel at their pain, yet aware of his own pain, though was not quite up to communicating the depth of his feelings. Standing off to the side and back of the congregation surrounding the grave and minister (whose words resonated like a broken record), were two latecomers. They had barely been noticed, other than by the occasional glance of a few beleaguered eyes which looked then sank back into their owners' selves.

The man and woman stood under the boughs of a huge fir tree, with expressions not tearful, but downcast; there was an ethereal sadness in their eyes that spoke of mysterious ways and distant places. The woman had a pale translucent complexion with natural rowanberry lips and startling hazel-green eyes, medium length ash-blonde hair and a Venusian presence that embodied the very essence of womanly grace. The man stood only a few inches taller but appeared much bigger through the powerfulness of his build, which exuded a raw energy. He was dark, prominently browed with black hair, dark eyes, a square jaw, strong nose and a full mouth; yet, for all his controlled fervent energy, a gentle warmth made itself felt in the twinkle of his eye, a warmth that contrasted sharply with the otherworldly reserve of the woman; there was a kinetic force between them that contrasted sharply with the homogeneity of dark attire and umbrellas.

Upon the completion of the ceremony, the minister extended to the small group the Georges' open invitation to their house for drinks and brunch.

Shaking off their umbrellas, everyone trudged into the front hall of the Rosedale house. The lights were all on, illuminating not only the dark day but also the haunting mood of the passing. And yet, the monotony of the interior decor gave forth the pallor of a funeral home. Drinks were served; friends and relatives spoke quietly; younger children wandered in and out aimlessly, adding their cheerfulness to the all-consuming atmosphere which would one day oppress them too.

Standing in the front hall with drinks were the minister, Ronald Morgan, Charles Willobie, Sadie McPherson, and John George, all light-haired, ranging from the minister's ultrawhite to Sadie's ash-blonde. The doorbell rang and John welcomed the strange man and woman standing there. "Please, do come in," he said. "I don't believe we've ever met."

"Hero and Niko!" said Ronald from behind. "My God, I wondered where you'd got to!"

They entered. Niko put their umbrella in the corner. They took off their raincoats.

"Here," said John, as he helped Hero with her dark burgundy mackintosh. "The weather agrees with our sentiments."

"We're devastated," said Hero looking at them all. Her black dress had a deep sangre rose sown above her left breast. "Hello, Ronald," she said, giving him a peck on his cheek. "Charles," she said turning to Willobie. Niko then shook hands with Ronald and Charles.

"Hero St. Germain. How do you do?" she said, introducing herself to John and the others in her sweet French tinctured English. "Nicholas Fitzooth," said Niko, doing the same. "But do call me Niko," he added in his crystalline English accent.

"John George," said John. Then Sadie and the minister introduced themselves. "I've heard of you both," John went on, "but that's about all; I'm sorry we must meet like this. Would you like something to drink? Scotch? Gin? Brandy? Beer. Red or white wine? Anything."

"A glass of red wine, please," they both said. Sadie left to get some.

They all stood there for an awkward moment, looking at each other. Hero and Niko's composure was deceptively calm. Hero, at least, had an axe to grind with John George, the father who wouldn't compromise his business relations for the sake of his son; this was probably just as well though, she decided, otherwise Pedro never would have come to Europe. There stood Ronald, the supercilious young scion, who always gaped at her with love-haunted eyes when she knew him in Wales years before. Hero thought he'd probably eat most people for breakfast but acted like a whipped puppy when around Pedro and her. Then there was Sadie, Pedro's teen love. Hero could see how far apart they were now, and most likely were then too. She recoiled at Pedro's involvement with these people. How galactic his isolation must have been!

"What the hell was going on over there?" probed Ronald, lording it over Hero. "He's the last person that would drive over a cliff; I just can't figure it."

"We hadn't seen or heard from him in months, Ronald," said Charles, taking the onus off Hero but looking at her for some explanation to fill the abyss of Pedro's fate.

"Hero and Pedro had separated," said Niko, easing scrutiny away from Hero too. "Not that there was anything anyone could do about Pedro's reclusive behaviour; you know how he always got so wrapped up in any new interest."

"We hadn't actually seen him in months," said Hero. "I'd been back in Paris working on a show; Pedro and I thought it best we didn't see each other at all for awhile. It was completely mutual; I'm in the dark as much as you."

"So, I gather," said John, "no one had seen or spoken to him for a couple of months, even you, Niko?"

"I attempted to reach him on numerous occasions without success. He was simply being particularly elusive; God knows he's done that before, but sooner or later, he always turned up again; even August hadn't seen him this time, although he was expecting him to arrive before June to recommence their dig."

"Yes," said Charles, a man with a mid-life corpulence and depressing disposition to boot. "When I spoke with August before I flew over, he said the last time he had spoken with Pedro was in March."

Sadie came back with wine goblets for Hero and Niko. Then she retrieved hers from the radiator cover and raised her glass.

"I want to propose a toast to Pedro, the most beautiful friend one could have, and how he will be missed forever." On the last word her feelings gave way and tears of grief once again welled up in her eyes. The others lowered their eyes, except Hero, who went over and gave Sadie a hug. Sadie felt Hero's warm energy transude into her, reminding her of Pedro. She realized how insecure she was feeling with Hero, just as she had felt with Pedro; there was something unfathomable about them, something both foreign and strange that made her cling to them all the more. After her devastating break-up with Pedro, she had taken years to crawl out from his maze. However, in time he had come to realize how interesting and important Pedro really was and how he had opened for her a much broader life than she had been prepared for. In her professional field, this had led her to soberly document things of the unknown and the unexplained, to expose not only for herself, but others, the significance of supernatural phenomena. "Pedro the Enigma," said Sadie, releasing Hero. As she did so, looking the latter in the eye, she observed that cross-eyed brujo-like expression she had known with Pedro years before. Hero too, thought Sadie, was possessed with a missionary zeal for the netherworlds, reflecting an off-beat hallucinogenic conformism. In the old days, Pedro would call it Sunday school and dispense with Spike Hammerstein's three-eyed-toad-blotter-acid — he and his wild friend Spike, the quiet and the solicitous — now both dead.

Hero, meanwhile, was conscious of Sadie's pain and then her own welling up inside; tears trickled down quietly and she remained speechless. She was feeling terribly vulnerable, still raw from Pedro and her own separation which was now permanent. Part of her was angry, angry that he could have cut himself off so completely, ignore her overtures, and then die without the slightest warning. Pedro wouldn't just die like that, she kept repeating over in her mind, letting the idea of his death consume her; yet she felt something was subtly but palpably wrong in this whole mess. It was the feeling of guilt in a complicity in silence, which was Pedro's silence. Sadie and Hero were both aware of their respective relations with Pedro. Hero saw in Sadie the perfect youthful match: her slightly gregarious personality, athletic build, large blue eyes, long natural eyelashes, and thick dusky blonde hair that fell to her shoulders. On the other hand, she could see that Sadie felt uneasy around her and kept a cautious distance while being mutually intrigued.

"How long did you know the deceased?" the minister suddenly asked

Niko in a voice tinged with a disdain that seemed to insinuate that Niko and Hero were not as welcome as they'd like to think. He appeared capable of bringing out a cross and hold it menacingly in front of them.

"About seven years," said Niko carefully.

"When did you last see him?" he persisted.

"March equinox, at Professor Woods' cottage," replied Niko.

"March equinox? Well, you and the Professor must be the last to have seen him before Pedro, by all accounts, vanished," intervened John George.

"Spring came early this year," said Niko, not liking the inquisitional direction of the conversation. "That was over three months ago."

"We never saw him at Easter," drawled Charles Willobie in his mellow-somber way. "I do remember Anne saying she saw his car drive up August's road."

"Why didn't Anne come?" queried Ronald.

"She simply couldn't bear it; she was fond of Pedro and loved him like a son. Besides, she feels his spirit resides on our estate about 'the lake and ruins and meadows', quote unquote," said Charles apologetically.

"Please excuse me," said John to Niko and Hero. "I would like to find Connie; she would love to meet both of you." John left, and Charles and Sadie excused themselves too.

Ronald, who had been standing there bursting to express himself, finally had his chance. "So, when did you last see him, Hero?" he asked.

"A good while ago," she said guardedly. She didn't like the tone of his voice, sensing in it an arrogant intrusion into her somewhat diffident suffering. "You know how close we were," she added in a tone calculated to signify the obvious.

"Pedro was my best friend," he announced, "even after the notorious family feud, which wasn't my doing, as you know; don't get me wrong: I honour his memory." He couldn't help but lower his eyes to her breasts where her nipples made gentle, well formed protuberances against the confines of her silken dress. He lowered his eyes further to her crotch.

Ronald smiled. He warmed to a pink glow that suffused his sharp, acerbic features and trim blond hair. He emanated a certain fecundity toward the object of his desire.

Without changing her stance, Hero looked him steadfastly in the eye, and waited a well-timed moment before uttering, "Still the same old Ronald. Your reputation precedes you. I once heard you spiked Connie's drink with acid at a teen party, then fucked her in the rec-room. Is that true?"

"Excuse me!" said the minister, out of his element and striding away with an Anglo-Gothic gait.

"Charming, Hero, charming," said Ronald half-amused. "We seem to have lost a member of the elder generation. But don't you think your timing was a little off."

"On the contrary, Ronald; I'm sure it's been a while since you've been put in your place," said Hero casually. "In deference to the departed, however, I shall raise my glass to Pedro, and of course, the triple Goddess. Come to think of it, Ronald, you'd make a good male sacrifice. Would you like to offer yourself at the next Wiccan feast?"

They were laughing as John and Connie came up to them. "Connie, meet Hero St. Germain and Nicholas Fitzooth."

"Oh, I'm happy to meet you," she said. "Peter never spoke of his friends much, and you've come all the way from England; you must've been very good friends."

"Yes, we loved him very much," said Hero, distancing herself from Ronald. She had clearly mixed feelings about this reception. She had lost her grip and everything seemed to be spinning out of control. Even the illusion of Pedro's death was simply too close to home.

Through pressure from the Canadian Embassy, the British authorities appointed Inspector David Thomas to undertake an inquest into the death of Pedro George. With the request, Thomas reconsidered that quite possibly he hadn't been as thorough as he could have been. His country posting had made him slightly soft around the edges. His dear wife Eliza and he operating their little hobby farm, were so satisfied with their life, it was difficult for him to be the hard-edged man he had been back in London. The presence of the umbrella under the front seat made him think there was a chance that it had been used to depress the accelerator, although no one seemed to gain by it. He thought that at least he should investigate further by visiting the Willobie estate, which initially he had had the local police undertake, to confirm Mr. George's death.

He drove his Range Rover up the long valley to Caerymwy, the beautiful little Welsh village nestled in high hills, from whose heights one could see the sea far to the west. The air was fresh and fragrant from the rain the night before. Pockets of mist lingered in meadows and glades, still unvanquished by the warm and brilliant sun, but soon these too would dissipate. Moisture and sun could then perform the miracle of drawing the rich verdant greens from the ground, which stirred even the dullest of heart-strings. Thomas smiled to himself. He loved this country far removed from the dark factory towns to the south; he loved this life, his wife, the mysteries of the ancient land. A sensation of power filled him despite the task at hand to investigate the young man's tragic death.

He believed it would be prudent to begin with the Willobie estate, having no decent alternative. Everything begins with a single step, he thought. He also happened to be interested in the old professor who was digging there around some site or ruins. The case, although seemingly routine, had begun to intrigue him. For some inexplicable reason, this ill-fated Pedro had captured his imagination — why Pedro from Peter?

He came to the Tudor village of thatched cottages, stone-and-beam buildings snug and settled along the little river, adjacent pastures running down from every side. Some children playing in the street stopped to look at him as he drove through, past an nondescript pub called "The Turk," then, farther down, a store by the old bridge. Once through, the road traversed a thicket, then forked. David Thomas took the road on the left which headed up the valley again. At the top of a steep vale was the stone gateway to the Willobie property. The lane leading from the gateway followed a creek to a manicured pond then ascended a rise. Gradually, above the rise, the nineteenth-century mansion itself came into sight. Of cut fieldstone, it consisted of a central edifice and a portico with two symmetrical wings, one on each side. Large oaks and willows and assorted gardens were arrayed ideally about the lawns.

At the sound of the motor, two black Labrador retrievers came from around the corner of the house and milled about him a little cautiously. Thomas parked in front and stepped out to enjoy the magnificent view of the whole valley dropping away in front of him in the direction from which he had come. He stood for a while, letting the breeze revive him with a hint of the sea, mingling scents of heathers and flowers.

A woman's voice spoke up from behind. He turned to see the woman, wearing green work pants and a mauve sweater, approach him. She was fortyish, with a kindly face that was both disarming and austere. She was highbrowed, and quite provocative, he decided, with champagne eyes, ash-blond hair tied in a short pony-tail and a bronzed complexion. She was the epitome of health.

"Inspector Thomas, I presume," she said, extending her hand. "Anne Willobie. We deserve yet another visit?"

"Good day to you, Mrs. Willobie; grand place you've got," he said, looking about. "And yes, I too make my rounds. This case warrants a little examination, shall we say. From on high I might add. Mr. George had influence, it seems."

"There's little more to say," she said, flicking a loose strand of hair and looking to the ground.

"One never knows what to say," he went on, shaking his head. "From what I gather, he must have been an extraordinary lad."

"We were very fond of him. I couldn't even bring myself to go to the funeral . . . I'm not good at funerals. Charles, of course, went . . . Pedro was like a son of ours, one we . . . " She talked with an uneven rate but flat; her voice had a sweet tenor, though transparent, as if she were putting up a brave front, revealing no emotional loss. Thomas felt instinctively that she was far more complex than she acted.

"Mrs. Willobie, this inquiry won't take long; all I ask for is your cooperation in answering a few questions about the deceased and permission to walk up to the ruins, or where Mr. George worked."

"By all means; I was going to suggest something of the sort. Come, let's go around to the other side and I'll get some refreshments . . . then we can sit and chat for a while."

They walked around the west wing through dazzling gardens and chirping birds and came to a patio with white steel garden furniture and a marble-top table. Inviting him to sit down, she disappeared into the house.

While waiting for her to return, he looked about curiously and saw sheep in pastures beyond the trees and gardens. His senses were fully activated now, and the feeling came over him that he was being drawn into something not at all familiar.

Mrs. Willobie returned, carrying a tray with tea and biscuits. She placed the tray on the table, poured the tea, sat down, and crossed her legs.

"Charles flew over yesterday for the funeral today," she said. "He was absolutely devastated. He kept saying, 'Not Pedro, not Pedro.'"

She stirred a little honey into her tea. "As I've said before, I'm not much good with funerals; I don't like them, though I suppose they're necessary enough."

"Did Peter-Pedro . . . Why was he called Pedro, by the way?" asked Thomas.

"I asked him that very question when he first came over here . . . He told me all his friends called him that; it made him happy . . . somehow . . . I asked him if he didn't like Peter; he replied pointblank, 'I'm not Peter anymore.' End of conversation. I'm inclined to think it had something to do with his youthful fascination with Don Juan."

"Don Juan. A committed individual, I'd say," said Thomas, as he poured a little cream into his tea. "Did he like to drink?"

"Almost never, as far as I know; he did, however, have an impulsive side . . . in which case he might have done so on a whim, but that's only what I gathered from some passing remark from Hero or Niko the few times they stayed here."

"They didn't stay here much? Where did they stay?"

"Well, they stayed with Professor Woods or camped."

"How would you describe Professor Woods?" asked Thomas with the growing sense of being left in the dark.

"Eccentric, a little neurotic. Pedro and he were very close."

"Interesting. I look forward to meeting him."

"He is rather private. We do let him work on our property about the lake. Pedro, of course, was working with him. The professor had a grant, and we chipped in an equal amount. We're very interested in what they've found. Did you know Pedro discovered some ancient runes?" queried Anne with the teacup at her prim lips. Her eyes took on a languid air, which effectively sent a shiver down the nape of Thomas' neck.

"No. Were they deciphered?" he responded automatically.

"The professor's working on it; that's the last I heard when they finished last fall. I think they're trying to prove that a supposedly mythical kingdom called Argeia was indeed situated by our lake. August has been at it this spring; he may even be back there now, taking up the project again."

"You mean he didn't go to Toronto either?" asked Thomas, raising his eyebrows and putting down his teacup.

"He called to say he wouldn't go, that Pedro did a rotten thing dying like that in the middle of their dig, and that furthermore it was completely out of character for him."

"What a strange thing to say!" exclaimed Thomas. "What did he mean by 'out of character'? Never send to know for whom the bell tolls. Or some such thing. Accidents happen."

"Very good Inspector; it tolls for thee, present company excepted," she said, suppressing a smile. "Yes, it must seem strange that he didn't go either, but you must understand that Augustus never goes anywhere. And Pedro was part of this land in ways most of us cannot comprehend."

"I'm not sure I follow you," he said.

"I want to show you something." She stood up and went into the house, returning shortly with a piece of paper. "Read this," she said, handing him the sheet.

He took it and saw that it was a poem written in a hand that had a sensual derangement to it; it wasn't the rapid scrawl of desperation, nor was it messy; it was simply obscure. He read:

> I am the impartial bard,
> The wanderer amongst trees,
> From the vale of Ebron,
> To the land of Albion. I, of summer stars,
> Born of hag Caridwen,
> Raised to stir the cauldron,
> Inspired from hellish brew. Natural in the secrets
> That Templars sought to know,
> Natural in the spheres
> Where Lucifer fell. I was with Turketul,
> I was the grail,
> I was with Yeshu,
> He wore my skin. The nine-fold sisters
> Have sequestered me
> To run as the Roebuck
> To the tree in the sun.

He looked over at Anne Willobie. She seemed to divine what it was that he couldn't put into words. "That should give you an idea of the sort of things going through his head," she commented in a wry sort of way that Thomas couldn't help notice as being rather cold.

"I see what you mean," he said, with a sad smile. "I haven't a clue what it's all about. Packs quite a wallop, though, doesn't it? Who's this Turketul and the rest?"

"August would oblige you on that and do much better than I," she said, with those champagne eyes doing their hypnotic ream.

She petted a black cat which had jumped up into her lap. The cat's tail pointed straight up as she purred, rubbing her head into Mrs. Willobie's breast.

David Thomas pondered the little poem for a few moments, trying to ignore the cat and Mrs. Willobie, who now gave him a most definite uneasiness. Yet, something in the poem gave him a feeling that here was someone who loved life as he himself did — albeit from a different vantage-point. Though, in fact, far beyond Thomas' rather safe existence, this young man appeared to have been on some kind of romantic quest or search for knowledge. The thought kept ringing in his head: no relatively sober-minded individual was going to just drive off a cliff unless of course he was asleep at the wheel. It just didn't fit, yet Pedro was gone. And if he'd wanted to fake his death for some inexplicable reason, certainly money wasn't a motive, as there wasn't any life insurance. Who would be most inclined to know anything about it? Was there foul play?

"Mrs. Willobie, was Pedro depressed? Could he have committed suicide?" probed Inspector Thomas.

"Absolutely not. He met every challenge in life head on," she said emphatically.

"Did Pedro have any enemies, anyone that might have liked to see him come to harm, Mrs. Willobie?" he asked pointblank, looking into those eyes that blinked slowly.

"Pedro? Never," she said. "Everyone loved him."

"You mentioned someone — Hero was it?" he followed up suddenly.

"Yes, Hero St. Germain, his supposed girlfriend soul-mate," replied Mrs. Willobie casually, seeming to enjoy the exchange.

"Where is she from?"

"Originally Switzerland; she now lives in Paris. She's an artist-astrologer — a very shrewd woman."

"Why do you say 'supposed' girlfriend?"

"Well, from what I gather, she left him quite cold-heartedly, which seriously depressed Pedro, then she took up with Pedro's best friend Niko, but don't quote me on that; they were all so damned tight. One really didn't know who was doing it to whom. Pardon me." She turned away with a firm but almost hurt expression.

"Do I sense a note of . . . let's say frustration?" he asked.

"Actually, Inspector, no. Their youth was simply infectious, that's all; Christ, I do miss them."

"Did Hero make it to the funeral?"

"I don't know," she answered almost curtly.

"When was the last time you saw Pedro or either of them?" He kept up the pressure.

"About three months ago. March."

"And no one has seen him since."

"Apparently not, but for Pedro that's not out of the ordinary; he would sometimes disappear for longer periods. You could leave messages with Niko, but Pedro was absolutely inaccessible. It was infuriating when his mother, Charles's sister, wanted to reach him."

"Connie."

"Yes."

"What of Niko?" asked David Thomas, persisting.

"Niko? Rock of Gibraltar; there isn't a more down-to-earth fellow; he's a relation of mine; I'm a first cousin of his mother, Countess Huntington. It was during a visit, oh, five or six years ago, that Pedro met him here. It was funny, you know. They became fast friends just like that, as if they were long lost brothers or something. The bond was never broken; Niko revered Pedro, which in itself is curious. Niko's only twenty-nine, I think, but he's already taken over the helm of his family's small, exclusive investment firm Fitzooth & Fitzooth. His grandfather, the late 16th Earl of Huntington, died and left it in his care; Pedro, on the other hand, couldn't be more opposite: just absolutely wayward, no financial responsibility whatsoever, compelling Niko to actually support him without reservation.

"Niko's mother had Niko when she was twenty years old but never married. Nicholas Fitzooth, the 17th Earl of Huntington, is the son of a Greek freighter captain by the name of Hermes Metropoulos. She did have a flair for the exotic; she once told me that we English aristocrats are far too inbred. She's actually quite a snob."

"Interesting" was all Thomas could come up with. He noted his earlier contact with Fitzooth & Fitzooth. Pedro's death was beginning to acquire definite outlines for him. There was something emphatically cultish about it. As his imagination raced on, he realized how much more there was to know about this Pedro George. It was all just too pathetic, futile: here was Anne Willobie and the Professor, two of the closest people to the deceased, who really cared for him but wouldn't go to the funeral for apparently selfish reasons. Something askew was all he could reason. However, his curiosity was sufficiently piqued to find out everything he could about Pedro George.

Pedro hovered in his sleep in a mass of coalescing images which formulated themselves into an expanse of stony ground from which sprang a growth of rough gorse and dry stunted trees. To the west, the sky was deep purple; to the east, the stars materialized into a cascade of celestial sparkle. The setting evoked the supersedence of a foreign universe. Pedro knew no other.

He heard Aeneas quietly and sure-footedly following him as they made their way along the dark thin ribbon of a path to a grassy field now rendered silvery by the full and luminous rising moon. Occasional wafts of sweet lavender growing in patches along the ridge drifted pleasantly across their nostrils. Trees loomed larger, and the darkness of a forest lay ahead. They moved swiftly along as they had been directed, seeking a place where, it was claimed, lived a goddess in a sacred grove by a water source of miraculous power. A small group of devout men were said to guard this deity and had lived here as the perpetuators of a cult for many generations. Each goddess was succeeded by another when the men felt their powers had waned (usually the first sign of aging).

People came from all around to drink from the pool and catch a glimpse of Ariadne, as the goddess was called. If there happened to be a full moon during any equinox or solstice, a male sacrifice was performed in her honour; or if she happened to look a man in the eye, his life was forfeited. Ariadne, however, made rare appearances and usually kept her eyes lowered. The situation was beyond her control as the men guarded her as a prisoner of the laws they had created and thus victimized themselves. Such bondage was common throughout much of the pagan world; yet this particular goddess, who commanded tremendous respect, held power and was known to pardon certain transgressors.

They saw the fire on a distant rise to the north across a large field. They stopped to rest and looked on silently for a few minutes, feeling the adrenalin surge into their hearts, irresistibly yearning to find that goddess who drove them on heedless of any danger, in awe of an unknown future.

Troylus was the son of King Priam, once the mighty ruler of the Trojan world, which had capitulated to the Greeks led by Agamemnon and Ulysses. Troylus's people had scattered in every direction, searching for a new homeland. He and Aeneas were themselves nomads on an epic migration to Avalon, a mythical land to the north. In their travels they had heard of a northerly land called Albion and believed this must be the same place. According to old wrinkle-eyed Gomer, the sea-faring Phoenician who had been their navigator in travels to and fro across the Mediterranean in recent years, their assumption was, in fact, correct. He had met sailors in his youth who came from there. Old Gomer had agreed to come with them across land — ancient Gaul — on their quest;

but no sooner had he left his beloved sea than he succumbed to the balm of eternity. Only a fortnight ago, he had been killed in a fight with a marauding band of vagrants on the Rhone.

The two men began to cross the field toward the highest part of the ridge, which stood out black between the field and starry sky. As they approached, they could hear a strange high soprano voice calling out religious incantations. The language was unintelligible. They reached the trees and crept warily until they could easily see the proceedings. Reassuring themselves by handling their swords and bows and arrows, they positioned themselves strategically behind some bushes and watched as a dozen naked men with elaborate masks and body paint danced about the fire to the singing in strange mimes. Behind the fire, partly obscured by the smoke and flame appeared to be a hairy monster tied to a stake. The latter was slouched over and seemed resigned to his fate.

"Such a beast," whispered Aeneas, crouching with one knee against his bronze breast-plate.

"A sacrifice," added Troylus.

"We must move to higher ground," said Aeneas.

"Let's take her while they're too busy to notice; we've got to act now."

They advanced, circling round the ritual taking place on a gentle slope under large coniferous boughs. Stealthily they crept along, passing in and out of the dancing light of the fire. Beyond the level of the Hairy Man, they came upon a trickle of water through an orderly grouping of rocks; then they continued until they came to a path parallel to the stream and followed it back to a pool.

"The source is by the temple," said Troylus under his breath. Instinctively, they left the path and the sounds of the ecstatic drones about the fire. They were hardened survivors, taut from meagre rations of dried meat and grain and long inured to the apocalyptic destruction of the Trojan civilisation. Ages ago they had shed their last tears over their miserable fate and loss of loved ones. All Troylus and Aeneas had known in their young lives was war; after this destruction it was their destiny to carry the seed of a new beginning, a new tree in the sun. They were the only ones left capable of doing so. Most of their people had died along the way or in Italy where their settlement had been overrun by the Etruscans. Others had chosen to integrate into that civilization, which was thought to be fair. Troylus, in disgust, outlawed himself. He became a king in search of a kingdom.

A new home in a new country required the love and support of a special woman. Troylus, when he first heard of a goddess living far inland in an area remote from any travelled route, had no doubt that she would be the woman he needed. Women of his royal caste were few and far between for the dispossessed. He couldn't shut the goddess out of his mind; he needed her to fill that emptiness in his breast and strengthen his resolve to continue his line; wisdom alone, without love and procreation, would not suffice. The fiercely loyal Aeneas was ready to lay down his life for his great friend and master.

Ahead, they could see torches flickering through the trees and a light breeze causing the flames to perform a mesmerizing dance under the dark canopy of the forest. Troylus and Aeneas waited, then moved along the edge of the darkness, following the torches until they saw the temple above the stream's source. The structure was modest — approximately ten metres by seven, with columns in front, white stone walls and a red tiled roof. A tapestry hung in the doorway, and on the steps were strewn bunches of fresh herbs and flowers. They noticed a guard standing off to the side; he was slightly in the shadows with a sword and spear, but they could see that he wore thick protective leather armour, a mask, and a helmet with plumes. The man appeared uncommonly large and was most likely a eunuch as was customary.

With a quick look at Troylus, Aeneas slipped away to approach from the opposite side. Troylus pulled an arrow from his quiver and held it ready in his bow; momentarily, he pulled back the bowstring and took aim. The arrow ripped through the air and hit the guard with a thud, square in the solar plexus. Without a word, the guard looked down and grabbed the arrow which had barely penetrated his skin but suddenly, before his reflexes took over, a shadowy figure jumped out from behind, slitting his throat. He fell over, croaking and gurgling, blood pouring down his chest. The whole incident was over in a matter of seconds, so precise and efficient were these two errant warriors.

In another instant, Troylus bounded up the few stone steps of the temple and held aside its tapestry. There, before him, was Ariadne. The sudden shock of their meeting left them both mute; his taut, tanned face was now wild with perspiration and his dark, unwavering eyes gave forth a mysterious intensity. Her light brown hair, hazel eyes, luminous skin and parted ruby mouth radiated an impenetrable magic. Thus they stood, the unspoken revealed in a moment's look.

Aeneas entered and took her arm, motioning her to keep quiet. They then departed into the darkness to the north, not before releasing the Hairy Man from his imminent doom, among the stunned worshippers.

Hero sat on a stool in the Georges' kitchen, her hand clenching a wine goblet filled with a hearty red Burgundy. Across from her, Sadie propped her head on her hand and rested her elbow on a white table, turning a large cognac glass full of wine with her fingers. An open bottle of red wine stood between them.

They had been speaking of Pedro's astrology. Sadie had discreetly steered Hero away from the Georges after the minister had complained to her of Hero's bombshell utterance. But, having spoken with her sufficiently, Sadie perceived that Hero was more vulnerable than she showed. And because of Hero's stoic exterior Sadie felt that she possessed considerable talents, one of which was being a sorceress; in fact, she was anxious to know her better, especially her relationship with Pedro. There was something inscrutable behind those hazel eyes. Her only hope was that Hero would open up about Pedro. Sadie also felt some responsibility toward the Georges, notwithstanding her own curiousity. Hero, on the other hand, knew only too well Sadie's thoughts. She held no sentimental attachment toward Pedro's family and friends (although she could undoubtedly sympathize with their loss), but she was deeply concerned with her own loss — Pedro — who had been irreplaceable, and she had not much come to terms with his apparent cataclysmic death. But Pedro wasn't dead: she had an uncanny sense of his existence! What she could not tell, however, was whether he was actually alive or merely existing as some kind of lingering entity. She understood Pedro, knew his life, knew his particular history; yet she couldn't perceive the outcome of this turn of events. She feared having to continue to play the marionette to Pedro's puppeteer and was at a loss to define what would be expected of her. Pedro's death had in effect become a virtual reality. She emptied her goblet and then refilled it.

Hero could not resist feeling that Sadie was an exceptional and kind woman and wished to be her friend. Moreover, Sadie must become her friend. The plot was thickening, she ruminated.

"So Pedro was an Aquarian. How do you interpret that?" asked Sadie, following up on the conversation concerning Pedro's use of astrology in his past life readings.

"Well, that's a rather loaded question. I believe we know too little about astrology to treat it as anything more than an addictive hobby," said Hero downplaying both her need to delve further at that time, and her knowledge of astrology.

"Pedro was into it," rejoined Sadie, prying for more. "Though I never really paid much attention. Do you think it works? I'm a Libra, but nothing written about Libras seems to fit me, so I don't believe in it," she said, quite sure of herself.

"You probably have a dominant ascendant or ruling planet that downplays your sun position. Let me digress, Sadie. You have shopping-mall-type astrology on one hand, which most people read, and then you have the science of astrology which Pedro and I use. Galileo and even Newton practiced this kind of astrology. It's quite valid, although it has been often maligned."

"What did Pedro think about it?" asked Sadie.

"Well, like me, he always said that your sun sign, albeit the most powerful force, is only one influence and that we carry all the signs of the zodiac in our cosmic imprint, if you will; it depends on where the emphasis is placed in the sign and house. There is an ineluctable resonance emanating from the planets and universe that astrological systems have attempted to define for thousands of years. The sun represents all the changes that we have not yet made or experienced but are headed toward. It is the identity of the self, the wellspring. On the other hand, the moon represents our feelings, memories, habitual thinking, and the subconscious. Then there's Mercury, representing the mind, and all forms of communication; then Venus, the appreciation and attraction in love and values; and Mars, the planet of inner motivation and emotion that drives us; then Jupiter, the planet of success, expansion and vocation, the guru or luck planet. Then we have Saturn, the law-giver of limitations and time; Saturn is the old man tapping you on the shoulder, teaching you to be careful; it defines and crystalizes and represses . . . " Hero hesitated for a moment to drink from her wine before continuing. "The outer planets are also important with their relative influences: Uranus — impulse, Neptune — vision, Pluto — regeneration, and of course, the rising sign, or ascendant, which indicates your external nature or how you present yourself. The synthesis of a chart can be a complex undertaking. But, to answer your question, Pedro's particular astrology in a nutshell — and I'll say this only for you — was that he was the kind of idealist that had the right stuff to make something happen. Nothing deterred him. Pedro once said that he was the purest, most ingenuous healer possible."

"I didn't realize he was a healer."

"As an astrologer, he could perform more healing in an hour than a psychiatrist could in a month or year or ever. Once you get the natal blueprint of someone's astrology, you have captured the essence of their being;

it then becomes easy to pick out their nature, both good and ill. The stars tell us all. For example, you may come across more as a Cancer than a Libra because of a strong ascendant, say in Cancer, with the moon also in Cancer on the very ascendant, but I'm just guessing. I'd have to draw up your chart to be accurate."

"Interesting. What was Pedro's chart like?" persisted Sadie.

"Pedro, where are you?" Hero called out suddenly to the ceiling. "I know you can hear me! You're not dead, are you? You're out there. What the hell is going on? Niko and I have come to take you home! Pedro, hear me!" She bowed her head and took another gulp of wine.

"What are you talking about?" exclaimed Sadie.

Hero just swirled her wine.

"Hero?" she asked again.

"He's out there, Sadie. I know he is," Hero said, looking intently into Sadie's eyes. "You prick!" she called out again. "You should warn me when you die!"

"Hero, take it easy," said Sadie, as she got up and put her arm around her. "Pedro knows how you feel."

"Oh, you're an angel, Sadie; I'm okay; I just cannot believe what has happened."

"Death doesn't post a timetable."

"Pedro was fascinating, Sadie," said Hero sadly. "He had a six-pointed star and a grand cross — an Aquarius Sun, Taurus Moon in the twelfth house with Taurus Rising . . . You know, we were pretty damn tight until he didn't want to have sex anymore; he went celibate on me. I think I understand: it was like he had risen to a sphere that I couldn't reach; I needed him and he didn't need me."

"You mean he didn't love you anymore?"

"I don't want to believe that," said Hero.

"What then?" Sadie suddenly thought she was being too compulsive with Hero as if she were conducting an interview. "I'm sorry, Hero. I didn't mean to stir up . . . so much."

"Oh, he loves me all right," replied Hero confidently and ignoring Sadie's deference. "But he moved into a higher realm. It was his way of telling us it was time."

"Time for what?" asked Sadie, once again the concerned advocate.

"Time to die."

"You . . . you think he took his own life?" said Sadie incredulously.

"Oh, God, no, he would never take his own life. He couldn't have been in that car. He just can't be dead."

"Now I'm completely confused; one minute you say 'It's time to die'; next, you say, 'He can't be dead.'"

"Something's wrong," was all Hero would say.

Sadie sat down and sighed, disturbed. She couldn't rationalize Hero's behaviour as simply grief. She had the feeling Pedro was hovering over them in casual observation, and she looked up to catch this impression in the shadow of the finely gold-etched glass fixture of the ceiling light.

In the living room, Niko and Ronald were quietly conversing with John and Connie George and Connie's brother, Charles. The mood of the group was indeed sombre: Connie had a seemingly perpetual handkerchief to her teary eyes, but was being brave and conscientiously performing her duties as hostess. The conspicuous absence of Anne Willobie hadn't been brought up, but their awareness of this was certainly simmering beneath the surface. Amongst the Canadian side of the family, Anne's sometimes peculiar behaviour was well-known. Often she had simply chosen not to participate in family functions and either would be elsewhere or if, present, would remain self-absorbed in her own affairs, leaving even the cooking to Charles or to Gwendolyn, a local Welsh girl who worked for Anne. But with this sudden family tragedy, Anne had simply overextended her personal freedom.

Charles especially felt the absence of solidarity and more than once apologized for Anne's strange neurosis about the funeral. (Indeed she had excused herself over the phone prior to the ceremony.) Naturally she was forgiven, but she raised eyebrows and doubt was cast on the stability of Charles's marriage. And, of course, Ronald hadn't heard any comment on the matter, so when the thought occurred to him, he quickly resolved to inquire.

"So, Charles, I'm surprised not to find Anne here. She was more than fond of Pedro."

"Yes, I know, but Anne was just too upset to travel . . . "

"Of course," said Ronald commiserating with him about the tragedy, but adding, "though I always thought Anne so well composed."

"Well, she's a softy underneath," said Charles apologetically. Charles, blond like Ronald, though his hair was shorter and receding at the corners of his brow, found Ronald a bore.

"What about the professor?" asked John, looking at Charles. "I gather he and Peter were the best of friends. Not a telegram, call, or anything, and Peter's been gone for two weeks now."

"Well, he's quite anti-social. And if it hadn't been for Pedro, we most probably would have had little to do with him. He was too wrapped up in his anthropology to even notice us when we happened to come around the ruins. Pedro, of course, would explain what was being done. It miffed me, because I had put up a few thousand pounds."

Until then, Niko hadn't spoken unless spoken to; but hearing Charles talk about Augustus as a self-centred egoist compelled him to interject.

"August can be a bit irreverent," said Niko, "but he is also very sensitive and wouldn't be party to a death that he couldn't really believe in. He thinks Pedro is still alive."

Everyone within earshot suddenly turned to look at him. Niko looked about, taken aback at the effect of his words.

"My God, is there any truth to this, Niko, or is the professor as wacky as I've heard him to be? You must agree, this is outrageous, and I'm quite upset I hadn't been told anything about it," said John with growing anxiety.

"All I really mean is that the professor has suffered enough. He lost a close grand-nephew a number of years ago and then his best friend, Anne's father, shortly thereafter. He wasn't quite the same afterwards," said Niko.

"But why would he speak of Peter like that?"

"All I know is what I'm telling you," said Niko, without revealing his own deeper convictions. "Let Pedro rest in peace. Don't mind the ravings of an old man; Pedro was in full charge of his capacities." Niko regretted he had spoken at all.

"August once told me," intervened Charles, "that Pedro was too reckless in a cerebral kind of way."

At that, Niko excused himself and left the room with Ronald following. They entered the kitchen where they caught Sadie and Hero hugging.

"Hero, you're not bewitching my fiancée, are you?" said Ronald humorously.

Hero let go and laughed. "Your fiancée? Well, aren't you lucky, Ronald; and Sadie, if he ever gets out of hand, call me pronto; I'll whip him back into shape. All in all, congratulations are in order, my dear; he is rich."

"Hero, Ronald thinks the world of you, he does — honestly!" said Sadie, crinkling her nose at Ronald.

Niko sat on a stool at the counter, and Ronald sat across from Hero, who was now at the table beside Sadie. After pouring more wine all around, Hero yielded to an urge to tease Ronald. "You know Ronald, you couldn't have come in at a better moment; my depression was reaching its nadir, and now I can use you to bounce back on. Oh, Sadie, please forgive me, but he can be such an ass; yet he truly makes me laugh."

"If you were a guy, I'd punch your face in," said Ronald with a sincere expression.

"Ronnie!" exclaimed Sadie.

"It's OK, Sadie," said Hero, "he's still simmering from my intemperate comment in front of Ted the Minister."

"I used to call her 'the Witch', Sadie."

"You've been very coy about that trip, Ron; maybe now I'll get some answers," said Sadie.

"Well, it's not like we were going out then, my dear."

"Mmm . . . " she said, thinking this over. She looked over at Niko. "Niko, I know you'll give me a straight answer: was he notorious?"

"Nothing out of the ordinary. We were all four years younger," said Niko. "No one was more honest about his feelings; actually, he was fairly discreet and gentlemanly."

"Niko, you are a true friend; I needed that," said Ronald raising his glass. "And now I want to toast Pedro, who treated me with a respectful, bemused disdain; may he see me now." And addressing the ceiling, he called: "I hope to hell you hear me Pedro because if you think you can get out of this one you're dead wrong, but I sincerely wish that you're putting us on and you'll be back soon."

They all toasted Pedro with a laugh.

"But before you get too excited, Ronald, shouldn't you come clean with Sadie about that trip?" questioned Hero, persisting in her teasing.

"Come clean? Didn't you just hear the very reflection of respect and class in Niko's answer?" said Ronald bristling up again.

"Come now, Ronald, what's all this righteousness we've been hearing? I want to hear from you the aggressive, egotistical, hardball, spit-in-the-eye side; it just, oh, turns me on," purred Hero entrapping Ronald in her web. Ronald faltered, but only for a moment.

"See what I mean, Sadie; she's a witch. When I first met her, she turned me into a zombie. It was like she and Pedro were the king and queen and I was the envious slave of desire. We spent most of the time camping by the lake, drinking homemade ale and eating toadstools; you can only imagine how depraved I felt after a few days of that, with her running around in the buff most of the time."

"Hey, I wasn't the only woman there."

"Yes, there was Marsha," said Ronald resignedly, knowing the cat would soon be out of the bag, or weasel from the cage.

"Who was Marsha?" asked Sadie, a little miffed at Hero's insinuating treatment of Ronald, although she felt he deserved it at times.

"Marsha is a friend of mine; she also happens to work for me," answered Niko, gulping down his wine and getting up for more.

"A beautiful black of Ethiopian descent, I recall," said Ronald, attempting to deflect the direction of the conversation.

"And you were with?" prodded Hero. "Come on, Ronald."

"Ok, ok; there was Gwendolyn."

"And just who was this Gwendolyn, Ronald?" said Sadie, acting threatened.

"Well, ah, she was a local girl who worked for Anne Willobie."

Silence.

Everyone but Ronald broke out laughing.

"What the hell! Why is it I am always the scapegoat?" said Ronald, throwing up his arms in exasperation.

"Do you feel guilty?" suggested Hero.

"Sitting here, I do, under your spell; see what I mean, Sadie? She's a witch."

"So tell me about Gwendolyn, Ronald," said Sadie.

"She was a local girl."

"Yes, I know that."

"Hero, you got me into this, now get me out. Sadie, please, those toadstools were deadly."

They started to laugh again and couldn't stop. Connie marched in with some hors d'oeuvres and left the tray on the table, saying, "Help yourself. I'm so glad you're being festive; Peter wouldn't have had it any other way. Isn't that so Ronald?" She left as quickly as she had come.

They erupted once more, in surprise at Connie's remark, but Hero kept up the pressure.

"Pedro enjoyed your exuberance, Ronald."

"Yes," said Niko, "he once told me you were an interesting catalyst to behavioral improvement in others."

"I don't know if Gwendolyn saw it that way," pitched in Hero, still laughing.

"What on earth did you do to Gwendolyn, Ronald?" demanded Sadie above the commotion with finality.

"Put it this way," spoke up Hero, "we did large doses of Amanita Muscaria mushrooms. Well, it was excellent for enhancing male turgor, and I don't think Gwendolyn really knew what she was getting into; poor girl had to be carried home delirious. We told her parents that she had sunstroke; but, she still asks of you, Ronald."

"Ronald!" said Sadie shaking her head.

"What can I say?" said Ronald, mollified by the reference to his masculinity. He was smiling now.

Chapter Three

I am not of this world.

—Yeshu (Jesus Christ)

Completely naked, Pedro looked out of the window in the early dawn before the sun had risen in the sky, a bloody pink at the source ranging to dark marine blue at the far perimeter. The ascending earth held him mesmerized until the blinding sun finally shot streaks across the building, catching his figure obliquely. Brilliant shards of light silently, surgically, cut into his heart like lasers; enough was enough and in one slow, calculated movement, Pedro spun away from the window and walked across the room to the old wood, leather, and metal chest. In a moment he had it opened and was rummaging through clothes and various contents until he found what he was looking for: two paper rolls tightly held by elastic bands and a folder with assorted scraps of paper, notes, poems and the like. He put the rolls aside and opened the folder, removed a newspaper clipping; then putting down the folder, he went back to the window. The newly risen sun was already baking the room; the day was going to be a scorcher. He could feel the heat as a provocative portent of the emotional havoc that his basic existence would manifest for poor Donna del Rio.

As he resumed his earlier meditations of the clipping on the sill in front of him, his apprehension turned to pain as two tears rolled in glistening streaks down his cheeks. "I know, I know, I know, I know, I know it's gotta be," he said under his breath. "Gorgon has found the answer to the riddle; she knows me, the bitch."

He picked up the wooden matches resting on the armrest of the old lounge chair, took one out of the box and was ready to strike it, but hesitated; he spoke softly this time, saying: "She would have her hounds of hell sniff out the white roebuck in the thicket and bring him down to tempt the apocalypse, but this thicket is one you shall never penetrate, Gorgon; oh yes, I feel you in me, you are here too, pining and needing my love, and you shall have it, you shall have it, you shall have me and it will destroy you; you will be confined to your madness, weak and feeble — powerless — like the trembling mistletoe torn from its high oaken loft and now lying withered on the dank ground; I shall pity you in my offering." With that, Pedro struck the match and put the flame to the newspaper cutting which he read for the last time.

It disintegrated in a flash. Pedro blew the ashes into the street; he then turned away to put on a T-shirt and shorts. Standing, he surveyed the room where he had spent most of the last three months. He would leave everything except a small dunnage bag already packed, his sleeping bag, some clothes, and sundry toilet items.

He walked over to the table and pressed the play button of his cheap cassette player. "Na Laetha Geal M'oige," a traditional Irish song sung by Enya, meaning "Woe is Me, Woe is Me," began its hauntingly beautiful intonation as if from the mythic vale of Rhiannon. Pedro hung his head as the strange song resonated down into his soul-chakra, her euphonic voice singing down centuries of strife. Only the misery of Donna del Rio struck a deeper resonance in him. Pedro then picked up a pencil and paper and wrote what he knew she could not make much sense of, yet what might at least let him go, at peace with himself, because she would know that he loved her, loved her as a beautiful Buddha heart destined for more than Pedro's Holy Grail, an artifact that could bring about only self-destruction. The stakes were simply too high for her to get too close.

"Dearest Donna," he wrote, "To you, I give the tears of the sun, lost treasures of the wine-dark deep, and all the children of Atlantis, for you are the original progenitor and mother of goodness! May you not hurl a Heliconian landslide at me for callously slinking away in the early hours without so much as a peremptory peck on your cheek. My heart is heavy — how weighted it feels, like Atlas! Can you ever forgive me? I was up with the sun — so touching, sacred and damned melodramatic! And I shed a few tears, a bit for my own sake, if you only knew; and I know this sounds so childish and remote, or secretive, even delusional, but I insist — alas, maybe I'm truly mad — I feel rather like a castaway in a dream that began thousands of years ago after the Great Deluge, continued unabated after the Crucifixion, and can only end upon what is called Judgement Day. Have you ever heard of the Hyperboreans? Well, against my better judgement, no pun intended, I impart to you something that could be interpreted as phenomenal in this day and age. I can't totally repeat it, but because you are you and one with infinite wisdom, I will recite a small part of the Cad Goddeu, an ancient riddling maze of early Britain; in this I am also . . . an original, conceited as it may sound, for really I am only like the wind passing through, but such a wind that must battle the wicked Gorgon, the evil with a thousand faces; don't worry; it's my battle now, the never-ending Battle of the Trees — I am running on here, aren't I, but don't worry about me! Sounds like a long strange trip, doesn't it? Well, it is — a long one, and one that I'm tiring of; I would really just like to be Pedro and write poems. I hope you forgive all this rambling, though please, there's absolutely nothing you can do about all this. Please. There are forces at work extremely inconsiderate of human emotion and they desire nothing but the complete use of the creature given over to it, Mother Nature's innocent child, humankind. What are they, these forces? Well, as I've said, Gorgon is like Mother Nature fallen prey to the very vices we so carefully admonish yet cherish in our pursuit of knowledge; the sensation of enlightenment slips imperceptibly into seduction by virtue. You see, like yourself, we must taste the fruits; we must fall to rise, and spin forever on this wheel . . . I must go now. I begin to sound polymorphic, ironically an essential dichotomy . . . you are beautiful. Now the Maze:

> It is long since I was a herdsman.
> I travelled over the earth
> Before I became a learned person.
> I have travelled, I have made a circuit,
> I have slept in a hundred islands;
> I have dwelt in a hundred cities.
> Learned Druids,
> Prophesy ye of Arthur?
> Or is it me they celebrate?

Sweet Donna, I am not a Hyperborean; I am just Pedro. But what is simple is complex, indeed a paradox, and it is not Pedro that speaks here, but an ancient. You must understand. Pedro." Then he folded the letter, put it on the table, and went over to where his manuscripts lay, picked them up and put them on the table. He again took up his pen, with which he then wrote on the folded part of the letter: *"Everything here in my room is yours."*

Pedro walked down the hall with his small carrying bag. He stopped in front of Donna's apartment and very quietly slipped the note under the door with his key; he then walked down the stairs to the street. Out on the street he headed east. The delivery truck was still parked, but Giovanni was nowhere to be seen. Pedro looked into the bakery, but he didn't see anyone. He looked down at his feet, to his huaraches and began to walk, chanting a little prayer that he made up as he went along:

> I come out now to meet you Gorgon.
> You wanted me and I denied you.
> I pray now for you to pacify
> The unquiet ghost.
> I forgive you. I love you.
> For what harder fate is yours,
> That makes and unmakes her Gods?

> *Little did you know who I was,*
> *And you can only be hurt,*
> *I must not let that happen.*

Pedro looked up. Just then no cars were coming, so he crossed the street to the streetcar island and waited. A sense of great release swept over him; he knew everything was lining up perfectly and had been throughout the whole progression of events since that fateful sabbath of the Wicca years ago during the summer solstice. The High Priestess, Brigid, representing the crone (who hadn't actually participated, but was significantly involved), Anne, the mother, and Gwendolyn, the maiden, had performed the ritual with other witches, using Pedro as the Horned God. Their coven was an ancient one apparently, predating Roman times, and was probably the most exclusive and coveted coven in all of Britain. He wondered later, however, if Brigid had turned evil and was destroying the extraordinary power of their circle. Given her tremendous hold, there was nothing any of the other witches could do. At Anne's bidding, he had let himself be pleasantly subjected, as the only male, to some bizarre proceedings; but he had been profoundly shocked by Brigid's revelations to him in private after the rituals of that first ceremony.

Pedro put all of this aside now as he waited for the streetcar. He was in a nirvanic state of acuity, something so Uranian in urgency, he was even at a loss to know its full significance. He did think, however, that his deliverance, his sacrifice, his pivotal role and subsequent rite-of-passage was something he was powerless to escape from, no matter what action he took. He was a marked man. This whole process was something he did not begin, nor would he end; it was something he could not thoroughly understand. He could only, like the poet following his bliss, walk the path to slaughter, smiling fatally. "Let go, let go," he told himself. "I have eaten the fruits of Eden; now I have been challenged by Gorgon — a fair exchange in the nature of things. I am not Ovid, nor was I meant to be, yet my exile is similar. No oracle, no knowledge will come of this. The secret will remain; the old ways are the new ways. Regeneration, the altar of death and sacrifice is the legacy of the race. Wow."

The streetcar arrived. Pedro stepped in and sat down. He thought about Hero and Niko and knew they must be in town. It wasn't altogether a happy thought.

It was about a kilometre walk back from the house to the lake; the old lane exited the gardens between two giant willows, then went up a hill at a sharp incline, cutting into the side of the slope. At the top, a warm breeze blew back David Thomas's hair. It both buffed and buzzed about him, exacerbating the strange feeling that he experienced in his meeting with Anne Willobie. He sensed she was undoubtedly a duplicitous woman. On the surface, she seemed the very essence of English propriety and decency, but upon more careful scrutiny, he deduced from his experienc that she was the cause of a vertigo that was disproportionate to the circumstances, thus far. Yet, he knew he should tread softly with his imaginings or intuitions and fall back on basic procedure.

The property was far larger than he had presumed. He walked across the top of the hill until he came to a number of stone fences with gates. Some recently shorn sheep in one field ran away when he approached. He followed the lane down a gully into a valley and paused to gaze. Before him, surrounded by craggy hills, lay an adrenaline-pumping vista. Before him, a green paradise with an indigo blue lake as the quiet centrepiece sloped gently down through meadows and groves to the bottom, dropping about three hundred metres vertically. The blue lake was a good kilometre in length and half as wide, with a narrow extension to the north end. From Thomas's side, along the eastern shore, one could see the remains of the old fortification mound, judging from its great prominence at the northern tip of the lake, and the stream that emptied there. The west side of the lake was more rugged with rocky bluffs and sparse foliage spreading up the hill, with one unique exception: in the middle, along the shore, was a low lying area surrounded by hills. This area was covered by a dense mature forest. Noting all he saw, David Thomas began his descent to the lake.

He had been given the opportunity by Mrs. Willobie to explore this mysterious property to his heart's content. She had suggested he walk down to the lake and around to the north where the old Celtic fortification mound was situated. He had received the impression he had been given permission to venture into a rarified zone which, during his descent to the lake, gave him the distinct feeling that, indeed, like passing through an invisible curtain, he had entered into a special place.

It became warmer as he approached the lake. Large oaks, ash, and other varieties of trees he didn't know, loomed up around him. Wild flowers radiated their nectared scents. Raspberries, currants, and other bushes flourished in pockets here and there; the birds sang merrily, content in their idyllic home. Inspector Thomas couldn't help but smile. This was the kind of life he had dreamed of back in London.

Upon reaching the lake, he could see that its water was clear and largely undisturbed, but the lightest breeze dabbled playful patterns on its surface, a magical sheet of blue mirroring the mottled empyrean far overhead. The air was sultry, saturated with the heavy scent of vegetation. He walked around to the north end of the lake, where there was another stone wall and gate leading to more pasture. Inside, the grass had been levelled by sheep, so all around the ancient mound every contour could be vividly seen. There was very little in the way of ruins: on top of the mound, which had a diameter of only a hundred yards or so, were stones scattered about, vaguely outlining ancient walls. The ditch surrounding the mound was well marked and must have served as a moat.

For a while, Inspector Thomas stood studying the layout, attempting to imagine what life was like in Celtic times. The outside perimeter was probably made from oak. The inhabitants had been excellent farmers, both in respect to animal husbandry and cultivation of grain. Although they had been Christianized, they had retained their own particular pagan ritual which incorporated the ancient Mother Goddess, Rhiannon, and the male god who had successively incarnated himself in Apollo, Taliesin, and Christ.

Eventually, he turned and looked down the length of the lake in the direction he had come. He had been so exhilarated by this little sacred valley that he had forgotten all about Mrs. Willobie and his reason for being there. Lower down the gentle slope, near the water, was a shepherd's hut. He went over to inspect it more carefully; he could see the fireplace outside in front made from a crude erection of rocks. Inside the hut was another fireplace, a couple of old wooden beds, and coarse linen-covered straw mattresses. He thought that this quite possibly was where Pedro and his friends had camped. Outside, he looked down once again the full length of the lake and marvelled at its size. He noted the west shore from that vantage point and observed that the substantial bluffs, forming a rock escarpment, prevented one from easily skirting the shore on that side. Most likely one would have to hike back and take the rowboat or find a goat path. But what intrigued him was that, where the bluffs ended, there was that low forested stretch behind a small bay, while further down, the land rose up again, yet not nearly as dramatically as the closer bluffs. He was reminded of the possibility of meeting with Professor Woods, but Mrs. Willobie had never said where, assuming, Thomas supposed, that he might be found at the old fortification mound. He expected at least some sign of a dig, but he had come across nothing. He made a three hundred and sixty degree sweep round and scratched his head. Then, turning back to his original position, he suddenly froze and felt a tingle rising up his back; he glanced once more up the hill where he'd come from. No one was there, but he could have sworn he'd glimpsed someone on top. He looked down to approximately where the path descended, but it was obscured in overgrowth. On an impulse, Inspector Thomas walked briskly back along the lake then stopped where the path ascended the hill. He turned down the path to the dock and stepped into the rowboat, untied it, and began to row out onto the lake with long strong strokes. The act of physical exertion brought back some level-headedness. Why on earth, he thought, would he get so stirred up at seeing someone? Because he had thought he was alone? Maybe he'd seen the Willobie woman and his alarms had just gone off spontaneously, which indicated to him that obviously this was not an ordinary place. On the contrary, it was deeply enigmatic, containing secrets somehow connected to the death of Pedro George, whoever he was. In the absence of a corpse, however, he seemed more a creature of the imagination than a real man.

Inspector Thomas pulled the rowboat up on a short, stony beach in the little bay beyond the bluffs on the west shore. Immediately, he could scarcely believe his eyes at the size of the trees inland. Huge oaks with trunks five to six feet in diameter completely dominated the vegetation; the forest ceiling was a green canopy that arched like great cathedral ceilings between the widely dispersed giant oaks. Little sunshine filtered through, but because of the bright July day, leaves and grass formed a shimmering and dappled kaleidoscope of green.

He followed a path through the majestic forest. Looking up occasionally and noticing long mistletoe vines growing profusely up in the crowns of the trees, he knew from his reading of Druid history that this very likely would have been a sacred grove. He thought he must be one of the few people to know of its existence since he hadn't heard about it before and something of this beauty would otherwise surely have become a local landmark. The fact that it was relatively inaccessible and on private property had protected it from any exploitation. The old fortification mound would even act as a front, being the visible curiosity, aside from the beauty of the lake and its environs. Inspector Thomas was ready to turn back when he noticed that the forested area was now narrowing because of the steep surrounding hills. Then he came upon a clearing. It appeared to be well-groomed, and at the center was a neat circle of smooth hewn stones with a slight opening at one end, each a couple of feet in diameter. Opposing the circle, just outside the slight opening, was an erect monolith about six feet high. David Thomas stopped dead in his tracks. He cautiously looked around, thinking he had stumbled into a private sanctuary; he had the uncomfortable sensation of being watched.

Slowly, quietly, he walked about, looking for a trace of anything newly upturned or excavated to indicate some human activity. Only the birds with their incessant singing and virtuoso high-flying aerobatics were the observers of this ancient site. Thomas relaxed and sat on a stone. He gazed at the forest surrounding him. What a different feeling from the wind-blown hills above the lake, he mused. After a few minutes, Thomas relaxed sufficiently to think he was alone, when from behind came an "Ahhumm!" which literally lifted him off his rock a couple of inches, kinking his neck. Turning around, Thomas saw the old man stooping with a digging tool. "Christ! You jumped the bloody moles off me, man!" he exclaimed, jumping to his feet.

"Did you know this is private property?" said the man in a growly voice, looking right through the inspector.

"Yes, of course; I came from the lake in the row boat," he said, collecting himself. At least he had found the professor, he thought, relieved, but that didn't stop him from being shocked. He knew Woods was eccentric, but he wasn't prepared for the hostile introduction and above all the look of the man: he was positively ancient with a scruffy white beard, curly hair that went straight up, and two pilot lights for eyes set deep in his head; the tattered old tweeds he wore gave him the appearance of having slept in them for years.

"I know who you are," said the professor, "and I'll give you some advice: let the dead rest."

"I apologize for intruding. I did get permission from Mrs. Willobie, Professor," said David Thomas forcefully, attempting now to size up this character who, by appearances, could have come out of a Conan Doyle novel. "And how do you know who I am, sir, may I ask?" Thomas queried in his no-nonsense stride.

"The point is, sir, she wanted you to come here so you'd get off her back," said the professor toning down his show of hauteur, "then jump on mine!"

"I assume then that there must be a good reason why she would act in such a way, not to mention your own reaction," parleyed Thomas.

"Ahhh, ye damn fool, I know your type; you think there's a broken law under every stone! Well, let me tell you something: there probably is, and the bloody world won't reform for you."

"I don't expect it to; I'm simply investigating a rather peculiar death, the death of a young man whom I gather you were very fond of, yet whose funeral you and Mrs. Willobie would not attend; I understand you even expressed anger at the notion that Pedro was dead."

"Well, if I'm guilty of something, you'd better handcuff me and take me away, young man, because I have work to do; from what you've told me, you know more about this than I!"

"All I ask is a few minutes to discuss the deceased," said Thomas.

The professor remained silent, scowling into the oak forest. Thomas refrained from prodding him, as he needed a few moments to collect his thoughts and determine how best to breach the mysteries at hand. Clearly, the professor did not seem to be the candid type, at least not at first.

"Professor," said Thomas finally, "what are you working on these days? Mrs. Willobie said you and Pedro had found something interesting."

"I'll say this," he said, turning to Thomas more amicably, "I've lived here most of my life; in fact, this property backs onto mine over the ridge. For years I'd known of this wood, but I'd never thought anything of it except to admire its ancient . . . sacredness, shall we say." He stopped to sniff the air almost like a dog, before resuming. "I'd been trying for years to get permission from the Willobies to begin excavation at the old fortification mound and thereabouts; they were interested but wouldn't give me permission other than for superficial investigation and open visitation. Roger Fitzooth of Huntington, her grandfather, purchased the property at least sixty years ago and gave it to his second son, Reginald, Anne's father, who was a good friend of mine. He wanted it to remain in its natural state and willed it so, feeling that little would come from a dig. I respected his feelings, of course. Charles Willobie, on the other hand, after Reg died, seemed more open to a dig, but after my grand-nephew died, he ceased to be so interested."

"I wasn't aware, so . . . I'm sorry to hear your grand-nephew died. A terrible loss."

"He drowned in the lake when he was eleven years old, trying to save a friend who'd fallen in and couldn't swim . . . a tragedy that was very hard on all of us. The other boy was a local boy. I was responsible for them at the time. They had rowed down the lake while I was poking about the old fortification."

The silence that followed this revelation made David Thomas quake inside, not so much on account of the gut-wrenching admission, but for the old man sitting beside him now. It made Thomas realize that, for all August Woods' cantankerousness, it amounted to little more than a brave front for an old mournful gentleman fending off the buffets of misfortune. His compassion went out to him. It also occurred to him that the professor wished to speak his mind in his own idiosyncratic way.

"How awful. So sad," said Thomas, at a loss.

"It's the way of the world," said Augustus, visibly shaken by the remembrance.

"When did this happen?"

"Eight years ago."

The sky glowed amber. The sun had set, and dusk pervaded the blood-soaked field before the smouldering fortification. Olwen stirred from her seeming death prostration with agonizing motion. Her wounds had stiffened, and the slightest movement brought tears to her eyes. She had one serious gash where Vron's sword had miraculously missed her heart and main arteries, but cut almost cleanly through her shoulder, breaking her collar bone. It immobilized her entire left side and so weakened her from loss of blood that she could barely come to her senses, let alone remember what had happened. However, reaching down and tentatively feeling her nakedness, aware of the indecency, she moaned and twisted herself around, closing her legs. In doing so, she saw her sheepskin pants staked into the ground with a spear which she tried to dislodge with her good right arm. Finally the spear gave way quite easily because a weight on top of it fell with a thud. In the dimming light she couldn't make out what it was until, prodded with the tip of the spear, it rolled down the incline to come to a stop in her naked lap. To her horror Gwydion's head peered at her. Sobbing, she smoothed out the hair which was a mat of blood.

Unbeknownst to her, a shadowy figure was poking amongst the dead. When he came near enough to hear her crying, he immediately went to her. He barely saw in the fading light the unmistakeable, embroidered willow bough under the feathers sown onto the shoulders of her leather chest armour. "Olwen, Olwen," he whispered, as he approached her. He picked up her pants and covered her. She looked over and saw Elphin the Jester leaning towards her. "Elphin," she said, before passing out.

Elphin proceeded to put the pants on Olwen, which was difficult because of the tears and rips during their violent removal and because she wouldn't let go of Gwydion's head. Elphin persisted stubbornly and managed to cover her sufficiently, as it was unseemly for their prime enchantress and queen to be so otherwise exposed.

Under the stars and quarter moon, there was enough light for them to move toward the lake. Elphin, a wiry old bard, picked up Olwen, still holding the head, and leaned her against himself, then stooped and slung her over his shoulder. Nimbly he made his way around bodies, reached the cover of trees, and as he knew the way, soon arrived at the lake. There he uncovered a small bark that had been hidden under branches, gently laid Olwen in some kersey cloth on the boat's bottom, pushed away from the shore, and quietly rowed into the dark of the lake.

Across the lake, Elphin watched the pitch-black silhouette of the ridge and came ashore exactly where he knew the little stone beach to be. He hooted like an owl, and within moments a warrior came out of the darkness.

"Elphin," said a voice with quiet dignity which also asked that foreboding question by inference of its tone.

"She's alive, Bran! She's alive!" exclaimed Elphin in a loud whisper. "Gwydion's dead. She won't let go of his head. She's alive, but badly hurt; she was ravished by the monster; there was nothing I could do. I watched from the thicket; I curled up and cried."

Without a word, Bran reached into the boat and lifted Olwen, who was still clutching the head. Swiftly, he disappeared into the forest. Elphin pulled the boat into the thicket and followed.

Donna del Rio awoke with Pedro George on her mind. This was not out of the ordinary for her these past few weeks as her youthful emotions had travelled at warp speed from intense curiosity to desperate love. Pedro had become the Godhead of her life, an alteration which was throwing her new-found independence and self-centredness into disarray; what had been a pragmatic and orderly maturation of self-discovery was now a hornet's nest of confusion.

Nevertheless, her strength of character impelled her to confront the matter. She knew if he couldn't return her love, she would simply have to persist gently but firmly. She really didn't have any idea what he was talking about half the time; it was as if he spoke in a kind of riddle; everything he said had far-reaching implications and only the mediation of some higher authority winking in her direction allowed her to glimpse the workings of destiny. Holy smoke! she thought, raising her head from the pillow, blinded by the early morning sun. I know why he won't have me; he wants to be a priest! She stuck with that for a moment. No, hell, that isn't Pedro. He's probably recovering from an affair in Wales; he probably put all his love into the woman and she two-timed him. He really doesn't trust women! I must tell him I'm different! With that thought, she jumped out of bed full of purpose, and naked, bounced a half-dance to the washroom. After, she threw on a bathrobe, went to her apartment door, and was about to open it when she looked down and saw the note with the key.

She read the letter with almost one swoop of the eyes, not understanding much other than that he was gone and would not return. Instantly crushed, she leaned weakly against the wall, then slid along in mute oblivion to her bedroom, where she flung herself on the bed.

She began to sob, but sobs turned to exasperated beseechings, then anger, then finally, renewed determination. She got up with the letter in her hand and began to pace frantically, stopping fitfully to read and reread it. Words like "Hyperboreans" and "Gorgon" and the strange poem and the "Battle of the Trees" all rang through her head. For anybody else she would have dismissed it all as lunacy. She knew that Pedro, however, had the integrity of a saint; therefore, everything he said made sense. He knew exactly what he was doing. That, amongst other things, was what she loved about him: he had an awareness stretching beyond even the three trillion dollar "information highway" being built around the globe.

Swallowing her pain, she traced in her imagination the path he might have taken. Occupied thus, she quickly got dressed in dark red shorts, a beige shirt, and Birkenstock sandals, then went to Pedro's flat. Inside, she looked around the room at his sangre chair, his trunk, and the papers on the table. These she picked up and leafed through, her eye alighting on the titles "Gorgon" and "Journey to Albion" and various notes, poems, and scribbles. Then she sat down on the edge of the chair and began to read bits here and there of his straightforward prose describing events that had apparently taken place in ancient times. There was little description, only the tersest chronicling. She stopped reading and drifted into a reverie: she couldn't understand the reason behind his escapism. Why would he leave these things for her? She tried to remember anything in their conversations that would give her a clue to his whereabouts. He did say he'd grown up in Rosedale. She picked up the papers and went back to her flat. In the telephone book there was a listing for a George on Roxborough which, a brief perusal of a map informed her, was in Rosedale.

In moments she was going down the stairs and walking through the store to the back where she kept an old rusted Skylark. From behind the till Maria called out, sensing her disquiet, "Donna, honey; what's the matter?"

"Have you seen Pedro, Maria?"

"No, what's happening?"

"Donna, you don't work today?" came Giovanni's mezzo from behind the melons.

"Have you seen Pedro?"

"Yeah, he left a couple of hours ago; I saw him walking down St. Clair. Why?"

"Oh, nothing; I can't come in today. Which way was he going?"

"East. Donna, what's going on?"

Donna exited. Giovanni and Maria exchanged incredulous looks. They had never seen her so determined.

Donna drove down Roxborough Street, which eventually came around to a ravine. She found the house and went to the door. A woman answered, and Donna uttered a sigh of relief — the woman undoubtedly bore a resemblance to Pedro in her expression.

Connie George naturally hadn't any idea who this young woman was, but she was pleasantly surprised; any distraction from the pain of her loss was welcome. Connie was feeling much better that day and Donna's timing couldn't have been better.

"Mrs. George?" asked Donna with a glance past her into the hallway.

"Yes?" Connie said as cheerily as possible.

"I came by to see Pedro. Is he home?"

The question seemed to hang in the air like a moored Zeppelin the moment before a sudden gust rips away its anchors.

"Excuse me?" Connie said quietly.

"I was just wondering whether Pedro had come home."

"You're one of Pedro's friends. Would you like to come in for a moment? I think we should have a chat."

Donna followed Connie out to the back patio. They both sat down.

"Wow. Nice place, Mrs. George," she said, looking about half-expecting to see Pedro.

"Who are you, dear?"

"I'm sorry," said Donna, extending her hand. "Donna del Rio."

"Donna, I'm so sorry to inform you, but Pedro died a couple of weeks ago; he was killed in an accident in Wales."

The expression on Donna's face didn't change. After the hurt of the morning and now this, she had an hysterical impulse to laugh, and would have, if it hadn't been for the pained look on Connie's face. Donna was about to blurt out: "Dead? Whadya mean, dead? I saw him yesterday!" but checked herself, unsure of anything. The idea even crossed her mind that she knew a different Pedro George, but that, she thought, would have been most unlikely.

"Pedro dead?" was all she managed.

"We're all still in shock," said Connie, putting her hand on Donna's. "How did you know my son?"

It took a while before Donna could answer; her mind was a boiling cauldron of a rare recipe. She realized that Pedro, for some inexplicable reason, must have faked his death, only God knew why. Some of his evasions the previous day now made sense. She also realized that whatever his reasons, her being there could blow the whole thing if she said the wrong thing.

"I . . . I didn't know. I met him last year. He said to drop by if I was in the neighborhood."

"Oh . . . it's so sudden; nothing can prepare you for the shock. How well did you know him?"

"We were just friends. I met him camping in Wales."

"Oh, how nice. Did you see some of the work he was doing on the dig at Caerymwy?"

"Uh, kind of; he told me about the ancient Gorgons and the Battle of the Trees." She was surprising herself.

"Wasn't he something? Professor Woods thought the world of him."

"Yes." Donna wondered how she could ask Mrs. George where Pedro would go in Canada if he wanted to get away for awhile.

"What do you do?" asked Connie. "You're so young and pretty."

"Thanks. I'm a student, but I'm working in my uncle's store."

"A store?"

"Well, it's sort of a delicatessen-bakery-market combo."

"I'll have to go there. Where is it?"

Donna cringed inside. "St. Clair West."

"What's it called?"

"Giovanni's. Mrs. George?"

"Do call me Connie."

"Connie, didn't Pedro miss Canada?"

"Why do you ask?"

"Oh, just curious. I guess I'm so shocked about his death I don't know what I'm saying."

"I don't think he missed Toronto, but I'm sure he missed the north country where we used to have a cottage . . . When his father sold the property, he was quite upset."

"He mentioned Georgian Bay once."

"Yes. The north channel near Manitoulin."

"Was there a town or village?"

"Birch Island. Why?"

"That's what I was trying to remember. Birch Island."

"Oh, I see. Pedro probably wanted to take you camping there. How close were you, now?"

"I feel so empty , Connie; I just can't believe this," said Donna, in an attempt to sound convincingly depressed.

"Come with me, Donna," said Connie getting up. "I'll show you some pictures."

Donna followed her, smiling. Pedro was alive and well, and her love made her giddy all over; in her mind she became an accomplice in Pedro's scheme and it seemed to fill her spirits with the power of the sun.

Chapter Four

*In my woal life Ive only ever done that 1
connexion which Ive wrote down here I
begun with trying to put it to gether
poal by poal only my reveal dint come
that way it snuck me woaly. I were
keaping that in memberment now. Ready to
cry ready to dy ready for any thing is
how I come to it now. In fear and
tremmering only not running away. In
emtyness and ready to be fult. Not to
lern no body nothing I cant even lern my
oan self all I can do is try not to get
in front of whats coming.*

—Russell Hoban,
excerpt from *Riddley Walker*

Hero rose to the mauve dawn with only a T-shirt covering her nakedness. She sat on the floor of her bedroom in Ronald Morgan's house and began to stretch and do aerobic and callisthenic exercises. At the end of this routine, in a faint sheen of sweat, she sat upright in the lotus position and meditated. She considered that it was this devout methodical approach to the spirit world that had originally attracted Pedro to her. Over time, however, the trappings of these doctrines probably grated against Pedro's instincts which sought to untangle any kind of stereotypical behaviour. Without communicating his feelings, he had left Hero in the dark to understand what he truly felt. She had tried to be that Lapwing, that mythical creature of his imagination, but realized any superficial imbibing of such a thing could only crash around her. Therefore, retreating into the corporeal dogma of her own vision was the best she could do. In the course of her meditations she recited the ancient poem she liked in a tired voice:

> Not of father or of mother,
> Was my blood, was my body.
> I was spellbound by Gwydion,
> Prime enchanter of the Britons,
> When he formed me from nine blossoms,
> Nine buds of various kind:
> From primrose of the mountain,
> Broom, meadow-sweet and cockle,
> Together intertwined,
> From the bean in its shade bearing
> A white spectral army
> Of earth, of earthly kind,
> From blossoms of the nettle,
> Oak, thorn and bashful chestnut-
> Nine powers of nine flowers,
> Nine powers in me combined,
> Nine buds of plants and trees.
> Long and white are my fingers
> As the ninth wave of the sea.

After, she stood up and with a sigh whispered, "Pedro, have you really forsaken me?" She gazed out the window at opaque clouds. He was out there somewhere; she sensed his presence under the sky in his own myriad-minded world. Her thoughts clung like iron filings to the magnet of their past together: the wonderful moments and the horrific ones long ago. Or was it all perceived as a tapestry homespun from Pedro's cosmic loom? Thus occupied, she reflected on the ephemeral moment of change. All perfection in beauty and love, whose efforts are incapable of a sustained duration, evaporates, leaving behind only a bittersweet memory. It indeed seemed to her that their so-called Ring of Power, crucial in their relationship to each other yet all-consuming in resolve, was ultimately a transparency, an antiquated myth no longer viable. Old spirits had retired, leaving the ancient flame destitute and forgotten, cast off from the tenets of time. Even Niko was succumbing to apathy. Before retiring the previous evening, he'd expressed the desire to simply get back to his comfortable existence in London. It was as if the circle of lives from their past had truly come to an end (she had tried to fit into her purported role not knowing precisely what that was) when Niko decided he had had enough. Curiously, his attitude affected Hero like no other. Although she hadn't quite accepted her estrangement from Pedro, it had become apparent to both her and Niko that their own relationship had become genuinely wholesome and was revealing itself exponentially by the day. Yet Pedro the Roebuck was still in the thicket — still the Hart of the Wood — still alive and Hero knew it, but she hadn't a clue what that implied. All she and Niko seemed to be doing was beating about the bush, not knowing where it would lead to. She questioned whether she had been unwittingly drawn into an affair to fill a part that otherwise she would not have had any inclination to play, by being cast, rather than doing the casting, as the lapwing.

Whatever the outcome of her protective machinations, she at least felt relieved that the ferocity of Brigid's spell, directed at them all, had been allayed by Pedro's death and they had all remained relatively unscathed. Hero felt perturbed, however, about the awkward position she had been left in and blamed Anne, who, being an important witch in Brigid's coven, had on numerous occasions constrained Hero's perspicacity and natural ability. Brigid must surely have known of Anne's complicity and subsequently, Gwendolyn's; yet what could she do? She supposed she could always accuse Anne, but maybe Brigid had Anne doing her bidding. Hero had great respect for Brigid, but Anne was incessantly dissembling between the two. Hero felt Anne's enmity toward her had overstepped the sacred vows of the Wicca; she had crossed over to the dark side, perhaps malevolently, if she had, in effect, brought about Pedro's destruction.

Anne should have relinquished her assumed rein of the bloody mare. Brigid was very old and probably not fully lucid, and Hero felt she was being overruled by Anne. Anne had become selfish and tyrannical, which intensified her broom-wielding grip. And all for what? Possibly, it was because Anne was faced with the reality of her own mortality, possibly because of the envy of youth, which no power can bring back. Hero, Niko, and Pedro had possibly threatened her position. Yet it didn't seem plausible, thought Hero, for a venerated woman to taste the bile of envy, especially after such service to humanity! The festering of a brilliant blossom is a foul process. Anne's mistake, Hero felt, lay in her perceived notion that Pedro or she was attempting to undermine her own strength with a sublimated desire to control her coven, at least to influence it, and in Brigid's mind, destroy it. Yet, ironically, Hero got on well with Brigid in more than just a superficial or professional way. She would have to go back and get some answers; she was afraid she and Pedro had been set up.

It came down to opposing bloods, an ancient battle still being fought. Pedro had called it the Gorgon and Battle of the Trees. Hero assumed, in these simple terms, that Brigid and Anne were no doubt Gorgons attempting to turn to stone both Pedro and maybe herself. Or was she somehow an accomplice?

Hero meditated putting it all behind her, focusing on Pedro aspiring to his celestial command, if not flickering as of late like a rogue candle melting down before its time. She was determined to exalt him as one above reproach because of his extraordinary presence of mind. His craft was his mind and he didn't know it; this was his undoing, she thought. This contemporary culture, she reflected, with its material success supposedly given over to a "higher" consciousness, was yet predisposed to scepticism. In fact, she had read recently something about Nobel scientists signing a manifesto attempting to discredit astrology once and for all, when none of them knew anything about it. These are our scientists? she thought. She remembered also that the very mentor of western medicine, Hippocrates, had once declared that the man who did not well understand astrology more deserved to be called a fool than a physician. Then there was Niko, that arch-pillar of society, who believed in our special powers. His support was extraordinary and he at least shared his wealth with them. But this was only reasonable, given their supposed ever-living dilemma and battle for survival that they in turn accorded as a war waged to save the western world.

"How jaded I must be," said Hero to the window. There was a knock at the door. Her heart leapt. The knocking had a strange tone about it as if it signified something ominous. Hero, in a moment of intuition suspected something was about to happen.

"Yes?" she said, cautiously.

"It's me," came the reply.

"Come in," she said.

Niko walked in as she turned to him, naked. They were completely at ease with each other. She walked over to the bed and put on her underwear; he closed the door, and watched her get dressed.

"Don't you ever look ugly?" he asked, hoping to lift her obvious sombre mood. Niko knew her only too well.

"Don't you ever get horny?" she said.

"For you my eyes are sufficient; I wouldn't touch you with a ten foot pole."

Hero went to him and let him embrace her. Niko let one arm slide down her back to the swell of her buttock.

"With Pedro dead, you might with a ten foot hard-on."

"You have a point there," he said, wanting to caress her immaculate rump, but restrained himself with difficulty.

"Rather, you do," she said as she disengaged herself and testified to the sudden protuberance in his pants by swooshing her hand near it.

"Thank you for noticing."

"Something's happening today," she commented, looking out the window again.

"Are you referring to this," he said, motioning to his crotch, "or are you just being provocative at my expense?"

"I'm sorry. You might be right."

"Right about what?"

"Why are we here, Niko?" she asked as she plopped on the bed and raised her knees to her chest making Niko stare at her and almost buckle in lust.

"To mourn Pedro, obviously. Should I leave you to pursue the quarry on your own?" he asked.

The telephone rang down the hall, suspending their talk for a moment. The ringing stopped. Ronald or Sadie had answered it.

"God, things are untenable. I'd just as soon go back to London," said Niko breaking the silence.

Hero still sat on the bed. She looked at Niko with that cool, riveting gaze. Niko didn't care to speculate about what was going on in her head. He was blinded by his love for her; he always had been and always would be. Niko blinked from the strain of eye contact. This whole ordeal had been a nightmare. Pedro had been his best friend, and he wasn't sure he was dead or whether this potential fiasco of going along with Pedro's death was right or wrong. He was worried that his credibility might be on the line with some of his most important clients, the Morgans and Willobies, if they got wind of any complicity on his part. There wasn't, but he obviously knew too much. It was a testament to Pedro's tremendous influence over him. And now Hero was leaning on him in a way that he hadn't felt before; yet she was not ready to give her whole self to him.

"We haven't done anything wrong, Niko. You know Pedro," said Hero as though she was reading his mind. "He makes the intangible tangible; and now to live as we do, we must see him on through."

"How? For all we know, he's dead," said Niko, not wanting to give in to the alternative just yet.

"Yes, but we know that he must be raised."

"Shouldn't we let him be the judge of that?"

"I'm not so sure, Niko."

"Go on."

"Charles mentioned something about a detective going to see Anne."

"So?"

"He'll visit the professor too, no doubt," said Hero.

"Maybe."

"If he's worth his salt, he'll see the whole lot."

"You're thinking that if he speaks to them, he may get around to us."

"They'll put him on our trail if Anne hasn't already."

"We shouldn't have a problem with that; he'd get to us anyway, wouldn't he?"

"But with a bad attitude?" she said.

"We could hardly be construed of being guilty of anything. How do we know he didn't die?"

"I suppose, but do you really think he's dead, Niko?"

Niko shook his head after a respite of silence and sighed. He knew Pedro wasn't dead.

At the center of Ronald Morgan's backyard grew a massive catalpa tree. At that time of year it burst into thousands of little white flowers whose petals fell from the great height and created a summery flurry. Hero walked out the patio doors and down to the tree. Sadie was preparing an outside breakfast with Niko's partial assistance. It was truly a glorious morning. The air was sweet; the lawn was plush, and petals came down in an enchanting munificence. Hero spun around like a child, with her head back, under the spell of the sky overhead. A lone robin perched on a branch above, tweeting and twittering its proclamation of paradise, which in fact was a glut of worms.

Niko settled into a patio chair and, in the preponderance of his ambiguous mood, watched Hero. Whatever the complexities of his deep friendship with Pedro, even death would seem to impinge upon his desire for Hero, not that it would cause any antipathy between them. On the contrary, Pedro couldn't have been happier about the affair. Pedro had inspired him to rise up and out of his subordinate world of finance to be a fellow adventurer, but he was without Pedro's art, and his function became to follow, preside and preserve. Many of his friends and relatives at home saw him as a paragon of modesty. This quality, with his title, success, and influence at his young age, created a much needed counterpoise to his mother's extravagance. Her subsequent squandering of much of the family fortune compelled him to remain the "dutiful son." Yet he had a strong sense of tradition that had lured him to draw upon an archetypical mystery: namely Pedro and his ring — the ancient triad — the Roebuck, the Lapwing, and the Dog. And as such, he had become unwittingly one of the custodians of the secret of life like a Templar or Knight of the Sun. For these laurels of perfection in the application of life were, he felt, akin to long lost totems of western Man. Niko saw himself as the king or protector, Pedro as the spirit, and Hero, as the High Priestess.

Hero seemed alternately to glimmer and fade before his eyes. He smiled. Divine nature was exacting itself and reinforced what served to anoint the backdrop of his brooding.

"We are too insular," he quietly declared.

"Then we must be unequivocally parochial," said Sadie, picking up the thread of his meaning as she put a basket of croissants on the table. Ronald came from behind, carrying soft-boiled eggs.

"Hey, St. Germain, don't put a hex on our tree!" he called loudly, putting the eggs down.

"Don't mind me," said Niko to Sadie, reverting to their own exchange. "There's a lot more to Pedro's mortality than meets the eye, and I apologize for being so coy about it. There have been some peculiar goings-on over there; the professor's dig spurred some strange behaviour."

"Chow time, Pan-Euro-Pagans — that means you, St. Germain!" yelled Ronald in his supercilious way.

Hero came bounding up, refreshed from her ramblings around the lawn. There was a predatory look in her eyes.

"So, Ronald, have we had enough heralding of the dawn yet, or are you still swimming in a wet dream?"

Sadie began coughing as her grapefruit juice went down the wrong way.

"Hero, darling, your mind is the very marvel of purity, and good morning to you," replied Ronald.

"Same to you, hunk," said Hero, intimidatingly.

"Hunk?" exhorted Ronald. "What's with you?"

"How 'bout 'stud'," she said, smiling.

"Only if you really meant it," said Ronald sincerely.

"Okay, I'm sorry; accept my apologies. I can't help myself this morning. Sadie, you two are great together."

"Does that mean I'm not a stud?" asked Ronald.

"Maybe," said Hero. With that they began to eat for a moment in an awkward calm before Sadie broke out laughing, with the others following suit. The stresses of Pedro's death had brought on a voracious hunger as well as an off-beat humour.

"So, Niko," said Sadie, after a few minutes, scooping into her egg, "what's all this about strange things happening?"

Hero looked up at Niko. "What strange things?" she said.

"Well, there were inconceivable circumstances."

"What's this all about?" perked up Ronald. "Is our divine Pedro still roaming the planet as a ghost?"

Hero and Niko laughed.

"Fact of the matter is," said Niko, "I want you to be aware of things that Pedro knew about and subsequently discovered at Caerymwy in Wales, in that order. He had some uncanny connection to the place as if he had truly lived there before in another lifetime long ago. For example, he knew exactly where the burial site was of Gwydion, a Celtic warrior from 460 A.D."

Ronald and Sadie silently digested what they heard.

"You see," Niko continued, "Pedro felt he had been reincarnated, and there was nothing one could do to refute this belief because he really knew."

"Reincarnated from whom?" asked Sadie.

"Gwydion, of course."

"I wouldn't have expected anything short of that from Pedro," said Ronald. "He used to imagine things and attempt to make them come true. I remember one summer he bought a small herd of sheep — about a dozen — and started an organic lawnmowing service with a sheep shit fertilizer bonus. He had this portable electric fence, a beat up old army truck, and a dog. No kidding. He even found two eccentric customers on large properties. He'd set up the fence and graze the sheep; they would trim the lawn as smooth as a golfing green. Pedro would sit under a tree and smoke spleefs and play his blues harp. They finally shut him down when one time he had apparently fallen asleep under his tree while his sheep had broken through the fence and gone on a rampage through the neighbourhood. The city health people almost had him arrested, but he sold the flock fatted on Rosedale greens.

"Yes, your telling of that story provides new insight into our present difficulty, Ronald," said Hero with feigned sarcasm behind a wry smile.

"And just what is our present difficulty, my dear?" asked Ronald.

"That of finding some rational explanation for Pedro's supposed reincarnation, of course."

"The only rational explanation for anything to do with Pedro lies with Pedro and he's dead. Dead," said Ronald with finality.

"Personally, I don't think we've seen the last of him," exclaimed Hero confidently.

"Oh, this is good. Does your crystal ball see him rising from the ocean deep like a merman Lazarus? Give us a break with your cryptic visions, Hero babe. Okay, so he was better than me, though my memory of him is this side of idolatrous, but he's gone. Gone."

"No, he's not dead," said Hero matter-of-factly.

"Yes, Pedro has reincarnated back into Pedro," said Niko, quickly slipping into the dialogue.

Ronald broke into hysterical laughter, followed by Sadie, Hero, then Niko, the latter assured of his timing. "You know, I received a call from Connie this morning," said Sadie at last. She began to choke over a mouthful of croissant that had gone down the wrong way, then recovering, continued. "Excuse me. She phoned to ask me if I or any of you know a Donna del Rio."

They stopped laughing and looked at each other.

"Who is Donna del Rio?" asked Hero abruptly.

"Well, whoever she is," continued Sadie, "She showed up at Connie's door this morning looking for Pedro. Apparently hadn't the foggiest idea he'd died."

"Where does she live?" interrupted Hero.

"I don't know."

Hero stood up, swallowing her last bite. "Come on," she said, "We've got to find her."

"Why?" asked Sadie.

"Because she is the only connection we have to Pedro," replied Hero.

"Are you really all right, Hero?" asked Ronald sincerely.

"Never felt better in my life," she lied. "Come on."

The sun declared itself with a young intrepid virility — the colour an impossible vermilion, its heat already burgeoning in the cool shadows of the night. High on an escarpment and looking down the abrupt side of a gorge into a narrow river sat three travellers, a woman and two men. They were silent and pensive, for they had much to think about regarding their journey from which there was no return. Fair Ariadne hadn't spoken a word but seemed quite content with the situation. The ease with which she had fit into the two warriors' plans satisfied them and they trusted her. However, neither Troylus nor Aeneas could keep his eyes off her in the bright daylight because her quiet demeanour and beauty were so captivating. They had had only a couple of hours of fitful sleep after a frantic night spent running blindly north across fields, rough gorse, rugged slopes, and forests. Then they had crossed the river and followed it into the gorge. Upon finding suitable high ground they collapsed in a heap, scratched, blistered, and bleeding. The two men now wore pleased smiles. The goddess woman hadn't uttered a single complaint; furthermore, though they might have been mistaken, she looked very much as though she was enjoying their company.

Aeneas brought out some dried fish, nuts, and olives; it was almost the last of their food. They ate quickly and silently, and drank water from a flask. The woman now looked at her two male companions, then lowered her eyes self-consciously; she turned to the sun, and to the astonishment of Troylus and Aeneas, raised her arms. She began to sing softly in Etruscan, a smattering of which both men knew from their travels. She then pulled her tunic from her shoulders exposing them and pink-nippled breasts to the sun. After, she covered herself, turned to the wide-eyed warriors, and said in Etruscan, "Thank you for my deliverance. I am Sarah, daughter of Epanider the Merchant and Osea the Jew. I was kidnapped by the Gorgonians at the age of fourteen. These seven years I have been confined to their purpose. They are a fanatical cult; although they did not physically harm me, I have been subjected to many disgusting acts. I don't know how to thank you, whoever you are.

But I trust you and wish to give myself to you, Troylus. I am yours."

"I will feed you and protect you, Sarah," said Troylus. "We are going to Avalon where we will rule our own kingdom."

"The Gorgons will come after us. There are many."

"We will fight them," said Aeneas.

Sarah smiled and said once more, "I am yours."

Troylus, unable to show any sentiment, possessed a tremendous infatuation for this venerable deity. Awkwardly silent, both he and Aeneas had lost the ability to let down their guard, not such a steep price for survival, particularly considering the bounty life had just showered down in the form of Sarah. The stirrings of fortune were beginning to dawn on them; and so ingrained was their hard upbringing and sense of honour, that without some flagrant signal from Sarah, they would strictly observe their duty as warriors. After all, they didn't really know where they were going or what lay before them.

Perched on the promontory, stunned by conflicting anticipations and spellbound by Sarah's presence, they waited for the inevitable confrontation with the Gorgonians, an eccentric splinter-group of the Ligurian Celts occupying most of the region. It was imperative that they move north as quickly as possible, but their present advantageous position at the top of the gorge and the opportunity it afforded for rest gave them a needed edge. Thus, fed and rested, they were prepared for a fight. Their highly tuned senses alerted them to the slightest nuance of movement; their hunter's essence left not a windy shift to chance.

Sarah became aware of all this; she sensed an imminent danger and kept looking at them to see if they were feeling what she felt, each of her glances being returned. She finally spoke: "We must go away before they come."

Troylus said, "No, we must wait." He put his finger to his mouth signalling for her to be quiet.

Aeneas said, "We are the hunted."

Sarah didn't understand. They seemed to be squandering their advantage. Her intuition told her they must turn the tables and become the hunters, a position they were more comfortable with. She bowed her head in abject wonder. Never had she known such a powerful confidence as these two emanated: even so, she was unsure of their rationale, brave as they were.

"They are many," she reiterated quietly.

Troylus and Aeneas suddenly motioned to her to get down low, then scrambled for cover themselves. Down below, by the river, stood the Hairy Man looking up and down sniffing the air like a dog on a scent. Behind him were at least a dozen fully armed Gorgonian warriors with bows, swords, and spears; they had provisions sufficient for a long trek.

The Gorgonians stayed where they were, listening to something the Hairy Man was saying. The group then split up into groups of four, with the Hairy Man in one that came across the river in Troylus's direction till it disappeared below them.

Troylus and Aeneas helped Sarah climb a large conifer set back in from the escarpment. Relieved about her safety, they turned back to face the enemy. What was about to happen meant heaven or hell; their blood surged madly and they were ready to fight with the strength of ten.

Both now went in opposite directions, hoping to flank the approaching group of soldiers. Troylus crouched at the foot of a boulder where he had a good view of the valley. On the rocks below, he could hear the men progressing up the side of the gorge. Something leapt past the corner of his eye. Outside his flank, another group had crossed the river and was starting up the sharp incline. The battle would be dangerously one-sided if he and Aeneas had to take on all of them at once. They must kill the first group before the others arrived; he had only moments to decide on his course of action.

He jumped up with his arrow drawn in his bow and emerged above the climbing Gorgonians. The Hairy Man saw him first and ducked as the first shot struck a soldier in the neck, propelling him backward and sending another with him over the cliff. The Hairy Man scrambled nimbly up another route with other Gorgonians attempting to follow him.

They screamed to tell the others, but were cut down by another two arrows finding their mark. The Hairy Man disappeared into the bush behind them. Within minutes another group came out of nowhere with spears extended and charged Aeneas. Lightning-swift, he retreated with the Gorgonians in pursuit. Troylus, who brought up the rear, vaulted onto the last Gorgonian's back and buried his short sword up under his arm into his heart. The soldier let out a cry but it rose unheeded in the din-filled air as he slumped hopelessly toward the earth. Troylus had already shot another man with his bow.

Upon reaching higher ground, Aeneas turned to face his attackers. In a reckless move he leapt with his spear at the first assailant, struck him in the eye and in a continuous movement with his sword slashed a remaining soldier across the neck. With brutal precision he dispatched four soldiers. Two of these now lay dead; a third pumped blood in his death throes over the fourth, who was clutching his gored eye, gasping in pain.

Without so much as looking at each other, Troylus and Aeneas again separated to meet the second wave of Gorgonians, who had joined together down where the first group had been ambushed. The newcomers spread out in a single line, keeping ten metres apart from each other and moving back through the bush. When they came to Sarah's tree, they stopped to survey the carnage unleashed on their fellows.

In the ensuing silence, as they waited and looked around them, Sarah clung desperately to the branch above, afraid to breathe. The Hairy Man was nowhere to be seen. Troylus and Aeneas crouched in bushes not ten metres from the nearest man. A soldier, the leader, spoke out in an unintelligible language that only Sarah could understand. He said, "Ariadne, great Goddess, have you seen how we die for You? How we fight for You?"

Troylus let his arrow fly at the leader, hitting him in the neck and sending him to a choking death. A moment after, Aeneas fired an arrow into and mortally wounded the man beside the leader. The remaining soldiers charged the bushes where Aeneas waited. The first of these ran into Aeneas's spear, getting pierced for his trouble through the lower abdomen and crying out in agony. A small phalanx of spears now bristled in front of Aeneas, who had to bolt behind some rocks. Troylus emerged from his place and fired an arrow into a soldier's lower back. Troylus charged with his spear, only to face three soldiers with their spears who counterattacked with the desperation of men fighting for their lives. Meanwhile, Aeneas, fighting three soldiers with his sword, received across his arm a slash that cut into the muscle. In a frenzy of bloody madness, he lunged at his assailant, who backed away to let the others hit Aeneas from the side, thrusting his sword into his exposed parts. Aeneas knew he'd be finished if he didn't charge through and clear the foray. He tripped, luckily, causing the potentially fatal blows of the other soldiers to miss their mark and cut rather than stab, then, propelled forward, he lunged again at his enemy, this time catching him in the groin, sending him to his knees in mute shock. But the others had a second chance and in a flash had fallen upon Aeneas. "Troylus!" he cried, "Save yourself!"

Troylus, within seconds, redoubled his furious charge, deflecting one of the enemy's spears and sinking his own spear into one of Aeneas's attackers; but in doing so, he gave the three other soldiers time to turn and aim their spears at his back. They charged. Aeneas now rolled out of the way, while Troylus turned to face his adversaries, but it was too late: one of the spears ripped into his armour. He managed to hold the others off with his sword, but the new attack enabled the soldiers to strike him with their swords. Troylus attempted to break free, but the spear prevented his escape. Sensing Troylus' plight, Aeneas scrambled up, and ignoring his current adversary, now threw himself onto the other three to save Troylus. He plunged his sword again and again, hacking and stabbing. Now, with their attention diverted by Aeneas's courageous leap, Troylus could thrust at his attackers; but the one remaining enemy came behind Aeneas and raised his sword in a mighty swoop aimed at Aeneas's neck. Suddenly, the Gorgonian froze in mid-swing, mortified to see a spear tip, shiny and red, come through his solar plexus and leather chest plate from a blow so powerful it actually lifted him off the ground for an instant.

Then there was silence.

The Hairy Man stood up proudly from behind the impaled Gorgonian, clutching his spear.

The dead and the living were in a bloody heap. The battle had taken only a matter of minutes. Troylus and Aeneas held each other up, unable to tell, with all the blood, how many or how serious were their wounds. They looked at the carnage around them, the gruesome death masks, some still twitching, one groaning. All who had fallen, died. Aeneas and Troylus began to tremble from battle trauma and were too stunned to acknowledge the Hairy Man, who stood there twisting his spear out of that last victim's body. They did not, therefore, hear the tip scraping past bones, nor see its point emerge with a mass of flesh and blood attached to it. The moments passed. The birds began to sing again. The sun burned down through the sparse trees onto the thin turf and heated rocks, marking the settling dust with bands of light.

Troylus and Aeneas freed themselves from the bodies of the defeated and approached the tree to see if Sarah was still all right. She was high up, straddling a large branch, looking away as if oblivious or asleep with her eyes open. Her tunic hung loosely; she had seen the commingled dust and bright red blood and wished to look no further. Aeneas and Troylus had been outnumbered fifteen to two, now three.

Aeneas and Troylus now acknowledged the Hairy Man, who stood off to the side, waiting like a slave holding his well-earned spear that was now cleaned and shining.

The ship's loud horn blared, sending its salvo across the water as it approached Manitoulin Island. The sudden blast reverberated, waking Pedro from his sleep in the upper forelounge of the Great Lakes ferry

Chee Chee Maun, "Big Canoe." He opened his eyes to see a small Indian boy staring at him with a fixed expression. Pedro stared back with a smile on his face, happy at the child's interest, but happier in his own thoughts. The vestige of gored bodies and the glory of a battle won was fading. He derided himself lightly; how could he withdraw from that scene to face the present? Yet it was all so fitting, his coming north to Indian lands and leaving behind a bottomless maze of the past.

Pedro had taken a bus from Toronto to Tobermory, caught the ferry to South Baymouth, and was going to hitchhike the final leg of his journey across Manitoulin to Little Current. He had already asked the Indian boy's parents for a ride to town.

Sitting up, he slung his dunnage over his shoulder, stood up and signalled he was going outside to the railing. The boy followed him.

Outside, leaning against the railing, Pedro watched as the ship coursed through the fresh aquamarine Georgian Bay waters. Against the azure sky gulls screeched and beseeched passengers for hand-outs; for a while they would coast in the breeze, plummet to catch something, then rise again, sometimes soaring higher than before. Pedro relaxed. In the matter of a single day, life had become wonderfully simple; he felt secure in his obscurity — at the forefront of a new adventure — though slightly guilty for leaving things in the state they were in. He knew someday very soon all would be resolved for better or worse. The whole thing was outlandish anyway: his headlong plunge through several lifetimes. He mulled it over, conscious of the boat's churning toward the shore as a continuation of this process.

South Baymouth Harbour was now imminent, the shoreline rocky and windblown at the entrance to the bay, and the stunted pines standing fast and firm. Crossing the channel was like crossing the divide between the south and the north.

It was a perfect balmy heat. Even with the breeze off the cool water, the air had a northern dryness and faint scent that triggered memories of the youth Pedro had spent in those parts. The feeling of comfort and familiarity evoked in him a wonderful emotion: innocence. He was a child again, completely engaged in the moment. He thought of the secluded point where he wanted to camp near Birch Island, close to the Whitefish band village. It wasn't far from Dreamer's Rock, the ancient native fasting and vision promontory, from which one could see for miles around.

Once disembarked, they now cruised north in a rusty yellow Impala. A pair of oversized cotton dice dangled from the rearview mirror. Pedro sat in the back watching the side of the road and scenery. Jimmy, the driver, was speaking about his gambling exploits in Atlantic City, how he started out with two grand and now had fifty. The little boy remained quiet, as did the woman, as if what was happening was a normal occurrence.

On the main street in Little Current, Pedro got out of the car, said thanks and went straight to a supply store. With nearly the last of his money, he bought a small tent, canvas pack, axe, cookware and an assortment of other items. He packed the supplies, then went to the grocery store to purchase enough food to last at least a week or two.

As he ambled with his two packs down the street toward the highway junction, he saw a Native American art display in the window of a small gallery. He stopped and looked for a moment, contemplating the possibility of embellishing his campsite; but the thought passed and he turned to go when a heavy-set native man emerged from the gallery and stepped onto the sidewalk, almost bumping Pedro. Pedro, without looking, excused himself and walked on. However, the Native American called after him. "Excuse me too," he said, adding, "Hey, if I'm not mistaken, I've just seen a ghost." Pedro stopped and slowly turned around. He looked at the man and broke into a grin. "Big Dan," he said. "Holy Smoke!"

"Pedro George! God Almighty, a ghost! Only Pedro George can die, and still live! Shit, man, you scare me! I've been in mourning these three days since the news passed through. Couldn't believe my ears, ol' buddy — what da fuck's goin' on, man?"

"I don't know, some kind of temporal shift, Dan; the Great Spirit spit me out — don't believe everything you hear! How the hell are ya?"

Big Dan's mouth hung open. He looked him up and down, moved toward him, put a hand on his shoulder, and squeezed. "You're for real," he said. Pedro laughed. Big Dan was the stolid sure-footed type who spoke with an eloquent native quality which never wasted words. His people, having lived in those lands for thousands of years, had a bred-in-the-bone, indelible sense of humility in nature. Big Dan typified the patient, powerful purity of spirit in a proud people.

"I'll explain things later," said Pedro in a calm voice that eased the shock of their sudden meeting, "but if you have some time now, I could use a ride up to Dreamer's; then I need a lift out into the channel. I'm going camping — I need to get away for a short while; life, shall we say, has become a bit obscure."

"Obscure?" said Big Dan. "More like weird, man, weird." He dropped his hand and looked to the ground, his eyes straying here and there as if to give himself time to get his bearings. "You were really dead, weren't you, Pedro; I mean, I heard about it through the Wilsons; everyone was shocked. You're supposed to be fuckin' dead, ol' buddy!!"

"Dead is dead; there's nothing more dead than dead; anyway, apparently I'm not dead yet," said Pedro.

"Come on, Pedro; let's get out of here. Are you hiding from something?" asked Big Dan.

"Not really. You still driving that old beat up truck?"

"Hey, weren't you just looking at my art?" said Big Dan, referring to the display window.

"Those yours?"

"Yeah, I sell 'em all over the country."

"I never knew you as an artist."

"I never knew you as a dead man."

They laughed and turned to go. Down the street Big Dan casually lifted Pedro's two packs into the back of a new red Ford pickup. "You have some story to tell," said Dan as he pulled away from the curb.

"It's the way of the world," said Pedro, looking ahead.

The sounds of the old forest became audible again after the shocked silence following Augustus's revelation of the loss of his grand-nephew and best friend, Anne's father. David Thomas couldn't bring himself to pick up the threads of conversation again; he seemed even to forgive August's and Anne Willobie's refusal to attend Pedro's funeral. They were obviously so worn down from the pain of lost ones that more of the same was just swallowed up in their general despondency. Time does heal, thought Thomas, thinking of the recent loss of his father, but never undoes the scar. Any reminder of death can touch sensitive tissue and trigger an automatic defense, an attempt to deny. This repression can become a bulwark against the abyss of enduring grief, a tenuous step by which to crawl back, one hopes, to the wellness of life.

The tragedy of the young boy's death, for all its horror, can only have accentuated the great filling of a void that Pedro's shining light brought. David Thomas could sense the loneliness of the old man sitting beside him; it was palpable in the hunched shoulders and odd gaze, the way he held the digging tool. He seemed to be holding on for his very life. David Thomas supposed that August's cantankerousness was actually his rendition of a sense of humour and that notwithstanding the sad reality of tragedy, he truly worked hard at being happy; he had a wit that hit its mark and kept others on guard. He did not like being taken lightly under any circumstances. This trait was undoubtedly at the core of his tremendous aptitude for his life-long study of antiquity. And for anyone with a wealth of knowledge like his to find himself, out of necessity, trusting a young character such as Pedro, must have required quite a submission to some spell of truth from whatever Pedro had to offer. Thomas could well have transmitted this last thought telepathically to the professor, who suddenly turned and said, "So you're here to find out why an old professional like me would ally himself with a young upstart like Pedro, who among other things, had a notorious streak without an iota of experience in archaeology." David Thomas wondered how August could read his own thoughts. And this peculiar reverence for Pedro was tantalizing.

"Is your background Welsh, Professor?" he asked, attempting to penetrate the enigma in his own way.

"On my mother's side, without interruption."

"And your father?"

"What in Mordred's drawer does this have to do with Pedro?" said the Professor, irritated.

"Excuse me, August; I have my own method of deduction. I eliminate nothing and I circumnavigate a full scenario, in all honesty, to separate the apocryphal from the unlikely. You see, peripheral facts do tend to support what could be plausible."

"Mmph! Well, I think it's humbug!" responded Augustus, but without conviction. Then he stopped speaking and gazed off at the oak trees.

"Well, what of your father?" David Thomas was cut off.

"Well what, well what, well what of it?! My father was an Englishman! I grew up in Cambridge! Moved back here in my early thirties! Learned my native tongue! Never looked back! My colleagues thought I'd cracked! But came to me for opinions! Most of 'em, boneheads! Now what do you want from an old curmudgeon? Speak man, or be gone!"

David Thomas checked himself, not sure how sound this old man really was, but appreciative of his forthrightness.

"So tell me, professor, why was Pedro so notorious?"

"Ha ha ha ha ha ha . . . he was indolent and indulgent to a fault . . . in spirit."

"Yet you respected him for something."

"He was a genius."

"At what?"

"At life — knowing people — history — human nature — I don't know; he just knew things; he discovered all this," said August, gesturing madly around.

"I'm interested," said David Thomas. "You mean to say, Pedro came through here once and saw something you hadn't, in all these years?"

"Precisely." He pointed to the hills behind them. "Here, look." David Thomas followed suit and saw two small shapely, symmetrical hills that rose abruptly above the vale.

"I don't understand. So what? Anybody could see them," said David Thomas, scratching his head.

"Don't ye see? They're like two large tits!"

"Why, yes, I suppose you're right."

"When he saw the tits, the first thing he did was look for the cunny."

"The cunny?"

"The cunt for Chrissake!"

"What?"

"The cunt of the Great Mother, man! This was the site for ancient ceremonies, beginning who knows when, witches, Druids, and so forth. This was the heart of the wood, the heart of consciousness, the heart of life for the people who lived here. Hundreds of years ago it was somehow forgotten. Look at these oaks, the king of trees, symbol of mastery of life, omnipotence, wisdom. Derwydd means Oak-Seer, hence Druid in Celt."

"Where's this cunny, then?" asked David Thomas.

"Come, follow me."

Inspector Thomas followed Professor Woods back toward the two large mounds into a vale that abruptly ended at a crack-like female genitalia. All the bushes had been cleared and boulders removed to expose a tunnel. There were pits in various degrees of excavation alongside the sharp incline of the vale which actually ended with a cleft at the tunnel.

"Extraordinary," said David Thomas. "What was found in the . . . cave?"

"Follow me," said Augustus, as he disappeared into the cave. Along the ceiling, a series of lights at twenty foot intervals or so were strung, fed by a car battery at the tunnel's opening. The older man paused to flick them on. About fifty feet inside, the passage ended. Here they passed through a narrow opening into a larger chamber. On the walls, many beautifully preserved drawings and writings formed a strange calligraphy with Latin letters, but of a dialect unknown to Thomas. Some of the drawings were graphically erotic with oversized penises and female genitals. The women and men were naked and, in a sequence of drawings, performed a ritual of what appeared to be an initiation ceremony using the very same cave. The person being initiated was being led blindfolded into the cave from which he was expected to find his way out, supposedly reborn. On another side of the cave was a very different scene in which a large white buck was being chased by hunters with spears. Nearby was a lapwing attempting to divert attention and further on, a dog or wolf sitting like a sentry, guarding something (which appeared to be a head with a crown on it), presiding over an oak tree that seemed to indicate wisdom, authority or power.

"Absolutely astounding! Magnificent! So well preserved!" exclaimed David Thomas, at a loss and feeling out of his depth.

"That's not all. Pedro led us to this. Do you see that crack? See where it goes up into that dark chasm? There's a burial chamber there."

David Thomas helped Augustus lift a ladder up against the wall of the cave. The older man went first, teetering precipitously at the top as he climbed off the ladder. Having found footing, he knelt down and crawled into a small hole. David Thomas followed. Once inside the hole, they half-crouched to reach another small opening which went sideways into yet another chamber, one not so large as the other, roughly ten feet by twenty and ten feet high. This chamber was painted in brilliant blues, reds, and greens, depicting Caerymwy Lake and the fortification, drawn in minute detail with a battle scene in front. On the opposite side of the chamber, the lake was depicted in moonlight, and on yet another side was another battle in the trees of the oak forest outside. On the last side was a picture of three men and one woman with blond hair. "For a little piece of old Cambria, not bad," said Augustus, obviously moved by the tenor of his own voice.

"Was this a burial chamber?" asked the Inspector.

"Look here," said Augustus. There, at one end of the chamber, was another slight opening covered by an ancient piece of wood. The professor carefully removed the wood and gazed in. "In here," he said, "is a sarcophagus for three bodies in fetal position with swords, shields, jewelry, and assorted other things. One of the bodies is headless; the head's in the arms of the female occupant. Pedro named them Gwydion, Olwen and Bran. Over this past winter I deciphered the writing there on the ceiling. Guess what I found? The very same names. Pedro knew who they were, and don't, for goodness sake, ask how he knew this; but, then, this is what Pedro is all about."

They walked up the vale above the crotch, across the navel, and between the breasts. The forest at this point changed to firs, then hawthorn and scrub bushes, wild violets, hazel tufts and juniper. A missel thrush swooshed away, cuckoos called, and wrens, magpies and the odd robin twittered in a melodious racket. Across a grassy meadow, they came to a tumble-down stone wall with a wooden gate.

"My property begins here," said the Professor with a wave of the cane he had taken before the ascent.

They came to a modest flock of sheep in an old overgrown orchard dominating green misty vales and meadows behind and below. Down a slope to the left, the lane came to another gate. On the other side, the cottage could be seen, snuggled into the hillside. "That's Ralph the Ram," remarked August, pointing to a sheep tethered on his front lawn. "A Cheviot."

Down the path a lapwing hobbled on the ground nearby with a broken wing. David Thomas went over to have a closer look, but the bird hobbled away. He pursued. The bird hobbled again, then, in a sprightly flutter, obviously amused with the Inspector, flew off. "Little devil," said Thomas under his breath.

"They do take advantage," said Augustus. At that moment an old Shelty dog came out wagging from a niche in the garden to greet him. "Arthur, my friend, keeping the bad ones away? Meet Inspector David Thomas; he's come to have lunch with us." The dog rubbed its nose on David's leg and welcomed him with a friendly sniff. As he stood in the doorway leading inside from the flagstone patio, the Inspector observed the dark interior of the cottage and smelled the ever-burning peat. It seemed larger once inside, and was clean but cluttered with a thousand books, assorted archaeological specimens, and various photos of digs; it was very much in character with the professor, with little comfort other than a few old wooden chairs around the hearth, a table cluttered with papers, numerous empty ale bottles with candles and the absence of any modern amenity, including electricity. There was that unmistakable earthy smell of burnt peat, which, as fuel, undoubtedly kept Augustus warm during the winter.

Augustus returned to the terrace, holding two large glasses of dark ale. Accepting one of these, David Thomas followed the professor to the edge of the patio. In his dirty tweeds, Augustus bellowed a hearty "Cheers!" to the valley below. Thinking this was the proper thing to do, David Thomas did the same, albeit with half the gusto. Then they sat down in two rickety deck chairs.

"I'm warming up some leek soup with oat cakes, Inspector. I hope as an Englishman you take to our humble Cambrian fare," said August.

"'Tis my country now, too; much appreciated. For everything. I must say, I hadn't expected so much!"

"I don't take kindly to strangers, as you know. I'm thinking of having steel doors installed at the entrance of the cave."

"Do you really think you'll be able to keep your discoveries from the public indefinitely?" asked David Thomas.

"I'm going to try to satisfy their needs with a book I'm working on. It'll be illustrated with colour photographs."

The professor took a deep drink of ale.

"Ahh," he said, wetting his grey whiskers. They both sat there absorbed in their respective thoughts, looking out across the many folds of the magnificent green valley. One could go into a stupor with the serenity of it all, the thatched white-washed cottage surrounded by brambleberry bushes and the vines — just perched up there amid the elements. David Thomas had thought he'd found seclusion in his own pastoral place, but the professor's was certainly an eccentric notch above anything he could have imagined.

"How long have you lived here, Professor?" he asked.

"Two score and two years." The professor's voice rose automaticaly from the depths of some reverie.

"How do you get to town? All I see is a footpath."

"Precisely. I walk."

"That's quite a hike."

"I don't do it often; Gwendolyn does errands for me. What in Christ's name are ye driving at?" said the professor, coming out of his meditations.

"I'm only curious. I do have an investigation underway." David Thomas regretted his words as soon as they were out.

"An investigation? By God, I thought we had an understanding; there's nothing ye can do here, Mr. Thomas," the older man said matter-of-factly.

"Why is that?" the Inspector said, surprised at the confidence emanating from the old misanthrope.

"There's an old saying, Mr. Thomas, and you, as a servant of the law, would be wise to heed its relevance. Quote unquote: 'Give your servant a heart to discern between good and evil', Kings."

David Thomas mulled it over a bit. "You're telling me more than some old biblical adage, aren't you?" he said.

"Ha ha ha ha ha ha." The professor stood up and disappeared inside the woody dark of the cottage, returning eventually with a tray of steaming soup, butter, oat cakes and a few raw carrots.

The food was wholesome, and they ate without speaking. David Thomas wanted to speak but hesitated until the meal was over. He did not want to pry too eagerly.

At last, washing a final oat cake down with his ale, he said, "Tell me, professor, do you find Mrs. Willobie a little out of sorts? She really was quite uncommunicative . . . When I was there . . . What I'm getting at, you see, is that there seems to be such a fog around Pedro and no one seems to know where it begins or ends, and Mrs. Willobie was so . . . vague; yet she, if I may be so bold to suggest, is a little like you as a local . . . but you are a specialist, of course, a recluse and make no pretensions about who you are, but she . . . I don't know; I'm asking you."

"Annie. Annie Fitzooth. She died figuratively when she lost her father, who lived here until the end of his life. He died the same year my nephew drowned. Pedro brought her back when Charles couldn't. She's a witch, you know."

"No, I didn't; then Pedro must've had a tremendous influence on her. Does she go by the name Fitzooth?"

"I believe Willobie. She did give up her name as well as her witchery upon marrying Charles, but I gather she bounced back. I'm not certain, but she's next in line to be the coven High Priestess, or so I gathered from Pedro."

"My God, this puts a whole new light on my talk with her. She's a bloody witch! Then Pedro was obviously involved with witchery," said David Thomas confidently.

"Inadvertently, I suppose, but remember Mrs. Willobie wouldn't harm anyone; she's a wise woman. Most people think of a "witch" as a wicked old hag with a broomstick between her legs, the kind in the Wizard of Oz. Well, I'll tell you, and I'm as Christian as the next parishioner, historically witches were given a bad name because they didn't fit the Christian mold. They still don't, but that doesn't make them bad. They practice 'pagan' rituals, 'blaspheme' against moral principle. Bah! Hogwash!" said Augustus, as he took a quick drink, turning away with a scowl.

"I didn't mean to insinuate that she's a bad witch," said Thomas, swigging his own ale.

"She loved the boy more than she should've," said Augustus.

"That's quite an admission."

"Hardly. 'Twas common knowledge to all but Charles."

"She showed me a poem he wrote, if you could call it that; seemed like a riddle. He was on some ego trip."

"Some might call it that. Pedro left one here too."

"Really? Would you mind if I read it?"

"Not at all." Augustus pulled it out of his pocket. "He wrote this before he knew Hero."

"So you were going to show it to me if I hadn't asked, or do you always carry it around?" asked Thomas, smiling.

"Don't push me, young man, I'm doing this for Pedro and Anne, hoping you may set things right."

"What do you mean, Doctor Woods?"

"Just what I said."

David Thomas took the paper. Again he saw the strange scrawl. At the top of the page, serving in lieu of a title, was 'July 29.' Beneath this he read:

> *Blue friendly sky kiss me now,*
> *As I lie in your lap,*
> *By a bower of sun-warm flowers.*
> *The sea-wind caresses my naked body*
> *Against the hilly hills.*
> *Her touch is hardly different,*
> *Yet tinctured,*
> *In a faint nectar-scent.*

White petals and the pink pistil
Draw bliss from the stamen.
Must I conjure more
Than is my due,
Or give away what I have?
I turn to the salt sea-wind,
And vent a silent plaint.

"Sweet Jesus," said David Thomas. "There's much more to this young man than meets the eye. Something's definitely going on here; a witches' brew has loosed a spell, don't you think?"

"Maybe, but Pedro had nothing to do with it. He was simple, a healer at heart. More and more people around were seeking his help over that of the others. However, he wasn't quite up to fulfilling that role . . . he enjoyed life."

"He therefore may have escaped from that looming responsibility," suggested Thomas. "Or the witches . . ."

Augustus stood up abruptly and said, "We need a refill, Mr. Thomas." He entered the cottage and called out, "I'm going to tell ye a bit about Pedro George; I want ye to leave this place with some proper sensibility."

David Thomas finished his ale; he felt relaxed and drew in deeply the warm scented air wafting in from the garden. He knew he was on to something. He knew he must stay. The letter of the law would have to wait, or at least be suspended. He was in fact overjoyed, for he found this sort of intrigue exquisitely appealing.

"Yes," he said loudly to the valley, his cheeks flushed with ale, "I must know more." And then, quietly: "I must know why Pedro George has died, at least by all appearances."

Chapter Five

*I am the strong creature from before
the flood, without flesh, without bone,
without vein, without blood, without
head, without feet, in field, in
forest, without hand, without foot, as
wide as the surface of the earth, never born.*

—The Wind (Old Celtic)

Sadie McPherson opened the Georges' front door without knocking, and with the others in tow, went in. The house appeared to be empty. She called repeatedly and finally got a response from the back yard, where they found Connie tending the vegetable garden.

"Would any of you like some radishes or leaf lettuce?" Connie asked, pragmatically. "We always have more than we can eat . . . " Her voice trailed away when she saw they evinced no interest in this horticultural surplus.

Hero was in an intensely quiet mood, trying to contain her impatience, and Niko held her hand understanding only too well. Ronald seized the opportunity to explore Hero's somewhat uncharacteristic behaviour. "Connie," he said, putting his hand through his blond hair, "we're here to find out where this Donna del Rio lives; Hero's decided that her hurt over Pedro will be relieved if we speak to her; besides, she's bursting with curiosity 'cause neither of us has ever heard of her before."

"Well, she said she met Pedro in Wales," said Connie, leaning on her hoe in the sunshine. Her expression was blank and non-committal.

"Where does she live?" asked Hero, unable to mask her anxiety.

"What's so important about Donna del Rio?" queried Connie.

"Nothing really," said Hero, collecting herself and sprouting a sweet smile. "Just gives us something to do, you know."

"Actually, Hero's being quite intense, Connie; I believe she's jealous. More likely she wants to find Donna to see if she had what it took to enrapture Pedro," went on Ronald in his jocular vein of sarcasm.

"Pedro never mentioned a Donna del Rio, Mrs. George," said Niko, covering for Hero.

"Well, why don't you go and see for yourself," said Connie, shaking her head. "She said she lives above Giovanni's Groceria and Bakery on St. Clair West. You're all being rather funny about this, don't you think?"

Hero did an about-turn and went back into the house. On a table in the kitchen she found a telephone and leafed through a directory beside it. She found a listing for Giovanni's Groceria and dialled the number. Maria answered. "Hello, is Donna there, please?" asked Hero, looking around to see if the others were still outside.

"She's gone away for a few days," came the reply.

By questioning Maria, Hero learned that Pedro too, was absent. A shockwave ripped through her; not only because he was alive, but because obviously, something was going on between Donna and him. It wasn't only the existence of another woman that bothered Hero; something was amiss with Pedro. He had become so wrapped up in himself; the whole business of his death should have propelled him above and beyond romantic considerations (other than herself, of course).

Further news elicited from Maria was that they had left separately. Donna had appeared upset at Pedro's departure, and Maria thought they had gone up north somewhere as that's what Donna had said when she called to say she wouldn't be back for a few days.

She went outside again. The news left her bruised and vulnerable, but she now at least knew for sure about Pedro.

"Shall we go?" she said putting her hands on both Ronald's and Niko's shoulders. "I just found out where it is."

"Do let me know if you learn something unusual about Pedro," said Connie. "John and I want to find out all there is to know. Just maybe Donna didn't tell me more for fear of upsetting us, which is silly — I take great joy in my son's life; we were blessed to have him. He was more special than we could see until he was gone. Well, good luck," she said, her voice breaking on the last sentence.

They said good-bye and walked away. Sadie turned at the patio and called out, "Connie, I hope this reaching for straws is the right thing."

"Reaching for straws won't bring him back, but it may let him rest in peace if we can accept his end a little better," called out Connie with a wave.

"See you later for our tennis game," said Sadie, departing.

"Oh yes, I almost forgot. Bye." She waved again.

In the driveway, Hero sat in the driver's seat of Ronald's BMW. Ronald stood at the window and Niko and Sadie sat in the back seat with grin-and-bear-it smiles. Hero refused to move and faced Ronald with a defiance only her closest friends could appreciate.

"Hero, no one drives my car but me. What the hell are you trying to do? Please," he pleaded.

She sat there with her hand out for the keys. "The keys, Ronald," she kept repeating.

Ronald shot a frustrated look at Niko, who shrugged. Whatever Hero had in mind, Niko knew, was now irreversible. Evidently, she had found out something and was prepared to take them all with her, irrespective of the outcome. In her behaviour was a hint of desperation.

"Shit," said Ronald, at last dropping the keys in her hand. "St. Germain, women like you give the female sex a tarnished image."

"Women like me? Impossible, there's only one; anyway, men like you eat out of my hand; and as for tarnished, it's your type that makes us shine. You're all footmen and slaves in the end. Can't even shake you off." She smiled broadly in her rather tragic glory.

Niko and Sadie still smiled in the back seat. Traitors, thought Ronald, who was not amused. However, for some reason, he couldn't bring himself to be ruthless with this woman on account of Pedro's death, his fear of her wielding a metaphorical whip, and his deference to Niko for that matter. They had something over him he couldn't understand. He needed them; he needed their temerity and depth. Strangely, they rubbed his vanity the right way, but he didn't know that.

"So why is it so important that you have to drive?" said Ronald, as Hero ripped down the street.

No response.

"Then where are we going?" asked Ronald forcefully.

Hero kept her eyes straight ahead and said, "Georgian Bay."

"Georgian Bay!" said Ronald and Sadie in unison.

"That's north, right?" said Hero.

"Maybe we don't want to go to Georgian Bay," exclaimed Ronald. "Niko, what's gotten into her? She's bonkers!"

"Hero," said Niko, "couldn't you tell us what this is all about? Or do we play charades?"

"Life is a charade. Sadie, what's the fastest way north?" said Hero.

"Well, we should get on 400 north—"

"Sadie, don't. We can't go north!" said Ronald. "She's nuts; I always thought so, and this proves it!"

"Why not?" said Sadie. "It's a beautiful day."

"So just go ahead and do it without planning, or clothes, or nothin'!" exclaimed Ronald.

"Come on, Ronald. Where's your sense of adventure?" said Sadie.

"Adventure? The woman's a lunatic! She thinks Pedro's spirit must be in Georgian Bay! That's it, isn't it, Hero?" said Ronald, in exasperation.

"Donna del Rio went to Georgian Bay this morning," said Hero, after a moment.

"How do you know?" said Ronald.

"I called her place."

Ronald sank back in his seat and shook his head resignedly.

"Where in Georgian Bay was Donna going?" asked Sadie, with a smile on her face. She felt like a kid.

"Manitoulin," Hero guessed.

"Near Pedro's old cottage," stated Sadie.

"I know."

Hurtling up Highway 69 on the east side of Georgian Bay, Sadie couldn't help but reminisce about her ramshackle days with Pedro a decade earlier. They used to drive in something rather more dilapidated than a BMW, and were usually higher than kites. Transportation had been kind of a cerebral thing: leaving and arriving were interchangeable and rate of travel, incidental.

Sadie looked at the back and side of Hero's head. Her intent profile was unwavering, almost robotic; she might have been asleep, and the car, guided telepathically. No one had spoken for quite awhile, and Sadie's gaze passed from the car's interior to the view zipping by outside and back to the interior again. Niko sat looking out his window, unmoved and immersed in his own thoughts. Ronald's head was straight in front of Sadie and he seemed content to be mobile, having perhaps gotten used to Hero's driving, which was fast yet safe. The scenery outside had become flat, with extended miles of pinkish rock and straggly white pines. There was little traffic.

Contemplating the sudden effect of Pedro's death on her own life, Sadie attempted to put it into focus. With some success as a freelance journalist and part-time editor for a major magazine, she felt it was time to take on something more ambitious. The occult interested her; and Pedro in his abstruse way had a hold on her, which she naively attributed to some mystical quality of his. She still loved him in a way and would forever miss his tender endearments; but she also knew he had grown beyond her and accepted that. Judging from what she had gathered from Hero, he might well have grown beyond her too. Hero's present behaviour indicated much unfinished or unresolved emotional disquiet. But what could she hope to gain by chasing down another unknown woman? Much about Pedro and his life would probably forever remain hidden. She flashed back to the fumblings and innocent discoveries of that day when they lost their virginity together, picnicking near her parents' country place.

"How did you meet Pedro?" asked Sadie in a sudden tremor of possessiveness.

"Skiing, actually; in Wales of all places," replied Hero so candidly, the same thought could have been on her own mind.

"You must be a good skier, coming from Switzerland."

"Not bad. I used to race when I was younger, when I was fifteen and sixteen. I gave it up to study psychology at university in Geneva. Met a married doctor there who wanted to leave his wife for me; but I moved to Paris to study art and astrology and met a Welshman named Wyn Jones who modelled himself after his countryman Dylan Thomas. He was a riot, but a budding alcoholic. Anyway, we went to Wales once and there was this huge snowstorm. After we found some ski equipment, we drove north into the mountains, inland from Caerymwy and Aberystwyth to Plynlimon Fawr, a mountain, a huge one for Wales. It wasn't long after that we came to a place where they actually had a rope tow rigged from the drive wheel of a truck. There wasn't any grooming on the slopes — it was just wild — the atmosphere and this thick heavy snow, like cement! Wyn had just one run and basically rolled down the hill like a snowball; it was hilarious, but he wasn't too happy about it and ended up at a local pub to get drunk. Meanwhile, I made the best of it, and got caught in a slush-slide — nothing too serious. Well, who should come out of nowhere to see if I'm okay? Pedro. We looked at each other and spent the rest of the day together. The connection was immediate, deep, bonding. That was over five years ago."

"All because of a snowstorm in Wales; that's rare in itself, but then to meet skiing of all things!" said Sadie.

"We spent that first summer together camping on Caerymwy Lake. It was wonderful. Anne Willobie wasn't too thrilled though; actually, she took an instant dislike to me. Pedro and she, you see, had had a rather torrid affair, and she felt she still possessed him and was even getting ready to leave Charles. I have to hand it to her — there she was, green with jealousy, and us living on her property. But she never kicked us off. I don't think she ever would have. Pedro meant too much to her; then there was his work with August."

"My God, Anne Willobie and Pedro?" exclaimed Sadie.

"Oh yes," said Niko. "It was quite a thing, you know, with Charles away most of the time."

"That hound-dog!" emoted Ronald. "And he always comes out smelling like a rose!"

"Pedro did something to her," said Niko. "She's never been the same. We'd been drinking wine once, and Anne told me confidentially after supper when Pedro had excused himself, that she'd never achieved orgasm before Pedro. She was quite unabashed in describing the prolonged intensity of her experience."

"She was prone to imitate youth, of course," said Hero. "Anne Willobie was weak and spoiled; her father left her millions."

"Do I detect an element of envy?" said Sadie, smiling.

"Envy? Hardly. I was gloating in happiness."

"I think Anne is better than that, Hero," said Niko, "She was always her usual demurring self; if anything, Anne understates." This was Niko's way of portraying Anne's integrity. He had known her all his life and very much appreciated her familial warmth; indeed, she was closer to being a big sister than a first cousin once removed.

Niko's understanding of the undercurrents at work was a mishmash of ironic lives. He wasn't sure of the reasons and motives for the death of Pedro although he was prepared to follow his lead anywhere, even in this bizarre ploy of Hero's. Indeed, he thought it might be left up to himself, Nicholas Alexander Fitzooth, the earl of Huntington, to ease Pedro back to life, though where, when and how would, he hoped, become clearer as the opportunity presented itself.

Hero was frantic. Niko hoped that opening up about Anne might bring Hero out in the open. Yet he thought it better to refrain from speaking again, so he resumed gazing out the window to the northwest. Pedro was waiting.

Stooping over the tribe who sat in various groups around the clearing according to their age and importance, was Elphin the Jester. This evening he had put aside his festive role for that of arch-Druid and was wearing his white blue-fringed habit, the very image of authority in those times. Indeed, he was a rare being — a wizard and a man of knowledge who could take on many guises and walk freely even among his enemies. Such was his power and the fear he inspired across the land. However, not everyone respected him. The Saxons didn't. They were an unruly, barbarous horde that now threatened his people's very existence; they knew nothing of the higher arts of a more civil culture. What they respected was conquest — being a rapacious, bloodthirsty race. Elphin did not fear them, but wisely kept his distance.

Five months had passed since King Gwydion's death. His people, the Argeians, were severely weakened; more than half of their seasoned warriors had been killed. Outnumbered three-to-one, they had fought with unparalleled bravery beside their king, sacrificing themselves for the sake of the women and children and few remaining warriors including Bran, who now was their leader. Bran and the others had escaped to the sacred forest and grove, guessing rightly that the Saxons were more concerned with moving on to the next village and fortification than scouring unfamiliar territory for survivors. The Argeians were notorious guerilla fighters and would doggedly pick off any straying Saxon.

Olwen had recovered with the help of Elphin's healing herbs and powers and the tender care of the tribe women. She was still sore, although her wounds had healed, and she required gentle exercise to continue to strengthen her muscles. In her desire for revenge she was unshakeable; indeed, the whole tribe were silently and steadily preparing for another encounter. Even in their weakened position, they had a double advantage: they were now considered unthreatening and, above all, Olwen had heard Vron the Barbarian reveal their god's name when he killed Gwydion. Vron had thought Olwen dead. To have your god's name revealed to the enemy was a guarantee of defeat. An opposing enemy calling out their god's name simply sucked most of the fight out of their hearts, for that meant they had been betrayed and the greatest of secrets revealed.

Vron's horde were Gorgon worshippers. The Gorgons represented a perverted perception of the Mother Goddess and of feminine beauty. This was the hag Medusa and her specter of death in a cruel and base expression of perversion. Complete loss of innocence and submission to the entrapments of the flesh was the domain of the seductress Gorgon. Human nature being what it is, the concept proved attractive to certain deviants like Vron.

So, there stood Elphin speaking in his peculiar way. Bran and Olwen sat side by side on a log off-center from the gathering. It was naturally assumed that he and Olwen would now share the same home. They had always been like brother and sister, but she was still Gwydion's queen and woman and High Priestess of their band. Though she was delegating her authority because of her condition, no one would even think to dispute her sovereignty (as their tribe was a close-knit one). Even Elphin, who had the power to contend, was in fact a humble servant to the royalty and, when not required to perform a ceremony, became such a simple innocuous creature that the children played with him as if he were a child himself.

"We, the Oak people," began Elphin, "the children of Apollo, the new Cambrians, can never die. No one can know our God the unspoken and we will survive. We are the guardians of the secret of life. Our totems: the Roebuck, Lapwing, and Dog assure that no harm shall ultimately befall us as long as the secret remains sacrosanct. Our great leader, good Gwydion, has been gone five moons. We shall revere his memory forever more in ceremony, in song, in the celebration of life."

The tribe then chanted in unison:

> We are the secret of life.
> Great Oaken spirit guide us.
> Goddess Ariadne bless us.
> Sun King the Unnamed sustain us.
> We are the Earth.
> We are the Blue Sky.
> We are the Shimmering Waters.
> We are the Green Flora.
> We are the Secret of Life.

Elphin then offered brambleberry wine from a horn and cauldron, after which he once again raised his arms to the giant oaks and spoke: "I have cast a summoning spell to bring Vron the Barbarian and his horde before us next full moon. We will destroy him and all those with him here in our forest. It will be the Battle of the Trees. They will be trapped into thinking our High Priestess is alone here with a few children. The Ash People to the south have offered their warriors to help so we shall have equal strength. Vron will die a terrible death!"

The tribe called out: "Death to Vron! Death to Vron! Death to Vron!"

Elphin raised his arms again with a staff in one hand. It was hewn from the finest oak with inlaid brass and silver on which were inscribed runic letters. He spoke:

By this Holy Rood of our Creed,
And Memory's Siblings,
Our God Stands Unnamed.
On the Open Hill, in the Thicket,
Across the Dark Waters,
Behind the Stars We Remain.
In the Mirror of the Lake,
We shine in Mistress Moon,
For His Benediction.
He came as the Sun King,
As they said He would,
Out of the Mists.
He came from Asia Minor,
As they said He would,
With Ariadne.
After He came He was killed,
As they said He would,
For Being the Unnamed.
We came from Island Dryads,
Wild Women from the Groves,
Cast off from Men.
They bore Children who were Learned,
And brought us from the Island,
Here to Cambria.
Fire Shadows on Painted faces,
Dance Ancient Homage,
To our Old Race.

Then they all began to dance around the newly lit bonfire to the strains of Elphin's harp. Girls and boys paired off, young and old, Olwen and Bran; they all set themselves free from the grim reality. The orange dusky sky formed a strange backdrop to the solemnities. The dance became feverish, and horns of wine in profusion were passed around.

Olwen and Bran, having participated initially to bolster spirits, now left with Elphin, who passed his harp to an apprentice, and went off to Elphin's hut up the hillside out of the forest. There they sat on rocks around a fire in cheery silence that ebbed by abstention from the festivities. Like a heavy curtain, the forest muffled the distant exaltations of the dance.

Attired in her best embroidered tunic with sleeves and belt and little bells sewed into the fringes, Olwen sat crosslegged, ever-beguiling with her berry juice-darkened eyebrows, long braided hair, and blue eyes fixed and sombre. The two men, Bran, dark and foreboding, and Elphin, grey and lean with his kind eyes unsmiling, looked into the fire.

Fondling a gift from Gwydion, a gold, amber, and lapis bird pendant that hung around her neck, Olwen quietly spoke of feelings connected with the terrible injuries long since smothered by her steely resolve. Up to now she had been a ghost of her former self, saying only that she should have died with Gwydion. Bran and Elphin, patient and understanding, had said little to deny her sentiments.

"Gwydion was our King. There will never be another like him," she said.

The men said nothing.

"I am the Queen. I will rule as he did, with strength and compassion. Bran, you will be my consort, and also the father of Gwydion's and my child; I am five moons pregnant. It is a miracle the child was not lost; that is why I must live — that, and to destroy this Gorgon and his fiends from Hades."

Elphin and Bran bowed their heads in solemn assent.

"Bran," she went on, "you may severely maim the barbarian, but do not kill him. I reserve this honour."

Elphin now spoke to the Gods. "We have suffered more than is our share. We have known the greatest joys under King Gwydion. We are desperate. Help us Rhiannon, Goddess, Glorious Maiden, Great Mother.

Help us Great God, Sun King, Horned Lord. Help us. We need your strength."

Bran spoke. "Queen Olwen, High Priestess, sovereign of the Tuatha de Danann, Kingdom of Argeia, descendants of Troylus the Unnamed, receive my oblation: I will serve you and our people to my dying breath, Olwen." Olwen looked at him, her eyes pained. "Olwen," he went on, "I shall be all that you ask of me, to my utmost; my man's heart and love are yours."

Olwen gave Bran her hand. Elphin stood up and threw some magic dust into the fire which emitted a colourful, yet harmless spray of sparkles about them. Elphin then went into his hut and emerged in shepherd's garb with a simple staff. He bid them adieu and, stepping into the night, set forth on a journey to the coast.

The channel that runs by Little Current is an active summer tourist area. At one time it was part of the route taken by the voyageurs across the north channel of Georgian Bay between the mainland and Manitoulin Island. It is endowed with many little bays and coves, and its waters are tamer than the open expanses of the Great Lakes, which are like small seas.

Pedro and Big Dan waited at the drawbridge for a yacht to go through. The drawbridge lowered, and the cars that had been waiting began to cross. Big Dan took out a smoke and offered one to Pedro, who took it not simply as a smoke (he had quit long before) but as a gesture of friendship renewed after a lapse of several years. During Pedro's teens, he and Big Dan had spent wild summers camping, fishing, playing pool at the tavern, getting stoned, and going to the powwows at Wikwemikong. They had lived with a common purpose until the currents of life parted them and Pedro moved to Europe.

They cruised along the highway north to Birch Island smoking, and listening to the Allman Brothers' "Pegasus." Big Dan kept looking over at Pedro and wondered what his old friend had been up to; something deep inside him couldn't quite believe Pedro was real. Supposedly, Pedro had really died, yet there he was. Pedro had always had an otherworldly quality to him, but now it seemed a more potent compulsion. Big Dan, usually at ease in any situation, felt uncomfortable; his native spirit sensed a ghostly redolence, though he knew Pedro well enough not to be afraid of him. Aware of Big Dan's trepidation, Pedro mulled over in his mind how he could best enlighten his friend. He decided to just let it spill out naturally. He knew everything was all right now anyway. The spell had been broken; his real death — whatever that was — had been averted for the time being. By surviving, he had dealt Gorgon a stunning blow. The degree of vulnerability had passed. It was as if he was on terra firma again after crossing a rope bridge that had given way behind him.

"So, Pedro," said Big Dan, searching for ways to breach the distance between them, "What you been doin' all these years?"

Pedro hauled on the cigarette, conscious of the smoke in his lungs. It didn't feel as bad as the knowledge that he knew it to be unhealthy. The tobacco was very fresh. He spoke as he exhaled. "Well, you know I've been in Europe, Wales actually, for the most part, and London this past winter. I was working on an archaeological dig on and off for a few years; did a little genealogy on the side for friends of friends and so forth. Nothing extraordinary. Life's been healthy other than this death-trip thing; kind of a shocker for the living, I suppose. I'm still dead for most people, you know. I'm not sure how it's going to end. I couldn't imagine really dying. I guess it's like a general anaesthetic. God, tell you one thing; I'm sure as hell thrilled to be here now with you, Big Dan. I knew I'd run into you sooner or later; kind of a coincidence you were the first person I bumped into, though!" Pedro laughed, relieved by his friend's candour, and finding something diabolically funny in the situation; Big Dan, too, now broke up into a fit of laughter.

"Hey, my best memories are of you, Pedro," he said, composing himself. "Shit, and I missed the funeral!" Again they laughed, this time hysterically. The release had been spontaneous. Calming down at last, Big Dan said, "'Member that time at Wiky, 'bout ten years ago, gettin' pissed with those young squaws? 'Member how we got high on that black oil and went swimmin' skinny in the moonlight?"

"How could I forget?" said Pedro, looking out the window. His lips curved slightly in a dreamy smile as he gazed at the rock flats and stunted trees outside. White quartz hills loomed in the distance. "Beautiful, wasn't it!"

Of sex and death there is a strange symbiosis. Big Dan kept remembering things as if to fill with them the dark void left by Pedro's mysterious death; he knew that, basically, Pedro had told him the truth about everybody thinking he was in his car when it crashed in Wales, but had sidestepped important details connected with the falsifying of his death. Why didn't he put a stop to it? He obviously needed the cover. Big Dan sensed in Pedro something he had never known before: a deep ethereal sadness, a mourning behind his enigmatic smile and generally positive outlook. It had always been difficult to look at Pedro's eyes; they seemed to repel with their knowledge of hurt. Big Dan let it go; if possible, he decided, he would help Pedro, although the latter was too strong to ask anything for himself.

"Well, whatever got you into this mess, I don't know. That's your business, but I got an idea," said Big Dan.

"An idea? Now we're really in trouble."

"Yeah, I know just the thing to make you alive again."

Pedro turned to face Big Dan. "I am alive."

"Yeah, yeah, you know what I mean. Do you remember John Kineu?"

"John Canoe?" Pedro queried.

"KINeu, not CANoe. It means war-eagle," said Big Dan.

"You mean John the Medicine man?"

"Yeah."

"I never knew his last name."

"He's got a fishing camp near where you want to go. Sometimes he lives out there alone for awhile. Matter of fact, I think he's there now. Anyway, the place has a little sweatlodge back in the bush, and there's fresh fish every day. Why don't you go there?" said Big Dan with his eyebrows arched.

"I don't think he ever liked me."

"Don't prejudge him. He's tough but wise. He helped me off the bottle a few years back."

"I remember one time we went up to Dreamer's Rock," said Pedro, "and he was there showing some girl the four winds or something. I was curious about what he was saying, so I brashly climbed up and interrupted his thing. As soon as I appeared, he left with the girl. I had a definite impression he was quite angry with me; he had a feather, a pouch and stuff."

"That girl, Lisa, is my girlfriend now, Pedro; don't worry about that. I remember that too. In case you forget, we both interrupted that ceremony. Forget it; he'd laugh now."

"Well, if you think it's all right, I'm game. I can always make my own camp nearby."

They approached Birch Island and went straight to the landing. It was relatively deserted as they pulled up.

Big Dan steered his steel boat with the twenty-five horse power Yamaha motor across an open stretch of water where one could see the horizon line to the south. Behind them lay the inlets and channels of Birch Island and Dreamer's Rock, the Rock's height of land above the rest. As they rounded an exposed point of rock out in the open (known as The Point), supporting a sparse population of stunted pine, they came to a bay with a rocky beach. Pedro sat forward, looking this way and that, easily regaining his bearings despite his ten years of absence from the area. The deep, clear, bright blue liquid sprayed and dazzled in the sun. Pedro felt better than alive; a surge of joy swept through him at the prospect of the peaceful oasis that awaited him. Wet from the splashing water, he thanked the wind for its ablutions:

> *Little tears fall,*
> *All in all,*
> *Bright in the sun -*
> *Away, away.*

On the beach they steered to was another steel boat. They pulled theirs up alongside, then walked a short way inland to a wooden platform deck on which stood a white canvas tent with a protruding awning. Located on the deck, under the awning, were a couple of old wooden chairs.

"He's not here," said Big Dan.

"Maybe he's collecting firewood or something," said Pedro, scanning the area and noting its big white pines, scraggy oaks, and occasional slim maple. The ground was rough and rocky with areas of thin turf. Down the beach, as far as he could tell, conditions were very much the same — anywhere within sight was less than ideal for sleeping. "Do you know a decent spot where I could pitch my tent, Dan?"

"We're on an isthmus here; just down toward the Point it gets wider, but on the other side, there's some smoother ground; it's not as protected. It faces north."

"No problem; it's summer. Let's go."

Soon Pedro found a comfortable spot that looked out to the northwest with Dreamer's visible to the west. The sun, still high in the western sky, broiled down, despite a breeze that was gently rustling the vegetation around the site. After they erected the tent and made a little fireplace from rocks lying about, Dan sat down and lit a smoke while Pedro absent-mindedly tried to make himself comfortable against a hollow in a nearby rock. The hot, dry air was scented with sweet smells. Giving up on the rock, Pedro walked over to the shore, took his clothes off, and jumped in. The water's coolness sent a tingling aftershock through his body. Down he dove like a seal, coming up for air when he could hold on no more. Below him, as he swam, he could see the rocky bottom disappear over a ledge into a dark blue nothingness. After awhile he swam out farther into the lake with an even breaststroke, turning onto his back from time to time to float, looking up to the immeasurable sky.

Later, when they went back to John's camp, they found the owner sitting on a rock, cleaning a couple of black bass and a pickerel; with a nod he acknowledged the presence of his visitors, then peremptorily returned to cleaning the fish. Occasionally, he would look up from his work at Pedro, who was sitting with Big Dan nearby. He had been well aware of Pedro's death and, had he not been John Kineu, would have been astonished; but John Kineu was accustomed to taking miracles like this in stride, for he was well-versed in mysteries of the spirit world. Pedro, too, had always made an impression.

"Well, our old friend Pedro has decided to rejoin the human race," said John.

"Yes, I thought the prospect of eternal damnation too deadly to pursue," said Pedro. Sometimes, off-key, he would involuntarily exhibit an uncharacteristic jocularity, then as suddenly, regret it.

"Very wise," said John.

"Pedro has come here to escape his past," said Big Dan.

"Anybody looking for you?" asked John.

"Some close friends of mine."

"Why do you run from your friends?" persisted John.

"It has something to do with my life in Wales."

John Kineu stood up on his bowed legs, having finished his cleaning, and stretched. For a while his dark eyes scanned the south horizon; he had the face of an eagle with smallish eyes. Then he put his hand through his grey hair, sighed, and spoke. "Dan, go light the fire at the sweatlodge.

Tonight we are going to see if our friend Pedro is really a ghost or not." He looked at Pedro. "Now you," he said to Pedro, "can help me prepare this fish fry. Slice some potatoes. Make yourself comfortable."

"Thank you. If you only knew what this means to me," said Pedro. He had found the perfect place.

"Also pick some cedar leaves; the spirits are crying."

Donna del Rio actually arrived only fifteen minutes after Pedro at Birch Island. She had driven her dented mauve Skylark through Sudbury and come around to Birch Island from the north. The trip was farther but took less time by avoiding the ferry to the south; there was only mainland to the north.

She went straight to the landing where a number of cottagers embarked and disembarked for their respective retreats. There, she was told by the gas attendant that he had never heard of Pedro George, much less seen him. A middle-aged woman said she'd heard of him, but wasn't likely to see him because he had died, and the family no longer came there. Donna stood outside and scratched her head in the warm sun. Her sun-illumined hair and fair skin began to heat up in the hot sun as she stood beside the Skylark. A couple of young males about sixteen strolled by in long baggy shorts and T-shirts. They gave her a good once over, tried to resume an indifferent air, gave up, and stared wholeheartedly. Her striking and somewhat foreign appearance must have assured them she was worth pursuing, as a little further on, they turned around and came by again. Donna was too wrapped up in her thoughts to notice them, so they stopped in front of her and one, a stocky blond, spoke up politely.

"Need any help?"

"Oh," she said, startled, "I'm just waiting for someone." She looked around again and then back at the boys who stared at her with obvious craving. "Thanks anyway."

They lowered their eyes and began to turn away.

"Wait," she said. "Did either of you know the Georges?" The boys stopped. "Yeah," said the blond boy, perking up, "my parents knew them. Their son was just killed in a car accident. How do you know them?" he asked inquisitively. Donna heaved a sigh. The boy's mention of Pedro's death had been delivered with a tone of finality. Pedro is alive, she convinced herself; he is not a ghost, and she loved him whatever he was. However, there was a problem — the strange question: to ask them by chance if they had seen Pedro George out and about. To ask it after having been told unequivocally of his death would be awkward. Anyway, if anyone had seen him, his name might be reverberating around the landing by now. No. Pedro, if he had come here at all, would have gone to an old friend's or disguised himself, and most likely he would have found himself an isolated part of the area.

"I'm an old friend of the family," lied Donna. "We're still in shock about Pedro's death; that's why I'm here actually, and I know the Georges sold their cottage years ago, but I had a request from Mrs. George to visit Pedro's cottage friends when I passed through. They did mention the name . . . " She feigned shortness of memory.

"The Wilsons?" said the boy with long brown hair.

"Yeah! That's it," said Donna, feeling at once guilty and cunning with her deception.

"They were neighbours of the Georges," said the boy.

"Yeah, that's them. I'm a little spaced from the long drive," said Donna.

"Do you need a boatride out to their place?" asked the blond. Both boys thought they were charming the pants off Donna and smiled to show it.

"You know, you guys are too much. You're sure it's no trouble?" Donna couldn't believe her luck; everything for the moment seemed to be falling into place. But where was Pedro?

She parked her old car and followed the boys down to the dock. The blond boy steered; the other sat in the middle; and Donna stationed herself in the bow where she faced them with her little canvas pack between her legs. The cruise out of the bay and into the open channels and islands was Donna's first experience of being on open water and a welcome relief from the hot sweaty Toronto summers. How invigorating and at the same time relaxing was this combination of lake spray and warm sun!

They entered a sheltered bay and drove up beside a large dock that jutted out into the water from the front of a cottage. Outside, a group of young people were sunning and lounging. Obviously, Donna thought, her escorts, Mike and Tom, wanted to show her off to their peer group. She would seem to fit right in with cut-offs and a vintage Grateful Dead T-shirt. The girls were friendly, and the boys, vainglorious. Mike and Tom smiled beatifically in their triumph and offered Donna a beer, which she accepted gratefully.

After a few introductions and their attendant banalities, Donna brought talk around to the Georges' supposed mission and sought what she wanted from a large framed, brown haired girl, Kelly Wilson. Her brother Tim, who was due back shortly from the landing where he had gone an hour or so earlier, had known Pedro.

While she waited, Donna relaxed over a beer and answered the teens' questions about how she knew Pedro. They supposed she had come from Europe. Then she extracted some more information from Kelly, who reminisced about when she was a little girl and remembered Pedro coming to their dock once with his girlfriend Sadie. "They were different, so . . ." Words escaped her. "Awesome," she resumed. "I was just seven or eight; actually, he was the perfect idol, as far as I was concerned." She told how she used to watch him roll cigarettes. "I was mesmerized. A few years later, someone told me he did something very bad — something to do with selling some dirt about a family to a national magazine. Then he left the country, I think. Never saw him again."

Donna ruminated in the sunshine on all that she was hearing, forgetting momentarily her reason for being there; she rather enjoyed the casual knowledge these teenagers had about Pedro. Pedro was becoming more real, a human being with a past; however, some of the cryptic things he had said to her before he left rose like a wavering discoloration in the air before her: "not long for this world," "on a dream that began thousands of years ago," "I am not a Hyperborean," "Gorgon — that takes on infinite appearances," "the Battle of the Trees." All this now seemed to border on lunacy. On this hot dock far away from the realities of life, why not just enjoy the cold beer and forget all that other heaviness, thought Donna.

"What's a Hyperborean?" she asked.

"A what?" said Mike.

"A Hyperborean. It's a word Pedro used once."

"Sounds definitively boring," said Tom.

They looked at each other. Out of politeness, Kelly said she would look it up in the dictionary when she went to the cottage. Without saying so, the teens began to think that, if for the most part Donna was pretty cool, something about her was also not so cool; and if she had a weakness, thought the male members of the group, would it not be incumbent upon them to infiltrate her defences? Already Mike had positioned himself next to her as if staking out his territory. Donna was rather amused by all this. She asked for another beer.

Kelly brought one down and reached across Mike as she gave Donna the beer. "It's from the north," said Kelly. "A Hyperborean is from the north. They worship the sun and Apollo. Was Pedro into mythology?"

"Very much so," said Donna absentmindedly. She was trying to figure out why Pedro would say he wasn't a Hyperborean; it seemed a strange thing to say. And Pedro was the very antithesis of strange in a strange kind of way. Donna felt an electric rush travel from her head to her toes. A notion flashed through her. Someone was trying to kill him! Maybe an ex-lover! So he had to fake his death in order to escape. It was a little farfetched, but knowing Pedro . . . In that moment she thought that maybe he was Apollo.

"I must be dreaming," said Donna, looking across the water and gulping some beer.

"Dreaming about what?" said Mike. The others looked on. "Oh, sorry. I was thinking about something," she replied. Mike inched a bit closer. "Something Pedro said," she added hurriedly.

Kelly's brother, Tim, suddenly arrived in possession of a couple of cases of beer and groceries. Beaming at the enlivening effect he had on the teens and with his eyes on Donna, he addressed them like an MC: "Well, my young cadets, as your chaperone for the weekend, vouchsafed by our too kind parents, who are off sailing the north channel, as your purveyor of party refreshments, and as navigator through perilous night waters, I ask you now, are you ready for The Point tonight?" There was an immediate burst of approbation, then layered "yeahs." The boys jabbed the air with their fists. "All right! The Point!" Great, thought Donna, very clever — with unerring instinct she had stumbled into a party of underaged adolescents babysat by a delinquent twenty-four year old. "Are you going to come?" said Mike twice before she heard him.

"I might as well enjoy myself while I'm here," she said ironically. "Besides, I still haven't found what I'm looking for."

Mike's ears pricked up. "Yeah? What?"

"A ghost."

Donna del Rio sat on a shelf of rock at the outermost point of land, looking to the southwest over a vast expanse of Georgian Bay. The sun was still a hot, burgeoning ball with at least an hour left of life before the behemoth earth rolled over and blotted it from sight. The agitated water lapped fragrantly, yet with little wind; here and there a seagull swooped past on the lookout for handouts. There were at least two dozen young cottagers, a couple of locals, and Tim, brandishing his beer like a rock star with a microphone, ready to gust up into speeches at the slightest provocation. His excesses beheld a note of pathos; he pawned his integrity for the glory of the moment like a cracked piper. Donna felt Tim's eyes on her but wouldn't look back, and he was not the type to pursue his quarry. While the others became more and more drunk, Donna turned inexorably into a wallflower, watching them laugh and sway around the bonfire. By dark the girls and guys had paired off slightly in a natural selection, leaving the loners to roll reefers in their little heaven. Donna considered herself one of them, emulating their bliss, yet remaining straight and sober. She was the mysterious guest from the unknown who knew Pedro, who remained only a visage of their imaginations.

Mike, who had gone off with Kelly, had by now been forsaken by her for another boy who was strumming a guitar. Mike now returned to Donna, who out of gratitude for the help he had given her, let him sit by her near the fire with his arm around her. She had, however, to fight back a laugh at the hilarity of it all.

"Mike, why don't you try it on that girl over there. She's not with anyone." Donna pointed.

"No way," said Mike. "You're the most beautiful. Hey, haven't I shown you a good time?" He teetered and slurred.

He placed his hand on her breast. Donna shifted and laughed nervously, removing the hand.

"Hey babe, I know you want this. C'mon, lighten up." The hand returned to the breast. This time she didn't tolerate it, and shoved him.

"Mike, I have a boyfriend, you know."

"Too bad for him. Where is he?" He turned to her and kissed her on the mouth. Donna stood up abruptly, leaving him in a dizzy rapture.

"He's around here somewhere."

"You mean the ghost?"

Donna bit her lip. In frustration she got up to walk down the shore in search of a dark, quiet place to sit.

"Hope you find your ghost!" The adolescent voice pursuing her had a suffocated, humiliated sound. "Pedro's dead, you know!"

The thought resonated in Donna's head. She felt like a fool. A voice from the shadows spoke to her. It was Tim.

"Donna," he repeated, "Come here. I knew Pedro."

Donna hesitated. She could vaguely make him out on the rocks with a girl whom she hadn't met.

"Yes," said Donna, walking to him carefully.

Tim was smoking a splif of hash and handed it to the girl. They were holding each other.

"Sit down," he said, "Want a toke?"

"No, thank you," said Donna.

"Mike's being stupid," said the girl.

"Yeah," said Donna, "So you know-knew Pedro?"

"Yeah," said Tim, "I was here once when he was here. I was about fourteen. He was a great guy. I'm really depressed about his death, a real tragedy."

"What was he like?" asked Donna without thinking.

"I thought you knew him."

"Well, I do-did, I mean. What was he like back then?"

"He was a philosopher; at least that's how I saw him. I thought he was like really smart; he kinda freaked me out. He was like . . . out there somehow; he scared me; he had a way of being rational. He brought out the good in people. I always tried to be big in his eyes, like grown-up; like I said, he was a great guy."

"Yeah, I know," said Donna, getting up.

"Where are you going?" asked Tim. "Stay with us."

"I wanna go for a stroll; I'll be fine."

She left the point and the party and kept walking down the shore, her eyes adjusting readily to the gentle, silvery light of the half-moon overhead. About a quarter mile down the shore she smelt smoke. She stopped and sniffed, then continued on until she came to the dark silhouettes of a couple of boats pulled up on the rocky beach. Inland, a small fire blazed, and emboldened by her unusual circumstances, she walked over to it.

Three men sat around the fire with illumed faces: two Native Americans, one of them old, and a white. To her astonishment, all three were naked and glistening with sweat. Her shock delayed any recognition. And as she approached, they politely covered themselves. Donna's ecstatic gaze drew a calm returned look of acquiescence, except from the young white man, who shot her a look of tender surprise. It finally registered within those fleeting moments. It was him. A silent thunderbolt fell and consumed her. He was not a ghost. He wasn't dead. He was very much alive, here, now on this very same patch of ground. Her legs gave away. The fire swirled. She could feel tears welling up from deep, deep within.

Chapter Six

A dream itself is but a shadow.
—Edward de Vere (Shakespeare/Oxford)

"So," resumed Augustus, sitting down again with a fresh ale, "I hope ye don't think I'm attempting to coerce the inspector in ye with this ale; besides, isn't this a grand day to simply sit and relax with ol' Bacchus, maybe tell a tale or two — heh heh heh! By your look, they didn't tell ye this ol' goat liked his ale!"

"'Fraid it was something we must have overlooked. I think I can handle it though; one doesn't often get to swash an ale or two with an eccentric old hermit who also happens to be an archaeologist working on probably the most exciting dig of the century; needless to say, you know the deceased, or should I say 'mysteriously ceased'?" David Thomas smiled in his beer. He abruptly had an intuition that both Augustus and Mrs. Willobie knew exactly what was going on, that Pedro was alive and well somewhere, and that it all had something to do with witchery. He recalled in a flash the umbrella in the Rover car and could have kicked himself for not suspecting that it had been used to depress the accelerator. But he was having too much fun for this seriousness just now, and there was so much more to learn. Besides, if Pedro was alive, there was no death, or homicide.

"You're a good man, Mr. Thomas, and I know you'll treat this incident with the utmost discretion," said Augustus guardedly.

"Do you think Mrs. Willobie would concur with this sentiment, Professor Woods?" asked Thomas, needling a thread into the seam of their rapport.

"Anne Willobie, God bless her, is a saint, though we aren't on the best of terms. She hasn't liked my company since her father died, which she took hard. Her own mother died of cancer thirty years ago. I have always had a weakness for Anne. Had I been a few years younger . . . but I'll see to it she'll be untouched by any . . . ill wind from your doings; these matters concern only the so-called 'deceased' and his lewd ways that have colluded with witchery to play out a damned pestilence upon all of us. Bad taste, I say. Bad taste." Augustus furrowed his brow, an act that made his eyes seem even more penetrating than usual. "I'll not have any scandal brought down upon us and this place. I think you are decent enough to understand that."

David Thomas kept a blank expression more from stupefaction than anything else; the professor seemed to have made an extraordinary admission between the lines and he wasn't quite sure how he was to react, knowing the professor's temperament. Thomas knew he couldn't yet lay any charge on these people; but he also knew that, when the cat got out of the bag, he might have to pull it down off the curtains, shredding as the cat clawed, although that in itself wasn't a problem as long as he could blame "this pestilence" on someone. He just hoped he and his department would not appear to be too incompetent in light of his initial report, not to mention the emotional chaos he had perpetrated by making official Mr. George's death.

"Yet Mrs. Willobie has certainly had an active role in these antics you insinuate," said David Thomas, stalwartly.

"Antics? My friend, you know not what is happening here. Even I am at a loss to fully comprehend. I can tell you Anne Fitzooth is a great woman. She takes on great responsibility in this area, notwithstanding the management of her vast property."

"Yes, yes, but how did this all come about? Who set the car off over the cliff? And where is Pedro now?" asked Thomas directly.

"The only thing I know is that Pedro didn't love Anne the way she loved him, and that is where it all begins. You see, Charles was away and rather a dull character anyway, nowhere near meeting the needs of Anne, who wanted children but was barren; I suppose they both put up walls that couldn't be breached; in fact, I very much doubt they'll be together before the year is out. When Pedro showed up one day about seven years ago, she found something to rejoice for in him, not that I condoned their behaviour. Pedro was naturally taken with this aloof debonair woman, and bent over backwards for her. This went on for a couple years until Hero showed up."

"Yes, this Hero was mentioned by Mrs. Willobie, not without some obvious rancour."

"Undoubtedly. But anyway, Pedro announced to Anne that their relationship as lovers was over. Charles happened to be home at the time, so the emotional fall-out was kept under wraps. Apparently, all went smoothly, but unfortunately Anne's hurt landed square on Hero's head. Hero, the younger more physically arousing, shall we say, played her cards very adeptly. Yet, for some reason, I could never fully trust her. Although I didn't approve of Anne's affair, neither did I see Hero as a good mate for Pedro; it seemed to me she was too good an actor, something too stereotypical. I don't know.

"I didn't fully comprehend this until more recently. In fact, I had only met Pedro on a few occasions, so how was I to judge, which was never my intention."

"When did you meet him?"

"It happened four or five summers ago. I was walking my usual jaunt down the path toward the Oak Forest to get to my rowboat I keep on the beach — I was doing a little exploratory digging at the old fortification at the time — well, I hear something; so I stop and listen. There was the natural clearing — at least up to that time I thought it was natural — the very same place you and I met, although it was only half as big then. Anyway, I walk along again and hear something moving up ahead in the bushes. I stop. Must be an animal or something, I tell myself. I peer through the foliage and see to my alarm a naked woman crawling around on all fours. She didn't see me. Well, talk about shock! I was about to confront her; I mean, here she was a stranger on private property and carrying on like that! Good lord! But I noticed after recovering myself that she was in some kind of deranged condition. She was drooling at the mouth, and while otherwise almost hugging the ground, had stuck her fanny up in the air quite provocatively. I confess, I was just so shocked I froze and didn't quite know what to do. There was this beguiling beauty, Hero, as I later found out her name, completely intoxicated on some kind of toadstool, crawling around on the forest floor with some vines wrapped around her head and shoulders. Coming to my senses, I again decided in no small way to reprimand this indecent behaviour, when out from a bush crawls Pedro sniffing like an animal: and up he goes behind her to mount her. At this point I just exited and walked home befuddled. Now, the next day I go down to find them encamped there with Niko and a black woman. The whole summer long, there they were, going to it, rutting day and night; I kept my distance mind you. Eventually I introduced myself — I have to admit a little intimidated by their proclivities — and, to my surprise, Pedro showed me the stones that you saw, only they were in their original positions; they had been on their side, covered with forest humus. Quite thoughtfully he went on to tell me about the cunny, and so forth. At first, I thought he was completely mad . . . he didn't know who I was or what I had witnessed there that summer." Augustus went off into a reverie.

Thomas swirled his half-mug and made an instinctive decision not to interrupt Augustus's truant thoughts.

"Did I mention the Ring of Power?" asked Augustus bluntly.

"Was it something you mentioned in the cave?"

"One evening I sat around with them by a good fire. Pedro was telling me about the Roebuck, Lapwing, and Dog, (a story that I had known through research) and how they guarded the secret of life — which is simply a way of describing the unnamed: in ancient times to have one's God (his or her name, that is) revealed to enemies was tantamount to self-destruction. Well, Pedro claimed that he, Hero, and Niko had been reincarnated from the Ring or Triad of Power, a supernatural aureole in the space-time continuum so to speak, that dates back thousands of years. This may have happened many times, but he had vivid recollections of two particular times: once as uprooted Trojan warriors from the second millennium B.C. and the other in post-Roman Britain. The Roebuck, Lapwing, and Dog are totems representing spiritual allies which in themselves are used in various forms by aboriginal people all over the world. To early peoples the mystery of life was no less compelling, of course, than it is for us; however, the method of interpreting and worshipping it has gone through many transitional leaps. The advent of Christianity brought about the transition of the 'moral' integrity of society. In pagan society it seems that moral judgements were precluded by the domain of the Gods and spirits which were figuratively shown respect and humility. The people were very much the instruments of the Gods. Do we not have the same parallels today? Well, in this little microcosm of the Ring of Power, we have yet another panacea to the strains of the cosmic dirge, the premise of which, as always, is that a particular quality of life has to be sanctified and preserved in order to survive intact. And how, you will ask, does this relate to Pedro? Well, he told me he was the Roebuck, Hero the Lapwing and Niko, the Dog. In essence, the Roebuck is the fable's ever-illusive, never-in-sight, most respected prey — yes, prey and ultimately doomed; he represents the vanguard of the secret of life — humanity's nerve centre — the very juncture of man the animal and divine aspirations, indeed the primary source of us all within us all. Running from all baseness, he does succumb, not to baseness, but to the hunter's spear, which in effect, is the human condition. Impaled on this, he is a prize, a trophy, a divine catch for all to see, venerate and mythologize. As such, he reveals our worst self and our best; in him we have an example to supervene. He dies so that the secret remains undiscovered — that is, the truth about the unnamed, namely we, us, those who have given names to everything, including the concept of God.

"Hero, on the other hand, is supposedly the Lapwing, the protectress: to protect is to manipulate; the secret is safe with her; she misses nothing and would do anything to preserve the sanctity of the Roebuck's impending martydom. She would deceive and destroy to hold true this purpose. She, therefore is not necessarily to be trusted.

"Then we have the Dog, Niko, the final defense, the true guard. As a physical and earthly power, none is so strong as the loyalty of the dog; he is the fabric from which the whole tapestry is made, and no coarse linen, but woven of the finest silk. If he is called upon, woe betide his adversary, who will be torn to bits. But without Pedro and by extension, Hero, his purpose is unresolved and fragmented. His duty is to serve the highest cause and only then will his power become manifest. But what is the crucible of all that this entails? Without exception or appeal, the Roebuck must sacrifice himself and die; to do so is his irrevocable fate. In the past, this was literally and ritualistically so, whereas today it is cloaked in a more subtle disclosure. Indubitably, the process, a natural one, is like the turning of the seasons or the change from dawn to dusk.

"Now you may ask, how does it happen that what initially begins as a seemingly innocent novelty, or arcane fixation of an extraordinary mind, self-abnegates into what must appear to the average layman as something akin to curdled cheese, i.e., pagan hogwash? What a defrocking of such noble charisma! Well, I'll tell you, I truly thought he was mad until he showed me the cave and actual burial chamber which he had discovered but which he himself had failed to decipher. When I studied the site, I was astounded because after reading the obscure Ogham lettering on the burial chamber wall, I realized everything Pedro had said was true; it was all there. Please let that sink in. It was all there — everything: the journey from Troy, the Battle of the Trees, his two deaths." Augustus stopped abruptly.

"Very intriguing," said Thomas, becoming increasingly less sceptical. He finished off his ale.

"So," went on Augustus, "how does this relate to this death of Pedro? Pedro, you see, was active in Annie Fitzooth's witches' coven. They needed him as their Horned God in their sabbaths, you know, Beltane and Halloween and the solstices and equinoxes, and so forth. Well, from this point on, I know little, and he didn't tell me much; but I'm inclined to think there was something between Hero and the coven, who felt Hero was perverting Pedro. Hero, of course, felt that if she couldn't belong to the coven — I think they feared her, actually — then the coven must have been perverting Pedro. It's all so damned banal and petty, but this is what you get when there is crossed love and emotions between very powerful sorceresses. Now, Inspector, if you choose to pursue this, you will, have to speak to those involved, namely Annie Fitzooth and Brigid Pyles, the old High Priestess — she's a good deal older than I. Christ, she looked old when I was a kid; she must be pushing a hundred or more. Lastly, you must see young Gwendolyn, the maiden of the coven, who works for Mrs. Willobie and me occasionally. She has spent a good deal of time camping with Pedro and his friends. I believe she kept Mrs. Willobie well informed of the goings-on. So, there you have it, my friend. Tread carefully among those witches; they might cast a terrible spell on you! Heh heh heh heh!"

"Do you think it is possible they faked his death?" asked Thomas, subtly dropping the question. "And if so," he added, "where did he go? Do you think he left the country?"

"Don't know. Don't care. I know one thing: Niko's father, Hermes Metropoulos, is a freighter captain who comes to Cardiff once in a while."

"Lord knows where he might be," said Thomas, looking down the valley.

"Poor Pedro," said Augustus, looking downcast. "I don't think he had anything to do with this, but it's been foretold; some things are inevitable."

"That's a rather cryptic thing to say, professor."

Augustus, too, stared out over the valley.

"By the way, Dr. Woods, who is Turketul?" asked Thomas, remembering the enigmatic poem Mrs. Willobie had shown him.

"Turketul? Why he was a knight errant in the ninth century who resurrected King Arthur's knights of the Round Table into the knights of the Grail. This was the beginning of a highly exclusive order that evolved down the centuries like the Templars. In effect, they were, I believe, an outbranch of the Ring of Power that purported to uphold the precepts of both Christianity and the ancient Celts, King Arthur's people. Pedro used to talk about Arthur. Why do you ask?" said Augustus, turning to face his guest.

"It was in a poem by Pedro that Mrs. Willobie showed me."

"I haven't seen that one. Good excuse for a visit." The professor turned to the valley again.

David Thomas decided it was time to leave, but just as he was about to go, Professor Woods turned to him again.

"Inspector," he said, "before you go, I think I should add that Pedro is a rare and exceptional human being; he's a bit like Hamlet, ambivalent, torn between his knowledge and the lack of fortitude necessary to carry through his convictions. As the result of this inconstancy, his belief in himself suffers. He runs from himself, his death, the irony being that he knows: it's as if a part of him is detachedly watching another part from a poetic height. Some felicitous bemusement scans the venue of his own humanity as it embarks on a collision course with tragedy." Augustus paused, then finished, "'Tis the way of the world."

The sea was a seething mass of grey tones breaking on the clammy beach under a low and forbidding cover of grey sky. The Hairy Man sat off to the side in one of his peculiar moods. He was fearful, fearful of the sea and the north, in which direction they now faced, looking out across that turbulent water between Gaul and Albion.

They had taken two months since the battle with the Gorgonians to cross Gaul from south to north, travelling over the high country of the Central Massif and into the verdant forests of Burgundy; then they reached the Seine and the Island Town of the Celts that one day, two thousand years in the future, would support Notre Dame Cathedral of Paris. They were actually treated with some reverence because of the motley nature of their band, which varied from the beauty of Sarah still in her Goddess tunic to the frightening ugliness of the Hairy Man, whom Troylus and Aeneas called Carbuncle from a mispronunciation of his real name. Luckily, Sarah was able to understand a smattering of the language, impeded in this endeavour only by the idiosyncrasies of her Ligurian vernacular. With the lines of communication open, they were able to tell their stories of travel and battle to the people who made fascinated listeners. In return, the people told them of an island off a section of the north coast of Gaul. This island was solely the domain of women who had been cast out or orphaned or had escaped from some tyranny. One of their hosts, a big boned man, suggested that they could start their new tribe with these women if they could be convinced. Troylus and Aeneas shot each other a fervent look of hope that the Gods had answered their most pious prayers. Sarah and the Hairy Man, on the other hand, were not so enthusiastic, seeing only a conversion of the Gorgonian male oligarchy into one of women.

The Celts had given them a small sea-worthy bark that now lay pulled up on the beach. Beside it were furs, hides, and dried foodstuffs such as meat, grains, herbs and fruit; there were also miscellaneous supplies for fishing, weaving, and other necessary activities. Patiently, they sat waiting for the tide to come in, with a small fire going and water boiling in a small metal cauldron — something they had shown the Celts how to forge with their advanced metallurgy. (In fact, they had exchanged knowledge for goods — for example, grains from which a gruel of crushed wheat cooked, into which Sarah now threw beets for a sweetener.)

Tethered on a grassy knoll was a she-goat with her kid; also grazing nearby were a young ram and ewe watched over by the Hairy Man. At the latter's side, procured in exchange for medicine, gamboled a young calf, which rubbed its head from time to time on his spear arm. Such was his natural affinity with animals.

The Hairy Man had proved to be of tremendous service not only in saving Aeneas's life, but throughout their travels in Gaul where he expatiated on the virtues of the flora and fauna of his native habitat. Along the way, too, he had entertained them with the story of his life and how he was the sole survivor of his tribe, which had been exterminated by the Gorgonians. The rugged mountains and gorges of the Cevennes west of Ariadne's temple had been his home. His people had lived there for countless generations, from long before any migratory influx out of the east. They had been killed because they were different looking — more exactly, their bodies, even the women's, had an unusually thick coat of hair. Although they were thought to be abominable, they were a passive, agrarian people with advanced knowledge of curative powers. In no time, through the use of particular roots and plants, Carbuncle had healed both Troylus's and Aeneas's severe wounds, enabling them to quickly put much distance between themselves and the Gorgonian search bands. Even when they came to unfamiliar lands, Carbuncle could guide them from his second-hand knowledge of certain landmarks or regions.

Sarah stirred the cauldron, contented in their present wealth of goods and peaceful coexistence. She was pregnant, the most wonderful thing that had ever happened to her. Troylus, the father, too, was overjoyed and exuded the virility of a biblical patriarch. Their lovemaking had taken on such a significant delight in their travels that daily, time was methodically if silently given sway. Only Aeneas was feeling the strain, as his cohort had slackened his fervent warrior's edge, which had to be made up for, notwithstanding Aeneas' own sexual yearnings prompted by Sarah's fantastic appeal. Nevertheless, he had never let down his guard and would suffer to the death for those whom he deemed his king and queen.

Looking out across that grey expanse, they wondered what to expect upon settling on the island. In the long run, they meant to go farther north, to Cambria, as they had heard or been told of a land there rich in pasture and forest and in rivers teeming with fish; a multitude of wild game, birds, and beasts too were spoken of. Also, these new lands would undoubtedly be wild, and nothing short of building a castle to protect themselves was their ultimate goal.

Sarah brimmed with happiness at the prospect of the kingdom they would find and her own contemplated role as its queen. During her bizarre tenure as Ariadne she had had many hours to herself; this solitude had led to her need for personal fulfilment of some kind. She loved to sing, and consequently, had made up many songs, some of which she had sung for the Gorgonians. Delighted, the Gorgonians had bestowed upon her the greatest of compliments, adopting her as the mother not only of life and love but of song and festivals. In this she had found a little solace and compensation for her bondage; but now she sang with the ardour of a freedom so exalted, both Troylus and Aeneas were abashed when she so expressed herself, as she had done for the various tribes they had encountered in their recent journey. Little did they realize, had it not been for her gentle, loving disposition, they might not have come nearly as far as they had, unscathed. Even now, stirring the porridge, she sang in that soft lyrical voice. Only the Hairy Man fully appreciated the radiant beauty of her gift and always tilted his head toward her as she sang:

> *Oooooolaaaeeehhhwaaaay*
> *Oooooolaaaeeehhhwaaaay*
> *The wind is soft on my face,*
> *The sun smiles on my lips,*
> *The water cools my mouth,*
> *I am nature's favoured friend,*
> *I am a lover's certain friend,*

I walk the earth,
I walk the earth.
Oooooolaaaeeehhhwaaaay
Oooooolaaaeeehhhwaaaay
My body will ease your sorrow,
My child will heal your pain,
My breasts will give you life,
You will find me in the meadow,
You will see me by the fountain,
I seek your love,
I seek your love.
Oooooolaaaeeehhhwaaaay
Oooooolaaaeeehhhwaaaay
You have known my ancient dance,
You have sought my willowy wisdom,
You have taken me in innocence,
I have fallen from the altar,
I have given all my lonely life,
I am a simple-hearted woman,
I am lorn from love and strife.
Oooooolaaaeeehhhwaaaay
Oooooolaaaeeehhhwaaaay

They entered the mist a short while after they lost sight of land. Holding their tack, they sailed in a north-westerly direction. Sarah had wrapped herself in a woollen shawl; both Aeneas and Carbuncle watched the surf and mist for any hint of dangerous rocks. Supposedly, the island was a good day's sail, and they had been out there ten hours. They had been warned that only on the lee side of the island, away from the prevailing westerlies was beaching possible.

Troylus stood at the tiller in a state of tense determination. He was a gifted navigator, for he could read the stars. In his twenty-two years he had sailed much of the known world. Troylus had a strong feeling that this Island of Women was the perfect stronghold in which to begin a tribe. If the women there bore sons, in time they could have a potent little force with which to settle in the mythical land called Cambria. This was his vision.

Suddenly, the waves began to break and the bark was surfing obliquely over a trough below which rocks could easily be seen. Troylus gripped the tiller firmly to hold the surfing craft above the trough, but another big wave came upon them and swept their craft along with it. Just then, miraculously, the fog lifted and a ray of sun transfixed them as the large wave rolled them gently into the bay of an island that rose up before them like a green vision of paradise.

Silently, as if in a dream, they drifted in to the shore. There they all jumped out and could not contain their brimming emotions. Troylus swung Sarah around in ecstatic abandonment; they all hugged. They had found a home. The sun was warm behind a big blue hole in the sky above them. Turning with a shudder from the sea, over which the wall of mist remained lodged like a magic shroud, and looking about, they saw groves and natural meadows good for pasturing, a small stream, suitable places to make shelter, but not a sign of the wild women nor of any human activity.

In order to pull the bark up past the high tide mark, they had to unload their little craft: the sheep, goats, and calf thus freed, soon found the edge of the vegetation and began to feed upon the rich verdant grasses that greeted them. The Hairy Man and Sarah prepared a makeshift campsite while Troylus and Aeneas went exploring.

At the summit of some high bluffs to the west of their landing site, the two men scanned the coast as far as they could see. The size of the shore's curve to the north gave them an idea of how big their new home was. The island, however, was much less lush at that end with sparse grasses and fewer, scragglier trees. Finding no sign of human life, they backtracked and went inland further; the women, they decided, must be at the far end to the northeast.

The rough terrain along their route gave way once again to a gentler landscape with groves and meadows in which numerous springs watered a seemingly endless abundance of wild flowers. Upon exiting a grove of trees almost large enough to be a small forest, they found a well-trodden pasture. In the distance a young woman was tending a flock of sheep.

Before they had a chance to show themselves, they were jabbed in the back by two spears. Both Troylus and Aeneas had their guard down, anticipating domestic, even docile, women ready to accept them ardently. Now, two strong, lean, hardened women with tight leather protective covering on their chests had them face down on the turf. In another instant they were relieved of their weapons, and a coarse rope bound their hands behind their backs.

Once the shock of being captured had worn off and they had seen their women captors, they began to smile again, notwithstanding their tarnished pride. They were thus marched past the shepherdess, who seemed more the type of woman they envisaged, as she eyed them with a knowing smirk on her face. Maybe their arrival was a common occurrence, in which case their anticipated subjection this strange women's tribe might cost them more than they had expected. Would they have done better to heed the Celts after all?

After walking through a deep forest and across some meadows, they reached the sea again. This bay was much bigger than the one in which they had disembarked. A path skirted the beach along a bluff. Finally, they came to a well-guarded little hamlet of stone homes with thatched roofs and gardens. Along the way a few people babbled incomprehensible things to them.

The women who had captured them were tall and blond, and spoke a harsher tongue than they had ever heard; however, on their arrival at the head woman's home, they were surprised to meet a soft-spoken, dark haired woman who spoke Phoenician, a Mediterranean language known to its sailors, and consequently a language of which both Troylus and Aeneas had a relatively complete working knowledge.

"My, aren't we far from home," she said. "Trojans, and aristocrats at that." She noticed the exquisite armour and family motto on the chest plate.

"We come in peace," said Troylus, looking about and liking the community instantly. Here and there played a few children of various ages, but if there were any men, he had not seen them.

"No man comes here in peace," she shot back with a laugh. "Are you alone?"

"There is my woman and a servant," said Troylus.

"We know. We saw you come. We have been expecting you. I wanted to be sure you were sincere. Come, are you hungry, noble ones?" She had an ironic abject look in her warm face.

They were untied and given tender lamb with an assortment of succulent vegetables. Little did they know that the hospitality shown them had serious ramifications. While they feasted, the women eyed them hungrily and laughed at their apparent fearlessness; only the head woman, whose name was Vera, seemed calm and collected. For a long while she stared, then said, "We get few male visitors." Troylus and Aeneas took no heed; they felt superlative as they knew they had found a home.

Hero's descent down the hill into Birch Island from the north was as steady and controlled as that of a seasoned racer. At the bottom, the BMW purred to a stop by the dockside landing, then idled for a moment to cool down and fell silent when Hero shut it off. They all got out and stretched and shook their legs from the five hour drive. Had they arrived a couple hours earlier, they could have joined Donna del Rio in the boat with Mike and Tom. As it was, Hero looked about furtively for telltale signs or in the hope of unexpectedly spotting Pedro. While waiting for her, Niko stayed cool by sauntering over to the water's edge and refreshing himself with the thought of its delicious quality in the form of a swim. Sadie and Ronald went into the store and bought cold drinks for everone.

Now, leaning against the car, they sought refuge from the sun's grilling heat in the sweet coldness of their Cokes and Sprites. Having reached their destination from such a bold beginning under the command of Hero, (most noticeably not her usual imperturbable self), they felt themselves further exempted from normal behavior by the hot, torpid sun. The death of Pedro had turned their whole modus topsy-turvy irrespective of any circumstance. Ronald, ironically, had replaced his earlier fustiness with an adventurous bonhomie; in fact, his energy was a little overpowering, and one got the impression that, given half a chance and nightfall, he might have glowed in the dark. His jet of radiance was a curious contrast to the dark and restrained knot of Hero's nervous tension which was like a coiled spring. Sadie, having watched her drive all the way from the back seat, sensed this, as indeed did Niko, who knew better, of course, than to interfere. While they were there, for whatever reason, they thought they might just as well enjoy themselves. She watched as Ronald's glance kept coming to rest on Hero and knew he was still enraptured by her Venusian presence, notwithstanding her strange mood. Yet she felt no jealousy or resentment; in fact, her knowledge relieved her, gradually solidifying into the conviction that something about her own relationship with Ronald was not right. For some time she'd been repressing this idea. Pedro's death and the arrival of Hero and Niko brought it all out; she knew now that she would soon have to come clean one way or another.

"This is great!" said Ronald, "I don't know why we came up here, but I feel great, all thanks to you, Hero." He stood beside her, attempting to get her undivided attention. Niko and Sadie looked at each other as Hero ignored him. "So now that we're here, how in hell do we know who we're looking for?" continued Ronald. "If she was just coming here to camp, no one here would know her either. Let's face it, she could be out on some island somewhere and we'll never find her. So what? I knew that when we left. Why don't we get some supplies and do the same. We'll have a blast! Sadie?"

"Yes?" she said, without enthusiasm.

"Where's the best place to get some camping stuff and food?"

But before she could respond, he went on: "Hey, Niko what do you think? Hero? Come on! Where's that Caerymwy spirit? We'll light a campfire and drink a few beers, or how about some wine? It'll be in Pedro's honour. How about it, our final wake! Just us!" Ronald focused on Hero again. "You're a genius, Hero; you knew this all along, didn't you? His closest friends up here alone camping In Memoriam!" Ronald brandished his Sprite. "All right! Pedro! Come on! Why are you all so repressed? Isn't this why we're here?"

"No," said Hero with candid finality. She now gave Ronald the undivided attention he had been craving; but by boring a hole through his head with her inscrutable eyes, rather than rejoicing with him, oddly enough she caused him to shut up for a few minutes.

"Well then, maybe you should tell us why we are here," he said at last. "Surely Donna del Rio can't figure in it. Where is she? Why don't you listen to common sense and let us do what I suggested." His tone had changed and was now mature and responsible.

"Ronald's right, Hero," said Niko, attempting to sidestep Hero's true conundrum vis-à-vis Pedro and her relationship which he felt was sadly and irretrievably over. Furthermore, he needed more time to convey gently to them the reality of their being there if he could just let them know innocuously somehow that, if it were possible, Pedro would simply resurrect himself before them all. Pedro would characteristically take it upon himself at that point to interpose with an appealing exposition of the politics of life after death. Niko knew Pedro would show up; he just didn't know when or where. Sadie, of course, might know a little about the area. "Sadie, do you have any idea where four outsiders could stay, some comfortable solitary space provided, of course." He looked at Hero. "We are all in agreement and we may procure a few supplies which I would be more than willing to pay for."

"We'll go halves," said Ronald eagerly.

"I think I know a place we can stay," said Sadie. She paused, looking at Hero, who was in such a strange mood she hesitated to go on. Her feminine intuition told her that Hero's intensity arose from jealousy, and the source of this was obviously Donna del Rio.

"Where?" said Ronald impatiently.

"There used to be a cabin, owned by the native band, that they'd rent near Dreamer's Rock," said Sadie, remembering her days there with Pedro, "but we'd have to see the chief."

It seemed like a sensible thing to do. They all looked at Hero. Naturally, Ronald jumped in.

"Well, what of it, St. Germain? Are the stars in accord? Well? Don't looked so damned serious. You were the one who brought us here."

"Yes I did, didn't I?" she said, turning to them now with a smile on her face. "I apologize for my mood; I just had to dig down in my lonesome soul and do a little scouring. And, you know? Everything's all right. Pedro's free to do as he pleases; that's the way it is." She laughed, patting her thigh with her hand. "Did you know?" she went on, seeming to laugh and cry simultaneously, "Did you know we were together in past lives? Yes, and Niko, vouch for me."

"Yes, it's true," said Niko, though noncommitally as he calmly watched the boats in the bay.

"But then we lost each other because he was always killed; and so it happens again." Hero circled out in front of them. "You see, this time, twentieth-century style, he doesn't just die and be done with it. Oh no, thanks to me, he comes back to life! Pedro lives! He's out there!" She swept her arm out across the expanse of the water as if casting a spell. "Isn't he, Niko? He's out there!"

"He could be," said Niko surprised at her sudden revelations. He had assumed that there would be a scandal when Pedro reappeared and that he, Niko, would have to do a lot of fast talking. Yet here was Hero, sounding like a madwoman, blowing the whistle herself. However, for that reason maybe it just wouldn't wash; no one would believe her.

"So all we must do," said Hero, "is wait for him. He'll come tomorrow evening. Meanwhile, let's go to this cabin at Dreamer's Rock; you know, where else would he come, but Dreamer's Rock?"

"St. Germain, you really are out of your mind, aren't you?" exclaimed Ronald. "You've always got some goddam rabbit to pull out of a hat, but this takes the cake!" Ronald broke out into cynical laughter. Hero and Niko smiled like gratified children. By contrast, Sadie, who thought Hero must be experiencing a nervous disorder, was less than charmed by her boyfriend's levity.

"Ronald, do shut up," she said, in a burst of impatience.

"Give me a break, Sadie! Hero just said Pedro is alive out there somewhere!" said Ronald, irritably.

Avoiding eye contact, Sadie looked out at the rippling waters again.

"And what's this lunacy about past lives?" resumed Ronald. "Christ, we're having enough trouble with the present one! Who needs a shitload of bad karma from who knows where?"

"You're right Ronald," said Hero. "Let's just go camping and have a blast; to hell with Pedro. If he wants to join us, hey, then we'll really have a time of it!"

"Now you're talking," said Sadie, relaxing in the comfort of Hero's supposed esoterics.

They went to find the chief who lived across the highway on another bay. After a couple of sets of directions and a tour of Birch Island including, near the lake, a rusty stretch of railway track on which Franklin Delano Roosevelt once apparently had his train car parked for three days during the Second World War, they found the chief who gave them permission to use the cabin near Dreamer's Rock. Sadie asked after Big Dan, who was the only Indian she remembered from the early days with Pedro. Big Dan was an artist and had a small gallery in Little Current, said the chief, adding that he hadn't any idea where Big Dan might be; he knew only that he lived above the gallery. Hero then asked if Pedro George was anywhere around. The chief replied soberly: "Don't know him."

In Little Current they stocked up liberally on food, and got some sleeping bags and assorted other supplies for a couple of days. Sadie then made a telephone call to Connie to cancel their tennis game. Afterward, they found the old, narrow window front to Big Dan's gallery. The Indian woman inside didn't know where he was but suggested they come back in the morning.

The cabin, or lodge, which was situated at the end of a long narrow bay on a point, was made from huge pine logs; it was spacious and able to accommodate at least a dozen people comfortably. Inside was a good sized fireplace, and a few other bare necessities, including beds and mattresses, a decent kitchen and firewood.

Across the bay, Dreamer's Rock rose three hundred feet above the water in a little round mountain. It's sides were decked with wreaths of white pines clinging tenaciously onto smooth white quartzite rock. From the cabin, the top looked like the giant hump of an albino mammoth. Dreamer's was surrounded by water, little bays and channels belonging to a larger maze of islands that opened up to the expansive waters of the north channel of Georgian Bay.

Once settled into the cabin, a process which took about five minutes, they decided to walk down the shore toward the open end of the bay in search of a suitable place to swim. (At the cabin, occasional band members and tourists would show up on hikes prior to or after climbing up to the Rock. The importance of the place was attested to by a cedar pole structure for native ceremonies that stood at the base of Dreamer's on an isthmus.)

Hero was first to shed her clothes and dive in. Ronald then whooped in unabashedly, followed more carefully by Niko and Sadie. Immersed in the glimmering blueness, cooling off from the sweaty heat and washing away the lethargy of hours of highway driving was truly a nirvanic undertaking requiring all their attention. They all drifted and dove, gladly oblivious of their previous cares, the metaphysics of time travel, and even the ramifications of a mystic Pedro, dead or alive. Eventually pulling themselves out and stretching naked on the bank, they let the sun dry the glistening water from their bodies. Sadie was becoming keenly aware of Ronald's infatuation with Hero, as he lay down beside Hero without so much as a look her way. For the moment, she didn't mind that much; Niko, who sensed her predicament, was being very supportive in a silent way. Meanwhile, Hero remained heedless of the chemistry at work in the cluster of bodies about her.

Sadie, lying there in silence, hearing only the wind sifting through the pines and smelling the aromatic scent in the water forgot her immediate need to worry about her and Ronald's newly ascertained polarity. She understood what Hero brought out in him: that kind of sparring he so thrived on, which she was incapable of mimicking. They had always had a working rapport; she in her quiet diligence, and Ronald Morgan, in his extroverted, materialistic self-indulgence. Sadie took a lighthearted view: he was easy, an automatic response, rather than some obscurity one was forever deciphering. In fact, she now saw that her relationship with him was very much a long-term rebound from the intensity of Pedro that had left her spinning and unresisting. Ronald then had simply moved in and taken her by main force. Pedro had at least let her come to him. How antipodal the two men were! Ronald had always been intimidated and controlled by Pedro's charisma. And now, with Hero, there was an opportunity for him to be consummately drawn. There was Hero, naked, pink-nippled, with beads of water clinging to her, her knees bent, legs slightly parted . . . and Ronald — you could almost read his thoughts like a running monologue on an information screen.

Later, over a meal of barbecued chicken and salad, as they lay out on the rocks by the cabin, they were wondering aloud what to do. Hero still talked as though Pedro were alive, yet offered no explanation for this belief. The idea became even more farcical with Ronald's exasperating rejoinders. Having initially revealed the truth as if from the throes of delirium, she now threw out crumbs of the same sort to antagonize Ronald for fun. Niko marvelled at how ironic it all was: when Pedro did show up, her own cock-eyed "wishful thinking" could still be perceived as innocent of complicity, yet eventually there would be a reckoning. Hopefully, he would be back in London before then.

"Pedro is with Big Dan," said Hero, stuffing her mouth with salad and pretending not to be interested in anyone's reaction to her words.

"Obviously. Who else would he be with?" asked Ronald, manoeuvering salaciously. "And when he shows up, I'm going to take him aside . . . and let him have a piece of my mind — the impertinence, the self-centredness — then finish him off myself. Think of it," he philosophized. "If he were alive, could any of you still consider him your friend? You see, Hero, Pedro would never do that. I'm being perfectly serious here; he was a true gentleman who considered others before himself." Ronald stopped, proud of having expressed such sentiments.

"Oh, Ronald," said Hero in a half sigh, convincing him that she had submitted to his point of view. Niko and Sadie began laughing.

"I think I'm going to hike up to Dreamer's Rock after supper," said Hero then, in the same docile way. "How does that appeal to you all?"

No one responded.

Sadie, by now sufficiently disturbed by Ronald, had examined his character from various angles. Owing to her passively tenacious instinct and loyalty to their engagement, she laughed nervously but said: "That's it. Ronald, I've had enough."

Ronald turned to her. "'Nough of what?"

"Enough of your preaching. Let Pedro alone; for God's sake, if he were alive, no matter how, we'd be overjoyed; Christ, it'd be a miracle. Now stop harping on it. We're supposed to be celebrating!" she said with growing impatience.

"Yeah, yeah, I'm just trying to get a handle on all this," he said, making a concession to Sadie's discomfort. "Sorry. Okay?"

"You know, Ronald," said Sadie, "being here with Niko and Hero makes me feel really wonderful; I feel we can say or do anything and be completely relaxed with each other. It's as if Pedro's spirit were hovering over us. Maybe this Donna del Rio is doing the same thing. Maybe Pedro is really here with us right now; Hero seems to think so. This could be what this is all about, not some power-tripping patronizing. Yes, I realize you just want things to be right, in other words, under your control, but that's not possible; you haven't the foggiest notion of what could really be happening here. It's like . . . I don't know what I'm really trying to say . . . but it's like . . . Jane Dawson."

"Jane Dawson?" said Ronald, cringing.

Jane Dawson was the pseudonymous writer of the article which exposed the Morgan family as having descended from criminal ancestors, that Pedro took responsibility for.

"Yes, and Pedro wouldn't say who she was."

"Yeah, so?"

"You're looking at her."

"What! You? You were Jane Dawson?" he said, aghast.

"I never told you because at the time I only wanted to do what I thought was a favour to Pedro; the article demonstrated his expertise as a genealogist and my revulsion for your family's past. Jane Dawson became my alter-ego. Actually, Jane Dawson still resents your family, even though there was something that really turned me on about you when we made our first strained efforts to get to know each other — your underdog sensitivity or something. I almost think I went with you because I wanted to hurt Pedro after he and I broke up and this grew into a dependency that somehow fed my needs. It was immature of me, Jane Dawson, or what you will. I've been so stupid! What I didn't realize then makes me squirm now. You represented something so foreign to my nature, so offensive, I actually enjoyed it in a perverse kind of way; that was the basis of my love. I just want to say I'm sorry for deceiving you; I mean, I really didn't consciously deceive you. I just didn't know myself very well."

"And you do now?" he replied, not knowing what to say.

"Yes, I think so."

"You think so? You just told me I'm repulsive and offensive!"

"I meant your ancestors. And I'm just saying this to get things out in the open. I still believe you're different. We're still engaged to be married and I'm not calling it off or anything."

"But you don't love me," he said, embarrassed.

Moments passed. She became silent and uncomfortable.

"Well, let's call it off then," he said, struggling to conceal his hurt feelings.

"Okay." The finality made her voice husky, tremulous.

"Hey, you two," chipped in Niko, "I'm with Hero; let's watch the sun go down up there on that rock. No need to hash it out just yet. We need a little more colour in the sky, the dramatic background you know. Too much talk, too little action. So let's go."

They actually all laughed. Niko stood up then and helped Hero to her feet, the latter appearing not to have heard any of what had taken place. "You know, what we really need now," he suggested, "is some gentle benediction."

Back in a deep, dark part of the forest where the turf formed a thick carpet over the rock and maples grew abundantly, displacing the pine that dominated elsewhere, stood John Kineu, Big Dan, and Pedro stripped naked. It was night, and the fire that Big Dan had started cast a glowing light high above, on the green ceiling of leaves. There was something quintessentially aboriginal about standing there naked in the "forest primeval," mused Pedro, looking at his surroundings. It was beautifully warm and quiet, the stillness sundered only by the crackling of the fire. Just to the east of the fire stood the little round sweat lodge. About four feet high at the centre, it was covered in birch bark, cedar and pine branches. Underneath this roof was a plastic tarp that really kept the heat in.

John Kineu had told Pedro that, since he was still dead in the eyes of the world, he must enter the womb of Mother Earth, symbolized by the sweat lodge, and purify himself of all he had been encumbered with, in order to be born again and live naturally. According to John, Pedro was actually the spirit of Odaemin, who died to find out from the great spirit how to heal the people. The great spirit, in response, told him how to build a sweatlodge in which the people were to purge the evil spirits. Odaemin was thus given back life to heal his sick people. So it was that Pedro, too, must live to tell the people how to heal themselves and by extension, the sick world. They rubbed some sweetgrass smoke on their bodies in order to enter the sweatlodge as clean as possible. Then John Kineu said in Ojibwa a prayer so mellifluous it blended with the environs, synonymous with rustling leaves that occasionally stirred overhead. After, they each took a handful of crumbled cedar leaves and threw them in the fire which sent up, in token thanksgiving, a flurry of sparks into the night. Then they walked clockwise around the fire, and Pedro and John entered the pitch black of the interior of the sweatlodge. Big Dan remained outside as the Fire Keeper; he would bring in the seven, good sized, red hot rocks that would sit in a slight hole in the centre to heat the lodge. Already, in the darkness, Pedro's mind careened in a whirl of brightly coloured images that changed course with every dense boom resounding from John Kineu's mysteriously obtained little drum. The intermittent booms came at even intervals between wonderfully eloquent Ojibwa prayers. As Big Dan brought in each of the red hot stones, John Kineu told a story about the sun, the moon, the earth, the four winds — all had an important place in the evocation of spiritual life. Once all the stones had been placed in the center of the sweatlodge, Big Dan sat down to the right of the entrance across from John Kineu.

Pedro was at the back, in the centre, facing them. By the time the last stone had been placed, Pedro was hot and wondering how long they would be in there. He knew, however, that he must be strong and not succumb to the heat; he must show his friends he was worthy since they had attended so patiently to his extrication from his denouement, and indeed harboured his swirling soul which had burst in a way beyond even the sight of the wind.

In the pitch black, Pedro began to feel he was burning up. He could sense an ambiguity of gravity approaching vertigo. He made himself one with the heat, one with the sun: from the sun we come, from darkness to light, and from light to darkness we go. Pedro felt he didn't have a body any more; he was mere consciousness in the heat of the void. Boom! The drum sent a heartbeat of the universe through the black heat. Big Dan would sprinkle water on the stones, the hiss of the steam reminding him of mortal life. John would chant the native incantation: heyyyehh-hyehhhyehhheyyyehhheyyyheyheyhey heyyyeehheeeyyyeeehhheeeyyy-eeeehheeeeyyyeeeeehhhheeeyy. Pedro was consumed in the heat of drumbeats and chanting. The images in his mind loosened their grip. Pedro soon was clear of any impedance. All that had led up to the present moment was insignificant: the slate had been cleared. The collision of Brigid's psychometric spell and Hero's uncompromising counterspell had propelled Pedro unwittingly to his death. In order for him to be saved, he had had to be killed, or so he presumed. In other words, his fraudulent death countermanded the potentially real one — he had been supposedly cured of death — the roebuck would live. Pedro still believed that nothing in the world could save him from that fate. In the beginning, nothing could touch him; he held sway over all, in the exuberance of youthful omnipotence. Now he was merely human. Yet the memory was sweet, except that poor Charles had been dethroned as the Horned God on account of Pedro in Brigid's coven, which undoubtedly was the beginning of the end of Charles' and Anne's marriage. Pedro's amoral part in that affair had come to haunt him. He felt that both he and Charles were casualties, but Charles was the oblivious one. He was a hard worker who took an active, if not amused, interest in his wife's supernatural proclivities. Anne, of course, with her background of proper appearances, had betrayed, with the advent of Pedro, that "mere convention of marital fidelity." Yet, as a well-meaning woman, she could not live with the deceit for long.

Pedro's life had reached its zenith by his initiation into Brigid's coven. He didn't heed the warning of his death when it became obvious to Brigid that there was little she could do, short of destroying him, to stop his complete domination over all the witches involved. Like a mysterious Christ of Eros, Pedro took a bemused interest in the solemnities. Graciously, he agreed to take them on a psychometrist's voyage into the undiscovered country from which a traveller may not return. The necessary prelude was to offer himself physically on their altar, in a curious ritual during which some of the witches had sucked some of his semen and used it to enhance concoctions they were brewing. This unique ingredient apparently heightened their clairvoyance remarkably. It seemed that Hero, thought Pedro, as a neophyte accomplice and a disturbing beauty, had also no recourse but to kill him, as Brigid had warned. Hero could have been the one to cast her net of illusion to make it appear so; yet unfortunately in the process she would lose Pedro, who had given himself over to the ritual of death in light of his past lives. This reasoning seemed to fit so perfectly. However, this was simply speculation; what appeared to fit wasn't necessarily right at all.

It had come as a terrible surprise the last time he saw Hero and Niko at Augustus' and before stowing away on Hermes Metropoulos's freighter in Cardiff bound for New York. Hero had kissed him on both cheeks, wetting him with her tears; and only later, as the ship ploughed across the swells of the Atlantic and the horizon's circle of blue on blue bore down on him, did he realize the pain of their loss. They had loved with a surreal intensity. But he couldn't reconcile that with the looming visage of Gorgon. Whatever it was, that chameleon of darkness implanted itself into everyone around him, unknown to itself: who is who is who is who? And if he was pure light, what horrified him more than anything, other than Brigid's dark eyes, was that time he had seen Hero shed a tear, not just a tear of love, but mourning for his impending death that she herself must have presaged. He knew then something he had never known in himself — fear: the fear of the Gorgon, his nemesis dating from long ago in his audacious past when he dared brave battle to steal from the Gorgonians. He could still smell the lavender scent on Hero's neck.

Niko loved Hero. Only this consolation enabled Pedro to extricate himself from her; he and she had meant so much to each other, like two conjugal stars, but ones unable to conjoin too long for fear of a supernova. It had been a love based on need and desire in a woebegone world. But he wasn't sure about Hero's motives: somehow they didn't gel with the feminine incarnations of his past. He felt as though she were perhaps some not-so-innocent imposter. The whole concept of his purported clairvoyance sickened him, and he didn't feel like being a martyr any more. Nor did he want to make martyrs of anyone else; he simply wanted to live, for a change.

When they came out of the sweatlodge, even the hot and muggy night air sent, by the effect of contrast, a thrilling coolness over their heat tormented flesh. In smiling silence, the three men walked back slowly in the dark toward John Kineu's camp. Their passage was distinguished by their soft barefooted steps on the earthen path. Pedro felt his destiny behind him, like a ghost quietly surrendered. The ghost was now dead; he was a babe in arms ready to be carried, loved without question and allowed to emanate an innocence of nature without the entrapments of the flesh. He was truly free; he could return to society; there was nothing to hide; there was no mystery. They sat around the smouldering fire. John Kineu was on his knees, putting small sticks on the coals. Soon the flames blazed up nicely, not too hot, but bright enough. As John Kineu sat, he spoke of the old ways, his youth, and a tuberculosis epidemic in which everyone had lost a loved one. Throughout history, his people, destitute in their pain, had died like flies during various epidemics. "There were abandoned children in winter camps," he said, "children who were barely old enough to survive; others starved or froze. Some were found crazy from the windigo spirit roaming the wild forest. All breeds of men and women have known such hardships in their pasts. Yours, Pedro, the white race of Europe, did once have the pure blood of an aboriginal species, but it has been much diluted. The white race is like the prodigal son who has lost his way but whose ingenuity could reconcile him in a spirit of true oneness to his Mother Earth. I for one am an optimist and believe our white brother will give himself over to the sanctity of the earth which he will discover is our benefactor. We have been chosen as humans to tend the garden, smell the beauty of the blueberries in the sun, see the great sun melt from so far away the winter ice and breathe the gift of life in the clear air. It is in such things that the value of life lies, and they cannot be bought or sold. Yet the politics of survival stipulate to incite the great dilemmas. Now how's that for speaking English!!" boasted John Kineu, breaking out into hearty laughter. "The sweat," he said, "has cooked my brains enough now that maybe I could pass as an eccentric Englishman, a sort of inverted Grey Owl. Grey Owl, you know, was an Englishman who fooled everyone including himself into believing that he was indeed a great Indian, so I'll call myself Jack English an Indian who pretends to be an Englishman!" Both John Kineu and Big Dan got a great kick out of this notion and laughed until tears came. Pedro smiled broadly, thinking that this locution was somehow directed at him. He had told them virtually nothing about his death; and here they were, simply accepting him in a way that effected a lesson in humility. So he thought he should say something to impress upon them that his supposed death was no more than a prank gone wrong; a prank he had nothing to do with it. He still, however, felt at a loss for words because of the immensity of what had transpired, not only the sweat which now signified an ultimate release, but the light-headedness and frankness with which he could see himself fading before his eyes. He felt as if he barely existed! He got up and walked to the water ten metres away. At the gently lapping water's edge, the slick element glistened in smooth eternal ripples. Above, the stars spread out like a spray of milk against the celestial silence of deep dark space. Pedro then turned to the slow curve of silvery rocks along the shore, following it to the point at least a quarter mile down. He thought he heard women's voices and laughs rising on a waft of balmy breeze; then he recalled the Point from another time. The sudden thought oppressed him. How alien he felt; he wanted to walk down and see what was going on but his body wouldn't move. He inhaled deeply and held the air in his lungs for a moment before slowly exhaling. His anonymity was beginning to bother him. He reached down and scooped up some water and splashed himself. After a drink of the lake water which left a distinctive aftertaste of rocks and flora like a subtle tea, Pedro turned and went to sit down again. A sheen of sweat still covered the men.

"There's a gathering on the Point," he said to the other two. "I used to go there myself."

"I remember seeing you there once," said John Kineu. "I watched you from the trees, but there was too much smoke. You had a big smile on your face; and so did you, Dan."

"We had good times," said Big Dan. "We blessed the sky spirits in a big way, made many offerings, eh Pedro?"

"Sure did. Did some of that in Wales too. But different." Pedro waited for their reaction, but getting none, he elucidated, "I had money in my pocket, freedom. I'd left behind yet another aspersion; I was good at that sort of thing; however, being dead doesn't give much room to manoeuvre."

"What's this aspersion, as you call it?" asked Big Dan.

"To begin, I was a genealogist. I did family trees for people. You know, ancestors. Well, I got into trouble when I did a certain family and unwittingly gave the findings to Sadie McPherson, who pseudonymously had them published in a magazine. The family never could find out who wrote the article, but I became the scapegoat. I couldn't deny my findings. They saw to it that I was publicly made out to be a charlatan and incompetent in my field.

"It was time to leave. My mother's brother had then just recently married an English woman he'd met in London society where he spent a good deal of time with the family business, Morgan-Willobie Inc., a multinational that financed venture capital. Anyway, they lived on an estate in west Wales, Caerymwy, to be exact; it had been inherited by his wife from her father, who was peerage and owned numerous estates. They welcomed me with open arms; it was like it was my place too. Anne Fitzooth actually took a bit of a shine to me. Her marriage hadn't turned out that well. She told me, "marriage from love, like vinegar from wine" — she was into Byron. They couldn't have children as she proved to be infertile, and this unfortunately grew into their undoing."

On the last syllable, the night fire crackled up. John Kineu and Big Dan remained inscrutable. The former squinted up at Pedro, gnarly-eyed from the effort to assess his story. "When she offered herself to me," continued Pedro, "I had no idea what I was getting into. I was beginning anew, and a start like that was an adventure, a very narcissistic one. In no time, we were full-blown lovers, but I was playing along with increasing trepidation, which was addictively exciting, and like a good boy, I did her bidding. My Uncle Charles was away for weeks, sometimes a month at a time; it was like I became lord of the house. We were insatiable — anywhere, anytime, anyhow. Then one day, naively thinking Anne would approve somehow, I brought Hero around, as she had expressed interest in the coven. Then shortly thereafter she spurned me, saying only that Brigid was the High Priestess of the coven which I had the privilege to be a part of. Brigid was your honest-to-God old witch, though of good repute, a wise woman who had mastered the healing arts and ancient spells. She is as real as the night. I had heard about her but had met her on only one occasion. Anne would never talk about her, and I assumed she knew nothing. But was I ever wrong. Anne turned out to be Brigid's apprentice and next in line to be High Priestess. Let me backtrack. One night, long before I met Hero, I was camping in my usual spot near a clearing in this beautiful oak forest. I was camping most of the time then and spending as little time as possible at the house; anyway, this particular time, I was camped on a little knoll away from the clearing. I was sleeping fitfully, but all of a sudden I was aware of women's voices, strange voices chanting incantations of some sort. It was the summer solstice ceremony. I walked to the clearing where I found them all naked; they had a fire and a makeshift wooden altar on which stood an array of things, a cauldron, candles, incense, a pentacle, a sword, a dagger, a wand, some salt, wine, water, ivy and flowers. To my bewilderment, Anne was performing the ceremony; she said the prayer:

> *O gracious Goddess, Queen of Night,*
> *I ask you to accept this rite,*
> *And send me all your mystic power,*
> *To aid in this important hour.*
> *In castle, cottage, sacred glade;*
> *Where ere the circle shall be made.*
> *I pray that you will grant this boon,*
> *O lovely Goddess of the Moon.*

I was watching from the shadows in fascination when, to my astonishment, after a half hour of chants and prayers, Anne called out my name as if she knew exactly where I was. She told me to remove my clothes — which, minus socks or underwear, I had scrambled into before the ceremony — and to present myself quietly to them so they might achieve the greatest power on Earth — the power of love and regeneration to work, in reverent, bounteous good for all. I found out later, I had replaced Charles because of Anne, of course. Anyway, it was a ceremony of marriage between the Horned God or Wild Hunter and the female Goddess or Green Goddess of the Summer. As if under a spell, I did as I was told and presented myself to them. Anne was the acting High Priestess because Brigid rarely took part any more. They welcomed me like a God, kissed my feet, my body, fondled my genitals, sang sweetly; it was the most bizarre thing; only Anne refrained. I was to be wed to the 'maiden,' a young woman by the name of Gwen. She has raven hair with white skin. She was only sixteen at the time and had worked for Anne; still does. She'd be about twenty-two now and a full-fledged witch. She teased me and worked me up to a severe erection and under no compunction was she to release its 'sacred burden'; it was the object of their desire and the source of the power that had us all enthralled. So there I stood, the centre and culmination of an ancient rite; I was truly flattered and at ease, as if this was what I had always been meant to do. As it turned out, that night was the pivotal point of my life; it was as if all eternity according to Pedro lit up for me — my past, present, future — my destiny made clear as a bubbling spring."

Pedro stopped for a moment to collect his thoughts. He breathed deeply as if preparing himself for the great discharge of his monologue. Big Dan, although refraining from comment, couldn't help but smile in wonder at his old friend. Dan's expression contorted and he looked down. He realized that for all Pedro's innocent wonder, there lay a life experience far beyond his own comprehension; it even made him look at John Kineu to see if any indication of the same was visible, but his face remained inscrutable and passive.

"After the ceremonies," began Pedro again, "they all frantically worked on my orgasm like hungry wolves after a scrap of rabbit. I ended up doing it with each of them over the course of the night. There was Gwen, and Anne of course; Beatrice Turnwell, a buxom middle-aged woman from Lampeter; Tilda Meade from Anglesey, who had braids down to her knees, and Kerry Mara from near Londonderry, a red-haired Catholic, who was one of Anne's best friends. Afterwards, we bathed in the lake, dressed, then rowed the two rowboats across the lake and hiked up to Anne's house. The sky was just beginning to lighten in those early hours about four a.m. We went inside. Some classical music was put on, Antonio Soler I believe, and tea was prepared. There were six of us sitting there, drinking tea in silence, as the sun peeped over the horizon and turned the treetops into golden crowns. Feeling a little strange sitting so formal and correct, I excused myself to go to the washroom. What I had in mind was to lie down in the bedroom where I would sometimes have a nap; naturally, just now, I was feeling a bit drained. When I entered the room, I went straight to the bed. The curtains of the room were drawn so it was reasonably dark. As I was about to take off my hiking shoes, I felt a cold draft run up my back. I looked but I saw that the window was shut. Something flashed past the corner of my eye. I froze in shock. She was sitting in the rocker in the dark corner of the room as quiet as if she were dead but looking directly at me with those black eyes of hers. In the poor light, she looked strangely young. She wore a long, black dress with white trim, that appeared to be out of the last century. Yet in spite of the darkness, a shine was visible from her black eyes; my first impression was of evil. I felt duped because there had been nothing in the room to tell me it was occupied. For a few moments we stared at each other. I wanted to call out in surprise but couldn't, as if I were mute under her spell. In a voice that sounded hollow but unexpectedly clear, she told me to sit. I obeyed, sinking passively down on the edge of the bed. She began to rock gently and asked if I had enjoyed the ceremonies that night. I replied that I had and that it was a unique experience. Brigid — that was the lady's name — went on to say that she hadn't approved of me but that some greater force was at work that she could do nothing about. Then she said that Gwendolyn was her great-granddaughter and the spitting image of herself when she was sixteen; she said Gwendolyn's grandfather, and Gwendolyn's father, among others, had once been Horned Gods. I then asked if that implied something ominous, because Gwendolyn had told me both her great-grandfather — Brigid's husband, John Pyles — and grandfather had died under mysterious circumstances, one in a barn fire and the other in a shooting accident. And she replied an emphatic 'Yes.' This startled me, but my first response was one of disbelief; I had an impulse to laugh, yet refrained. She went on, to my total wonder, to say that I would try to bring about the destruction of their coven, which had been connected to her family for hundreds of years. Again, she restated her reluctance to have me; then she had the audacity to ask how Gwendolyn had performed. It was apparently Gwendolyn's first serious participation in Wiccan ritual, which she had been groomed to do since her thirteenth birthday. Gwendolyn, I admit, had a rather strong crush on me; I knew her, of course, through Anne Fitzooth. She was Anne's loyal helper around the house, as well as Brigid's and August's. At any rate, I could not bring myself to humbly decline any further involvement with these unique women. Aunt Anne even insisted I stay; she said that Brigid was just bluffing and really enjoyed having me around. This baffled me even more. In fact, I was told by Kerry that Brigid was the one who had suggested me in the first place but Anne wouldn't let on to this, saying only that a meeting of minds had been able to come up with just one choice. Apparently, I had been regarded as too good to be true. And well, naturally, I remained their Horned God for a whole year until I met Hero. I knew these witches intimately and even visited their homes which was quite a bizarre treat. Anne even approved. Then there was Hero. I met her skiing of all things, in the Welsh mountains. Now Hero, the extraordinary creature that she is, insisted that I have her brought into the Wicca because she wanted to get in on the action. So, through my intercessions with Brigid, Hero apprenticed with Anne, who agreed to her joining with reluctance because she, as it turned out, was incredibly jealous of Hero's youth, beauty and talent. The whole scene, actually, was becoming a little ridiculous for me. In time, Anne and Hero's female animosity, for all their good will, could only drive a wedge through the coven; it seemed that Brigid's prophecy had come true and that she had used Hero as a pawn to achieve the prophecy. To defuse the situation a bit, I backed off and used my power, and ransomed myself against their need and desire; but this backfired as Brigid demanded that I remain and 'run the course' until they could find a successor. I attempted to enlist an old friend from Toronto, Ronald Morgan, but he got so excited that he just about raped poor Gwendolyn, who actually liked him because he was my friend. In any event, none of the other members of the Wicca would even consider him and thought it was a joke. When he was rejected, he rushed home to Canada, depressed and inconsolable. My friend Niko now put himself forward — Niko, by the way, would have been great, but I couldn't bring myself to let him participate; I felt he had only volunteered to help me rather than out of genuine interest; I also had in the back of my mind lingering doubts as to the sanity of it all; things were a mess as it was.

"Then the bomb. Brigid, that very first night, uncannily had mentioned something called Gorgon. She said that I had been having dreams about it. I had in fact dreamt about this Gorgon, a spectre of death in the form of the ancient myth of Medusa and other evil apparitions. I asked her, without letting on that she was right about these dreams, what was Gorgon. Without answering my question, she simply said Gorgon would never show itself. I proceeded to give her a taste of her own medicine by accusing her of being Gorgon, which she laughed off in that cackle of hers. I was doomed, she said, by my own innocence and refusal to acknowledge her authority which would help me. Now it was my turn to laugh; I really thought the whole thing a rare joke. Gorgon, I said, could kiss my ass. And she said Gorgon would, many times. She said this soberly, almost sadly. I asked again who Gorgon really was. She reiterated Gorgon would never reveal herself, but that I must realize that she would get inside me, making me my own worst enemy. She said the only way I could conquer Gorgon was to conquer myself and that I could not do that alone. I thought that this was just her way of hooking me. I couldn't accept this supernatural freak, Gorgon. As far as I was concerned, Brigid was Gorgon and I wasn't going to let that old crone reject me on account of a stupid myth. I think then I was turned on by the spectre of Gorgon.

I wanted to know if it was real: the ancient evil bitch myth. Gorgon was a challenge to take up, which you might think I'd come to regret, seeing the extreme nature of my present predicament. Well, I had these dreams, you know; in the past, like way back, I had been sacrificed brutally. Brigid said that my death was imminent and the Wicca would unwittingly have a hand in it. This was too much. I got up and left, and I swear, when I walked by her, she reached out and grabbed my arm with unbelievable strength and said: The Wicca is not what it used to be. You have changed all that, Pedro. Welcome, let us serve the Good Goddess together and maybe things will be all right. I left without saying anything. I walked down to the lake and rowed back to the Oak Forest. That same day, I discovered the stones buried under forest residue toppled this way and that. I had actually noticed them before. Then I discovered the cave and some more ancient wonders. Anyway, when the runes were deciphered, I saw that the secrets they contained corresponded to everything I had dreamt and even written down, and further, had begun to come true. I knew then I was on a death trip. And life, by that same token, now became magnificent; I was in love with it, and it loved me. The Infinite, the Great Spirit had set me on a path I had no choice but to follow. I had always lived by my impulses, and so I would die by them, although I was confident nothing could harm me; it came upon me in my naivety, that I had to save the Wicca from themselves and lead them away from Brigid's terrible power. I would raise myself to be their Apollo. In this I was successful. Hero and I became the unspoken rulers. Brigid then cast a spell on me. I don't know what she did or how she did it, but it worked. Even Hero with her astrology saw it coming. Even Niko warned me; it seemed they all had it in for me. Of course, they were looking out for me, but that is precisely what Brigid wanted: for me to think they were all protecting me. I didn't believe any of it; I laughed away their fears; Brigid laughed with me. Then disaster struck, or as near as I could get to disaster. During an incredibly violent lightning storm last summer, a number of massive oaks six feet thick were split asunder top to bottom as neatly as a small log by an axe. I had been camping alone for a few days. Anne had gone away; no one else was around except old Augustus who was there in his cottage up over the ridge. In the middle of a dark night, the storm struck, turning the forest into an electric nightmare. The most frightening explosions rent the air. You could hear the massive old trees ripping apart in agony at the onslaught. I scrambled out of my tent and sat under the awning in the front to watch. The shards of lightning were closing in on me fast and furious. I bolted into the rain in my bare feet, clad only in shorts and a shirt, and made for the cave, but more lightning barred my way. I ran back to my tent only to see it disintegrate before my eyes in a fireball that extended from the top of an oak right through the full extent of my campsite. Everything I had with me there was destroyed. Panicking and in shock, I blindly ran for the hills or, more precisely, the vale that heads up to August's place, and an hour later, drenched, bleeding and bruised, I banged on his door. The lightning had followed me to his paddock then ceased as abruptly as it began. After that, the fear was in me; I was caught in the spell. Brigid had me on the run. Hero and I eventually split up. I couldn't bear to bring anything down on those I loved. Then, one day, I was driving my old Rover car down to the coast and was coming around the corner when a huge Roebuck bounded out of a ditch by a forest and straight into my car; it was killed instantly, its neck broken. I veered off the road, just barely missing some rocks. Notwithstanding my crippled car, I came through physically unscathed; my mind was another matter. The Roebuck was my ancient totem; within the Wicca and my triad with Hero and Niko, a pact we made in view of my dreams of the past, I was the Roebuck. Still, undaunted, I refused to abandon our coven. I was the Green King, the Sanguine Mystic, and the Fool. Then, as if I hadn't had enough, I was attacked by a rabid fox which had entered the cave unbeknownst to me. If I hadn't put up a ladder against a ledge inside just the day before, I would have been savaged. The fox eventually wandered off. Then and there I was convinced of the spell. The Wicca, or rather Brigid, was too much for me. I had to retreat. I assumed that the witches were all entangled in a movement to bring about my demise. Call it Gorgon, call it fate, but everything had become evil and suspicious. Yet I still refused to give up; I would stand and fight in my own way until I was so thoroughly infected with the poison of the spell, I could feel death's rank breath sticking to the back of my head. I wanted to see Gorgon face to face. But inevitably, I bolted. Last March without telling anyone — I had an opportunity to stow away on a freighter bound for Montreal. No one except Hero and Niko knew I came to Canada. Everything that has happened since is beyond my understanding. My death. What a freak out. I can only guess the Wicca or Hero cast the illusion of my death and brought me yet again to the fore in their own strange way. Hero and Niko are look . . . "

Pedro stopped mid-sentence. There on the other side of the fire stood Donna del Rio, gazing speechlessly in his direction, but looking as if she wasn't quite sure who he was because of the obstruction of the fire. John Kineu casually covered himself. Big Dan and Pedro followed suit. For extended moments, the answer to infinite questions was hanging mid-air between Pedro and his visitor; it was then going skyward in the heat of the fire, and might have been sending smoke signals to the stars. For a while the two of them were too bewildered to say or do anything. Through the incandescence of the firelight galvanized in their locked vision, Pedro saw Donna's countenance change before his eyes. She appeared for alternate moments to be Sarah the Jew, Olwen the Celt, then back to Donna del Rio. His retrocognitive visions were almost always accurate.

John Kineu began to laugh. Big Dan was too caught up in Pedro's tale to do much besides wait expectantly with a thoughtful expression on his face.

Pedro was suddenly taken by a terrible longing. Donna del Rio. Donna del Rio, who knew nothing. Or was she onto something? How had she gotten there? He wondered. A spasm of his old fear came upon him but passed off as quickly. The truth was he needed her now as a friend and ached for the natural and spontaneous playfulness that had consistently formed a part of their friendship. Each interchange had seemed to predispose them to the next and the next, until . . . gradually, effortlessly, irresistibly, it seemed only right to love her as it was meant to be. But he had resisted crossing that line and was resisting that idea even now, though he was seized with yearning for her. And that was the healthiest thought he'd had in a long time. Donna appeared to stumble. It was a curious stumble like a faint; not a full-fledged pass-out, but a gentle crumpling to the ground. She put her hand on the hard contour of a rock in a slow calculated motion as if she had rehearsed the very move. Pedro felt that he had rehearsed with her. In a flash Big Dan and John Kineu were at her side, gently helping her into one of the simple wooden chairs on the deck. Having thrown on some clothes, they quietly allowed her to introduce herself. Pedro held her hand. In his eyes was a bemused shock. They spoke their names but nothing else made sense. Pedro was overwhelmed by this freak of coincidence. It was so good that it actually grounded him. She, nonetheless, felt the same way; it seemed mortifying to have such good fortune. Although Pedro's extended testimony, interrupted by Donna del Rio's intrusion, had lost its tension, the hyperbole of the whole affair summed up the unspoken. Both John Kineu and Big Dan were all smiles. They had witnessed a most marvellous and revealing scene, notwithstanding their curiousity as to who this extraordinary young woman was. Pedro's angel, they decided, had found her wayward love. And it was no accident.

Chapter Seven

Often, often, often, Christ walks in the guise of strangers.

—Celtic rune

Alone in his room the same afternoon that Hero and Niko raced up north, Charles Willobie lay back on his bed with tears in his eyes and mortal hurt in his solar plexus, feeling as though a vacuum had sucked out his guts. He had just returned from a tennis game with Ronald's father, Frank Morgan, and on an impulse, telephoned Anne. Regretting the call the moment Anne lifted the receiver, Charles felt his throat tighten and his words cease as she calmly told him she wanted a divorce. Her words, uttered so simply, carried no resonance at first; they sounded muted and perfunctory, like dense little Morse codes not understood upon first reception. She had begun by saying Pedro was alive and that she and he had had a "torrid" affair a few years back which ended with the arrival of Hero. Anne went on to say she "suspected" Pedro was alive, but wouldn't elaborate. Before Charles finally could stammer, "Wh . . . wh . . . what did you say?" out it came: their marriage was finito and he needn't bother coming back at all. According to their premarital agreement, he couldn't make any claim on her possessions — not that he would, of course, in any case; besides, he was already a wealthy man. By the time it was all laid out for him, taking no more than a minute and prefaced with pleasant introductory remarks, she was already countering Charles' response before he could articulate it. "We've been through this before; I can't take it anymore; my whole being screams out for living honestly, straight up. I'm the one who's been dead, not Pedro; I'm moving back to London for awhile; I'll have my lawyer contact yours. I'm sorry Charles. I feel rotten about it, but I've made up my mind; it's taken years. Good-bye." Click.

So there it was. He lay back with his leather and canvas shoes on, and felt pain course through him like a chemical through his veins. His mouth became dry and stale. His pale hazel eyes felt shrunken, deep in their sockets. His appetite vanished. A burning mental crunge could view only one looming image: Pedro and Anne making voracious love morning, noon and night. He was the cuckold of the century. He could see the open window in the master bedroom with curtains gently flapping in the breeze, silver shadows of the Welsh moonlight caressing the writhing bodies in their ecstasy. Pedro was no longer Pedro, but some phantom. Over the years, Charles had summoned up in himself a thoroughly positive approach to help Pedro through the thick and thin of the latter's troubling ways. This all reversed. Charles couldn't stop the dawning reality as it began to manifest. Memories flashed up one after the other. He remembered the Wiccan ceremonies he had participated in years ago, never understanding what they were all about, but letting himself be swept up in the general revelry. The unique archaic ways of enhancing supernatural powers and the healing were all acceptable to him. He then bowed out for Pedro at Anne's behest. It was true that Anne's talk of her "witching" had at first been a turn-on. But the lengths they went to in order to acquire power and insight into the supernatural through sexual rites had at last made him pass it off as excessive. He had embarrassingly dabbled in it those times for her sake and knew he hadn't been regarded in any great light. Then Pedro. Always Pedro, his sister's son and only child. Pedro. Pedro was alive; maybe, he thought. This truth reverberated in his brain. He recalled his first memory of Pedro as a little boy of five or six, up at the Morgans' farm in King Township, north of Toronto. There was a meadow behind the shed where Pedro had found a fieldmouse nest and was guarding it from the calico cat, Murphy. When Charles, just twenty, asked what he was doing, Pedro replied with another question: did he know that there was a dog buried in a glade of trees right there? Charles, who had said that he hadn't heard but didn't think so, found out later that the boy had been right. The dog had been a pet of the previous owner, an elderly man. Charles attempted to find out if this was true but was unsuccessful until, coincidentally, the grand-daughter of the previous owner came by shortly thereafter to visit the place she had remembered as a child and told Charles that her grandfather did indeed have dogs, two of which had been buried exactly where Pedro said. Pedro just somehow knew. It always rankled him. How did this kid know and why? And that kid had been fucking his wife! And he was alive! Alive! What a self-centred little prima donna if there ever was one, he fumed. What a bastard! He hated him. It was the first time he had ever admitted it to himself, and it felt good, at least better. With these last thoughts reverberating in his mind, Charles stared at the ceiling and the light fixture. He loved Anne, and her words hurt viciously. The pain came on deep and numbing. He knew he could not hope for reconciliation: Anne was a real bridge burner. And this time it was clear she had withdrawn to her netherworld never to return. She, the incumbent High Priestess, was casting her nets farther afield, atop the unbridled mount, a wild stallion that only one person in the world was capable of dismounting: Pedro. And he would have no such designs unless Hero wanted Anne's position for herself and this was all some intricate scheme or counter-measure in a power stuggle. Yet they all must have been in league somehow to pull off Pedro's fake death, an illusionist's coup de grâce. And what of Brigid? thought Charles. She may well have been in on it too. She may indeed have been behind it all. Anne had told him once that, from the start, Brigid had been dead set against Pedro as the Horned God and she may have pitted herself against the others who called for the illusion of his death to protect Pedro. Brigid's spells were frightfully intense; yet it all made little sense; poor fools, they were all so deluded. What good could come of it all? He found solace in this reflection and release. What a blessing; he felt, that at least he had come through intact and not warped like the others. He clung to this idea. It softened the impact of Anne's betrayal.

As Charles realized his new freedom, a latent pragmatism sprang into action. He was a businessman, after all, who had personally doubled the assets of Morgan-Willobie by some very deft dealings in the U.S. and Switzerland. They were almost debt-free because they had invested with Swiss francs. Subsequently, the U.S. dollar devalued precipitously, enabling them to pay most of their debt in U.S. funds exchanged from the Swiss francs. Anne Fitzooth had been influential in the actual deal which bought them substantial ownership in a Swiss technological engineering company holding the patent for a revolutionary generator that ran on a form of hydrogen fuel. The company was a multinational, well diversified in technological production and at the cutting edge of research, the envy of both the Americans and Japanese. Charles's investors were well satisfied with his transactions. The demand for new technology was unprecedented. These thoughts relieved Charles; he had been a success after making a faltering start in the family business. His father, now deceased, had never fully recognized his potential. Yes, he had, of course, taken him on as his successor, but he had died before Charles earned his spurs. Ronald's father, Frank Morgan, on the other hand, as the chairman, although extremely cautious, had all the confidence in the world in him. Charles could count on a great bulwark of support in Frank, concerning this present malaise. Frank had little patience for the eccentricities of the likes of Pedro and Anne.

The telephone rang. Charles picked up the receiver. It was Sadie calling from Little Current to say she wouldn't make the tennis game with Connie. Charles, too dazed to question what she was doing in Little Current, simply said he'd pass the message on and signed off.

As Charles's mind began to clear, the visage of his older sister, wonderful

Connie Constance, came hurtling home to him. How was he to tell her that Pedro was alive? His whereabouts were unknown, as usual, but he was alive. Furthermore, on top of his own estrangement from Anne as a result of Connie's beloved son, how was he to absolve himself of his partial responsibility for the way things ultimately got out of hand? Unwittingly, he had let Pedro pursue the path of self-destruction, hand in hand with his own wife. He should have insisted that Pedro go somewhere else. But then there was Pedro's discovery and his association with Augustus. There was no way Pedro would have left; he would have laughed in Charles's face.

There was a soft knock at the door. Connie called him.

"Yes," said Charles, "come in."

Connie quietly entered the room. Charles looked at her strange, consternated eyes of worried sister-of-mercy blue. They looked very much alike in a depressive sense. Their eyes, mouth and nose were practically identical, all slightly drooping yet fleshy except for the eyes which held up the face like ballasts astride the nose; they were good looking and unique. Connie's hair was tied in a loose pony-tail with some loose strands straggling over her ear. She was wearing her workshirt and slacks and bore the marks of her labour, duly noted in the grass stains on her knees and dirt in her finger nails. For a woman in her early fifties, she was very sexy. But to Charles, she was big sister. "Who called?" she asked. "I was in the garden." But sensing Charles' temperament, she queried, "Is everything okay?"

"Not exactly." He sat up at the edge of the bed and was silent a moment, letting Connie take the lead.

"You don't seem yourself. What's wrong?"

"Anne's leaving me. We're getting divorced," he added, therapeutically admitting it to himself.

"What?" Her eyes opened wide in shock.

"She called to say good-bye and not to bother to return, among other things."

"Oh Charles! What on earth brought this about?"

"Now brace yourself. She had had an affair with Pedro. Quite intense, I gather," said Charles like a wooden soldier.

"Oh my goodness! Pedro?" She stood there gaping.

"Ready for more?" Charles now found some demented delight in expressing himself.

"More? What?"

"Sit down, make yourself comfortable."

Connie sat down in the sofa chair, where she held herself upright, her breath becoming short and her heart beating rapidly. Charles went on matter-of-factly.

"Connie, apparently Pedro didn't die. I don't know where he is or how this could be, but Anne just told me he's alive." Connie froze into pure electric paralysis, her expression impassive, except for the slight beginning of a little tremor on her lips. A metallic sensation developed in her mouth. Charles's voice thudded lifelessly in her ears. The very view before her seemed to fragment into a Cubist painting. Her eyes opened wide.

"My God!! That WITCH!!! SHE KNEW MY SON WAS ALIVE?"

"That I don't know. I mean, I don't know how she knows."

"But Peter is ALIVE? She said he was ALIVE?"

"Yes. I think I understand what happened, but I'm not absolutely sure. It must have been something to do with the Wicca."

"I can't believe this!" Connie stood up and paced, trying to get a hold of herself. Her mind rankled with questions. "How is it he didn't show up?" she muttered, in mid-stride. "What's been going on? Where is he, then?"

"I think that circumstances set in motion a terrible thing. We've all been deceived, myself, the worst. I wonder how much Hero and Niko know. I sensed something strange, at least in Hero; although from her it's to be expected, and I haven't any idea where he could be."

"Charles," she said with a slow, pensive emphasis. "What on earth is going on? How would Hero and Niko know? I mean, they were at the funeral! Do you think they could know something like that and still come to the funeral? I won't believe this. I can't believe this. Listen, we must call John. Here, let me." She reached the phone before Charles did and dialled her husband's club, then hung up after asking for him. "Damn, he's left."

"Connie, you're making me nervous. Sit down, and let's think this through. Christ, I'm glad for you, but I've still lost my wife over him. I could kill him now that he's alive!"

"Charles, calm down: I know Anne; she'll be thinking of you. You mean so much to her. Don't give up. You've been through too much together to give up."

It was Charles's turn to stand. Followed by Connie, he went out into the hall, descended the stairs to the front foyer, and exited through the back of the house.

"Hey, Charles, settle down. Take a deep breath of fresh air."

"Stuff the fresh air. See you later, Con. By the way, Sadie called to say she couldn't make the tennis game."

"What's she doing?"

"I don't know. She called from Little Current."

"What? Little Current?"

But Charles had crossed the patio to the lawns that rolled away in an easy decline to the edge of the ravine. Connie stopped on the edge of the patio to watch him go. The bliss hit her then. Her son's death had all been a bad dream.

Charles sat revelling in the vicissitudes of his martyrdom, tightly holding his glass of scotch. He felt slightly sheepish about leaving Connie like that, but the stroll through the ravine and his subsequent beeline to a local pub were definitely what his angel ordered. Just now, he was quite drunk but held it well in the dark end of the bar where he huddled innocuously on his stool.

While his brain danced the usual alcoholic delusions of introverted glory, Connie had waited impatiently back at home for the return of her husband, who had actually gone to the Canadian Tire store for a new lawn hose. She finally phoned Frank, who callously bemoaned the reversal of tragedy and quipped about the long shadow of Pedro, who, he said, was obviously still feeling sorry for himself. Connie had registered only the superficiality rather than the substance of the remark: how could Pedro not feel sorry for himself? He could have at least, however, shown up before his own funeral. But the pith of those thoughts was lost in her as soon as the notion occurred. The mother's instinct for the love of her son nonetheless stood as a continental shift of force. There was an incorporeal innocence in her that Pedro himself had so blatantly inherited. A furrowed brow replaced her giddy looks when she faced the possibility of her own responsibility in the matter. The sudden visage of Ronald Morgan conjoined with her in acidic ecstasy seemed to penetrate the piety of her self-esteem.

"Forgive me," she whispered to the mirror in the front hall as John George walked in the front door.

Charles never knew about that terrible faux pas of his sister, which was just as well as he worked closely with Ronald Morgan. Charles was more actively spiritual than Connie, having read the Tibetan Book of the Dead, and a variety of mystical or occult authors like Ram Dass, Edgar Cayce, and Crowley. For several years in his early twenties he had travelled to the Far East where he had placed himself under the tutelage of a guru master possessing encyclopaedic knowledge of the Hindu teachings. These pursuits fizzled out, however, when he got caught up in a materialist phase, not to mention the fascinating lures of Anne Fitzooth.

Charles was thirteen years Pedro's senior, and had always resented Pedro's natural attraction as some kind of hobo mystic. Charles recalled an instance when they were discussing Edgar Cayce, that humble, religious farm boy who was also the clairvoyant genius revealing the subconscious mysteries of mankind and cures for its sicknesses. They broached the idea of Cayce being a special vessel, one of millions on the river of humanity, to authentically prove the omnipotence of spirit. And Charles in his then quixotic optimism had taken the young initiate Pedro into his secret confidence only to be subtly challenged by a vain appraisal of Charles's munificence.

"All that stuff goes in one ear and out the other," said Pedro. "I function purely in the salient. I suppose I take it for granted. What is, is. Do you think we would be civilised without the status quo? Take science: it can be as ignorant as the bloody church; in a sense science too is a church — the Church of Progress."

Charles shook his head in remembrance and kicked back his third double on the rocks, numbing his teeth on the ice. Absent-mindedly he spoke out of his stupor: "What an ass-hole!" Then, sucking the last hint of scotch out of the icecubes, he mumbled, "Takes one to know one."

"Excuse me," said a voice beside him.

Charles turned awkwardly to look, his receding grey-blond hair out of place on his forehead.

"Are we being hard on ourselves?" said a middle-aged woman who had recently sat down on the empty stool between him and some younger men.

"Very verily," he replied, trying for wit as he looked into his drink. He had been comfortable in the solitude of his own misfortunes, drinking his elixir of narcissism.

"Striking up a conversation with a stranger in a pub is not something I do every day," the woman said with dignity, sensing his reluctance to communicate.

There was something in the woman's voice that struck an solid note, something genuine in her manner that had stood well against the buffets and beatings of life. He reflected now on the wellspring of his spiritual being and the divination of destiny. How odd, he decided boozily, that an angel had come to console him. Why me, he thought, a poor bloke whose emotional life is as checkered with failure as a Greek tragedy.

"You said, 'we'; that must mean you are feeling empathy rather than sympathy," said Charles. "Care to keel the pot of a witch's brew?"

"Sorry, I didn't catch that?" She leaned closer, struggling to hear through the hubbub raised by the jocular bunch on the other side of her.

"Just as well. A tale told by an idiot."

"You've had a falling out with your wife?"

"Something like that," he contented himself with saying, though the question cried out for something much more brilliant.

"What are you drinking?" she asked, changing the subject and pulling out a Peter Stuyvesant cigarette and lighting it.

"Scotch."

"May I buy you one?"

"Why not? I'm drinking doubles. I'm Charles," he added.

"Angie," she said.

Reinforced by this further drink, Charles shifted his pained vigour to a more relaxed eloquence. He couldn't open up just yet about his marital demise. His failure to do so gave Angie the lead in a depression competition. Candidly, she told the story of how she had pined away for a man for ten years, done everything for him and had been ready to marry him at a snap of the fingers only to be dumped ignominiously. She said that he was now engaged to someone whom, for most of her life, she had regarded as one of her best friends. The jerk, she said, had always appeared the very soul of romantic ardour and attentiveness, but had been "fucking" her friend all along. Some friend! Angie just laughed it off now, as if the whole affair were the story of some third party's heartbreak, not her own. Betrayal, as "Geronimo" Charles said, had a nasty way of turning the heart.

Charles ended up at Angie's place, a nearby, impressive condominium. They were both admirably, rather than disgustingly, drunk and began necking while saying good-bye, which invariably was prolonged. She strip-teased for him to the songs of Billie Holiday singing her lustier renditions doused in booze and heroin. The atmosphere was perfect, however, and Charles, succumbing to Angie's wiles, soon sprawled naked over her couch, albeit quite dissatisfied with his middle-aged body which made him think of a bloated white albatross. Their subsequent pungent-fumed love-making failed to reach climax though they tried for an indeterminable time, giving up exhausted at last in her queen-sized bed. With his head now pounding war drums of migraine intensity, Charles felt horrible — the whole night after the mutual pickup in the bar had been a pedestrian farce, though exciting. It nevertheless cheapened the state of sublime melancholy he had achieved earlier in the evening. On reflecting thus, he thought it a good time to leave and at least retrieve a remnant of his martyrdom. He wasn't quite ready to be happy yet. It was at that precise moment in the early fresh summer dawn, nestled in beside Angie the Angel, who had positioned her wet sex against his awakened member, that he had a swift intuition of Pedro's whereabouts. While Angie whimpered deliriously as he eased into her, the warmth overwhelmed the previous inhibitors and her movements squeezed every ounce he could muster. Even still, in the ecstacy of the moment that purged his hammering headache, he felt with little premonition that the little swine was quite possibly up on Georgian Bay, somewhere around Manitoulin. As Angie released herself, shaking Charles in the process, he pondered the events of the day before. During a long drawn out afterglow, Charles remembered that, earlier the day before, Connie had mentioned a visit from Hero, Niko, Sadie, and Ronald. Hero was supposed to have acted quite peculiarly when Connie told them of this young woman Donna del Rio, who had come by early in the morning looking for Pedro. The said Donna had met Pedro in Wales and was obviously ignorant of his death. But then she had asked about Georgian Bay and Pedro's old cottage. So, thought Charles, Hero gets wind of something in this Donna del Rio, and then they all take off in Ronald's car to look for her. Where? St. Clair West. Connie called there later to speak to Donna only to find out that she had gone north. Georgian Bay, undoubtedly. Why? Pedro was up there. It all added up in a strange kind of way. The only problem was that this Donna woman must have known Pedro was alive somewhere, which appeared to be anomalous in view of the fact she was oblivious of his death and very upset hearing about it, unless she was deceiving Connie. Furthermore, Charles had certainly never heard tell of this woman in Wales.

Charles finally released himself from his warm mooring, did a gentle roll, and swung himself up over the side of the bed.

"Charles, what are you doing?" purred his bed partner.

"Gotta go, Angie," he said under his breath. "Call you later."

Angie turned around, exposing her small breasts. "Let us not let a one-night-stand get in the way here," she said sadly. "This was an aberration for me."

Charles came around to her side, half-dressed and hugged her. "Never."

"Will I hear from you?" she asked groggily rubbing her head, not without a tremor of vulnerability.

He held her back and looked at her. "I promise. I think you're beautiful." He then wrote down his telephone number.

"Thank you," she said, writing her own.

She watched him finish dressing and leave.

Trudging down the vale from Augustus' aerie past the purple heathers and the deep cym where the silver-streaked waters of the mountain stream tumbled below into the oak forest, David Thomas felt in his ruddy face the effulgence of heady ale and smelled a hint of ancient peat that followed him from the cottage. He looked to the sky, now a mottled pewter, and the distant grey-blue mountains of Plynlimon Fawr. His mind and the rushing waters were one; there stirred in him the longings of a troubadour with a pneumatic wanderlust endemic to the Welsh — hiraeth, that soul-bond stronger than the specter of death.

David Thomas revelled in his flight and soared higher, wheeling about the names of great Welsh: Boadicea, Caracatus, Gwion, Dafydd ap Gwilym, and Owen Glendywr. And there was the long line of earthy Welsh women, with their dark hair and pale skin, who in essence gave birth to the civil and religious liberty of civilisation; for it was in their bosoms that the vital principles of equality and justice were nourished. Thus he ruminated: hiraeth, the magic spheres of longing in the mystic land.

Once down in the dark oaken substratum of forest, David Thomas came back to his preponderant senses. The darkness of the woods that afternoon contrasted sharply with the intoxicating light of the morning. He looked around in watchful anxiety, expecting to see a witch dressed in black standing beside a tree but then immediately scoffed at his own imagination. The Wicca was honorable; they were a tradition that had run up against the wall of an avaricious Christianity bent on eradicating every vestige of earlier spiritual forces. Did not the Wicca seek to uphold the very grounding of humanity's goodness in nature rather than the wasteland of ecumenical dogma? David Thomas was surprising himself. Here were thoughts he had always done his best to repress (often in deference to Eliza, his wife, who was a pious parishioner). But obviously the gravity of the strange pedigree of lives he had found himself involved with provoked those latent thoughts.

On his arrival back at the lake, David Thomas pushed the rowboat off the pebbled shore, embarked, and began to row across the now slate-black waters. He watched the oars dip with a refreshing sound into the oily smooth, gentle billows. Who were they, these people in their cynosure? It seemed they existed in a land apart where the governing laws had no connection whatever with the real world. Had they broken the law? Someone had certainly caused the destruction of an automobile. Pedro might have to answer for that, he thought, since the car was in his name. Did anyone intentionally fake his death? It was hardly provable, but the circumstances made it likely. Pedro might have to answer for that too. He was guilty of a crime, not to mention the agony he had most certainly put his family through. But what was the purpose of all this monkey business, he mused, as he approached the dock across the lake. Was it an ultimate test of Pedro's guardianship of this "secret of life" thing? What, essentially, was the outcome? Was it some ridiculously cultish scenario only a pagan society could comprehend? Was it really a life and death struggle? Who could he charge? What use would it be to charge anyone? The case was definitely a strange one. He would have to solicit Anne Willobie for some answers. Would she be candid, he wondered, so that at least he might satisfy his conscience, vis-à-vis the law, and convey something respectable to Pedro's mother and father, who undoubtedly would want further proof either of their son's death or of his survival and possible whereabouts? Could the tragedy have been as futile as it was beginning to appear? Ah, what the hell, he thought, just about everyone could be incriminated, including himself for just getting to know about Pedro. Guilt by association. Pedro himself could well have consciously chosen a path doomed to end in tragedy. Into the valley of death rode Pedro, not to reason why. Or was it preordained?

He hiked back along the lake and up the hillside to the pastures. The sheep had disappeared and the wind had picked up. Cymru, Cymru! What a land, he mused, as he walked beside the old stone wall. Up ahead he saw the dip of the hill and the treetops of the glen where the Willobie estate lay. Suddenly, in the east toward the mountains, something moved, some small fragment of the landscape across the field by the stone fence. He remembered the person on the hillside in the morning. As he approached the stone fence to investigate, the wind carried a muffled cry of anguish toward him; the wind had picked up even in the moments he stood there. Like a symphony, it weaved the anguished cry in and out. Intrigued, he continued along the wall but did not see anything but empty pastures. When he came to the corner, he entered through an open gate the next field. About a hundred metres back along the other side of the same wall from which Thomas had just come, sat a young woman who evidently had chosen the spot for its protection from the wind. She held her head in her hands and was still unaware of him. Once, she gently pounded the ground with her left hand. David Thomas approached slowly to avoid surprising her, hoping she would see him. As he came closer, he could see that she was dressed in black leotards and a dress with a grey wool cardigan.

"Hello," he called out above the wind from about fifteen metres away from her.

At the sound of his voice, she looked up immediately. She had been crying and, embarrassed, wiped her eyes with her sleeve. David Thomas paused about fifteen paces away, with the wind fiercely gusting over the top of the stone wall and pealing in his ears. In that moment he knew who she must be and wondered if she might have some inkling about him. Of course she might, he thought, if Anne had told her.

She had raven hair and pale white skin, and was quite buxom. Her face reminded him of many of the young girls in the villages; at once she seemed quintessentially typical, yet untypical or remarkable, perhaps for her burning green eyes and red cheeks.

"Yes?" she said in Welsh with a jaded eloquence, surprised at his intrusion.

"Sorry for intruding," Thomas said in English. "I thought I saw something move down here and took it into my head to satisfy my curiosity. Everything all right, Miss?" He walked closer to within five paces.

"Oh, does it show?" she replied in English, looking away, seeming to be unconcerned with his presence.

David Thomas couldn't decide whether she was being sincere or sarcastic.

"I heard you a minute ago, actually. Naturally, being the way I am, I had to investigate. Inspector David Thomas, by the way — I've been spending some time on the property, with Mrs. Willobie's permission, of course." Gwendolyn recoiled for a detectable instant. Then she tried ineffectually to smile.

"I didn't know," she said. "I haven't seen her." She looked straight ahead across the intense green of the field.

"It's a wonderful property," commented Thomas.

She shrank from beginning a conversation. Although the Inspector seemed congenial to her, she appeared to feel unsure of how to proceed in her vulnerable position.

"I've just come back from Professor Woods' cottage," said David Thomas, deciding to plunge right in. "We had a grand old time. I learned quite a bit about you all; I shouldn't worry though. As far as I'm concerned, there's little sense that I can make out of your ways other than that the principals atone for any misdeeds they may have done. Since everyone seems to be innocent, there's nothing to prosecute, much less anything to prosecute with. In other words, you could say, I wish I could wash my hands of it. You see, I believe our Pedro is alive therefore, he's the one to blame, if anybody is for this scandal, don't you think?"

Gwendolyn's green eyes screwed up at him contentiously. David Thomas hardly knew what to expect. She reacted so strongly to his remarks, he thought for a moment she might hit him, but instead she turned abruptly away as if too perturbed to say anything. Thomas decided to try another tact. "My wife, Eliza, you know, dabbles in herbal remedies and the like," he said. "I place the knowledge on a high pedestal in the scheme of things." He was unable to back away from this verbal cauldron of chance with this abject young woman. "Mrs. Willobie is quite the adept, I hear. I'm interested, you know, Gwendolyn — and it is Gwendolyn, I presume — I'm interested in knowing your views about Pedro and this fraudulent death. I must point out that if you know anything at all about his death, you are obliged by law as an intimate to the 'deceased' shall we say, to reveal any information concerning the whereabouts of Pedro. I may be the Dyfedd District Inspector, but I don't intend to press charges in this case unless the law has been broken. I don't, however, think the brevity of this scandal warrants a barrage of public scrutiny. Don't you agree? And I believe that's the last thing any of you . . . Wicca would like. What is your last name, Gwen?"

The sun broke through a giant crack in a cloud. Its light was dazzling and compelled David Thomas to sit down beneath the wall a couple of metres from Gwendolyn. "Don't mind if I do," he said contentedly, "out of that blasted wind."

Gwendolyn turned slightly to face him and, fidgeting with some grass, reluctantly answered his question.

"Jones."

"Jones. Gwendolyn Jones. Do you know a Geraint Gwynedd?" probed Thomas.

"Why do you ask?" she said cautiously.

"He's a professor in Aberystwyth."

"So?" she asked, looking up curiously. Her eyes seemed to turn from green to darker green.

"Once I called the university in response to a complaint and asked to speak to the head of the English department," said Thomas.

She looked away, not wanting to be part of this inquiry.

"You don't know?" he persisted.

"Should I?"

"You don't want to remember."

She pulled at the grass.

"Someone was apparently raped. It was my first case here, almost five years ago. The victim dropped the charges, claimed her mother made her say it."

"Oh?"

"She claimed it was a mistaken identity."

"Did you believe her?" she asked facetiously, looking away.

"I don't make judgements."

"So what made her drop the charges?" she said coyly.

"The supposed rapist was her father."

"Too bad."

"She said it happened at her father's place. The story went that she'd been drinking in the pub and got drunk. The father didn't even know it was his daughter because he hadn't seen her in fourteen years. But, of course, nothing was corroborated."

"I like my father," she said tearfully. "So what do you want?"

"Yes, Ms. Jones. Gwendolyn Gwynedd-Jones. Small world."

The whole story given to the police had been a fabrication. Her estranged father had been innocent. Gwendolyn began to cry again. David Thomas watched sympathetically. He wanted to comfort her, but kept his distance. He remembered the case; the young woman in a delirium from some strange intoxication and the mother insisting she speak to the police, the girl not knowing who he was but recounting lies between fits of laughter to appease her mother when in truth Gwendolyn protected the identity of whoever was involved and didn't describe what had actually happened, all the while her mother being hysterical.

The sun went back behind the grey clouds.

"Do you know where Pedro George is right now, Gwen?" he asked.

She was silent.

"Why are you so upset, Gwendolyn?"

"Don't you know what's going on around here?" she exclaimed. "Anne's going back to London for an indefinite time. They'll all be gone. Everything's over. It's just me that's left. Just me!"

"What happened that time a few years back?" asked David Thomas, on the outside chance she might open up to him.

"Nothing."

"Did Pedro have anything to do with it?"

"Are you kidding? I told my mother I had sunstroke."

"Your mother didn't believe you."

"So what!" she said defiantly.

"Your mother thought you'd been raped."

"She's neurotic."

"Why did you lie to her, may I ask?"

"I don't know; she didn't want me to be a part of the Wicca, you know." She stopped ripping the grass.

"Then she knew about your involvement with the Wicca."

"Geraint Gwynedd, my real father, is Brigid's grandson. My mother remarried shortly after he left."

"Ah, I see. So why blame whatever happened on your father? That's a very serious accusation."

"My mother always said he was a cad. I didn't know any better; it just came out. I don't know. He left us when I was two. He's a witch too, you know, but not our kind."

"Which is?"

"More practical," she said after a pause.

"So you don't know where Pedro is?" asked David Thomas, making a determined effort not to sound impatient.

"No."

"Does Mrs. Willobie?"

"You will have to ask her."

David Thomas sat quietly for a moment. He realized that he would get little from Gwendolyn. She was either the loyal Wiccan, an innocent participant, a foolish young woman, or all of the above. And whatever had happened to her years before that had brought on the charges against her father, absurd as they were, was obviously just to lead away from any scrutiny of the Wicca, or whomever had caused her apparent "sickness". There was little more Thomas could extract from her in her present mood.

"What do you plan to do with yourself Gwendolyn?" asked David Thomas.

"I want to run a farm, you know. My great-grandmother said she'd give me hers. Meanwhile, I'll stay here; I do odd jobs, you know, but mostly I look after Anne's farm."

⁂

The two black Labs greeted David Thomas with friendly wags of their tails as he again approached the venerable trees and gardens of the old manor house. He walked to the front. The big, beautiful oak door opened, and there stood Anne Willobie radiant as the sun. She had changed into a burgundy dress but was wearing the same mauve sweater and brown leather loafers. She looked as wholesome and happy as a nuptial smile. David Thomas stood there for a moment in a quandary over this strange levity.

"Do come in," she said. She had to repeat the invitation before he finally heard. As he stepped into the hallway, she directed him to the living-room and solarium, where he was to wait while she put on some tea. It was all very matter-of-fact; her manner was rushed, but replete with confidence. She swung around, flipping her brown hair, and striding off in a light gait.

In the living area David Thomas turned an appraising eye on the rustic contents of the place. Arrayed before him was a hodgepodge of furnishings and antiquities whose procurement must have required an intensive scouring of the country. The effect was a little cluttered but simple. He sat down in a cushioned wicker chair near the solarium, which was virtually a jungle of plants.

"I'll get around to sorting this out when I get back," said Mrs. Willobie, entering the room.

"The plants do proliferate!" Thomas quickly responded. He was adjusting to her uncanny presence, and the small talk gave him a few needed moments to summon his own sense of power and ease that otherwise came naturally to him. In fact, he was restraining himself from gloating, which would only fall flat against her bouyant psychometry and champagne eyes.

Standing up by an adjacent chair with her hands on its back, she turned away from his obvious scrutiny.

"Yes," she said, "I do so hate to cut them. It must hurt."

"So I gather you're going back to England for awhile," he said, attempting to start a dialogue on his terms.

Pedro the Enigma 187

"Yes. Tell me, how was your jaunt down to the lake?" she asked, steering clear of her own plans, at once aware that his tone of voice had given away his officious side.

"Absolutely wonderful. It is an incredible property," he said, blithely playing along with her evasions.

Her expression changed, assuming something implacable; she seemed to gaze into the air over his right shoulder. "If you have something to say, please say it, Mr. Thomas," she said with a sudden abruptness, now looking directly at him on the last syllable.

"There are many things I would like to say, Mrs. Willobie," said Thomas coolly. "But first, I would like to express my sympathies to you on the loss of your father some years ago, whom I gather you were very close to, according to Augustus."

"Thank you, Inspector. How is Augustus?" she said, cutting him off.

"He seems very well," said Thomas, uncertain of how to proceed with her gusts of wind shift.

"Did he tell you he was once a Horned God, Mr. Thomas?"

"Ah, no, I don't believe he did," said Thomas a little put off by her question. "I must say, though, if he were, it must've been good for him. He's a healthy old fellow, honest and forthright. I certainly enjoyed his company-"

"Yet rather a serious omission, Mr. Thomas. How credible do you think he is? I find him fawning. He worked with Brigid before my time, or maybe even yours."

"He mentioned her. Quite an old witch."

"Yes, well, let me fetch the tea, then we can . . . let's say, dally in the subterfuge, shall we, Mr. Thomas?"

"If you insist, Mrs. Willobie."

"That was a joke, Mr. Thomas."

"Ahum, yes, ha ha."

"And it's not Willobie anymore — it's Fitzooth, Miss Fitzooth. I am divorcing Charles."

"I'm very sorry to hear that, Miss Fitzooth."

"It has been coming for a long time. He's quite impotent."

"Yes, I see . . . a rather personal thing . . . one must be happy," said David Thomas, a little put off by her candid remark, yet hoping she was raising her veil for him.

"Oh, I'm happy all right, but the love we shared simply couldn't hold up. Sometimes one must start anew. Just a moment." She swung around and left the room. Some music started up from the kitchen area. Kate Bush, thought Thomas; he had heard the song before on the radio. He sat there contemplating the information he had received that day and which he was now in a position to act upon. He looked at the plants and decided botany wasn't one of his better subjects. A thought struck him: it must have been Gwendolyn, the lonely shepherdess who had seen him that morning from the high pasture. He wondered why that kept nagging at him? He sensed a complicity between Anne and Gwendolyn that was a little frayed around the edges. One or both of them were very worried about his presence. It also occurred to him that he must get directions to Brigid's farmhouse.

Anne Fitzooth returned, carrying a tray with tea and scones, a small pitcher of cream and some honey. She quickly set it down and poured two cups of tea, giving one to Thomas. "Please help yourself," she said, sitting back in the other chair.

"Your hospitality is much appreciated, Miss Fitzooth," said David Thomas. "But I do not want to take up any more of your time. I now have as good a grasp of this case as can be expected at this point in time. Let me be frank: Augustus alluded to the possibility that Pedro's death has been a hoax. I would like to know your position on this. I hope I make myself clear, because I do not in any way condone the spillage, so to speak, of witches' brews outside their private domain. I also need directions to Brigid's place. At any rate, I think, as I said, I have some grasp of the problem with Pedro . . . I might add, a most peculiar individual."

"Mr. Thomas," said his hostess, interrupting him again, "no need to explain. To tell you the truth, it's been a bloody nightmare. I don't know what Augustus has told you, but I'll tell you flat out, Pedro was or is one powerful human being and had a tremendous influence on all of us, one way or another. We all wanted him for ourselves — myself, as you're probably aware, included. Now, (and I speak for the others too), we're not fools who read lurking spirits into everything, but Pedro crossed the line. He took advantage of us and our ways, not becoming for an apprentice witch."

"What do mean 'crossed the line'?"

"He challenged Brigid for the control of our coven. Brigid didn't even have to try and 'do him in', not that she ever would. Pedro set himself up to 'die,' unwittingly I think, as a challenge to his own nemesis, Gorgon, an evil specter haunting him down through the ages. We all loved him, including Brigid. Christ, she even warned him the day they met."

"I still don't follow you. What is Gorgon?"

"The Gorgons in mythology were supposedly monstrous females with pigs' teeth, claws and snaky hair, the most notable of whom was Medusa, who turned her victims to stone. It has been said they were only personifications of the terrors of the sea. Take it one step further: the sea was always a feminine symbol, like the moon, by which men may feel threatened. Man fears the power of women."

"Are you trying to tell me Pedro feared women?" asked Thomas, becoming more sceptical.

"Possibly. That's why we liked him. We certainly were not threatened by him."

"Yet he 'crossed the line.'"

"Politics, Mr. Thomas."

"So why would someone want him dead, Mrs. Willobie . . . Miss Fitzooth?"

"Not dead, but removed." She turned to look out the window; the wind was not letting up and could be heard in the trees. It was an eerie sound under the circumstances.

"It appears he removed himself by faking his death," said Thomas, sipping his tea. The whole scene was becoming ludicrous to him. "All rather redundant," he added. "Unless, of course, he was murdered."

"Murdered? Are you kidding? He was not one to dramatize his entrances and exits, Mr. Thomas, not that he wasn't beyond setting himself up or was set up to die. But I can tell you, even if he was, I certainly would have had nothing to do with it."

"Well, who did? Gorgon the creature of myth?" exclaimed Thomas, suddenly with impatience, pleased with the effect he had on her.

"I don't know," she said, "but things happen."

"Are you trying to tell me a creature of myth stalked Pedro?" said Thomas waving his hand in the air.

"No, but where do myths come from?" she responded coolly.

"Why, I don't know really," he said with feigned exasperation. He perceived her reasoning to be deranged.

"Reality, Mr. Thomas. Myths are based on reality. Oh yes, they've been distorted, displaced, but they are as real as you or me." She put her tea down and took a scone, which she spread with cream.

"Yes, but how does such a mythical creature plot to kill Pedro?"

"It's not the creature, it's the reason the creature came into being, our natural destiny as humans that's at work. When you create a God (and embody it) in the flesh, you kill it. Or it kills you."

"Why?" asked David Thomas, completely lost.

"That's like asking why they killed Jesus, or Pan, or Osiris, et cetera. I think it's like sending 'divinity' back to its proper sphere, heaven or the infinite."

"I still don't understand," persisted David Thomas. He couldn't make head or tail of her talk; they all seemed to be playing games — forbidden games guaranteed to twist your mind so far out that monsters such as Gorgon became living flesh in the guise of whomever you might imagine. Talk about delusion, he thought.

"Brigid did put a spell on Pedro, not to kill him, but to save him. He didn't see it that way, of course, but it worked."

"People shouldn't meddle with lives like this," commented Thomas, trying to give himself a little space to think the puzzle through. "What is a spell?" he asked after a moment. "And what makes you so sure it worked?"

"A spell? It's really just psychic domination — power over an individual. Witches use it to enhance healing. It can get unwieldy in the minds of neophytes. Psychometry is not to be played with, at all; it is to be used solemnly and with great respect. Young adepts should only use it under the strict guidance of an elder, such as Brigid. I hardly consider myself qualified. Pedro, on the other hand, was a born natural and had it without trying. He got what he wanted, well, until he came up against Brigid."

"Brigid Pyles," he said, remembering her last name.

"Brigid Argeia."

"Argeia? Isn't that a mythical Welsh kingdom?"

"Yes, whose center was once this property."

"Really? Why did Augustus call her Brigid Pyles?"

"That was her late husband's name, though he died fifty years ago."

"Gwendolyn said she was Brigid's great-granddaughter."

"So you met Gwen. She's wonderful, isn't she!" said Anne Fitzooth beaming.

"She was upset you were leaving, among other things."

"It will be good for her. I hope she goes back to school."

"What is her family connection to Gwynedd?"

"Gwen is descended from Brigid's daughter, Olwen, who married Geraint Gwynedd and then died in childbirth. Brigid's grandson, also Geraint, or Olwen's son, is Gwen's natural father. Gwen's mother then remarried a fellow named Jones."

"Goodness, there's quite a history in all this," said David Thomas. They both sat quietly for a moment, Anne sipping her tea and David Thomas eating a scone.

"Pedro's parents know he is alive by now. I spoke with Charles in

Toronto, earlier," she announced, staring out the window again quite comfortably.

"How do they know he's alive?" exclaimed Thomas.

"I told Charles," she said evasively. Her black cat jumped in her lap.

"How do you know he's alive?" he persisted. "Where is Pedro? Why didn't he come forward if he was indeed alive?"

"Call it psychometry, Mr. Thomas. I just know, and I haven't any idea where he is; nor do I know how or why this has all come about," she said with conviction.

"Psychometry? I need proof!" he said adamantly.

"Where's the body, Mr. Thomas? That's proof enough in a court of law."

Thomas refrained from responding. He knew only too well his responsibility in this matter. He then decided upon a different tact. "All right. Say he is alive. Where do you think he would most likely be?"

"Probably Canada. He would have taken a rather abstract view of his funeral."

"Quite the cool customer, I'd say. How could anyone stand aside and see his family and friends suffer unnecessary bereavement like that? It's downright sadistic."

She laughed.

"You're a pretty cool individual yourself," said David Thomas. Although he had begun to find her intriguing, her laughter now made him angry — angry at himself for his poor judgement concerning that damned auto accident.

"Pedro is not sadistic, Mr. Thomas," she said, "I insist. To understand him, you must accept his martyrdom; I wouldn't even be surprised if he'd actually gone to his own funeral."

"You're not joking?" he asked incredulously.

"Hardly. Well almost."

"One doesn't know where you all stand," said Thomas.

"How so? I'm telling you the truth," she said.

"Why didn't you tell me this morning?" he said, prying.

"Because I hoped the whole thing would blow over; but, after meeting you, I knew you would get to the bottom of it. I just wanted to make sure that you would have to 'discover' a few things for yourself. My deceit this morning — in fact, these past few days up to the funeral — has not sat well with me. It's been hell."

"You don't seem to have much respect for the law, Miss Fitzooth. But since you have repented, I shall not take any further action — unless of course, you have lied to me."

"I respect the law, Mr. Thomas," she said flatly.

"So who do you think actually rigged the car, then?"

"Certainly not us, Mr. Thomas; probably Hero St. Germain, who practices her own particular brand of sorcery which I find nauseating."

"She's a good witch then. Am I correct?" he asked.

"Oh, she's good all right; she and Brigid were quite close too."

"I didn't know that, and naturally you and Hero were not on the best of terms . . . Pedro seemed to have both of you quite involved." Thomas was having fun now.

"Are you suggesting we were rivals?" She was aroused.

"I don't know."

"Well, to tell you the truth, if there was anyone who could have led Pedro to the brink, it was Hero; they were very strong together. I accepted that. I accepted her because of him. I loved Pedro, Mr. Thomas."

"I'm aware of that."

"If you think I'm a cool customer, you don't know what that means until you meet Hero St. Germain. I envy her. I swallow my pride when I say it, but she's a lot more witch than I am. Brigid recognized this too, but I have more experience, and I've been much more involved with the community and Brigid over the years. There is a social subtext to all this, you know. St. Germain is through and through both occultist and artist; she walks a fine line between what the Wicca propounds and the impulses of a voyeur. To be fair, I would say she has tremendous potential."

"Where does your cousin, the Earl of Huntington, fit in, Miss Fitzooth?" As he said this, Thomas glanced through the window and noticed Gwendolyn outside, walking around the house. How strange, he thought, I'm in the midst of witches.

"Niko loves Hero. Need I say more? He's a willing player, but no witch. Niko and Pedro are bonded in eternity as long lost brothers or something; nothing can come between them. Everyone looks up to Niko; he's his own person, successful, tremendously well respected amongst his peers in London; but when it comes to Pedro and Hero, he's their slave and master. Ironic, isn't it?" she said in her gentle English accent.

They could hear the front door open and close. Soon, Gwendolyn stood impassively before them; then with a slight gesture of her hand and a half-smile, she turned and disappeared into the kitchen.

"She's getting herself a teacup," said Anne knowingly.

"I'm glad she could join us."

"You're a good man, Mr. Thomas. I hope my being frank with you about this denouement hasn't prejudiced you against us. The powers that be were unleashed briefly, but have been contained with only a little 'spillage,' as you say. Sorry about the emotional fallout vis-à-vis the family and so on."

David Thomas refrained from responding to Anne's compliment. He knew he was handling all this very well from the Wiccan point of view. He could have charged in like an impossible bureaucrat, been less tolerant, blustered, or threatened charges. Had he done so, however, he may not have discovered anything about this scandal until it blistered out with the reappearance of Pedro, if he was alive. But where was he? Bloody witches' nest, he mused.

Gwendolyn pulled up a chair and sat down, then poured herself some tea. The room darkened as the weather took a turn for the worst. The windows began to reverberate slightly in the wind from a threatening storm.

"Gwen, I hear you've already met Mr. Thomas," said Anne.

"Yes," she said, smiling politely.

"I'm glad you've joined us, Gwen," said Thomas. "We're having a delightful discussion about Pedro and the Wicca. I never imagined how deeply engrossing it all is. You've grown up in an environment saturated with this doctrine. It's curious, really; I just hope you use this knowledge wisely. I think, if I may say so, one should counterbalance this doctrine with conventional study, say university. Were you not enrolled at Aberystywth?"

"No," said Gwendolyn, before adding, "Maybe I would like to try. Annie thinks I should. But I doubt it. I like it here."

"Good," said Thomas, "if it suits you. Now."

"Gwendolyn," said Anne with a slight urgency, "Inspector Thomas needs your help to find Brigid's place. Would you mind going with him; it's not the easiest spot to find."

Gwendolyn looked as though she were about to complain but looked down without saying anything. After an awkward silence, she mumbled, "I suppose I could."

Thomas, who would have been content simply to take directions, sat back and observed that late afternoon tea, now ensconced in momentary silence. He believed that Anne's articulate candour was further testimony to her particular deceit, yet he was unprepared to pursue it at that time. Rain had begun to drive against the solarium windows, and he became aware of a racket made by branches scratching too. The dogs were barking madly to be let in.

Elphin the Jester woke to the virtuoso performance of a cuckoo which spurred the thoughts of a good omen. No sooner had he come out of his bush by a cleft in a projecting rock than a sorry group of four young women walked past, being led by a dozen Saxon warriors bearing the standard of Vron the Barbarian. Elphin had heard that Vron had set up his little army from hell in the village of Aberystwyth, on the west coast of Cambria. Up to that moment he had not known how he was to get inside the Saxon fortification on some reasonable pretext in order not only to save his own life but also to lure Vron back into Argeia, Gwydion's little kingdom. At the moment when the women and their guard went by, it dawned on Elphin that he could come across their path as a gleeman, a kind of mad poet who could trump up and pander glorification of Vron's odious exploits. Such a ruse might just appeal to Vron's vanity. How to entice the Saxons to reinvade Argeia of their own volition would have to be worked out later. Entry into Vron's inner circle was the present challenge.

    Elphin immediately went into the lane behind the group of travellers and called out like the cuckoo bird which had initially wakened him. Adding dance to song, he jumped up and down in his nimble and scrawny way to make it obvious he was a fool rather than an armed threat or decoy and was assisted in his intent by the area's open country and sparse woodlands which were not conducive to ambush. The band of Saxons turned around and walked toward him with their spears and arrows poised, ready to quickly dispatch this wild-bearded old man in rags, armed only with a crooked staff. For a few moments Elphin hovered between the thought of his previous freedom and of the great dark void that loomed ominously before him. Instinctively, he sang out a ballad off the top of his head to hold their attention for a few more moments and give himself time to ensnare them in his ploy. The Saxons, twitching in their discomfort and glaring murderously, came irritably to a halt. Elphin sang:

> *Down from the east he came like the wind,*
> *He came like the wind, he came like the wind,*
> *Vron the Great, leading brave fighting men,*
> *Brave fighting men, brave fighting men,*

He comes to this land to claim his find,
To claim his find, to claim his find,
And free the poor from bad King Gwydion,
Bad King Gwydion, bad King Gywdion.

We all rejoice to sing his praises,
Sing his praises, sing his praises,
Vron the Great, leading brave fighting men,
Brave fighting men, brave fighting men,

In battle cry his banner he raises,
His banner rises, his banner rises,
Over the dead body of bad King Gwydion,
Bad King Gywdion, Bad King Gwydion

"Cease, old man!" said one of the warriors in a broken vernacular of the Cymraeg tongue. The others lowered their weapons. The young women, dishevelled, in torn clothes, hung their heads. Elphin assumed a twisted posture like that of a deformed tree and prayed for his stars to hold constant. Ah, how his heart cried out for the poor women who were to be meted out a fate worse than death. He recognized them from a village south of Caerymwy on the river Stywyth. Remaining contorted until he was sure of his having survived this first phase of his induction, Elphin the Jester raised his staff to the sky and gave thanks.

"Thank you, Great Father," he said, pausing briefly then touching the ground with his staff. "Thank you Great Mother. Thank you for delivering me into the hands of my master, Vron the Great. I am safe from the unbelieving tree-people-"

"Shut up, old man!" said the leader from ten paces. He was large, blond and brawny with dull little eyes. He then grunted at two warriors — one dark and sinister, the other young and blank faced — to bring the old man into line with the women. The latter remained mute and uncomprehending.

The warriors hastened them along, beating one woman who was falling down and ready to kill her, had Elphin not helped her along. The spumy grey waters of the Irish sea came into view, and soon smoke from the village palisade could be seen. Once inside the well-guarded compound, the Saxons were cheered, and the poor women were sized up for their ability to satisfy lust. Elphin was led from the central area where a hundred warriors had gathered (by the same two that initially found him), to a small outbuilding guarded by another two warriors. They passed by heaps of corpses stacked crudely along the wooden wall of the fortification. As they went, they saw two old villagers carrying the bodies one at a time under guard to an outlying area for burial. Elphin was shoved into the dark entrance of the building and took a few minutes to adjust to the light. It was cold and damp, so he found a corner and hunched down to keep warm while keenly eyeing a small pile of wood against the other wall. From beneath the thatched roof and walls, slight bands of light filtered in, one shaft falling directly onto a dark lump across the room.

The lump moved and raised itself up. He could see it was a young girl of about fourteen, dark haired and fair-skinned. She remained as quiet as a ghost, staring at him with frightened eyes.

"Do not be afraid, young one," said Elphin in a low, clear voice that dispelled her fear and replaced it with a little reassurance. "What has happened here? Is this where Vron now stays?"

The young girl refused to answer but did utter a little cry. Plainly she was badly traumatized. Elphin went over to her slowly, saying, "I will not hurt you. Have you been hurt? I am Elphin of Argeia, a healer. Do you know my name?"

She remained quiet, but now at least her face wore a pensive expression. Elphin held out his palm with a few hazelnuts in it. She hesitated but took them and hungrily began to eat them. He gave her more, and had some himself. Then he saw that she was shivering, so he took his old outer sheepskin mantle and put it around her. She began to cry again, but leaned onto him. So to comfort her, he put his arm around her and held her gently. Soon she was asleep.

Elphin realized that they had been set aside for something special. He was right where he wanted to be if he was correct in thinking that only for Vron would they be spared. The young girl, most likely, had been saved for Vron's pernicious pleasure that evening; and he himself, a gift from the blond brawny Saxon, would provide the entertainment. His captor would undoubtedly earn a commendation of some sort from his heinous master. Elphin closed his eyes to rest.

Not long after, both he and the girl were stirred by shrieks from a woman fighting a bitter and losing battle against some of the despoilers. Her cries became long, agonizing moans, then finally ceased. A terrible silence followed. These barbarians, thought Elphin, were a blight requiring nothing short of extermination.

The young girl now seemed to have revived somewhat; although terribly frightened, she was more relaxed. Elphin released her from his comforting arm, stood up, and investigated the premises. A small crack through the corner of the rough stone wall permitted him to see out, but there was little he could see; except the movements of the cruel marauders to and fro.

"We have little chance of escape," said Elphin, attempting to communicate again. If he could win her confidence and enlist her help, his task might be made much easier.

"What is your name?" he tried again.

"Eorann," came her reply. Elphin was surprised by the firmness of her voice. She spoke a heavily accented Gaelic.

"You are not Cambrian," he said gently.

"I am Irish," she said, with greater conviction.

"What has happened?" continued Elphin.

"These bad men killed my people. We had come from Eire to trade for gemstones. They captured us with the rest of the village. My father and brothers are dead. I am orphaned. I will be next. I will not give myself to that monster," she exclaimed venomously.

Elphin waited a minute in silence in respect of her loss before saying, "I feel your loss as I have felt mine."

She stared glumly into the darkness.

"Eorann," said Elphin gently, "maybe we can work together. But first, do you know of any back entrance to this fort? Sometimes a secret tunnel is dug for emergencies," said Elphin, coming back to sit down beside her.

"There is one, but it was discovered and is probably being guarded. Some of the women and children escaped but were caught and brought back."

"Eorann," began Elphin, "we will have only one chance to escape. At night while these despoilers have drunk themselves senseless, we will be compelled to serve as base amusement. You are being saved specifically for the enjoyment of Vron the Barbarian, their insidious leader; I think I am to sing his praises — they think me a bard. I will give you this." Elphin reached into his pouch beneath his tatters and gave Eorann a little wooden vial. "It is a sleeping poison, belladonna, if mixed with ale. You must slip it into his drink at the right time, just before he takes you into his private quarters. You will have to use your feminine guile to know his mood. Do not hesitate! Your life depends on it. Do you think you can do this?"

"Yes, I have had suitors; my father was a wealthy merchant."

"And you are indeed a lovely girl," said Elphin.

"But, if I succeed, what should I do? Kill him?"

"No, do not try. He must lead his horde back to my land where we will destroy them to the last man. It is only on our own battleground that we will be able to finish them with the element of surprise. They are too strong otherwise."

"How will you lure them?" she asked.

Elphin paused.

"I don't know yet," he said with a furrowed brow. "But at least you have a chance to escape through the tunnel. If my plan comes together, I shall go with you. You may turn out to be a prized possession that he will come after. We will leave a trail that will lead him to his death."

"He would not value me, she said. "I am nothing."

"How can you be sure? He has put you here for some reason." Elphin stood up and began pacing, worried that his plan might fail.

"He values his sword more than a woman," she said.

"His sword," said Elphin, abruptly turning to face her. Light from a crack in the wall marked a stripe across his long beard which seemed to tremor in his fervent desperation. "His sword," he repeated. "What does it look like?"

"It is unlike any other, so beautiful, with silver and jewels. It shines in the sun, but loses its lustre in his hands. He captured it from a king."

"Gwydion's sword," said Elphin ecstatically. "This will be the lure. He will come after Gwydion's sword."

"Do you wish me to steal it?"

"Yes. You must; it is our only hope."

"I will steal it," she said proudly.

Elphin began to pace. He knew how he was going to deceive Vron's horde. "Where is the secret tunnel?" he asked.

"At the other end of the fortification," she said, "in a similar hut used for storing dry peat."

Long after dusk had descended upon them and the night's horrors were underway, Elphin and Eorann huddled together in the cool, damp hut. The raucous yells and background uproar from the main building were becoming more vehement. Never in his varied life had Elphin encountered such a depraved band. Had he not subtly importuned the Saxons, there would be little chance of cozening them to reinvade Argeia at the place of his choosing — Caerymwy's oaken epicenter. As it was, Elphin knew that all the knowledge, craft, and sorcery he had ever learned would be put to the maximum test. As bait, both he and Eorann could just as easily be swallowed up without effort as inconsequent victims of Vron's frightful holocaust. He heard footsteps and voices coming their way. The guttural mutterings now outside could mean that his or her presence had indeed aroused some interest and that there was possibly a chance that Vron, in a fit of stumbling lust, might provide Elphin with a precarious advantage. He gave the inert Eorann a little shake and, removing his arm from around her, went to sit in another part of the room.

"Eorann," he whispered, "remember our plan, and if I should die, save yourself; save yourself, child. Go east to the hills of Caerymwy. Seek out Bran the Warrior and Olwen; they will care for you. Do not come back for me."

The door opened, and a torch protruded, lighting up the area. The figure behind the light, ignoring the girl, called out to the old man to rise and come along. Elphin put on a pretence of acrimony.

"Ye sluggards, ye leave me in this hole with an Irish bitch; she's as cold as the very ground!" he said, getting up sullenly. He walked out and shut the door, leaving Eorann behind. From this moment on he knew he walked a tightrope; one slip, and death was certain.

His escort led him through the dark, lighting the way with torches. On the way, they passed stark frightened figures cowering in the shadows from the sudden onslaught of light. It was a dark world of enforced shock for anyone who had survived Vron's bloodletting. After awhile, Elphin and his guard came to the main building, which was lit up with torches around the entrance where two dozen Saxons were drinking from clay jugs in a disorderly fashion. A number of women there appeared, by drunken fawning, to have ingratiated themselves with a few of the barbarians. To Elphin they seemed like broken women, or remarkable actors; their sultry looks and crazed tempers almost repealed the fear in himself except for the off-chance of their betrayal if they recognized him. Yet the moment he passed, the ale-dulled silence in their traumatized eyes falling upon him was all the response he got.

On their entry into the Grand Hall, the boisterous crowd parted, as if he were the Grand Vizier. In minutes he found himself alone under the timber-trussed ceiling of the central area, adjusting to the illumination of the many torch lanterns evenly arrayed about the hall's rough stone walls. The drunken crowd that greeted him uproariously now fell silent. Elphin looked about at the sea of murderous faces. He was impassive. His powers set in like a second wind and he almost relished the challenge. Here was a mob of hot-blooded morons and the sense of a distinct advantage began to inspire confidence in him.

Turning to the long oak table in front of him, Elphin pretended to acknowledge the central authority of that degenerative horde, the muscularly corpulent beast, Vron the Barbarian.

Rather than kowtow to the tyranny, he felt that to provoke their obvious rancour might just engage them enough as a whole to hold their attention, if slight, in his favour over Vron. It was not that it would impute disfavour but, on the contrary, garner temperance. Elphin sensed that these Saxons, being so flagrantly unpious, were captivated by plain dumb braggadocio.

Elphin began to laugh. What began as a fake guffaw developed into genuine hysterics. He was soon shrieking in honest ribaldry. The Saxons, nonplussed, began to murmur to each other and cast looks at Vron. But before disaster could strike, Elphin restrained himself and called out in Cymraeg, "Where's my ale? Where's my ale? Ye God-forsaken bastards!"

"He asks for ale!" someone called out, translating.

Another uproar. Someone came out with a tankard and poured its contents on Elphin's head. Elphin got down on his knees and licked what he could off the floor then, comically, did the same to his hands and face, crying for more. This seemed to elicit sympathy or amusement and a couple more Saxons came out and repeated the ale drenching. The crowd once again burst into pandemonium. Only Vron, glowering, stood up and growled something. Everyone quickly shut up.

"Who are you, old man?" he said in Saxon. Someone translated. Elphin turned to face the boar's head with the shiny little eyes. As he lowered his own eyes in expedient submission, he did not fail to notice the hilt of Gwydion's sword at Vron's side. "I am Elphin the Sillurian, your eminence. I have heard you are in need of a gleeman, so I have come to laud your conquests and sing the praises of your glory for the simple fee of food and lodging."

"It is said that one should not trust old men with beards in Cymru," said Vron in his gutteral drawl.

"I am Sillurian, Vron. We spit on the Cymru."

"What will it matter then, old man, if I kill you? You are all the same to me. KILL the mongrel dog!"

As several Saxons approached with swords in their hand, Elphin knew then he had only one chance. He also knew he must have been lucky enough to have lived as long as he had with them. Vron's policy was simply to butcher everyone.

"Vron," he called, "I have some information for you. I speak the truth. There is an army waiting for you. You will surely die, if you do not heed my intelligence."

"Where, old man?" he growled.

"Argeia, your Lordship."

"Argeia? They were but a day's revels!"

"They have joined with others."

"They run before us like rabbits."

The blond, brawny Saxon then spoke up. "Do we kill him?"

Vron hesitated. One Saxon had his sword raised. Elphin felt unruffled. He was prepared to die. Vron raised his hand. The Saxons backed away. Vron began to laugh. The whole horde began to laugh. The challenge to their might by an awaiting army had heated their blood sufficiently to distract them from Elphin. And Elphin had succeeded in creating an illusion of his importance to the Saxons, even if the result was only a bit of borrowed time. The night wore on. Elphin summoned up all his strength to play first the puppet then the marionette.

In the early hours of the morning, Vron retired with Eorann, who had been brought in after Elphin, and Elphin managed to slip all of a pouch of powder he had into the remaining barrel of ale. The men eventually dropped off like flies; those on duty were so drunk they merely simulated attention but soon slouched over into glassy-eyed unconsciousness. With ease Elphin found his way in the dark to the now unguarded peat hut. Saxon defences that night were so lax, a surprise attack, had there only been one ready, would then and there have destroyed them. They undoubtedly realized this or would not have allowed themselves their present state of relaxation. Nevertheless, the seeds of their doom had been sown.

Elphin huddled in the hut, listening to the faint vestiges of revelry across the fort. He found the hole in the center of the peat pile and could have escaped, but he waited for Eorann.

It was like a miracle when silently through the dark crawled Eorann, pulling the beautiful sword. She entered the hut, whispering softly to him. Elphin, without a word, but whispering her name, took the sword and followed her swiftly down into the hole.

Vron the Barbarian and his horde did precisely as Elphin intended them to do. They went straight back to Caerymwy where they were ambushed on all sides in the Sacred Forest. Bran and Olwen commanded their entire army to chant, "Gorgon, Gorgon, Gorgon!" as they mobilized for attack. Gorgon was the Saxon's unnamed Goddess who, being exposed during the initial strike, wreaked havoc on their morale, which in turn had them in disarray and fear. Every last man was slaughtered. Their blood so thoroughly soaked the earthen forest floor, it was said the ground remained red for days after.

Vron was spared in observance of Olwen's wish, only to be blinded, castrated, and silenced by having his tongue cut out. He was then set free to roam the rest of his days in terrible depravity. No one killed him. He was made to suffer by being kept alive and taunted by all; but he perished within a fortnight, uttering his gutteral curses to the end.

Chapter Eight

Here with a Loaf of Bread beneath the Bough,
A Flask of Wine, a Book of verse — and Thou
Beside me singing in the Wilderness -
And Wilderness is Paradise enow.

—Omar Khayyam

Sadie McPherson remained resolute in her changed attitude toward Ronald Morgan in spite of much beseeching from him on their hike up to Dreamer's Rock. They were alone together, having been left behind on the way by Hero and Niko, so they had ample time to come to terms with their sudden falling out. This had come on unexpectedly, like a giant storm cloud emerging out of nowhere on a sunny day. Ronald, so secure in his engagement to Sadie, had behaved like the new owner of yet another chattel and unwittingly exposed himself by garrulous overtures to Hero. Sadie, the chattel, had the unnerving experience of divining what marriage to him would be like: discord such as they were experiencing now, without their present independence from each other. Her freedom, Sadie realized, gave her leverage to execute a necessary control over Ronald's sexually egocentric side. As long as this was in place, she found him exciting and indeed loved him for reasons she was not fully sure of. And Ronald, when receiving her affection, was more than falling over himself in gratification.

"*Sadie, please listen to me!*" said Ronald behind Sadie, on the path they were following beneath a cliff in the forest. "Please," he repeated, more calmly. He then grabbed her arm, but was shaken off.

"No! I don't want to think about it now."

"You can't just one minute say we shouldn't be together, then the next refuse to talk about it!" bellowed Ronald, stopping.

Sadie turned around and shot him an anguished look, her big blue eyes like orbs of electricity that made Ronald want to go up to her and kiss her all over. He knew she was his woman and thought she just wasn't quite yet sure herself. Meanwhile, Sadie was thinking that, once she had made Ronald vulnerable, as Hero could so easily do, he really was quite the little puppy. If only he could just be a little more sensible. At almost the same moment, another thought occurred to her, that their relationship was becoming a runaway train.

"It's just that I'm not sure I love you," she said dejectedly, looking down on the word "love."

"Whaddaya mean, you don't love me?" cried out Ronald with his hands raised in exasperation.

"Why don't we just go up and enjoy the view, Ronald. Let's just forget about this for awhile. There's always tonight," she said provocatively.

"What's that supposed to mean?" he said, a bit mollified.

"Nothing. I just want to be open about things."

"Precisely. But is it you or your alter-ego, Jane?"

"Me. Shall we?" On that, Sadie spun around and continued to climb.

"You said some pretty rotten things about me, Sadie," said Ronald seriously and refusing to budge.

Sadie continued up the path.

"Well?" he called out.

"Okay, I'm sorry," said Sadie to the trees but not stopping to turn around.

Apology accepted, Ronald resigned himself and followed.

Already at the top of the promontory called Dreamer's Rock, Hero first, then Niko, quietly surveyed the vast view, turning slowly around three hundred and sixty degrees. To the south, they could see the main part of Georgian Bay, a brilliant blue that extended to the horizon. To the north, the white quartzite Cloche mountain range, mottled with the perennial green of pine trees, spread from east to west, interrupted by the bays, channels and inlets between Manitoulin Island and the mainland. A warm west wind stroked their souls in a generous lambency. In silence they both thought the same thoughts: ancient quests and Pedro, affinity and absolution being a paradigm of something most stupendous — a happy melancholy.

Their revolving gazes simultaneously met in each other's eyes. There they stood unwavering, knowing implicitly the very wiles of each bodily expression. At that moment an invisible curtain rose from between them, revealing an intimacy impossible before. Yet it was something they had always known somehow; what is meant to be may simply come to find its rightful place in the gravitational mindfield of life. Hero turned and leaned into Niko; they held each other quietly in the caressing zephyrs, then Niko kissed her tears and she kissed his. They found their lips, wet and moist, their warm tongues, hungry.

Hero, on an impulse, drew away from Niko's strong hold to look into his eyes; they were full of love. She blushed. Niko gently laughed, sighing through his nose. Hero turned away and laughing in her penny-pinching way, stretched her arms lovingly.

"Well, you were true to form hiking up here, the mountain goat that you are," said Niko, retreating slightly to their regular level of platitude. "I could barely keep up."

"Oh yeah? Tell me about it; your Greek side's no slouch for Thiran foot paths," she rejoined delectably.

"Greek mountains are no match for Swiss, but I accept your ploy of parity," said Niko with a twinkle.

"Now, now, Huntington, I know your subtle patronizing. Just because we kissed, and it was good, don't think this girl has got it made for you!" She gave him a squeeze as she circled around him.

"Do I look exasperated?" he asked, letting her hand slip away.

She didn't answer, but posed a more thoughtful bearing.

"Niko," she said sweetly, "Pedro will come here to see us, won't he?" Her eyes were set to the east, to where, in fact, without her knowing it, Pedro was camped across the large bay a half-dozen miles distant.

"So you think he's here?" he said.

"Of course, he's here, and I'm certain he knows we're here."

"He'll come then."

"Oh yes, he'll come. Tomorrow very likely, with the del Rio woman . . . it may be difficult for me . . . and Pedro."

"But everything will be all right now," said Niko to reassure her.

"We'll have to exit pronto, Niko. Why don't you come to Paris for awhile?"

"Love to, after I check in, in London."

Sadie and Ronald finally appeared. They both seemed more at ease as they climbed up the last stage of the ascent to the rotund pinnacle of Dreamer's. Ronald put a hand on Niko's shoulder, huffing and puffing. "Well, I'll be damned; we made it!" He gave Sadie a hug.

"In more ways than one," said Sadie.

"So," said Hero, "you've got him trained again?"

They laughed. "I'm not sure. He's on trial."

"Is that so, Ronald?" probed Hero.

"Yes, Sadie is my true love, not Hero St. Germain the fantasy; I have been finally humbled; Iron John I'm not, just candy-assed Ronny (the barbarian) Morgan. I'm a new breed. Now, who's made more cosmic leaps than me, eh?"

When the laughter stopped, Sadie suggested that maybe Pedro had made more cosmic leaps in that he had definitely been reincarnated.

"What's so hot about Pedro?" said Ronald. "He wasn't any great sage or anything — more like Tom Sawyer on acid."

Sadie, rather than admonish him in his attempt at self-aggrandizement, embellished the allusion by saying she must have been Becky

Thatcher lost in the cave with a melting candle. This expression of their respective personas at that moment raised them to a new plateau of polemics. The very Rock itself lent them the added aero-arpeggio of wind and tree from their height in the sunset — the northern spectre made more beautiful in that severe clime, which had them now sitting with their feet dangling. Sadie's quiet determination had found its center in her assertive rebuttal of Ronald's interminable energies.

For better or worse, they were compatible as long as she held the reins. It seemed in their renewed harmony, Niko's earlier request for benediction had been granted. It was the purest, most immaculate granting of a wish she had ever experienced. Maybe it was the anointing aero-arpeggio, or better still, Pedro's presence and old Indian spirits; but whatever it was, they savored it like a gentle tea without a ripple of requiting necessary. They were humbled.

In the stillness, the old sun finally set, leaving only its ever-residual afterglow fading into the nocturnal sphere. The smell of dusk now wafted up out of the forests below and with it came mosquitoes. It was with reluctance that they decided to quit the warmth of their rocky ledge. Standing up, Ronald cursed the bugs with impetuosity.

"See how we suffer on your account, Pedro!" he shouted to the darkening gloom. "May you be reincarnated as a mosquito! Ha!!"

"Ronald, you really do have a peculiar sense of humour," said Sadie.

"He can settle his score with Pedro tomorrow," said Hero, as she nimbly stepped down off the Rock.

"There she goes again. You really believe Pedro will arise from the dead like a lost Lazarus, don't you, Hero?" said Ronald with a toned down sarcasm.

"He'll be here," she said, walking down through the rocks.

"What's with her, Niko?" asked Ronald.

"She's convinced, Ron; I don't think Pedro died. It was a mix-up. The witches' field day, you know. Let's just wait and see. Come on, let's go," said Niko lightheartedly.

"Are you kidding?" said Sadie, following. Ronald stood there with a dumb look on his face.

"They never kid, Sadie," said Ronald soberly.

"Oh, yes, they do," she responded contrarily.

Their walk back to the cabin was a solemn one. Ronald, in his reverence for Niko and ineluctably for the strange Pedro, was in a quandary over what was going on. Enough was enough, he thought. He didn't understand his disquiet. Sadie, on the other hand, felt a sudden surge of longing for Ronald. He was like the rock. One knew what it was. Hero and Niko, though she empathized with them, had become a notch too beguiling in a far-out kind of way. She had a sudden vision of herself tumbling rapidly, uncontrollably, through distant reaches of outer space.

That night Sadie and Ronald made prolonged love. Their transports went beyond sex. This was exceptional. In the cocoon-like security of their double sleeping bag amidst their sweaty raptures, they seemed now to reach a new, previously unexplored realm of sexual experience, a mountainous terrain in which they ceased to function as two autonomous units and grafted or fused together to form an invincible one. Although Ronald had always made commendable efforts to please his partner, he had hitherto favored a he-man, jack-hammer approach to love-making. He now transcended these methods and achieved the gentle intensity Sadie needed.

Hero and Niko had zipped together their single sleeping bags, but refrained from actual intercourse since Niko wasn't quite ready to achieve the turgor required. He was too adrenalized for spontaneous copulation. His mind was not at ease because Pedro, as his guide into the stateliness of spirit which he so fed on, was not dead, at least not like before as Troylus and Gwydion. Hero, naturally, had few reservations when she grasped the immensity of Niko's dilemma. She cupped and cradled his privates with such skill, that he did find release with a moan unlike any she had ever heard. They clung together like wet worms, happy that they had gotten over the hump. He was an uncommon man, and she knew that he would be hers forever.

※

After a breakfast of French toast, they decided to go back to Little Current and find Pedro's old friend, Big Dan. They knew he had a little gallery and lived in an apartment above. The day started out hazy and humid, but the radio predicted cooler weather toward evening and warned of the possibility of thunderstorms. Ronald drove with Sadie beside him in the front. Hero and Niko were in the back. They were all in a jovial mood and had their windows down to take in the warm air.

When they reached the main street of Little Current, they stopped and parked to wander about, then headed toward the narrow storefront that read N'Daki Menan. Here they entered and browsed around. Sadie spoke to the native woman behind the counter, who was reading a book. Big Dan, said the woman, hadn't returned from fishing. Nor did she know when he might, but she suspected he would be back sometime in the afternoon. Sadie left a message with her that some of Pedro's old friends wanted to speak with him and that they could be reached at . . .

No sooner had she finished than the large frame of Big Dan entered the store. He was indifferent, but smiled when he recognized Sadie from years before when she was with Pedro, and even gave her a little hug. Big Dan could be as imperturbable as Sitting Bull himself, but at the moment he felt the awkwardness of the situation and was a little at a loss as to what to tell his visitors. Were Sadie and her companions the friends Pedro had mentioned confiding in about his continued existence? Big Dan decided to feign ignorance of Pedro's circumstances to safeguard any unwanted publicity until he could get back to the Point.

"Good to see you, Big Dan," said Sadie.

"I never thought I'd see you again," said Big Dan, sticking to small talk, "so I'm glad you refute my thoughts."

"So, I guess you heard about poor Pedro, Dan. He apparently found his Maker, although lately . . . " Sadie paused to cast a suspicious glance at Hero, "I'm beginning to think Pedro hasn't thrown in the towel yet."

Big Dan looked at Hero and Niko, inhaling their strange foreignness. Ronald he all but ignored, confining himself to shaking his hand. "Yes," said Big Dan, realizing at once that Hero and Niko knew about Pedro, and that by their synergy, they would be sure to understand his own position. "I was deeply affected by all this," he said. "My head's still reeling."

"Same here," said Sadie. "The funeral was just the other day. Hero and Niko here came over from Europe to attend it. Now we're on a kind of visit; another friend of Pedro's, someone we've never met, a Donna del Rio, supposedly came here. Well, it's all a bit crazy, but Hero thought by coming up here we could kind of put Pedro's spirit to rest. Am I making any sense?"

"Sounds okay to me; you came to the right place. His spirit is very real. Maybe we can find it together, later this evening; but today I have some business to tend to."

"Thanks, Dan," said Sadie. "By the way, is there anything to do around here today? Hero and Niko have never been here before."

"There is a Pow Wow in West Bay this weekend," he said.

"Hey, that's something," said Sadie. "What do you think, everybody?"

"Sure," said Niko.

They left Big Dan's gallery with the strange feeling that he hadn't seemed at all affected by Pedro's death and was paying lip service to the expected commiserations. Hero and Niko wore knowing, otherworldly smiles.

Spurred by Big Dan's suggestion, they drove to West Bay, Niko in the front with Ronald, Hero and Sadie chatting in the back about the Wicca. Hero was describing the powers of her coven, and how its members really controlled, or at least channelled, nature's energy. If something were set in motion by ritual or spell and their powers were not abused, nothing could prevent the desired outcome. If the powers were abused, and the uses to which they were put were malignant, undesirable results snowballed exponentially, usually returning sooner or later to strike the originator of a spell with a karmic thunderclap. These disclosures led Sadie to question whether Pedro had been the object or initiator of such a spell and had thereby become an unwitting victim. Hero refrained from answering for a moment, seeming to relish the deep blue of the North Channel beyond the highway across some cultivated fields. She then said in a quiet voice that Pedro was innocent of any wrongdoing, and that, in fact, no one could be blamed, because all wished him well. As a seeker, Pedro had entered into realms of human exaltation like a deranged missionary, offering his tortuous testimony of heaven's byways. He had offered himself up, it seemed, as a willing sacrifice. But he had been much too hard on himself.

No kidding, thought Sadie. But what floored her, and it was something she had definitely begun to suspect, was Hero's insistence that Pedro was alive and well, somewhere in the vicinity. She now asked Hero point-blank how she could be so sure, but all Hero would say was that her Wiccan powers told her so. There must have been a damn good reason to counterfeit Pedro's death, Sadie concluded. Was his "death" that simple logistical step contigent on a new Pedro-designed immortality? What kind of trip was he on anyway? Hero ceased speaking after that, appearing to acquit herself of any complicity.

Ronald brooded on the possibility of Pedro's survival, wary of Sadie's sensitivity toward the idea, though he decided to play along. He was not so much intrigued as flustered since he felt restrained to voice his opinion because his and Sadie's earlier falling out, from which he had not fully recovered. He was also suspicious of Hero's witchery, which he believed had as much to do with this calamity as any wrongdoing he may have committed. Yet he could not stop himself from admonishing Hero for preventing the funeral. And not quite sure what to believe but leaning to the sceptical side in interpreting Pedro's supposed resurrection, Ronald elicited an ebullient round of laughter from the whole car by saying quite seriously, "I give up. Sadie? I will buy the rights for you to write the authorized biography of Pedro George. And if that won't do, I'll simply fund an unauthorized project. What do you think? Are you game?"

Hero, still laughing, kept up the pretense of seriousness by saying the official pronouncement of Pedro's demise was something she was not about to challenge, despite the fact that she knew more than she ought to under the circumstances. And who was she to dispute Pedro's death, she went on; she was as genuinely devastated by the whole episode as anyone. Ronald brooded again, not having received the expected praise for his benevolent gesture.

Niko saw that Ronald was waxing indignantly again and intervened to say that if Pedro wished to be dead in the eyes of the world, he would have to live down the cryptic nature of his actions. "All the more grist for the mill," he said. "So what if this episode spins out of control. Pedro is still with us, if he would only make a miraculous entrance."

"Fantastic!" said Hero. "What a story."

"Personally," said Niko, "it makes me feel wonderful."

"Wonderful?" remarked Ronald. "How 'bout ridiculous! Are we now to become disciples and kiss his ass?"

"Ronald!" exclaimed Sadie.

"Sorry, I couldn't help it," he said, smirking.

They all quietened. There was a strange incumbency to this situation. It was like writing a letter. The sentiments seemed truly exceptional when first written down, but it would be preferable to wait a few days before posting it. Ronald concluded by saying he would cooperate if only he could see Pedro with his own eyes.

They arrived at West Bay and found the Pow Wow grounds. Out in the open the heat hit them like an inferno. The glare of the afternoon light penetrated like a knife. But their discomfort was forgotten when they noticed that some dances were underway. The Aboriginals were in their full traditional regalia. Amid a whirl of exuberant colour and sound, the dancers pounded out their rhythms in a large circle about the beating drums. Ronald made a joke about the whereabouts of the cavalry. Niko stood mesmerized while Hero and Sadie wandered off and did a casual circuit of some of the vendor booths.

Niko, finding himself alone, soaked in the sun. He found it soothing; it reminded him of a summer he had spent in Greece with his father's family on the island of Thira. He was thirteen and fast approaching puberty. The incendiary heat of Greece in July-August and his inexperience because of his temperate English background combined explosively and off he went on an incontinent spree. Lady Huntington, his mother, true to form, had sent him there for "further experience," knowing full well this move was akin to shock treatment since he had never met his father or known anything about the paternal half of his family. The Metropoulos family was the best thing that ever happened to him. Not only did he shed his upper-crust armour to the wine-dark sea breezes, but he had a series of interesting siestas with an island native, Zita who, being older, introduced her young friend to hyacinthian honey foraged from the wilds. Niko came home to England sun-baked, a true English explorer, and exuding confidence, thereafter readily accepted by all who knew him.

An unusual burst of noise and animation from the dancers winding up a movement of the dance brought him back. He turned to see where Hero was, and having caught sight of her, began to review lovingly in his thoughts the previous night's tenderness. He knew he had always been madly in love with her. He revered her cool wisdom, her Swiss meadow ways and health. She was the only one he could imagine bearing his children, a possibility that was swiftly becoming a firm reality. He was getting caught up in the holiday excitement of the event, treading on air. Things had progressed well. Pedro would show, and Hero and Niko would leave for Paris, chapter closed. He thought that maybe Pedro had succeeded in extricating himself from the chains of his past, which in effect did the same for him and Hero. The roebuck was free and all else memory.

～

Pedro George awoke that morning curled up next to Donna del Rio, not only with a severe erection that she kept naively attempting to manipulate in his delirium but with the vestiges of a most peculiar dream. Donna, on the other hand, had stirred from her fitful slumbers in anticipation of the very appendage that now rested obsequiously against her bottom. The one sleeping bag they shared like a duvet with John Kineu's cotton coverlet as a pad was enough on that hot, humid evening and they should have been perfectly comfortable; the ground, however, was very hard and knotty from protruding roots. Donna was not used to this kind of roughing it although she was tremendously obliging, given the bizarre circumstances. While Pedro was still sleeping, she had gotten up to leave the tent and relieve herself; then getting under the cover again, she couldn't help but notice gentle Pedro in his nudity; her desire piqued and she resisted touching him with difficulty. But snuggling in had to suffice, and her movements yielded her the longed for arousal. Lying there in the early dawn had her smiling serendipitously. She just hoped that Pedro would not think her recent pursuit of him too aggressive.

Pedro, having stirred from his peculiar dream, was succumbing gratefully to the warmth that enveloped them. For a few moments, he searched nonchalantly at the tail-end of his dream and was just about to get a grasp on it, when Donna turned to face him, sending a fragrant token of her body his way. His dream clouded over immediately, and he now started to sink fast into the pair of eyes only a few inches away from his own, losing himself in their simple but unmistakeable message: make love to me, now. Pedro realized his days of abstinence were over for awhile. He couldn't deny Donna or himself. He had been released from the temerity of his tumult, and now was obliged with the blessing of the infinite to offer himself up wholeheartedly on the altar of true love, in a humble but worthy relinquishing of his chastity.

Donna del Rio lost her virginity to Pedro. with his gentle guidance, and her subsequently unavoidable pain was soon overcome by their conjoining and synchronicity of hearts amplified in the very essence of physical bliss. The way Donna would move her hips and gasp had Pedro exultant in wonder at his lover's naturalness. A woman's secret, he thought, and moved on her as if he were not excluded from the innocence of experience. It was a new life, this procreation. Her auburn hair fell about their famished kissing; her white, pink-nippled breasts, pushed eagerly against his chest, enticing his arms and hands to pull her still deeper. They released simultaneously, like two supernovas, in a rare ecstatic wonder. The shock of this revelation made them moan and melt for such a time that not a word could be spoken for the paralysis of a glowing mute magnificence. After a time, when the hot sun had well arisen, they quietly and still without speaking a word, left the sepulchred tent to swim naked in the glittering waters.

Their almost bashful feelings for each other in that sudden outpouring of love and loyalty tingled all over in the crystal water. The water, like silk, enveloped and cleaned their love-sensitized skin. They tumbled and dove like two happy seals. After, dressed only in his shorts and T-shirt, Pedro started a little fire to boil water for oatmeal. Donna, in similar attire, came up to him by the fire. He put his arm around her and they kissed.

"Good morning," he said.

"Isn't it though!" said Donna, hungrily.

They watched the fire and smelt the driftwood smoke like incense, unwilling to move a hair's breadth lest the aura of nirvana be altered. Herein lay the core of their existence, that they admire each other eternally. Their glances brought coy smiles to their faces; it was better they didn't look.

Suddenly, during these timeless moments, they were interrupted by movement in the bushes behind them. It was none other than Mike from the Point, looking for the lost angel who had appeared the day before leaning against the mauve skylark. His intention was honourable, for he was afraid she had spent the night huddled in a shrub somewhere, or worse still, been dragged off by a bear. He had initially walked as far as John Kineu's tent to be directed by its amused occupant through the bush to the other side. Young Mike, thoroughly shocked by the presence of the native American, conjured up in his mind a terrible scenario in which he saw Donna being raped by a drunken war-party and left to crawl in the direction John had pointed.

Seeing Donna obviously in complete harmony with her friend and the crackling fire, her hair wet from a swim, and the smile of sexual wisdom beaming broadly from her and her companion's faces just about made Mike want to fall to his knees and cry, especially after his fantasy of heroically rescuing her from a fate worse than death.

Discountenanced, choking a bit on his words, he said, "I thought you were lost or something."

"No, I found my ghost," said Donna.

Mike laughed nervously, having never known Pedro, but resenting him for embodying what, in adolescent fashion, he himself wanted to be — the mystery man. Pedro, unintroduced, sensing that unmitigated repartee was the only honest approach, thought that no matter what he might say would come across as pretense. Pedro had always been aboveboard in all his relations. Truth was his God. But to Pedro truth wasn't the whole truth because he knew God was more than a literal concept. Poor Mike, he thought.

"Hi, Mike," said Pedro continuing to stir the little pot with the wooden spoon. "You probably wouldn't remember me; I'm Pedro. I gather you and Donna are acquainted. You hungry?"

"Hi. No," said Mike, looking at Donna who apparently couldn't get her uxorious smile off her face. What did a guy say to an apparition from The Twilight Zone? Pedro George had died. Was he not now almost a myth in these parts? So, what was a live Pedro, in a word, Donna's ghost, doing crouching there?

"Are you from around here?" he said, playing it safe. If Pedro was dead, then this had to be a different Pedro, that was all. But Pedro's looks rang a bell, from back when he himself had been six or seven. How could he forget Pedro, the Pedro his mother had pointed out with the Indian Big Dan as being into drugs? "Just look at them," she said. "They're lost in space." It always stuck. And here he definitely was, the guy "lost in space". Wow. Yes, this Pedro didn't look as forbidding as he remembered, but it was definitely the same guy.

"I used to have a cottage here. I remember you," said Pedro.

"I was little," said Mike afraid to ask the question.

"Point hasn't changed much," said Pedro.

"Yeah, it's the same Point."

"You're welcome to have some porridge, Mike," said Donna, attempting to steer the conversation and wanting Mike to go away, fast.

"Ah, no thanks," said Mike, feeling uncomfortable. "I think I'll go back now. I'm glad you found your ghost."

"'Fraid there's been a bit of a misunderstanding," said Pedro.

"Uh-huh," said Mike, beginning to back away.

"Well, take care," said Pedro, tending the fire.

"Thanks, Mike," said Donna.

"No problem." Mike walked away down the shoreline back to the Point. On his way he came across a squirrel. "Take care?" he said to the squirrel. "Take care?" The squirrel eyed him curiously, then ran for it. "Holy fuck!" said Mike.

Mike's arrival had temporarily broken the charm of Pedro and Donna's magic morning. "Now, where were we?" they both said at once, eager to resume. Sharing the spoon and the pot, they alternated mouthfuls of hot oats and honey and began a new quintessence of joy by feeding each other like silly adolescents.

"I'm sorry," said Pedro more soberly, after dribbling a dab of cereal onto Donna's thigh from the spoon.

"Mmm, all the more for me," she said, scraping up the spilled porridge with a finger.

"You know what I mean."

"Oh," was all she said, unwilling to abandon her joy.

"I had to, but it's over now."

"What?" she said, still smiling.

"My death, you know."

"O yeah, your death." Her smile waned slightly.

"I had to be dead; I don't even remember anymore."

"Neither do I." She looked at him impassively now.

"I think I love you," he said.

"I think I love you too," she said.

"That's good."

Without replying, she clasped his hand with a sudden urgency and pressed her lips to it.

They put down the spoon and pot and went back into the tent and undressed. Lying on the sleeping bag, naked in the warmth of the early sun, they began exploring, both tasting of scented water. From time to time a soft lake breeze fluttered up and beguiled them with its light feathery caresses.

An hour later they were in their shorts again and walking down the shoreline. Along their route rose up Precambrian granite rock, cracked and scarred with time and breached everywhere by stoically tenacious trees. The waves of the bay lapped endlessly forward to greet the rock. Here was a destiny of eternal vigilance that plied nature's elements. He was their delicate child, said the waves and the rock to Pedro, something of them distilled into the bare essential of themselves, the union of earth and ecstacy. Pedro and Donna were the new genesis. They were the immaculate ones.

They stopped and went for another skinny dip. Afterwards they dried off in the sun on a hot rock, their bodies again stirring to the warm upwelling of a kundalini rush. Practical concerns, however, claimed their attention; they chose to simply convene a more cerebral incandescence resisting the embryonic empathy of desire.

"Pedro, we haven't used any birth control," said Donna.

"I know. I hope you're pregnant," he said with a grin.

"Are you serious?" she replied.

"Yes."

"But . . ."

"We can get married. Do you want to?"

"Pedro, are you serious?"

"As the sun is my guru. Yes."

"I . . . I . . . yes, yes, of course."

"I could be a baker with Giovanni for awhile — we'd work together, all of us; and you could finish university," said Pedro, seeing the beauty of their life in the loom of his imagination.

"Oh, I know we can do it!" cried Donna. "But Pedro, you don't just want to be a baker, do you? What about your archaeology and writing? Shouldn't you pursue them?" suggested Donna, taking stock of the logistical patterns within her own horizons.

Pedro gave this idea a nod, but was too swept up in his own bright imaginings to give it anything more. The very notion of conforming to any conventional view of what he might be expected to do made him queasy. His whole being took refuge in the peace and tranquillity of Siddhartha on the river of the grocery store.

"Those are my interests," he replied sincerely.

"What about your ambitions?" she said softly.

"My ambitions?" He looked with intense eyes as if in awe of something that had turned up under a rock.

"You know, fulfilments," said Donna. "I don't see you being happy at Giovanni's."

"Don't you see, that's where I might be quite content," he said, then added, "for awhile."

She put her hand on his and said, "There's no rush."

"I have my ambitions," said Pedro coming, to the erudition of his thoughts, without conceding to Donna's rationale. "They are the interests I have stated. My death resulted from these very ambitions. I didn't know that before. But now I understand my ambitions. Ambitions are the reasons for personal volition. I chose to play at being a witch because they desired it. They desired me. That was very ambitious of me. I honoured ambition. And the price for that honour was death. It began millennia ago, and it begins again with us. It used to be more serious in ages past, when we had to deal with apocalyptic desolation, like what's happening in other parts of the world today — Somalia or Bosnia, for example; so this time around, so far, I've managed to enjoy myself a little without the threat of extermination. You see, a grocery store is amazing. All that food, delectable breads, vegetables, fruits, everything — it's like Eden. And every day the truck brings more."

"Pedro, what on earth are you talking about? Who is they and what's this about being a witch?" asked Donna curiously.

"Donna," he said, "the reason I died happens to be the unintentional result of being involved in a witches' coven during my stay in Wales the last six or seven years. I wanted to tell you in Toronto . . . but I kind of felt caught up in the whole thing — the death, and couldn't bring myself to let anybody else in on it, even you. Death is . . . I think, a personal thing."

"Yeah, I guess so," said Donna, a little unsure but ready to ratify his peculiar cant on death. "But what were you doing with witches?" she questioned.

"We were harnessing the powers of nature through plants, chants, and . . . dance . . . in a rather metaphorical way. We made medicines, charms, potions, spells . . . it was fascinating. There was this old woman — Brigid, who knew everything. Everyone in the area knew her and feared her, but she was like the matriarch who was called upon for any number of problems: sickness, stress, love, hate, pregnancy . . . she was well respected and had a number of apprentices and accomplices. I was the only male, however. There was ritual."

"This is incredible," said Donna excitedly. "What was the ritual?"

"You know, full moon ceremonies, equinox and solstice, Beltane and Halloween, all necessary to stay tuned with psychic intuition and enhanced personal power which should convert to healing power," said Pedro quietly so as not to inspire too much curiosity but appease the need to know.

"So, did the faking of your death have something to do with these rituals?" asked Donna, looking across the water.

"To tell you the truth, Donna, I don't really know; I just went along with it. It was some kind of statement, I think, or counterspell to ward off threats to my life prophesied by Brigid."

"So Brigid did it?"

"I don't know. Probably. Or the others at her behest; still it all seems so out of character. But I will take responsibility for it because in a way I asked for it, not literally, but through my actions."

"How so?"

"Being . . . purposefully prodigal . . . or something. They kind of put me on a pedestal . . . I had power."

"Wow, you've been through so much. Why didn't you come forward or tell me before?"

"I don't know. It was all so strange. I think I was studying the situation. After awhile, it kind of appealed to me. I'm really sorry about it now, but it was something I had to do; it cured me of the spell."

"What spell?"

"Someone put a spell on me to get rid of me."

"Why?"

"Like I said, I wielded too much power; that's all I can figure out."

Donna shook her head. "Strange way of doing it."

"You can say that again."

"So, what did Brigid prophesy?" persisted Donna.

"That I would be haunted by Gorgon."

"One of the stories you left me."

"Yes. But the weird thing is that Gorgon came to me before Brigid told me. It came to me in a dream," he said.

"The Gorgon in mythology is Medusa, who turned people to stone," commented Donna as a matter of fact, remembering her Greek mythology course. "And Perseus slew her with the help of Minerva, right?"

"Yeah, but in reality, what we perceive to be the good avenging the evils of Medusa is all wrong. In fact, Perseus didn't kill Gorgon. He listened to her story that she was once a beautiful maiden whose gorgeous looks and profound intelligence aroused the ire and jealousy of Athena who had the power to destroy her, which Athena did with poison, thus rendering her ugly by horrible disfigurement. Medusa was the victim as well as Athena, one from envy, the other from simply being the wisest and most beautiful. And that's the point: Gorgon is the specter of circumstance that pervades the circle of karma from one victim to the next. Gorgon is the rage, fear, or insecurity that drives one to do terrible things, or on the other hand, to be a victim of those circumstances. Gorgon is a metaphor or concept that is the folly of our ways, by which we are so victimized. So Perseus is made out to be the killer just as society is a killer. Medusa in fact committed suicide. She offered herself to Perseus' sword as a sacrifice."

"How do you know this, Pedro?" asked Donna.

"I dreamed it. I am Perseus and you are Andromeda, my wife. And we are the happiest couple in history."

"You're kidding?"

"No." A big smile came across his electric face. His eyes were brilliant.

"I hope not," she said, poking his shoulder.

"I had another dream this morning," said Pedro tacking higher into the wind of the moment, "that showed me love, when I reflect on it. Last night, when you appeared to me, you made me believe in miracles. I hurt you by leaving you the way I did in Toronto, though not deliberately. I had to get over my death. My friends John and Dan and I had a sweat last night before you came. I sweated out the toxins of my past, and like a child, embraced a new life. You are part of this fresh start, not like a plan, or piece of the scenery; you are the miracle. This is very profound for me, because I have lived as a miracle in the design and purpose of my own making. We are all miracles, but to truly understand that, you may suffer horribly in the process, as I did. Last night replaced my miracle with a human being again.

"In my dream I was wandering over a kind of landscape that seemed to comprise a microcosm of human habitat. I couldn't see who I was with; every time I looked around to see who my companion was, she would disappear. There were banks of grass, waterways, roads, boats, woodlots, beaches, buildings, clouds, wind, groups of people. There was a certain blandness to it all, but I was humbled by some inner reason obscure to myself. Frankly, I am at a loss to know what I was doing, where I was going, or whom or what I was looking for. Yet this female presence was there. It was like I knew who she was, but didn't. She was leading me somehow, and yet I was alone. As I came to various people, people I don't think I have ever known, I would be repelled like a ball in a pinball machine. I became very frustrated with this limbo, this strange phantasmagoria that I was witnessing. Everyone seemed to know what I was about, except me. I sat down on a bank of grass and watched some moored boats with masts that started heaving in a rising grey sky wind. I could hear their masts and lines clatter and ding. How, I wondered, was I to know where I was if I didn't know who I was? I thought to try and exit this hellish park in a kind of car somewhat like a go-cart, which was old and worn but actually started. I followed a road that wound around a grassy plateau and when I came to the edge and was about to see the horizon, which I had begun to feel was my salvation, a large, bright red racing car came out of nowhere and drove right over my go-cart jalopy. Somehow, I was not in it at the time of impact but I knew somebody was. I quickly got the race driver of the red car to back off and rushed to the jalopy to look but saw only a pile of earth with a few remnants of the car. The occupant's head peered up from beneath the earth. I'm sure it was me, but I didn't know who I was and felt too inhibited to confront the individual, yet I helped him out of the debris. He was very sore and shaken, but miraculously unhurt, except that he began to bleed profusely out the back of his head where, oddly, I saw no wound — the blood just seemed to stream out directly and incessantly. The best we could do was wrap his head in a cloth we found lying nearby. There was some urgency to our actions becauset we were to continue our search for whatever it was at all costs. The red racing car, meanwhile, had been replaced by a red canoe. We got in, laying our mysteriously wounded friend on the bottom, then we pushed off the edge of the plateau. Now we were on a river with someone behind us, and were hurtling through rocks and rapids while being shot at from behind with arrows. Eventually, we got jammed on a rocky bar where the river trickled down to nothing. The assailants behind us were fast catching up, and I remember looking up and hoping to see some way out of the spot we were in. I noticed that our bleeding casualty, sensing our peril, had also begun to help. However, when I looked up again, I noticed we were now in a giant, corrugated tunnel with light at the end. We began to move more quickly, and as we approached its end, we knew that we were no longer being followed. At the exit we hesitated because the light was so brilliant we couldn't see beyond. My female friend told me it was all right to go on. So we did. The wounded person's head stopped bleeding. That was the last thing I saw. I became blind. My female escort took my hand and led me back to the place where I had started from. I asked where the wounded fellow was. She told me he was safe. I said I couldn't see. She said I would see if I opened my eyes because the bright light had gone. I opened my eyes, and it was morning and you were snuggling against me."

The sound of the waves coalesced with his voice as he stopped speaking; it had the effect of stopping the train of thought. A little bird, a white-winged crossbill, with its brilliant dabs of red, perched above them and cocked its head. It had come out from its low-lying creek to essay the open spaces.

"That was beautiful, Pedro," said Donna dreamily, pulling her shapely legs up to her chin.

"I've never been separated from myself like that before, not knowing anything. I suppose it's all right to dream like that when I'm around you," he said, looking out over the bay.

"Pedro?"

"Yes?"

"I met your mother."

"I thought you might have, but you didn't tell her?"

"No."

"Why not, may I ask?"

"I believed in you. Pedro?"

"Yes."

"Who were the others, those women?" she asked, delicately.

Pedro told her about Hero, Niko, Augustus and Anne Fitzooth. He talked about how close they all were but couldn't imagine they would be capable of sending his car over a cliff, at least willingly. It didn't matter anymore.

She asked him about the letter and what he had meant. He said, "I don't know" and "nonsense". This was true; he really didn't. Words and thoughts just came out of him. There was something definitely profound in it all, but who was to say that what he said was meaningless? Even his most glib statements like "I don't know," evoked a cauldron of possible, tangential romances.

Pedro could be just as easily hated as loved because everything he said seemed to insinuate this subterfuge of possibility. People either believed in him or resented him. They resented his dreams and the way he could make his dreams come true. The bigger the dream, the more he did. Pedro's dreams were in constant flux. How was he to be trusted with his dreams? Was he good enough for them?

Donna del Rio couldn't hope to understand him; no one could. Not Hero, not Niko, not anyone. Donna knew this. She had known the minute she met him that he was one in whom the image met the real thing. She did understand that he needed her. It was as though they had been married and just misplaced each other in this lifetime, but finally found each other. She even knew that she was pregnant.

Donna remembered the first time she met him and the way he couldn't make up his mind about which loaf to buy — French stick or crusty Italian. He settled for the Italian. Shortly after, she had moved in next door above Giovanni's store. She didn't see him for days and wondered what he was doing. He didn't go out much at night or during the day. Yet, for some reason she loved him the minute she laid eyes on him. He was intelligent and so obliquely pained; his smiling melancholy was too much for her to resist. He was too damned different. There was no other man in the world, as far as she was concerned, who could come close to Pedro. She finally got up enough nerve to invite herself into his flat one evening. To her great surprise and blessed relief, he was not only what she had imagined, but considerably more. Alternately, he had entertained her with fascinating talk about all the things she could never put into words; and then he would tease her too, even about the crush she had on him. Uncharacteristically, she let him get away with it and yearned for more. He could have twirled her around his finger, but he kept an honourable distance in deference to their friendship. During those sexually electric moments, she even offered herself to him, albeit in a subtle way. He remained chaste and so did she. Undaunted, she set him up to find her naked once when he came over before they went out one evening to see a movie. He saw all of her and said, "You have beautiful breasts." Embarrassed, she then covered herself. He later apologized for commenting about her breasts, saying, "I didn't know where to start." She tried to entice him by replying, "Start anywhere." Still, he would not be tempted.

Pedro now stood up on the rock and nimbly stepped down to put on his shorts. Out of one pocket he revealed a piece of paper and then came back to sit down beside Donna.

"I wrote this for you yesterday," he said, giving it to her.

She took it carefully. Her eyes lit up. "A poem."

> O happy blue.
> It will happen.
> I saw your eyes reading the letter.
> The richest green from sodden dew.
> I wish the sun would dry them.
> I wish I could kiss them.
> If ever there was an aching heart
> Assail me the billions for my loss.
> The sky is blue.
> The lake is blue.
> The sun is blue.
> O happy blue.

A year had come and gone on Vera's Isle, as they called it. Troylus and Sarah had a baby boy named Ganymede. Other children were begotten by both Troylus and Aeneas. Vera had decided to welcome the newcomers on the condition that she could exact an undisclosed price for her concession one year later. There was something remarkable about these errant warriors that she liked in the way they carried themselves and enthusiastically gave their utmost effort toward the domestic responsiblities. They were undoubtedly the most earnestly honourable men she had ever come across and also Mediterranean, like herself. Meanwhile, all of them were a closely knit cohabitation. Vera herself took Aeneas as a consort, had a daughter by him, and was now pregnant with her second child.

The Hairy Man, known as Carbuncle, lived by himself with his herd of goats and cattle. He traded medicine for livestock, and also managed Troylus and Aeneas's share of stock. Sarah minded the gardens while Troylus and Aeneas tended a few hectares of grain and oversaw the munitions and defenses. Ultimately, however, this domesticity was not altogether satisfactory to the intrepid Troylus and Aeneas; they became restless for adventure and conquest. It was in their blood to seek out new lands. They talked about Albion and the prospect of conquering a small area to gain a foothold. They were told by Vera, who had reformed her own feelings about these strangers within the first month of their arrival, that Albion was a dangerous land in which to covet even a portion for themselves. They may have come from a great and powerful background, but they were no match for the wild Picts of the north. At this juncture, Vera decided to exact her fee, contrary to her original plan to send them away or kill them if they resisted as she had fated other men who had come, some of whom she had dispatched without so much as a word of greeting. She decreed that Troylus must go alone to Albion as a traveler with trinkets for no less than a year to find out what was out there. If he refused, she would expel them all. Aeneas vehemently protested, insisting he take the journey himself, and after a wine-soaked and orgiastic repast, prevailed upon her to change her mind. The truth was that she didn't want to get pregnant again for awhile and had a difficult time abstaining from Aeneas's ardent demands on her.

The day came for Aeneas to depart. Vera no longer had any real power over them, as it was almost two years since their arrival. The fee for their indefinite tenure on Vera's Isle was of no consequence as they would have gone to Albion anyway. So Aeneas departed as Vera's emissary-of-sorts with the Hairy Man as his cohort. Vera was tearful but wise in knowing that at least, this way, they would hopefully return and then surely realize that their own island was the paradise they desired. Unfortunately, the inordinate annual rainfall did not boost their appreciation of Vera's Isle.

One day that summer following the spring Aeneas left, two of Vera's warrior women came running into the hamlet calling out in their own tongue that two large boats were approaching from the east. Vera ran up to the lookout to see for herself whether they might be friendly or hostile. When the sailing vessels came close enough for her to tell, she shuddered for the boats were not just hostile, they were more malevolently hostile than anything she could remember. They were the Gorgonians, at once recognizable by the horrible masks the priests wore and trademark visage of the Medusa head on the sails. It just so happened that like Sarah, Vera too had once been subjected to a cult domination. In her youth, she had been abducted by a vagrant band of pirates from the Balearic Islands in the Mediterranean. She had been repeatedly raped and finally sold to a tribe on the coast of Spain. There, she was sold again to a splinter group of Gorgonians from Gaul, with whom for ten years she wore out her youth in service to an insidious priest named Vacuna. Despite terrible hardship at first, she ultimately had some good fortune by escaping and eventually, after much travelling, founded the women's island, a refuge for dispossessed women and children. The children, as they grew up, were taken to the mainland and turned over to the various tribes who were in constant need of augmenting their work force and into which they easily integrated. Though eccentric, Vera and her clan had earned respect by their tough attitude toward unwelcome visitors. The local mainland inhabitants even warned them when they could of impending danger. But nothing prepared them for this intrusion.

Once they knew the extent of the danger confronting them, Vera and Troylus immediately directed Sarah and some of the younger children, including Ganymede, to set out from the other end of the island on a small sailing bark reserved for emergencies, to get help from the friendly coastal tribes. Troylus and the warrior women then went into hiding to prepare guerilla ambushes, leaving the hamlet deserted. Vera and a couple of the grown children and the youngest went into secret hiding places used for just this type of crisis.

Some of the women thought that, since the Gorgonians must surely be coming after the famous Ariadne, they would not harm innocent children. As religious fanatics they presumably only cared for their stolen Goddess. Vera knew better.

About one hundred Gorgonian warriors disembarked and quickly surrounded the hamlet. Discovering it deserted, they fanned out in four squads to seek the inhabitants. Troylus and his warrioresses surprise attacked one of the squads but were repelled by the arrival of another squad. Even with Aeneas and the Hairy Man, it would have been doubtful if they could have overpowered the hardened and fully armed Gorgonians without a major loss of life. The Gorgonians had started a war over Ariadne. Such was their devotion.

They sequestered Vera's house as a holding cell for the warrior women. In the front yard, where their handiwork could easily be seen from the cottage's window, they tied Troylus to a gate-post. Determined to know where Ariadne was, they attempted to beat this information out of Troylus but they broke his jaw and fingers to no avail. At this juncture, Vera and the children were brought forward, having been ferreted out by one of the Gorgonian squads. Vera began to scream obscenities at them, especially at one particular Gorgon priest wearing a mask representing a face contorting in a death grimace. She had recognized the priest as Vacuna, the man who had subjected her to unspeakable perversions for ten years. Her screaming, however, merely stoked the flame of their sadism. They brought forward some young children who were crying and beat their brains onto the turf. The warrioresses who were the mothers let out great wails of anguish from their prison. Eventually, they cried that they knew where Sarah was and would tell them if they would spare them all. Gerta, one of the tall blonde Germanic women, was brought out. The Gorgonians seemed to know where she was from and marvelled at her size. They had her stripped naked and held her while their leader, Arog, fingered her to smell her scent. After a moment, he smiled and said, "Man eater."

Troylus knew that, if they revealed Sarah's whereabouts, they would be lost, and he would die; he only hoped his death might somehow avert the deaths of the remaining children long enough for the coastal tribes to arrive and fight the Gorgonians.

"Gerta," said Troylus through his teeth, "protect our children." Before he could continue, a Gorgonian hit him in the face, knocking him senseless with the shock of pain. Vera began screaming again. "Take me! Take me!" she cried. Gerta looked around, unsure of what to do. The Gorgonians stood a tearful little girl in front of Gerta and threatened to kill the child if Gerta lied.

"They went to Albion," said Gerta, "to look for a new home with Aeneas and Carbuncle. They left not two moon's gone. Do not hurt our innocent children. The others will return next year."

Arog spoke quietly with Vacuna to the side. They laughed. Returning, he told Gerta that if the warrioresses wished to save their lives, they must kill the Trojan and eat him. They knew Gerta was from a Germanic tribe that worshipped a God-king or poet-king for a year then killed him ritually. The Gorgonians wanted to see this death-rite performed. When Gerta refused, they threatened to kill the girl, so she acquiesced. Vacuna pushed Vera forward to help.

Gerta, with the help of the despairing Vera, laid the delirious Troylus on a wood table and were about to dispatch him with a quick, merciful stab to the heart, when Arog intervened and claimed that, according to what he had heard, they were not enacting the ritual properly; they must conduct it with all due attention to its authentic form. The warrior women had no choice but to comply. Vera didn't understand completely, but Gerta did. She had witnessed this event when she was young. With tears in her eyes, she cut off Troylus's testicles. At that moment, as Troylus lay bleeding profusely, white-faced, and teeth clenched in agony, the Gorgonians chanted to Gerta and Vera, "Eat! Eat! Eat! Eat!" Then they again threatened the girl who now lay petrified with shock on the ground. With a shriek, Greta consumed one testicle. Vera, looking down, ashen with nausea, steeled herself and ate the other. The Gorgonians were well pleased and let the women finish Troylus with a swift stab to the heart. Troylus saw the grey sky obscure and fade as darkness fell before his eyes.

The Gorgonians celebrated that night in a brutal orgy, mollified by the sacrifice that had been made in Ariadne's honour; especially gratifying to them was the knowledge that Ariadne's abductor was the bronze Trojan. Thus their rampage had all the justification it needed.

In two days, an invading horde of Celts swarmed over the island, and outnumbering the Gorgons two to one, chased them into the water where they slaughtered half of them, including Vacuna. The remains of Troylus and the two dead children were buried in the oat field. So traumatised were Vera and the others that poor forlorn Sarah persuaded them to abandon the isle and seek a new home in Albion. Aeneas and the Hairy Man returned the next summer to a subdued colony still in mourning for a Troylus now revered as a god. Aeneas fell to his knees and raised a cry for his loss that reverberated into the memories of all those present. Sarah went to him and cried with him.

Finally, Aeneas, Sarah, Ganymede, and the Hairy Man, with half the colony, departed for Cymru, according to Aeneas, a beautiful land teeming with game and fish, blessed with rich valleys and verdant forests. Vera, at the last moment chose to remain where she was, with the others' promise to visit.

Chapter Nine

> Deep, it is like the ancestors of the myriad creatures.
> Darkly visible, it only seems as if it were there. I know
> not whose son it is; it images the forefather of God.
> —Lao Tzu

Under the massive dark shadow of the storm clouds, Inspector David Thomas drove his Range Rover down the steep vale back into the valley where Caerymwy village was situated. Beside him sat a quite apprehensive Gwendolyn Gwynedd-Jones, whose compliance was derived from loyalty to Anne Fitzooth. Anne had seemed keen that she go with him. Gwendolyn had borne a great deal of the burden of the Wiccan involvement with Pedro on her young shoulders. Except for Hero, she was the one who in the past few years had had most contact with Pedro. She had also suffered the most and was one of Caerymwy's permanent fixtures, like Brigid. When Anne had her affair with Pedro, Gwendolyn was the girl-housekeeper, always around, performing various errands. She would make the lovers' bed, look after the groceries, mail letters and keep mum about all the secrets. And testament to her determined character was her agonizing crush on Pedro that even Anne didn't fully comprehend, although one was never too sure with Anne. Pedro was everything to Gwendolyn. It was Pedro more than Brigid or Anne who inspired her and formed her thinking about witchcraft. She would even copy his manner and ragtag clothes. She was happy to serve Pedro in any capacity whatsoever. Unfortunately, Pedro didn't entertain the same regard for her, so caught up was he in his own propinquity. He did, however, suffer too on her account; he empathized with what he saw in her and was curious about her feelings. She couldn't express herself or exude the right chemistry; as a result, she was like a poor relation struggling needlessly to be equal amongst people who did not acknowledge any such disparity. All her gestures toward him seemed banal or redundant, yet he was gracious and wanted desperately to be as good a friend to her as possible. In the Wiccan rituals, they had been married several times; they were very good together, the best the others had seen in those circumstances. For Gwendolyn, until Hero disrupted it, there had been no other such intimacy in her life until Pedro's friend Ronald arrived for an extended visit, which wasn't the same at all. She went with him only because she loved Pedro. By giving herself wholeheartedly to Ronald, she had hoped to show Pedro how she could love and possibly elicit a jealous reaction from him; but this plan backfired when to her great regret, Ronald proved to be too demanding on her youthful temperament. It was Pedro, in fact, who put a stop to Ronald's strenuous subjection of Gwendolyn when she lost control in a feverish toad-stool induced frenzy which brought on her sickness and her mother's calling the police after the girl had been taken home delirious. Moreover, the arrival of Hero, prior to Ronald, had altered the status quo sufficiently to upset her equilibrium, hence the crisis. Her intoxication knew no bounds in that their substance abuse had broken the parameters of orthodox witchery set under Anne and Brigid. To the others, she came across as a sort of happily dissolute young bohemian. Her whole life and hurt graduated into something far more than she could get a handle on in her simple charm and village ways. Only now was the karma finally coming home to roost, and she wanted, like Pedro, to come clean.

    David Thomas sensed Gwendolyn's discomfort, but chose to relax in the silence between them. In his own way he understood her youthful sacrifice to the expectations of her Wiccan peers. He concluded that the

Wicca had shown scant consideration for her youth and the needs of a person her age to mature normally without their kind of interference. Her closest friends of the past five years had gone, and now her mainstay, Anne, was leaving indefinitely. It was no wonder she was as depressed as she most evidently seemed.

The rain battered the windshield in sheets.

"A far cry from this morning, I'd say," said Thomas, attempting to start up a conversation.

"Mmph."

He gave up on this train of thought and tried a new direction. "Do you have any non-witch friends, Gwendolyn?" he said, looking over at her, backed into the dark corner between the seat and door with her black looking consternated eyes and tangled hair about her pale face. She appeared to almost recoil in fear.

"Of course," was all she said.

"Would it not be wise to back off the Wicca for a spell?" he continued, slightly intimidated by her fear.

She wouldn't answer.

"Gwendolyn," continued Thomas, "how long have you known Mrs. Willobie . . . Miss Fitzooth rather?"

"All my life."

"Did you know her father?"

"Of course."

"Did you like him?" Thomas asked.

"Yes. He and Annie were very close."

"Did she change when he died?"

"She married Charles."

"Who didn't make her very happy," he commented.

Gwendolyn wouldn't elaborate.

"Was Anne angry with Pedro for leaving her?" he persisted.

"No," she said, and paused before saying, "I heard them argue once, you know."

"What about? I didn't think Pedro was the type to argue."

"Over Hero. Anne despised Hero."

"Did you?"

"No, Pedro loved her. At least I thought he did."

"Then he broke up with Hero," said Thomas.

"Yes, and left us," she said sullenly.

"You had hoped he would stay with you. Am I right?"

Gwendolyn fell silent. Inspector Thomas could almost feel the emotions suspire around her. He chose not to push her too hard. It was obvious she had loved him deeply and painfully.

"I did the car, Mr. Thomas," she said suddenly.

"You did the car?" Thomas's heart leaped. He never would have believed it.

"Yes," she said defiantly.

"On whose instructions?" he probed automatically.

"No one's."

"You did it by yourself?" he persisted.

"Yes."

"What on earth for?" said David Thomas, not wanting to sound so exasperated.

"I realized it was up to me to tell the world about Pedro, you know, his powers."

"I don't follow you. What does destroying his car have to do with his 'powers'?"

"So we could resurrect him, of course," she said stiffly.

"And was this 'resurrection' some conspiracy of silence between you all?" he asked incredulously.

"I did it, Mr. Thomas. I did it all by myself and I think it was the right thing to do, you know," she said defensively.

"What do you mean?"

"Well, he never came forward to disprove his death, so I know he wanted it. It was a symbolic death. All those involved with him understood, including Pedro, especially Pedro." She sat up straighter with the sound of his name.

"You mean a symbolic death like something religious?"

"Maybe."

"How do you know that he's alive?"

"Pedro is numinous, supernatural, you know," she said, gesticulating with her hand, ignoring his question. "He was a healer too. Many people believed in him."

"Oh," said David Thomas, indicating by his tone of voice that he took this seriously. He thought that in reality maybe Gwendolyn had to kill Pedro, at least by illusion in order to deal with her loss of him and carry on. Gwendolyn was not well, he presumed. "Who else was involved?" he reiterated.

She would not respond.

They drove into Caerymwy, past The Turk pub.

"Turn right," she said.

They turned and soon exited the village again, back into the gloom of a forbidding countryside. The low clouds now engulfed the hillocks of the vales as the Range Rover wound around a large slope.

"There's an old stone foundation around the corner. Turn right again in the lane."

He did as she directed. The lane, which had not been gravelled in quite awhile, was slippery, but they easily made it up the first incline with the four-wheel drive. Now on a level stretch, they passed through a wood and over a stream, then up a pasture to a dark cottage nestled in a grove beside a small stone barn. The spot seemed ominously desolate.

"Rather bleak," said David Thomas. He was glad Gwendolyn had come with him.

"It's charming in the sun, you know," she said defensively.

"How long has she lived here?" inquired Thomas, as he turned the motor off and the sound of the wind became louder.

"All her life. This was her mother's place too, you know. Well, there was the Great War — she did move to London for a few years. She was a nurse then, and got married."

They got out of the Range Rover and hastily walked through the enclosure's gate to the door of the old cottage. The absence of wires indicated its lack of electric power and telephone. It was preserved in its ancient state. A few chickens poked about and a goat with her kid were tethered to stakes in the yard. David Thomas wondered how she managed here at her great age. The place was certainly antiquated, although not unkempt. In the inclement weather it seemed strangely protected, as though it had an affinity for adverse conditions which thereby granted it a dispensation from the effects of their visitations.

Gwendolyn entered the dark cottage without knocking while David Thomas remained on the threshold. Suddenly Gwendolyn screamed, "Grana!"

Thomas moved into the gloom, slowly letting his eyes adjust to the dark interior. "What is it?"

"Oh, Grana!" was all Gwendolyn said.

David Thomas entered the old kitchen with its ancient hearth where a fire had burned for hundreds of years. On the floor, lying on her side, was the body of Brigid. She was old and puckered and, in her black apparel, looked like a dead crow with its feet curled and tucked. Gwendolyn was holding her hand and leaning down to see if she was breathing. David Thomas crouched beside her and felt for a pulse. She was stiff. She must have been dead for a day at least.

"She's dead, Gwendolyn."

"It's all my fault," said Gwendolyn, sobbing at this new tragedy in her life. "It killed her, my spell on Pedro. I killed her! I know I did. Ohhh."

"My dear, you have done no such thing. Your Grana was very old and died naturally by the looks of it. Do not torment yourself like this. Stop all this delusory nonsense," said Thomas gently, but firmly.

Gwendolyn was inconsolable. Lifting her to her feet, David Thomas led her out of the cottage back to the car. Then he drove directly to The

Turk in Caerymwy and phoned the coroner from there. He also called Anne Fitzooth, but she was either ignoring his call or had made a quick exit. Then he called the constabulary directly under his own jurisdiction so that all was taken care of for the time being, except for Gwendolyn, who now sat at the bar with a bitter. He approached her. The bartender stood and looked at him and said "Is there a problem, Inspector?"

"We just found Brigid Pyles dead in her cottage," said David Thomas, loud enough for other locals within earshot to hear. There was an instant lull in the hubbub. One older man spoke up to the whole establishment. "The old witch is dead. Brigid Pyles is dead!" The man then turned to the Inspector. "Was it natural, officer? You know she was prone to meddle."

"Excuse me, what do you mean by meddle?" asked David Thomas.

"Don't get caught up in his talk, Mr. Thomas," said Gwendolyn. "Willy here's a gossip who talks to his cups more 'n his kin."

"Ahh, Miss Jones," exclaimed Willy, "would I were the buck I was, I'd move you like I did once t'your Grana. I did her chores as a boy an' more. Ha! Gentlemen, and ladies too, here's a toast to the old woman; it'll never be the same 'ere without her!"

"Mr. Webb, I know what she knew, you know, so don't go on thinkin' you're the strutting rooster," said Gwendolyn sharply. Willy Webb took a long swill of his draught to restrain himself. There was, in fact, in those people present, a deep respect for the dead and they all felt the loss of Brigid Argeia, the old sorceress. Young Gwendolyn knew her people.

David Thomas had watched the short exchange between Willy Webb and Gwendolyn with keen interest. The people here had been genuinely upset. Brigid was obviously notorious. She had certainly been respected, yet feared. Willy Webb knew when to back down. A few of the villagers consoled Gwendolyn and she went to their table. Thomas then asked Willy what he knew of Pedro George.

"He was a quiet lad," replied Willy. "Tragic loss of life, that was. Many of us knew him. He'd come like water and like wind he'd go. He helped me once when I was on the tiles and too drunk to go home. He gave me a lift and stopped by the next day. I didn't know why he'd come, but Missus told me what he'd done. I tell ye, I didn't drink so much since then. The kid made me feel queasy at the thought, somehow. Damned if he was a witch, but bless him anyway."

"Gwendolyn said he was supernatural," commented Thomas.

"Ah, I dunno 'bout that. She's a wily wench an' plum tart t' boot an' would a' had 'er hooks in him. 'Twas plain t' see. But I tell ye, he had the magic in his eye and stood apart."

"Do you think there was foul play?"

"Naa. Now you're barkin' up the wrong tree."

Later, Gwendolyn and Inspector Thomas drove back to Brigid's. He asked Gwendolyn what the spell was that Brigid had put on Pedro. He said that, according to Anne, Brigid was trying to save Pedro from Pedro; apparently, a phenomenon called Gorgon was out to destroy Pedro, something that had targeted him as a sacrificial victim. David Thomas wanted to know what she thought of that.

Gwendolyn, having drunk a bitter ale in her manically shocked depression, revealed the reverse reaction by coming across as superficially buoyant. Every so often, one or the other of her hands would nervously flutter up to sweep her hair over her head. David Thomas's mention of Gorgon appeared to be having a decided effect. At first, she diverted the question with a reminiscence of a particular evening of drug-induced revelry with Pedro, Niko and Hero, just the four of them. It was at the beginning of Pedro's relations with Hero; they were entranced by each other. Hero had wanted Gwendolyn to show them some of the Wiccan rituals so she could participate. At first, they pointed out to Hero that one could not just participate. One had to be introduced and accepted by all the witches. It sometimes took years for an outsider to be allowed to enter the circle. They had, in fact, been quite discouraging, but then Pedro had gone on to deliver a sort of deranged sermon about something called Gorgon, a being which sought suitable male victims to be sacrificed. A woman was sometimes involved unwittingly. She would actually love the man to death, such was her power.

They arrived at Brigid's again and waited in the car for the arrival of the coroner and local police. The wind blew unabated. A sense of Brigid lying dead inside the house weighed heavily in the air between them.

"So, what about the spell?" persisted David Thomas. "Was Pedro's life really in danger? And if it was, from whom?"

"From Hero, of course. Brigid was attempting to separate them."

"But Brigid and Hero were supposedly on the best of terms, according to what Anne told me," stated Thomas.

"Yeah, they were, in a way, you know. Hero was exotic, just absolutely unique; she added wonderful new blood to the coven. Like, she turned me onto astrology and things. She's amazing, you know, in her own way. Then maybe Brigid used her."

"Then why the spell?"

"Well, if I say, will you give me immunity?" she asked lightheartedly.

"Immunity? I don't understand. From what? You haven't hurt anybody." David Thomas let her have the slack. He knew he was getting to the crux of the matter.

"Well, I guess not. You see, I cast a spell on Hero that would cause a rift between her and Pedro. I wanted Pedro for myself. I did everything for him. I loved him. She screwed everything up. That time Pedro was sermonizing about Gorgon, she and I ended up doing a pseudo-ritual on Pedro after which he did both of us — you know, screwed us — but he ended up with her. Niko watched, then I went with Niko. I really liked Niko but my displacement rankled; it should have been me with Pedro and Hero with Niko. I know Niko wanted it that way too."

"Did Anne know about your spell?"

"Yes. She found my altar and charms in my room and the materials I used. She knew I had Pedro's wallet and some of his clothes. I stole them from him, you know. I told him, after, but he never asked for them back. Anne knew what I'd done before I told her, but she didn't do anything about it either — she had her own bone of contention with Hero. Her honest side prevailed, you know; and in the best interests of the coven, she made a full disclosure to Brigid about what I'd done. Unfortunately, the spell had been cast, so there was nothing that could be done to stop it. And I'd done it right, but I'd also set Pedro on a collision course for self-destruction, at least that was how Brigid saw matters, because he was too vulnerable — his dreams and past lives, you know; it was like he was an open book — and she would resist any attempt to undermine his and Hero's solidarity. My spell could only throw a wrench in the works, play hob with his destiny and would cause not only his fall but also all of ours."

"So you made a serious mistake," said David Thomas, hanging onto the thread of her bizarre confession. "If I'm not too bold, maybe Anne had already put a hex on them. And quite possibly she knew about you doing the car."

"No, no, you don't understand. Pedro could have died! It doesn't matter what Anne knew! My spell inadvertently, although simple, was dangerous, very dangerous, yet he persevered somehow from imminent death. There was something more powerful at work on him, you know."

"You just wanted to wreck his relationship with Hero?"

"Yes, but things kept happening to him; he was almost killed on numerous occasions all because of me and my stupid spell. Brigid, Anne and I were frantic, so Brigid did a spell that would protect him. But unfortunately this crossfire of spells pulled him away from all of us. Hero and Niko smuggled him out of the country on a ship captained by Niko's dad which had come to Cardiff. I followed him there in March, when he left Augustus' place. Pedro severed the Gordian knot of our coven; we became feeble, so I took it on my shoulders to undo what I had done and 'kill' Pedro. It worked. I lost Pedro, but we regained our power. I didn't tell anybody. It looks as though Hero and Niko also knew he was alive and they didn't speak out. You see, killing Pedro saved us and him."

Thomas remembered Anne's talk of killing the God.

"When you said his 'imminent death' before, was that to do with your spell? Why was his death imminent?" he asked, perplexed.

"You know, Gorgon. Gorgon was onto him, and literally loving him to death," she said. Her voice fell away sadly. "Hero was Gorgon, or maybe me, you know."

"You mean, you were Gorgon too?" asked Thomas, unbelieving.

"Yeah, you see Pedro and I started at the same time. I was barely sixteen, you know. I used to tell him I was Gorgon and was going to eat him up. We made love lots of times. He liked it when I was Gorgon; it kind of turned him on to me, you know. Brigid told me about Gorgon at the beginning."

"Yes?"

"She said Pedro should not have been chosen."

"Why?"

"He was too good and would destroy the coven, you know."

"How?"

"He played with us witches, and we were powerless to stop him. For him the whole thing was a game, a challenge. His role became dominant when he should have been more serious about contributing to our cause: that of healing and serving our community. I know you think we're all cuckoo, but we're really just simple people. Pedro changed all that. He showed me . . . Apollo, Perseus or something. I think we all went a bit overboard, you know."

"So you were Gorgon?" he asked again.

"All of us, I guess; you know, I had a spell on them, and it worked," she said proudly.

"Was Hero upset when Pedro broke off their affair?"

"I bet she was, but you could hardly tell. She's cool, you know. It was like she accepted what was going on. I feel rotten about it — that's why I'm telling you, you know."

"Yeah, I know," mimicked David Thomas with a hint of sarcasm. "You could have just kept him with the love charm."

Pedro the Enigma 247

"I did, often," she said sincerely.

"It still seems to me there was more going on than your jealous spell. Maybe Pedro actively sought some kind of death trip. He sounds like a voyeur par excellence."

"Well, if he did, he sure had me figured out."

"Didn't he introduce Gorgon, at least the theory?"

"Yeah."

"It obviously haunted him."

"Yeah, I guess."

"Well, no matter, just don't be so hard on yourself, okay?"

"Thanks. You're not so bad, you know," she said.

"Just what was this spell anyway?" Thomas asked.

"Spells are secret, you know," she said.

"Well, it isn't secret anymore, you know." he said.

Gwendolyn laughed, which made Thomas truly wonder about her sanity, considering her Grana was lying out there dead in the stormy darkness on her kitchen floor. Then she smiled and chanted mischievously:

> Double, double toil and trouble:
> Fire, burn; and, cauldron, bubble.
> Fillet of a fenny snake,
> In the cauldron boil and bake;
> Eye of newt, toe of frog,
> Wool of bat and tongue of dog,
> Adder's fork, and blind-worm's sting,
> Lizard's leg and howlet's wing,
> For a charm of powerful trouble,
> Like a hell-broth boil and bubble.

"I'm just joking," she said impulsively, after seeing the adverse reaction of Inspector Thomas. "For Grana," she added, then laughed again. Thomas chuckled, albeit suspiciously, at her dark humour.

On his way home that evening, David Thomas could only shake his head in wonder at the course of the day's progress. He had started out on a routine, if not slightly dull investigation concerning the tragic accident and presumed death of a young man named Pedro George. By the end of the day, he had not only come across another death — a real one — and had also uncovered the mysterious circumstances surrounding Pedro George and what turned out to be his non-death. The general scandal seemed quite clear to him; yet he remained puzzled by the fact that there didn't seem to be anyone guilty of wrongdoing other than Gwendolyn Jones in her destruction of Pedro's car, an act which he had already decided to overlook in light of the unusual case — a conspiracy of confounded emotions. Quite possibly, after all, Gwendolyn had been psychometrically coerced. Only Hero, Niko, and Pedro himself could ultimately provide the final answers now that Brigid was dead and they were safely out of the country as far as he was aware. Then again, this ostensible madness would probably come full circle. They all probably knew more than they were saying, except maybe Gwendolyn, who ironically indicted herself by her soul-sweeping disclosure.

As David Thomas descended from the high country, the ceiling of grey mottled cloud receded to a far more unthreatening height. It really was a different country back up there with the wind in one's ears and clouds seeming to brush over the top of one's head. He left behind the mysterious off-beat tracks through meadows where Augustus lived and Brigid died, and where Gwendolyn gathered up her capricious sheep in her black shepherd's garb, summoning from her fantastic youth ecstatic visions of Pedro joined with her about the Beltane fires and nights spent in the dewy wood. These thoughts entangled him like ivy vines hanging from the towering oaks. How easily seduced they all were, how easily ensnared! But was it fair of him to judge? Theirs was a separate reality where secrets slept, to be wakened from the dungeons of the mind and archetypical mirages few dared to venture into. He had certainly been given a severe induction.

He had driven Gwendolyn back to Anne's place. Although Anne had departed, the dogs were there and would keep Gwendolyn company. Now she would begin a lonely stretch of her life. Was it her chosen path after all? Hopefully, he thought, — and he would follow up on the matter — she should reconsider going back to school and really put to good use her Wiccan study, though he doubted that she would. She was as wild and free as the wind in the trees.

They had left Brigid's once the local authorities arrived; there was little more they could do. The coroner's first impression was that she had had a massive stroke mid-step. She simply blanked out. Thomas wondered what her last thoughts were. What were the thoughts of a hundred-year-old witch? A well-tuned pitch to the moon, spheres, and herbal powers was only as good as the practitioner's subtle adjunctive skill to heal. They would read the prescription in the eye of the being and tincture of the skin. But there was the spiritual side which grew with age and transformed the holy body of ecstatic rapture into wisdom, or want. Brigid had tried to hold up the integrity of her coven, to be thwarted by licentious and amoral youth, symbolized in that strange Pedro, who now arose in David Thomas's mind like a Mephistophelian prodigy. He wondered what Pedro was really like; he certainly had taken on rather mythical proportions. One thing was for certain: both Brigid and Gwendolyn caused his downfall for very different reasons, or did they?

David Thomas arrived home. He had a farm overlooking the Irish Sea. The house was modest, only twenty years old, and had a garage. Eliza, his wife, was in the garden, doing some random weeding. She came to him as he parked the car, giving him a quick peck and telling him that he was late and that the phone had been ringing all afternoon. Why hadn't he called in at the station? David Thomas brushed the question off, saying he had been investigating a case back in the mountains. All he wanted to do was sit down, put his feet up and look at the book he had been reading about the presumed discovery of the Ark of the Covenant in Ethiopia, where it had lain guarded for almost three thousand years by an archaic sect of Jews who had become Christians. The Templars had been privy to this knowledge and it all seemed very plausible. But as soon as he took out his dinner, which had been warming in the oven, the telephone rang.

As soon as John Kenneth George entered the front hall of his Rosedale greystone, Connie rushed from the telephone, which she had just hung up, with the wonderful news that Pedro, their wayward son, was alive. John George thought his wife had gone over the edge and told her to relax.

"But he is!" she said.

John George burst out laughing, something he rarely did. The last time he had truly laughed had been on the occasion of Pedro's twenty-fifth birthday when he attempted to reach his son in Wales but was told by Anne that he was living in a shepherd's hut and had forsaken such amenities as telephones for the time being. At present, he didn't cease laughing until he had a drink in hand to fortify himself. Only then did he yield to Connie's beseeching to be serious and sit down quietly before her. Just then the doorbell rang and Frank Morgan entered. Frank also found a drink and sat down, cursing all the way about what people would think about the new development. Finally, he stopped and said, "John, you're my best friend, but I pity you with that son of yours." Then he too broke into a fit of laughter. Connie could only watch them, nonplussed, until the inanity wore off.

At first, they blamed the "mistake" on the ineptitude of the Welsh police; then they blamed it on Anne for remaining silent about what she knew; then they blamed it on "all those witches"; finally they blamed it on Pedro because he did not come forward and put a stop to the shenanigans. Connie defended her son by saying he obviously didn't know of his reported death; he probably went travelling somewhere and was oblivious to the whole scandal. This idea got John and Frank laughing again, convinced that Pedro had probably orchestrated the complete fiasco. Frank summed matters up by saying half seriously that there was something fishy in Pedro's very dying. "Pedro die? I'd have to see it to believe it!"

"I don't think our son's death is anything to joke about," said Connie firmly. "There's more to this than you're willing to admit! But anyway, I for one am overjoyed at his being alive!"

"Of course, of course," they conceded patronizingly. At this point, they began to make telephone calls to get to the bottom of the scandal. They telephoned Anne first and received no reply. Then they telephoned the number they had been given for the man in charge of the Welsh investigation, an Inspector David Thomas, but were told he was unavailable that day. Miss Abigail, Thomas's assistant, did upon John George's insistence, give out Thomas's home phone number; but when they tried to reach him there, they got only his wife, Eliza.

The discussion changed to Charles's disclosure of Anne's affair with Pedro. They thought Anne's behavior, as well as Pedro's, lewd, and derided the immorality of the whole Wiccan group. Connie, now distraught as she was, defended her son again along with his friends. "Unhappiness," she said stubbornly, "is what leads to extramarital liaisons." But this direction of the dialogue both Frank and John ignored, preferring to return to the insipid details of Anne's adultery. Having speculated that Anne must have faked Pedro's death, they presumed she went mad when spurned by him and, being a witch, of course resorted to drastic measures. Connie held this view because it absolved Pedro who she felt was still young and impressionable. Charles, unfortunately, was holding the short end of the stick but would be better off without Anne; he had always considered her too selfish anyway. Frank was the only one who defended Anne Fitzooth, but he did so because she had once impressed him with tremendous inside savvy of British commerce, knowledge which subsequently led them to Fitzooth, Fitzooth years before Niko had assumed the mantle. There had been little activity since Charles's big move into Swiss technology, which is why they hadn't met Niko before the funeral, This led them again to speculate what role, if any, Niko and the beguiling Hero may have played in Pedro's disappearance. Connie countered this suggestion since they were his best friends after all and it seemed unlikely they would have come to the funeral had they known more than they did.

"What would they have to gain by being involved?" said Connie dubiously.

"With Peter incognito, Niko could move in on Hero," commented John. Frank nodded his approval. These tactics seemed to be acceptable reasons to implicate Niko and Hero. Connie again had to rescue the integrity of those wonderful friends of Pedro. Hero and Niko were going out together, she said, after Pedro had already stopped seeing Hero. John George suggested that Pedro might have become depressed as a result of this crisis and faked his own death in an impassioned fit.

"He must be apprehended," said John George.

"How dare you talk about your son like that!" exclaimed Connie sternly. "I'm sure there's a good reason he's done what he did. We know our son better than that."

"We have to be objective, my dear; we simply don't know anything," he replied in his cool, adroit way. "Let's call Anne."

They called but only got her answering machine. They began to wonder about Charles. He was probably getting drunk in some bar, they decided. They would have to wait until he returned to get any further information from him. And Hero and Niko had gone up north with Ronald and Sadie and could not be reached. They thought this peculiar, and Frank was now upset with his own son, Ronald, for having taken them sightseeing when they were most needed there. They digressed into comments on the "mixed up" younger generation in general.

"Wait a minute," said Connie, "I'm the elder end of that generation!"

John George rang David Thomas again. This time Thomas had just arrived home. But the conversation that ensued was not pleasant. Actually it was awkward; John George began disparagingly. He had had three drinks, none of them singles, in not much than an hour and accused the Welsh policeman, who happened to be English, of gross ineptitude causing terrible emotional havoc.

"What kind of Mickey Mouse operation," he blared, "are you running anyway?" But as the conversation wore on and he heard first-hand all that David Thomas had to say, he became more and more compliant. Thomas was both eloquent and thorough in his response. John George finally signed off, having attained some needed explanation for peace of mind; indeed his son was alive. He exclaimed loudly, "He's thought to be in Canada! Christ, and he didn't even let us know he was alive! He apparently boarded a freighter in Cardiff last March bound for Canada!" David Thomas didn't spell out, however, the now saturating Wiccan involvement and details of Gwendolyn's obsessive act. This left the onus on Pedro and made both Frank Morgan and John George very angry. They called the police.

In half an hour Detective Dumont of 52 Division rolled up outside. In the living room John George told Dumont all that he knew. Dumont, uncertain of the authenticity of the claim since he hadn't heard anything official, could only gape and assume the worst. Pedro had committed fraud, and Detective Dumont wanted to know whether they, the parents, were prepared to accept the consequences of an investigation. First of all, Pedro would have to be found; and if he didn't want to be found, it might take a long time.

John George paced up and down the livingroom; Frank sat to the side on the couch. If it became clear that Pedro didn't want to be found, what alternative did they have but to hope that Pedro would come back himself; after all, he was a grown man. Connie suggested they wait at least until Charles returned before involving the police. He knew more about the matter than anyone there. This course was agreed upon and Dumont left.

Shortly before 8 a.m. the following morning, Charles arrived at the

Georges' house a little dizzy from his sultry, though propitious solstice. John and Connie were both priming for the day. Connie had them sit at the table on the patio and brought out a breakfast she had just prepared. On the glass table top, hot croissants, soft-boiled eggs, freshly squeezed orange juice, jams, and steaming Jamaican Blue coffee were arrayed. Charles, not wanting to focus on the many charged questions coming from John George, delayed the onslaught by tending to his immediate need: that rich coffee. He methodically spooned in his honey, poured a little cream, and held the cup close to his lips, savouring the aroma.

"I must collect my thoughts, John," he said, "I've just been dropped into an Abyssinian hell-fire; moreover, I was plucked from the flames by the Queen of Sheba and I am saved." He sipped his coffee gratefully, aware of its caffeine beginning to course through his veins. "She's in advertising . . . named Angie, . . . granted me the keys to her kingdom. I have to say I was impressed, and, lucky boy that I am, I intend to follow up on this acquaintance.

"Now, if you both hold on to your seats, I will expound my knowledge of Pedro et al once I have sufficiently fuelled my rather sacked system. Thank you, dear Connie, for this excellent breakfast."

They all began to eat.

"You're obviously feeling much better today," said Connie, with her mouth full of croissant. "Why did you come back so early?" Her smile gave away her teasing.

"I needed some air, early morning air. Everything has been rushing like river rapids. Think of surviving a Niagara turbine; I'm a bit flushed out," said Charles happily transformed.

"Are you not going to speak to Anne?" asked John indifferently.

"Not a chance. It's better this way. Did Connie tell you Pedro was fucking her?" he said angrily. Charles and John were never the best of friends. Their respective cynicisms could find no point of accord.

"Charles, let's keep our heads, shall we?" said Connie with a big sisterly tone.

"Well, that son of yours has really fucked up this time. I take it quite personally. I think he should suffer the consequences," said Charles, eating more voraciously.

"We don't know where he is. We've told the police—"

"He's up north; I'm sure. Probably Manitoulin."

"Manitoulin! Ronald Morgan drove up there with the others," stated John George. "Do you think they knew?"

"Maybe. I don't know. Maybe this del Rio woman knew."

"How do you know he's up there?" persisted John.

"Where else would he be?"

"Who knows," stated John.

"Believe me, I know he's there. Put it this way: I have a very strong intuition. Where there's smoke, there's fire; and where there's fire, there's Pedro."

Big Dan came huffing and puffing over the rocks with the padded gait of giant bear. He sniffed the wind and looked up and down the shoreline, then he saw the tent and walked toward it. From its interior he could hear the clear tenor of Donna del Rio's voice. "Hey," he called out, "I always heard the white man liked to sleep in, but this is more than I can take." Pedro replied heartily that the red man was known to take a good long siesta and they were simply following local customs. In a moment Pedro came out in his shorts, his white skin tinted red by the sun. Donna came out after him.

"All well in heaven?" asked Big Dan. Pedro responded that he was gratefully dead, the only problem being that like Odaemin, he wasn't sure if returning to the living was going to change anything. Donna crinkled her nose and cocked her head, missing the meaning. Big Dan explained that the previous night John Kineu had said Pedro was like Odaemin, who went to the Great spirit only to be sent back to the living to heal the sickness among them.

"And how is he supposed to do that?" she asked matter-of-factly.

No one answered. Instead, Pedro began to describe the times they lived in as a fat age that subscribed to the Church of Progress and was presided over by its own brand of clerics, the scientists, politicians, and administrators of the status quo. It was no different in this respect from times past, only now people refused to acknowledge the wisdom of the ancients because it hadn't run the gamut of modern qualification.

"Look around us," he said. "Look at what the Church of Progress has done to this planet. Any advantage we have supposedly gained by our technology is nullified if we cannot survive the ecological or sociological holocaust that man is perpetrating."

He went on to say that only the hard lessons of experience would teach the human race to live in accordance with nature. Essentially, nature hadn't any agenda that insisted the human race be a part of it. So Pedro spelt out his thoughts, feeling obligated to express in a constructive way the reality of man's relationship with the Great Spirit and his destiny as a species.

"The changes that must come have always been in motion," he said. "The answers are within us; it may be necessary to invoke a new symbol or mythology to help establish the change. Notwithstanding the errors we have made through the Church of Progress, I believe that science must open the doors to the greater universal mind over matter, which the Aquarian Age will manifest. A far greater society will emerge. I believe this will come to pass, but possibly with far diminished numbers."

Pedro put his arm around Donna's waist and she leaned her head on his shoulder. Big Dan said there were two things he had to tell him: one, that John Kineu wanted to see him (he had some fresh fish), and two, that Ronald Morgan, Sadie McPherson, Hero St. Germain, and Niko Fitzooth were at the log cabin near Dreamer's Rock.

"I knew the day would come," said Pedro, "but Ronald and Sadie too? Wow, this should be interesting."

"They probably found out that I came here," said Donna, sticking out her bare foot for balance as they teetered a bit.

Big Dan said he had met them at his gallery in Little Current and had suggested they go to the West Bay Pow Wow. He would drive Pedro over to Dreamer's Rock later if he wanted to go.

"We must go," said Pedro. He wanted badly to see his old friends, now that the conundrum of their maelstrom had dissipated.

They hiked across the short peninsula to John Kineu's side where they found him sitting in his rocker on the tent deck.

"Hello," said John. "How is Miss del Rio this afternoon? And Pedro? I dreamed last night that you walked together hand in hand, true weed-jeewaugun — companions for life. It was a happy thought." He smiled brilliantly.

They attested to the well-being and goodness that were bestowed upon them by John, but few words came. A celestial silence fell upon them in a kind of prelude to the unknown that lay before them. Weighty things loomed up, countering their present levity. Pedro felt giddy at the thought of meeting his old friends, who he hoped would receive him faithfully, despite the audacity of his death and sudden love. But what if they recoiled from him now, deciding that in the end he was ridiculous? These were new thoughts, vulnerable thoughts, which actually made him feel whole. This sensitivity stimulated the desire to make amends, to release his bond with the abstract which had so dominated, having then plumbed the depths of their laity. He thought Hero and Niko must be under great pressure and wondered how they had managed to stand through the funeral, knowing they had seen him off from Cardiff three months before the accident. Then again, they might have thought he had returned to Wales and really did die. Curiosity now aroused in Pedro the need to know who set up his death; before, that need had been incidental and repressed by the very shock and actuality of it. Brigid, Anne and Gwendolyn appeared in his thoughts before him. Brigid was beckoning to him like a ghostly apparition which he didn't immediately understand; Anne was turning away in her most austere manner, casting one last glance with those champagne eyes; Gwendolyn was reaching for him, crying and mouthing words he could not hear. He knew somehow Gwendolyn had caused his presumed death; she appeared frantic as though she were losing her mind. Pedro remembered that she had had the extra set of keys to the Rover. He had given them to her in jest after one of their ritualistic Wiccan marriages as a token of marital conjugality. Pedro shivered to his core in compassion for Gwendolyn. He saw her suffering as something only he could comprehend. Had he been such a terrible burden? He pondered whether he would be a scapegoat.

As they were stepping into the boat, John Kineu called from his rocker, "Be tough, eh; don't let them get to you!" They motored across the vast channel toward Dreamer's Rock. The blue skies of earlier in the day had given way to grey; it was still humid though, with the smell of rain in the air. They sat quietly, with Big Dan driving from the stern and Donna and Pedro facing him from the middle seat, their hair blowing wildly about their faces. Pedro watched the spray and surf of the water as waves undulated in strange greys, blues and purples across the darkening expanse.

When Hero and her companions returned to the rented cabin, there was a distinct note of excitement in the air, even after the lull of their long drive. Hero kept looking up to Dreamer's Rock, expecting to see a smoke signal or some other sign. Ronald, a bit subdued, kept his eyes on Sadie. Sadie was living sagaciously in the moment, aware of something extraordinary in the works. By contrast, Niko was apprehensive, unsure of what to expect from Pedro; nevertheless, he was caught up in the current and let himself be swept along with an uncharacteristic optimism. It was as though they anticipated a great sporting event involving two equally matched teams.

They freshened up with a swim and afterward, stir-fried a vegetable curry with rice for supper. Then they sat, digesting it contentedly on the deck, looking out over the water. They knew something was going to happen, but what? Big Dan had said he would come by to visit. Hero and Niko assumed that Pedro would probably come with him. Certainly, Big Dan would have told Pedro by now that they were there; it was getting on in the evening. Suddenly Hero stood up and shot another attentive glance at the top of Dreamer's where the bristly pines stood like Gothic sentinels in the threatening skies. Something was definitely in the air, an ionization, a pressure shift from the earlier open-endedness of a hot carefree summer's day. The humidity was reaching the saturation point.

"I'm going up," she said and trippingly spun away, which seemed to indicate she wanted to go alone. Niko hardly budged, but Ronald impulsively sat up, ready for the clarion call to action. Instantly, Sadie put her hand on his forearm and without a word restrained him.

As Hero nimbly hiked up through the rocks and trees, the closer she got to the top, the better she felt. A certain measure of solitude was a daily need for her; it was her life's blood. She was not a group person. The hike relaxed her. In her childhood and adolescence in Switzerland, she would hike three or four times a week. Her body craved the expansion in her lungs as she breathed in time with her meditations; her mind, suffused in the distraction of watching the ground for little cracks in the rock, peculiar arrays of plants, the colour of the shades, or the density of the forest, kept her on guard. She was thus swept clear of love's fomentations. Her newly realized love for Niko was deep, satisfying, and stable; on the other hand, vestiges of that vast country called Pedro remained with her. The two attachments co-existing in her formed a problem that could never be resolved. Only time could teach a greater forbearance: the emotional quandary of her startling affair with Pedro had triggered a maze of verisimilitudes that only a cruel God could conjure. Destined not to be together when one's whole being felt otherwise was a personal tragedy's finest yardcloth.

She was not long in approaching the top on which was a plateau of large granite rock supporting a straggling variety of trees and plants. When she got there, she wandered unhurriedly in and around the various flora, up and down the diversified rockscape. She saw the prominent rock up ahead of her at exactly the same moment she smelled smoke. The odour lingered faintly in little pockets of air that circulated oddly about the hilltop even when the wind was moderate. But the weather was taking a turn for the worse, and it seemed unlikely to her that anybody would be there. As she rounded the last obstacle of tree and rock before the summit, however, she stopped dead. There he was, crouching by the fire, just as she had seen him so often before. He looked up, but not at Hero. Then a woman came from the other direction. Donna del Rio stopped in her tracks upon seeing Hero. For that initial moment, as they stood and faced each other and as Pedro turned again to the skillet heating on their campfire, neither of the two sensed or communicated by eye contact any negativity to the other. Hero, of course knew who Donna del Rio was but didn't show anything in her demeanour that Donna could construe as anything more than an innocent intrusion. Donna del Rio, however, unsure who Hero was, still sensed Hero's reaction to seeing Pedro as something more than a stranger's surprise in coming upon them.

Pedro turned his head instinctively. He was already smiling. Hero took a couple of tentative steps. He stood up. "Hero!" he called across the rock slab. They came to each other and touched each other's arms before they automatically embraced. "Pedro," she said. Their greeting was profound but anticlimactic. The passions of the present had forsaken the past. Theirs had been a love based on need, a consummate need destined for the mausoleum of lovers. Theirs had been a love that honour had reasoned to do and die. Theirs had been a love sequestered to hallucinate. It was a relationship that had floundered on the altar of love, and the flesh and blood experience could not hold. Whatever they felt for each other now was redundant and hollow. Pedro released her slowly and turned to introduce Donna del Rio, who stood there not quite understanding but patient. Donna and Hero shook hands and then Hero hugged her with tears in her eyes. "Don't mind me," she said. "It's not like I haven't been to his funeral!"

They laughed. Afterwards, the three of them sat around the fire sharing some blueberry tea from the one tin cup, conversing quietly about what a great place it was to have a fish fry.

☙

Big Dan was tying up his boat at the Birch Island landing when he noticed a small dot moving far away in the grey sky. The dot became bigger and bigger until it landed. The Twin Otter swooped in and coasted across the water to dock. In a moment the pilot stepped out, followed by Mr. and Mrs. George, then a fellow dressed in tweeds. Big Dan waited, and the Georges, who recognized him, stopped to talk.

"Big Dan, hello!" said Connie. "How lucky! You're just the person to help us. How is everything?"

"Fine," said Big Dan smiling.

"This may sound a little strange, Big Dan, but John and I are here to find our son."

"Pedro?" said Big Dan, regretting the way he said it.

"Yes," said Mr. George. "We've heard that Pedro is quite alive and likely somewhere around here. I'm sure, if he is here, you would know about it, Big Dan; he was your friend; I know this may come as a shock to you if . . ."

"Mr. George, Pedro or his ghost showed up here yesterday. I couldn't believe my eyes. We revived him, of course, and it looks like he's been through some kind of freak accident."

"But he's okay?" said Connie, needing reassurance.

"Oh, he's great, Mrs. George. Just great. A little hard to see, but great."

"Hard to see?" She opened her eyes wide.

Big Dan smiled but restrained himself to respond. His play on words about Pedro being a ghost didn't quite catch.

"Do you need a ride?" Big Dan asked, laughing to himself.

"I don't know," said Connie. "Do we need one?"

"If you want to see your son, you do," he said.

"Where is he?" said the Georges in unison.

"Dreamer's Rock."

"Dreamer's Rock?" said John George.

"Yes," said Big Dan humbly.

"Well, what are we waiting for?" said John George.

They all crammed into Big Dan's pick-up. As they got going, John George introduced David Thomas to Big Dan. "He's come from Wales to close the book on . . . Pedro George."

As soon as Inspector David Thomas had put down the receiver after speaking to John George, he resolved to defend himself in the matter of Pedro George. In a surge of energy, he telephoned the airport and arranged to fly at his own expense to Dublin on the next commuter flight from Aberystywyth's little airport. Getting up, he kissed Eliza full on the lips, and said, "I'm going to Canada to see for myself this young man who supposedly died in an automobile accident. It turns out he is apparently alive and well in Ontario. I will explain when I get back."

"David, you're what!? Going to Canada! Now?" exclaimed Eliza, confounded. She stood there plumply in her summer dress with her eyes squarely on her husband.

"Dear, I must satisfy my curiosity about this most peculiar individual. I feel I must go, if even to . . . to say I'm sorry to the parents of the young man whom I wrote off as dead. It's a tale too difficult to explain just now, believe me, but I must run if I am going to catch the eight-thirty."

"What about your supper?" she said flustered.

"I must run." He headed for the door.

"This is most unlike you, David," she said as he left.

He flew to Dublin, then took off immediately on the red-eye to New York arriving there in the dead of night. Early that morning he flew to Toronto, where he got in touch with Pedro's parents.

Being severely jet-lagged and driving down the highway with a North American native, squeezed into the front seat of a pickup with the parents of the infamous "deceased," had a macabre feel to Thomas that appealed to his vanity as a detective. At times, the country life he led wore on him a little claustrophobically. He needed the occasional release, and the spontaneity of this trip came to him like an impulse from on high. It was almost as if he had a calling to see Pedro George, not to mention the responsibility he bore in this case. David Thomas felt he had earned the right to see for himself how events would unfold. Had he not circumvolved the progress of a rather auspicious star?

They turned down a gravel road, following it for a quarter mile until they saw the cabin, the little bay, and the rise of rock and tree that ascended to Dreamer's Rock. As they approached, three people were walking along the stretch of road before taking the turn around the bay to get up to Dreamer's. It was Ronald, Sadie, and Niko. Big Dan stopped. They waved, then Sadie and Ronald broke into big surprised smiles at the Georges, without the foggiest idea as to why they were there. Niko, however, knew exactly, and had a sudden foreboding: if they were here with Big Dan, where was Pedro?

They greeted each other cheerfully. Connie looked beyond them to the cabin. "So," she said, "Where is he?"

"Where's who?" blurted out Ronald beatifically.

"Well, Pedro, of course," said John.

"Pedro?" said Ronald. "Pedro? What do you mean, Pedro?"

Big Dan and Niko looked at each other perplexed. Sadie's face altered from elation to shock.

"Isn't he here?" said John and Connie together. They looked worriedly at Big Dan then at Inspector Thomas. "Pedro's alive and he's supposed to be here!" said John emphatically.

"That's what Hero's been saying since yesterday!" said Ronald. "Don't tell me you've been seeing the same ghost!"

"Would someone mind telling us what is going on?" said Sadie. The dank humidity of the evening weighed heavily upon her. Now the sky, too, darkened with the emergence of an apocalyptically ominous cloud over Dreamer's Rock like a colossal flotilla of doom. Drops of rain began to touch them sporadically.

"Where is Hero?" asked David Thomas quickly.

"She's up there," said Sadie, pointing up toward the ridge. "We were just on our way."

"Could he be up there?" Thomas looked at Niko. "Lord Huntington?"

"I don't know," said Niko. "We haven't been up."

"Inspector Thomas has come all the way from Wales," said John George solemnly. "It's been found out that Pedro's death was feigned. Anne Willobie has said so, according to Charles. The cat's out of the bag; he must be here. Dan said he dropped him off over two hours ago." The rain came on progressively harder. They all looked up at the Rock again. Ronald and Sadie were speechless.

Niko took the lead. "Shall we go then?" he said. There was a rumble of thunder in the distance.

"Wouldn't Hero just come down? Or Pedro?" said Sadie carefully.

"I can't believe this!" cried out Ronald. "You think Pedro is up there? I can't believe this!"

Suddenly there was a massive explosion of thunder that had all of them ducking and ready to hit the ground. It was amplified in the concavity of the small bay and cliff, reverberating at length with an ear shattering report down the channel. Niko, who had seen the lightning bolt burst forth, its frazzled megavolt striking the top of the Rock, was temporarily blinded.

Once the blast's after-ring had faded, from way up the ridge, a prolonged shrill sound was heard, less noticeable at first then growing in volume, rising over the gentle pats of raindrops on leaves. It was a shriek of despair.

Niko bolted toward the path, Ronald at his heels. Then the rest followed in a panic, a cold blade of fear stabbing their hearts. In the dash, Connie stumbled, crestfallen and tearful, and was helped up by John George muttering under his breath. Behind them, with furrowed brow, strode a sombre Big Dan.

"The others should be up shortly," said Hero to Pedro, sipping the tea and tingling all over with a mixture of anxiety and pleasure from the beverage and the fire's warmth.

"Good," said Pedro, looking at both her and Donna who sat blithely beside him. "How is Niko?" he added.

"Fine. Great," she said, reluctant to speak of her and Niko's recent intimacy. She was suddenly feeling very vulnerable and noticed a big black cloud sagging precipitously through the surrounding grey, declaring its presence. Donna saw it too but failed to wonder at its intent, so caught up was she in the exotic Hero with her European obliquity. Sitting there with Pedro, she became aware of the grounded crosscurrent of familiarity flowing between him and Hero; still she was not unaware of Hero's self-control which was admirable, considering not only the second coming of Pedro but also the obvious vestigial depth of feeling she must still have for her ex-lover. Donna's thoughts darkened with the giant storm cloud approaching, and already sparks from the fire flew up about them with each gust of the heightened breeze. Still, the fire warmed them against the depressurization in the air from hot humidity to clammy cool. Immediately overhead, flitting birds were making last frenzied dives for cover.

"It appears you're over the hump, Pedro," said Hero quietly. "We're so relieved, of course; you know we had to be sure." She looked at Donna and, smiling but with sad eyes, asked, "Donna, have you really been to Wales?"

"Oh!" Donna laughed. She remembered what she had told Mrs. George. "No, actually, when I found out Pedro had died, I kind of reacted . . . instinctively. Boy, was I surprised — the shock of my life — I mean, I knew he was alive! I'd seen him the day before. God, what a freakish thing! I'm still reeling, even if I did the wrong thing by holding my tongue. It wasn't easy finding him, but I suppose that finding him was meant to be." Donna looked at Pedro for support. He simply smiled.

"You did the right thing, Donna," he said. "I did the wrong thing."

"You two look made for each other," complimented Hero graciously if not reluctantly. Pedro had fallen for a woman who seemed to both understand and adore him. She realized their own relationship had ultimately served only to reconnect Pedro with his true love. This did not necessarily placate her. "I didn't know what to expect by coming here, Pedro," continued Hero. "We just wanted to see you again. Do you realize we actually went to your funeral?"

"Did you really think I'd died?" he asked solemnly.

"We weren't absolutely sure; nevertheless, it still came as a shock."

"Who do you think did it?" Pedro suddenly queried.

"Who knows? Who cares?" said Hero nonchalantly.

"The important thing is that you're here, Pedro," said Donna.

"How long have you been here, on Dreamer's, Pedro?" asked Hero.

"We waited at the cabin for half an hour," said Pedro, "then we decided to come up here, maybe two hours ago. John Kineu gave us a couple of bass and we've been roasting these potatoes." The rain had begun to spit, and looking up at the cloud, he added, "We might be pushing our luck."

"Where are you camped?" asked Hero. She passed the tea to Donna. "Maybe, we should head down."

"Across the channel near the Point," said Pedro.

"Can you see it from here?"

"You can see the Point," he said. "I could show you. Have you been up on the Rock yet?" Pedro stood up energetically, followed on cue by Hero. Donna stayed to tend to the supper. Behind them came a rumble somewhere. Hero hesitated. Pedro clambered up the rock and pointed to the east. "Over there," he said, turning about. "Wow, look at that cloud!" he exclaimed, before turning again to Donna, and in a calm voice said, "Drama."

Hero made a step toward the sharp rise to the summit. Below her the treetops swayed menacingly in the restless wind. She reached out with her hands to touch the rock face for balance as she stepped, taking careful note of the Precambrian rock's density. Motes in the grain were the last thing she saw before the explosion. Suddenly, she was lying flat on her back, seeing stars. Specks of rain burned into her like witch hazel. She saw the Rock empty. A scream pierced the air.

Donna had turned the potatoes near the coals. They were almost done, and she decided to put them in the pan with the cooked fish. Then she looked for cover. Above, Pedro was pointing with his arm. Her eyes settled on him. She was concerned. He looked so exposed against the grey sky. The rain had intensified. Pedro stood there in his shorts and shirt and tire-tread sandals, with his white skin and wild wavy hair. His big brown eyes settled on Donna for a few silent smiling seconds as if to reassure her of his love when the bolt simply appeared. For an instant, frozen like a spectre of creation, he stood there in his familiar form, but aglow in the electrical arc. In the first milli-moments it sounded like a whisper ricocheting deep into the stratosphere. It was the finest, most delicate thing, before the blinding florescence, then the explosion, deafening to the ears, mortifying to the sight. And he was gone.

For Pedro, the moment of truth came not so much as a shock but as a most piquant sense of déjà vu. When he saw for a brief flash the marvelous fuse from the sky connect with him at his finger tips and course through his body like a microwave beam, he relaxed with the thought that a pantheon of lives had yet to be realized. Accompanying this prescience was a split second's cognizance of a multifarious past: Troylus stood smiling under the Trojan sun in splendour and pomp befitting his royalty. Aeneas was there with him, fierce and loyal. Gwydion, Bran, Sarah, Olwen, Elphin, and Gomer, and even the Hairy Man projected themselves processionally along the gilded cosmos. Then, last but not least, Donna and a little boy looked at him knowingly before he was taken up and levelled in a cushion of air, all atingle as if tapped on the head by a magic wand. Donna and the little boy were holding him from the anti-gravity of a galactic star dusting, but the axis of his being diffused in him before their eyes like a fleeting ghost rushing out from the vortex of time. Then there was nothingness — a density impossible to comprehend but a faint sensing of a light chanced to hover very near, just above, out of sight — the feeling of turning, turning, turning within an orbit of confinement, striving for that light, intensely, irresistibly, born of consciousness . . .

The End.